W9-BPS-716

Praise for the novels of Adriana Herrera

"Herrera is consistently one of the most prescient, thoughtful romance writers today, always finding compelling ways to weave vital topics into her scorching-hot love stories." —*Entertainment Weekly*

"Herrera excels at creating the kind of rich emotional connections between her protagonists that romance readers will find irresistible." —*Booklist*, starred review

"Sweet and thoughtful, but delightfully filthy, too." —*New York Times Book Review*

"Herrera's work remains compulsively readable. She crafts lively Latinx characters with instant, electric chemistry that sings on the page, and handles realistic obstacles in a relatable manner." —*Publishers Weekly*, starred review

"Incisive and modern, navigating the complexities of privilege, purpose and power, all while exploring intense passion." —*Washington Post*

"Herrera...deftly charts the struggles of finding love and friendship in unexpected places." —*Library Journal*, starred review

"Adriana Herrera writes romance with teeth—you'll laugh, you'll cry, and you'll be refreshed and inspired to fight even harder to create the vibrant, welcoming America in which her books are set." —*New York Times* bestselling author Suzanne Brockmann

"[Adriana Herrera] is writing some of my favorite Afro-Latinx characters and giving us beautiful love stories along the way." —National Book Award winner Elizabeth Acevedo

"Herrera masterfully combines the fun, gooey, interpersonal, romantic stuff with plots that are firmly grounded in reality and involve social justice. The result is contemporary romance that matters, stories that reveal an abundance of inconvenient truths about society." —*Book Riot*

Also by Adriana Herrera

Sambrano Studios

One Week to Claim It All
Just for the Holidays…

Dreamers

American Dreamer
American Fairytale
American Love Story
American Sweethearts
American Christmas

Dating in Dallas

Here to Stay
On the Hustle

Also available from Adriana Herrera

Mangos and Mistletoe
Finding Joy
Caught Looking
Her Night with Santa
Monsieur X

For additional books by Adriana Herrera,
visit her website, www.adrianaherreraromance.com.

WITHDRAWN
CHARLESTON COUNTY LIBRARY

A CARIBBEAN
HEIRESS
IN
PARIS

ADRIANA HERRERA

HQN

Recycling programs
for this product may
not exist in your area.

ISBN-13: 978-1-335-42751-9

A Caribbean Heiress in Paris

Copyright © 2022 by Adriana Herrera

All rights reserved. No part of this book may be used or reproduced in any manner whatsoever without written permission except in the case of brief quotations embodied in critical articles and reviews.

This is a work of fiction. Names, characters, places and incidents are either the product of the author's imagination or are used fictitiously. Any resemblance to actual persons, living or dead, businesses, companies, events or locales is entirely coincidental.

For questions and comments about the quality of this book, please contact us at CustomerService@Harlequin.com.

HQN
22 Adelaide St. West, 41st Floor
Toronto, Ontario M5H 4E3, Canada
www.Harlequin.com

Printed in U.S.A.

To my abuelas, Doña Laura and Doña Juana,
the Leonas of my childhood.

A CARIBBEAN HEIRESS IN PARIS

Life in the Caribbean had taught Luz Alana Heith-Benzan a few vital lessons. First, corsets in the tropics were the purest form of evil. Second, a woman attempting to thrive in a man's world must always have a plan. Third, a flask full of fine rum and a pistol served well in almost any emergency.

And most recently, if one was to ever find herself setting sail for the Continent in search of a fresh start, one must do so with her two best friends at her side.

"Can I go up to the Eiffel Tower too?" Luz's little sister asked, as if she could sense she had been left out of her sister's musings. "I promise I won't drink any of your champagne." Clarita had been attempting to commandeer their schedule while in Paris since the moment they'd boarded the first steamer in Santo Domingo.

"Clarita, you're ten. You would not get champagne regardless of the circumstance." That elicited a frustrated huff from the little monster, who at the moment was sitting primly by a bay window with the blue sky and water at her back, posing for a portrait.

"Stop needling her, Luz. You know how she fidgets, and I'm almost done with the sketch." The artist was Manuela, one of Luz's two best friends and Clarita's most fervent enabler. "Don't worry, querida. I'll smuggle you up the tower."

She was, at the moment, capturing Clarita's likeness while her sister sat with her hands crossed over her chest and eyes closed, affecting a disturbingly funereal air. One eye popped open. "Can we go to the catacombs?"

"*Don't* encourage her, Manuela. At this rate we will spend the summer traipsing through cemeteries."

Clarita responded by lolling her tongue, making Manu guffaw.

Luz's sister had become obsessed with the macabre after their father's death eighteen months ago. She'd tried her best to fill the void he'd left, but with both their parents gone, she also knew there was nothing that could repair becoming an orphan at such a young age. That still didn't make Luz any more inclined to haunt every graveyard in Paris.

The truth was that despite the hardships of the last few years, and her unease about what the future held for her and her sister, she *was* looking forward to the summer. Leaving Santo Domingo had been bittersweet: no matter how sound the reasoning, leaving home was its own sort of death. But there had been too much mourning in her life already. Looking ahead was the only alternative.

They were finally only a day away from the harbor at Le Havre. From there, another day of travel would take them to the French capital for three months at the Exposition Universelle. Three months of opportunities for her to meet buyers for her rum, Caña Brava. Three months in which to get her and her sister's futures in order, before the two of them were to permanently settle in her father's ancestral home in Edinburgh.

Unexpectedly finding herself at the helm of her family's distillery had been...difficult. On more than one occasion, Luz wondered if she was capable of stewarding their legacy into the future. A dream that had begun almost fifty years ago with Luz Alana's mother, Clarise, and her grandfather Roberto Benzan. A distillery owned and operated not by the children of Spanish colonials but by a Black family. Where every pair of hands that worked to make the rum—from cutting the sugar cane to preparing the spirits for shipment—was entitled to a share of the profits. Caña Brava from its inception had been an experiment in what industry without exploitation could be, and it had thrived for decades.

Her father, Lachlan Heith, a Scotsman who had arrived in the Caribbean looking for investment opportunities, had been the main investor of the distillery. It had not been long before Lachlan proposed marriage to Clarise, and for the next thirty years poured his life into her and her vision. After her mother's death, her father had continued their plans to expand Caña Brava's operations. Their rum was well-known all over the Americas. From the Unites States to Argentina, Caña Brava was coveted for its quality and unique smoky flavor. Lachlan wanted to bring the rum to European markets. His strategy was to elevate the spirit's image, to replace the bottles of brandy being served in the grand homes of Britain and the Continent with their Gran Reserva. Luz was more interested in making products for everyday people. Her father loved the hands-on operations, being in the distillery with the workers. Luz preferred to think of new ideas. Where he'd wanted to focus on selling their rum to the higher echelons of society, Luz believed the key to future success was to enlist the lifeblood of commerce: women merchants. The modern woman had ideas and preferences of her own and that were distinct from men's, and Luz saw the potential in focusing on them as a market. Her vision for the future of Caña

Brava was not quite what her father had wanted, but he at least recognized her talents and innovative thinking.

Which was why, she could only assume, after his death she'd found out that he'd passed the operations of the distillery to his second-in-command and left her in charge of the expansion to Europe. She'd been hurt by the slight, affronted that her father did not trust her with the business that her mother's family had built, until she realized that staying in Santo Domingo was much too painful. That she desperately needed a fresh start. And so, before her departure she'd transferred the majority of her holdings in Caña Brava to the people who, like her family, had nurtured it from the beginning.

She'd left with the promise to find them new prospects, new markets, new buyers... Building partnerships was where she'd always excelled. She hoped her skills would be as effective in Paris as they'd been in the tropics. Like her mother before her, Luz left with the intention to blaze a few trails.

"Did you hear that, Luz?" Clarita's voice, which every day sounded less like a little girl's and more like a young lady's, brought Luz Alana out of her thoughts.

"Sorry, amor. What did I miss?"

"Manu has made us appointments at the House of *Worth*!" Luz had to bite her lip at the reverence in Clarita's voice. The child also loved dresses...as long as they were dark as night.

"You have more tiny black dresses than I know what to do with, Clarita," Luz admonished. She'd been complacent in indulging her sister's penchant for gloomy clothing for months after their mourning period had ended, but she would put her foot down at acquiring more of them. "No more new dresses until you've had a chance to wear the ones Manu bought you in New York," Luz said, to which Clarita responded by making a very unladylike noise. Luz turned her attention to Manuela, who was still focused on her sketch.

"More gowns, Manu?" Luz asked and received a shrug in

answer. Luz's friend had wheedled permission to come to Paris with the excuse of securing a proper trousseau for her upcoming nuptials. Her betrothed and her parents, who had been waiting for almost three years for Manu to set a date, had agreed enthusiastically. So far it seemed Manuela intended to spend the man's money until he regretted ever setting his sights on her. They'd already spent a fortune in New York. It didn't matter: Manuela treated money like air. Something she consumed without any thought, always expecting there would be more when she needed it.

Their current accommodations were the perfect example. When Luz enlisted her friends to make the trip to the Universal Exposition, Manuela had written back insisting they travel in one of the new steamships from the French Line. This one had been decorated by Jules Allard, the Vanderbilts' personal designer. Because only a sea vessel outfitted for the likes of Alice Claypoole Vanberbilt herself would do. It wasn't that she objected to fine things: on the contrary, she quite liked the tearoom they were sitting in now. The pale blue and green damask drapes, the ornate Aubusson carpets and the velvet-covered armchairs built if not for comfort, certainly for broadcasting opulence. It was just harder to enjoy these things when one knew how much money was required to access them.

Luz hadn't exactly grown up without comforts either. Her family's business provided the means for that and more—but this was a different level of affluence. The kind of overt display of wealth meant to stun and intimidate. The kind of environment that usually brought with it people Luz had to mentally arm herself for. And it wasn't that she could not handle herself among this crowd. Two years in a Swiss finishing school had prepared her well for this, but it was exhausting. It was a world she always navigated with caution. She could never fully let her guard down among the so-called wellborn, lest one of the barbs they deployed so swiftly caught her unaware.

"I could get her just a few things, Luz," Manu muttered softly, still absorbed in her task, her countenance a study in concentration as her charcoal-stained fingers fluttered over the page. Luz noticed the dark smudges on the otherwise-pristine cuffs of her friend's lavender jacket and was struck by a wave of pure affection. Manuela, who loved baubles and expensive things, never thought twice of ruining them when it came to pleasing those she loved.

"Manu," Luz responded in an equally soft tone, because demands never worked with her friend, unless your intention was to get the exact opposite of what you were asking for. "You already bought Clarita four gowns during that outing to the Ladies' Mile in Manhattan." Luz ignored the huff coming from her little sister's direction as she spoke. "You know that until I'm able to get in touch with the solicitor in Edinburgh and discern what our finances will be like, I can't spend—"

Manuela opened her mouth to protest—and possibly offer financial assistance again—but Luz Alana held up a hand. "No, querida. You have already been too generous." She blew a kiss in her friend's direction in an attempt to soften the rebuff.

Luz would not budge on this. She could not be frivolous, not when the only thing she could count on at the moment were the funds her father had reserved for this trip and whatever income she would obtain from the sale of the three hundred casks of premium rum currently in the cargo hold of this ship. Her inheritance was inaccessible to her for now, and the future of Caña Brava was too uncertain for any unnecessary expenses. Despite knowing that Manuela truly wanted to help her financially, Luz also knew how fast women could become burdens and nuisances to their loved ones. She would stand on her own two feet.

"What has Manuela done now?" asked Aurora, startling Luz. The last member of their foursome strode into the tearoom, her long legs swallowing up the carpet as she arrived at their luncheon table.

"Me?" Manuela asked innocently, her hazel gaze the very picture of angelic virtue. As if she hadn't just been trying to convince Luz to buy dresses that cost as much as an estate in some parts of the world.

"Yes, you." Aurora chuckled as she bent to kiss the top of Clarita's head before dropping into an empty armchair. Aurora arranged herself in the corner they'd commandeered to take their afternoon tea, her ever-present Gladstone bag still clutched in one hand.

"How were your patients?" Luz asked as she handed Aurora a small plate full of sandwiches. Manuela stopped sketching and waved her hand at Clarita, who flopped down from her pose like a puppet who'd had her strings snipped. They all looked forward to hearing about Aurora's adventures whenever she returned from her rounds in the third-class cabins. They'd only been on the ship for eight days, but within hours of setting sail from New York, their friend had managed to avail herself to any passengers who needed a doctor and always came back with tales.

"So?" asked Clarita, who had a concerning appetite for the gorier details of the situations Aurora encountered.

"Everyone is doing well," she assured them with that satisfied grin she sported whenever she talked about her patients. Aurora was always happiest when she could put her skills to use and was never shy about offering them to those who needed them. "The young man with vertigo is improving wonderfully. And Miss Barnier may have that baby before we reach land." She crossed her legs, revealing her split skirts, which a few of the older ladies on the steamer called *grossly indecent*. A couple of heads turned, and quite a few eyebrows rose at Aurora's lack of concern with proper feminine posture.

"What were you frowning about?" she asked, circling a finger in the vicinity of Luz's forehead.

Luz spluttered for a moment but answered before Manu could. "I was explaining to Manuela that I can't afford more wardrobe-related expenses in Paris." Aurora was always her ally in matters of moderation and restraint.

"Well, you can't," Aurora decreed. "Not until the situation with your inheritance is sorted. You know that, Manu."

Manuela heaved a sigh, then pursed her lips dramatically as she reached for the cup of tea she'd handed Luz for a bolstering splash of Caña Brava. "Fine, no spending on *frivolities*." Luz was certain she didn't imagine her friend's mocking tone, but she refused to take the bait.

"Did you write your letter?" Manuela asked, taking the conversation in a different direction, which was her way of conceding to Luz's wishes.

"Yes." Luz nodded, folding the document in question to place in an envelope. After tea she'd ask the concierge to post it to Mr. Childers once they reached the port. "Hopefully, I'll receive some news within the next couple of weeks." Her friends nodded encouragingly while Luz's stomach twisted in knots.

Among the many surprises Luz had to grapple with in the past year, the most disconcerting one had been the realization that her father had never changed the conditions of the trust he'd set up for her when she turned sixteen. At the time, he'd arranged for it to be managed by Prescott Childers, an old friend in Edinburgh. It made sense then. She'd been young and could've used the help navigating her finances, but now, at twenty-eight, it was at best an inconvenience and at worst a potential disaster. The conditions, as they were, only granted her access to her inheritance with permission of the trustee or if she married and her spouse released it to her. To further aggravate her already-precarious situation, Prescott had been ill in the past year and had scarcely responded to her letters. The first she received in almost six months came only weeks before she departed from Santo

Domingo, informing her that Mr. Prescott Childers had passed away and the trusteeship had passed to his oldest son, Percy.

Percy was as elusive as his father.

She would never know if her father neglected to change the terms before he died because he assumed he had time or if he didn't trust Luz with the management of her inheritance. To think her father found her lacking in the ability to care for herself and her sister had been devastating. It still was. She didn't know if that wound would ever properly heal.

"Are you still with us, Luz?" Manuela teased. She'd been lost in thought again.

"My mind keeps wandering," she said by way of an apology.

"You have a lot to consider, Leona. Which is why we must make a plan for our conquest of Paris," Manu said kindly, making Luz smile at the nickname the three of them had acquired while in finishing school in Switzerland. The three Latinas who roamed the hallowed halls of the famed Ville Mont-Feu like a pride of three. Twelve years on and here they were, still ready to take on the world for each other.

"We already have plans," Luz reminded her, while she passed a biscuit to her sister. "You're presenting two of your paintings at the Beaux-Arts salon so all of France can witness your genius."

They all turned to look at Manu, who blushed at the attention. Manuela's art was the one thing she took seriously. She was talented—brilliant, even. Getting her work selected for such a prestigious event was evidence of that.

Luz Alana tipped her chin toward Aurora next. "Aurora has plans to meet with her group of women physicians at the exposition and formalize their international society of women doctors." Aurora, who had a true talent for organizing people, had been corresponding with other women physicians around the world for the past couple of years. A few of them would be in attendance to the exposition, and their friend had lofty plans for what they'd accomplish during their time together.

"You should make time to enjoy yourself too, Luz," Aurora said, uncharacteristically. If the woman whose idea of leisure was improvising a clinic in a steamer thought Luz was taking things too seriously, the situation had to be dire. But her friend lifted a hand before she could respond. "Enjoyment within reason, of course."

"Everyone brace for Aurora's list of all the things we can't do, see or touch." If there was one thing Manuela loved above all else, it was to needle their best friend.

"You are the reason I even make these lists, Manuela Caceres," Aurora retorted, falling right into the trap as usual.

Manuela leaned forward to cover Clarita's ears and whisper. "As long as your rules allow for our Luz to at least once kiss the wrong man for the right reasons."

"And *that* misguided request gives us the first rule," Aurora announced. "No falling in love."

"Love?" Manuela balked. "What does kissing have to do with love?" She was whispering but, given the gasps around the room, the acoustics were better than Luz would have thought.

"Concurred about the no falling in love. Not the kissing," Luz echoed as her friends continued to argue their differing views on what constituted enjoyment. It was not that she didn't yearn for love, for companionship…but those were for the Luz Alana who had parents and whose every decision didn't hang her sister's and her own future in the balance. Love was for girls who had someone to depend on. For her, it was merely one more item on the long list of things she could not afford.

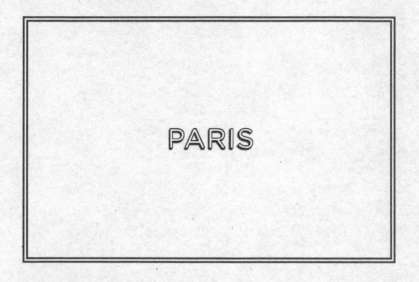

PARIS

One

Paris, May 1889

"No, absolutely not today," Luz muttered under her breath as she purposefully made her way through the thirty-meter-long maze of stalls and tables of the Palais des Industries Diverses. She kept the man currently disrupting the carefully arranged display of Caña Brava's offerings in her sights.

She'd come to the venue at dawn to set up her table. It had been an ordeal to even obtain a display space. Since the very idea that a woman distiller could be among the exhibitors seemed so distressing to the organizers, it had taken half a dozen attempts before she'd been assigned a table number, and this cad was apparently availing himself of it.

"What in the world does he think he's doing?" she hissed under her breath as she glared at the large man who was now picking up the bottle of Dama Juana she'd strategically placed just behind her Gran Reserva. She'd meticulously angled it so the light coming in from the electric chandelier overhead highlighted the roots and spices in the bottle. She'd had everything ready for the evening's judging, and now it was all ruined. Dozens of distilleries from around the world would compete for ribbons that could spark the interest of buyers. Luz was the only rum distiller in the mix, and she'd done everything she could to ensure her display was attractive to passersby, but now her table was in shambles.

The reception was the one event where she'd been able to pay an entrance fee without being required to offer an explanation as to why no man was accompanying her. The more fool her for thinking she'd get through a single day without losing her temper.

Luz was tired, *exhausted*, utterly done in by men. Long gone was the enthusiasm and optimism with which she'd boarded the train in Le Havre headed to Paris. Just that morning one more of her father's associates had told her to her face he simply did not "deal with women" before walking out on her. Which left her with less than a handful of prospects for finding a shipping partner in Europe and not a single buyer secured after a month—and now she had to deal with *this*.

"I've not seen him before. I would've noticed. He's...hard to miss." Aurora was rather breathless as she caught up to Luz.

"I would think not. He's the size of a mountain." Luz's irritation made it challenging to keep her voice down, and the man *was* startlingly large. Just then the big sod moved her hand-painted signs with the seal of Caña Brava to the side and replaced them with what she could only assume were his own bottles.

God, she could slap him.

"Ladies, if you'll excuse me, I have a man to verbally eviscerate," she said, lowering her voice to a barely audible, furious whisper. In any other circumstance she'd almost feel sorry for the man, because he was about to be the recipient of what amounted to thirty days and twelve hours of pent-up frustration.

She was armed for battle, wearing her favorite morning suit. The one luxury she'd allowed herself since she'd left Hispaniola. She knew she looked the part, a modern woman, a distiller, who had every right to be in this room. Feeling slightly less murderous, she tossed her head back and gripped the hard casing around her waist as she marched forward. If she was forced to wear all this armor for the sake of fashion, she would put it to good use.

The jacket was a blue-and-burgundy houndstooth and complemented her figure very well—with no bustle, because she had to move in these clothes and the corset was hard enough. She felt the hem of her long skirt flap against her ankles as she strode to confront the man, reciting in her head the words she'd volley at him. Though she did not reach the heights of the disrupter at her table, she was tall for a woman, and she liked that about herself. She stood at her full height in every situation, made her presence felt. Women had to fight for the very oxygen they breathed, and Luz purposefully claimed any space she entered. Leonas didn't cower to anyone. They roared.

"Excusez-moi, monsieur," she said in the most commanding tone she could manage with her ribs as constricted as they were.

"I don't speak French, lass," he said smoothly without turning to face her.

Charming.

The Scottish brogue made her stumble for a moment, not expecting to hear something so warmly familiar in that moment.

"I'm happy to communicate in English, sir." *This* finally made him stop. Luz was not prepared for what she was confronted with.

The man was irritatingly handsome. A face one could only call striking. It was the full kit. Red lips that curved into a perfect bow at the top. Thick sable hair was placated with some pomade, but for one errant curl which fell across his forehead, which she found oddly appealing. Then there was the beard paired with those dark eyebrows. They made him look a little dangerous, like a gentleman pirate. It was a most unsettling combination.

He kept his eyes on her face, his body tilting toward her, as if he wanted to inspect her more closely. She held herself tightly as he assessed her. His inquisitive eyes took their time exploring her, and she had to resist the urge to squirm. There was nothing she detested more than being looked at like an exotic animal. Although this was not the invasive, impolite examination she'd been subjected to more than once in the past few weeks. Instead of the familiar, uneasy prickle behind her neck, something much more distressing occurred. A warm and not entirely unpleasant sensation bloomed in every part of her body he focused his attention.

That was certainly not anything Luz could entertain at the moment.

"Has anyone told you gawking at women is extremely rude?" she asked peevishly.

"Where are you from?" he retorted, ignoring her comment.

She wasn't in the mood to give the man a lesson in geography, so she followed his example and disregarded his question. Instead she pointed to the bottles of Caña Brava and silk flowers, which were now fully shoved under the table. "Those go on top of the table. *My table.*"

He arched a sable eyebrow at that and leaned on the edge of said table as if he was settling in for a lengthy conversation. "*Your* table?" He was taunting her.

"Yes, mine," she practically spat. He just stood there impassively, like a gigantic, Scottish statue smiling at her as if she was the most entertaining thing he'd encountered all day. This— *this*—was the exact reason why she'd deferred dealings with other distillers to her father and she'd focused her energy in building relationships with women merchants. Men were impossible. Men were *infuriating.*

"I am an exhibitor at this event," she said, waving a hand over the pin on her lapel, which she noticed *he* was not wearing. "Or do you, like every other man in this building, have trouble grasping the concept of a woman owning a rum distillery?"

"I'm sure you're very good at it too."

Oh for… The man was scraping her nerves raw. She was feeling quite light-headed. Perhaps he'd brought on some type of rage-induced ailment.

"Although these don't look like rum," he observed as he picked up one of the bottles from the floor. That raspy growl of his was *unsettling*. Luz's heart raced as his massive hands engulfed the small squat bottle of Dama Juana. He turned it around, multiple times, holding it up so close to his face it almost brushed his perfectly trimmed beard. If she wasn't so irritated she would've laughed; he clearly hadn't the slightest idea what he had in his hands. He finally turned to look at her. Those amber eyes lit with curiosity, again she felt faint. It had to be the summer heat… yes, certainly the heat.

"What is this called?"

"It's a bottle of Dama Juana," she informed him curtly, and his nostrils flared.

"French, English and Spanish. Impressive," he offered in answer, seemingly oblivious to her increasing irritation. She bit her tongue, unsure as to why she was entertaining the man's questions. "What's inside of it?"

"Rum, *my rum*, soaked in roots and spices from the island. Some for flavor, others for medicinal purposes." She could just leave it at that, not give him what he wanted, but it was impossible for her to not explain the significance of that little bottle he was holding. "Every family back home has their own recipe for their Dama Juana, but my great-grandmother was a root worker, and her mixture was famous all over the island. I began to produce it and sell it in our local markets a few years ago."

He made a noncommittal noise and kept that unnerving whisky gaze on her. "How enterprising," he finally said, and something about his tone irked her.

Just like a man to disregard as silly feminine whimsy anything that was made for or by them. She should end this now. He'd already wasted enough of her time.

"Sir, I—"

"May I?" he asked, wrapping his fingers around the cork on the bottle, and Luz finally had enough.

"No, you may not." She didn't snatch the bottle from him, but she did manage to pry it from his unsurprisingly powerful grip. At the contact, a shock so intense ran up her forearm that she almost dropped the bottle. He reacted too, staring at his own hand with a puzzled looked on his face, then flexing it a couple of times. It made something hot and tight stir inside her.

She had no time to dwell on it since he went almost instantly back to being an irritating ass.

"That's not very reflective of the spirit of fraternité our French hosts asked us to embrace." He tsked, shaking his head from side to side like she was letting down the entirety of the exposition with her selfish attitude.

And *that* was when her patience finally snapped.

"*I* am the one fracturing the fraternal spirit of the exposition? Not every so-called gentleman who has gone out of his way to let me know I am not welcome here?" She was able to keep her voice low, but she was trembling from fury. She could not stop herself if she tried. The dam had been broken. "*I* am the one lacking in the right attitude when I've been ogled, insulted and harassed after I've paid my way like every other distiller?" Her breaths were coming in bursts, her breasts rising and falling as she glared. She was aflame with indignation. "Have you had to explain your reasons for entering this pavilion even once? Well, I have to do it every time I attempt to cross that threshold." Was her voice shaking? Oh God, she was going to cry. With great effort, she clamped her jaw together and tried to get herself under control.

His eyebrows were so high on his forehead they were practically at his hairline. She knew what would come next, and she braced herself for the insults, the sneer from him, but he only looked at her as if he was trying to decipher a very complicated puzzle. At length he finally responded, and it was not what she'd expected in the least.

"If you share the names of the men who have interfered with you, I'd be happy to acquaint them with the proper way to treat our colleagues." His voice was very even, but there was an edge of menace that made her stand a bit straighter.

He looked angry and...sincere? As though he truly intended to go searching for the offending parties. And a month ago she might've felt a small sense of relief at that, even felt gratitude for the gesture, but she knew better now. There would be no help forthcoming. All this man would accomplish was to waste her time and exhaust her patience.

You only have yourself to depend on.

"Right now, the only person interfering with my ability to do business is you," she told him, smothering the little voice in her head trying to convince her any offer of help was better than what she had now. "I am not moving my things," she told him stubbornly, returning them to the matter at hand. She was well past trying to make allies out of people who saw her as nothing more than a curiosity.

"I'm sure we can figure out an arrangement that works for both of us, Miss..." he said in that tone men used before they patted her on the head and told her to run along.

"Luz Alana Heith-Benzan." She straightened her spine as she told him her name. *Luz Alana: light* in Spanish and *beauty* in Gaelic. Light and beauty. That always helped, recalling who she was. That there was purpose in her presence here.

"Alana?" he asked, his brogue deepening even in that one word. "Are you Scots?"

"Dominican *and* Scottish." Luz didn't attempt to disguise her impatience.

"Interesting."

"My father was Scots," she bit out. "He came from Scotland to Barbados when he was a young man. But he settled in Hispaniola shortly after. It's an island in the Caribbean," she added before he could ask her. "Now that you've had your geography lesson, would you be kind enough to *move your things*?"

His upper lip twitched with humor, and she had to bite the inside of her cheek to keep from screaming.

"I know where Hispaniola is." It was truly exasperating how he handpicked which things to respond to. "My cousin was born in Jamaica."

"How nice for you," she replied in the most caustic tone she could manage, but the pendejo only laughed. That was it. She was done with this game. "If you'll excuse me, I have to fix this."

He just sent her another one of those bemused smiles.

"By fixing, you mean hiding my whisky."

She ignored him and continued to work on returning her items to the front half of the table. She dusted off her hands as she finished, piercing him with a challenging look. "Today Scotland and Dominican Republic will have to coexist on equal terms."

The naked astonishment on his face almost made her laugh, but if he ever saw her teeth they would be biting into one of those enormous hands pawing her things.

"Equal terms," he repeated, that seemingly ever-present mirth tinging his words.

"We can call it informal diplomacy. It's been done before," she said, waving a hand in front of herself. "I am living proof."

"You're very unlikely." He sounded so genuinely confused, Luz wasn't certain if he'd intended for her to hear that.

"I'm a lot less unlikely where I come from," she said wearily. "I'm not even that unlikely here."

She wasn't sure what to make of the expression on his face, and before she managed to decipher it he threw her off balance again. "I can see that for myself. Your presence is…undeniable, Miss Heith-Benzan."

His eyes on her robbed her of breath.

Luz was no ingenue. She'd been courted before and enjoyed a handsome man's attention well enough. But in the past—even when she'd been drawn to a beau—she'd found the gains that came from a man's attention to be sorely lacking if her independence was part of what was at stake. It was why she'd always felt in control in those situations: she'd accept the flurry of flattery and on occasion even allow a chaste kiss or two, then she'd walk away unaffected. Certain that what she'd left behind paled in comparison to her freedom. And now here she was, unbridled after merely minutes of this man's attention. She did not care for it.

"I'm curious to see just where we can take these diplomatic efforts." His voice jolted her out of her thoughts, and when she looked up at him, that devilish grin was fixed on his face again. "I'm positively brimming with ideas."

"And I'm positively certain I don't want to hear any of them," she retorted, making him tip his head back and laugh.

She would certainly not be charmed, and she would absolutely *not* dignify that with a comment. Since he seemed to be done with his observations on her parentage—and disturbing her bottles—she decided to take her leave while she was ahead.

"Good luck this evening. You'll need it."

And because, like her father always said, she could never just win, she had to trounce, she leaned in and whispered conspiratorially, "Caña Brava will most certainly win the overall selection, but there's always the grains-spirits category." Before he could get the final word, she turned and hurried off toward the doors that would lead her to the fairgrounds.

Just as she was about to step into the light of late-summer afternoon, she turned to glance back at the Scot and found him still looking at her. Except this time his eyes were sparkling in a completely different way, and *that* look was most certainly not what she'd come looking for in Paris.

Two

"*Do you know who that woman is?*" James Evanston Sinclair, Earl of Darnick, and the heir apparent to the Duke of Annan, asked his newly arrived friend and business partner, still watching after the force of nature as she swept out in a swirl of blue linen.

"What woman?" Raghav Kapadia asked in disbelief as he took in the remnants of Tropical Storm Luz Alana.

"The one who just walked off. She's the proprietress of the distillery that produced the bottles which are now comingling with ours," Evan clarified, but Raghav was not paying attention. He was much too distracted by the chaos on the display table.

"Did *you* move the bottles, Sinclair?"

"No," Evan answered distractedly, eyes still fixed on those delectable hips swaying out of the pavilion. "She did. I've been informed we've disrupted the rum exhibit and possibly incited an informal diplomatic incident."

Raghav made a noise of indignation, and from the clatter coming from behind him Evan assumed the man was rearranging things. Once Evan lost sight of her, he turned around to find his friend holding up one of the bottles of Caña Brava. "No, don't move the rum," he warned. "We're sharing the space."

"We're *what*?" This time Raghav's amazement was not feigned. "*Sharing?* I never knew you even understood the meaning of the word." That wasn't exactly true. Evan could be particular when it came to his whisky, but he wasn't territorial. Although, he could admit to not being one to compromise when it came to his business. Other than when Caribbean beauties were involved, apparently. "Is this heat finally getting to you?" Raghav's dark brown eyes twinkled.

"Someday you'll learn that you're not nearly as clever as you think you are," Evan quipped.

"I wasn't gone very long. How did our masculine and sober display get transformed into a tropical paradise?"

The word *paradise* evoked an image of loosening those mahogany curls draped lusciously over golden-brown shoulders. Evan required a moment to clear his head from that assault to his senses. "The owner of the artifacts we found on the stand this morning made an appearance. She suggested—" More like *demanded*, and Evan was still feeling the effects of that.

"Yes?" Raghav coaxed with a wave of hand.

"She suggested we share the display."

Raghav's gobsmacked expression would've been humorous if it wasn't Evan's own dumbfounding behavior that had provoked it.

"Since when do you comply with anyone's demands?" Raghav inquired, clearly astonished. "A complete stranger—" his business partner's index finger was now up in the air as he recounted what Evan has just said "—a *competitor* managed to get you to relinquish our territory? I must find this heroine, this master negotiator, who has bested the Braeburn himself." Raghav's voice broke on the last couple of words, laughter rumbling under his supposed astonishment.

"Sod off, Kapadia," he said without heat. "I don't have time to explain myself." The blasted man was still laughing. "We need a second table so that we each have space to display our bottles. Could you do that, please?" Evan held up a hand, knowing Raghav was probably thinking he'd lost his mind. "She seems to be here on her own."

She *had* looked exasperated. No, it was more than that. The woman seemed ready to crumble. She'd been close to tears, for God's sake. It wouldn't kill them to lend a hand, and besides, Evan had other things to worry about. "Apparently she's had a rough time of it. Other distillers giving her trouble." That last bit softened Raghav's expression.

"The Earl of Darnick has been disarmed. I am devastated to have missed it," the other man lamented, while Evan recalled the way she had stood her ground with him. He was a large man. His size alone usually had people treading with caution. But not Luz Alana Heith-Benzan. The woman was a firebrand.

"Now that I think about it, what are you doing here?" Raghav asked, finally realizing Evan was not where he was supposed to be. Which only helped to remind him why he'd been so cross before his encounter with the rum heiress.

"The meeting with the new buyers didn't go very well."

Raghav's mouth twisted in an acidic smile. "Right, the ones who won't deal with nonwhites for religious reasons." The same religion that permitted them to buy whisky by the cask prevented them from considering people with brown skin as human beings.

Evan sighed, recalling the shameless way in which they'd asked Raghav be absent of all negotiations. "I told them they could keep their business and that I refused to run interference between them and you on account of their prejudice."

Raghav shook his head adamantly.

"I told you making money off them is satisfaction enough."

Evan knew it was true, but blast it all, he shouldn't have to put up with this bloody nastiness. "I appreciate that, and typically I would agree. However, this isn't good business, Raghav. I don't run day-to-day operations, *you do*, and if they can't work with the general manager of the distillery, they can't have the Braeburn."

"All right." Raghav shook his head helplessly, but his friend's grudging smile told Evan he'd made the right choice.

"Is that for me?" he asked when he noticed the envelopes Raghav had left on the table. One in particular sent his pulse racing.

"Yes." Raghav handed him the bundle and pointed at the dark blue envelope. "From your mysterious ally." Evan knew he wasn't imagining the tightness in his friend's tone. He felt Raghav's penetrating stare on him as he turned around to open the correspondence. He didn't like lying to the people he cared about, but in this instance it could not be helped.

As always, the note was short and to the point.

There's been a positive development. Same place. Eight o'clock this evening.
ACSR

Evan placed the paper back in the envelope and slipped it into his pocket as he considered the cryptic message. It could be anything, really. It could even be the man trying to mislead Evan. He didn't dare get his hopes up. They'd thought they'd been close a few times before only to hit dead ends.

"Is it good news?" Raghav's voice jolted Evan, and he schooled his face before turning around. He knew his friend worried about his secret dealings with this enigmatic new associate.

"Maybe," Evan said vaguely. "I'll know more tonight." If Raghav only knew just how much hung in the balance. The future of the Braeburn and finally exacting revenge on his father all depended on this. Tonight it might finally be within reach.

"Do you think this person will really get you what you

need to get the Braeburn out of your father's control?" Raghav had asked this question before, confused as to why a complete stranger would offer to help Evan finally get the documents he needed to extract the deed for the distillery from the duke.

"I have something that is of use to him," Evan told Raghav, saying more than he should. His friend didn't look very convinced by that but let it go. There was a reason why Evan had made Raghav his general manager. The man was nothing if not pragmatic. He knew, as Evan did, that continuing to grow and expand a business that they didn't rightfully own was a particularly perilous game. Every year the Braeburn's success and profits grew, his father was less likely to see reason. It didn't much matter how he gained full possession of his business, as long as he finally got it out of his father's clutches, before it was too late.

Since he'd taken the helm of the distillery that had belonged to his maternal grandfather ten years ago, the phylloxera infestation in France had practically decimated the brandy market. Evan had been one of the first distillers to anticipate that the demand for whisky would grow as brandy production dwindled, and he'd made a fortune because of it. Everyone wanted fine Scotch whisky and while some of his savvier competitors had been able to quickly adapt as the demand continued to increase, Evan had had to cajole his father for every concession that allowed him to expand. He'd offered to buy the Braeburn outright on more than one occasion, but the duke had refused every time. The threat of selling the distillery from under Evan was too effective a tool to keep him docile for his father to ever consider letting it go. Which meant the offer to finally get his distillery and his revenge could've come from the devil himself and he would've taken it just the same.

"Evan, did you hear a word I said?" Raghav asked impatiently.

"Sorry," he apologized as he tore into the next missive, this one from the duke.

"Murdoch's telegram said he arrives this evening and also warned that Beatrice and Adalyn are on the same train."

Evan groaned but was not surprised about his sisters—they did not like to be left out. His cousin Murdoch was, like Evan, part of the consortium of private businessmen who were financing unofficial British presence at the exposition—since the Crown decided to boycott the event—and had been traveling back and forth between Edinburgh and Paris for months. He was an engineer, and his firm had been heavily involved with multiple projects being built for the exposition, including Gustave Eiffel's tower.

"I'm surprised they didn't come with Gerard," Evan said distractedly as he unfolded the two cards from his father. His sister Beatrice's husband, Gerard Ruthven—who was the son of the current British ambassador in France—arrived in Paris the week before heading a delegation of financiers who had descended on the French capital looking for investments.

The correspondence from his father was an invitation for the ball his second wife would be hosting in honor of the duke's sixtieth birthday. Evan refused to even think of the new Duchess of Annan as his stepmother, considering she'd been *his* fiancée before she decided being the wife of the second son of a duke was not nearly as appealing as being a duchess. That experience had cured Evan of any desire for romantic entanglements. His appetite for bedding a beautiful woman when the desire arose remained as healthy as ever, but allowing his emotions for one of them to rule his common sense or detract him from his work? Never again. In truth, he didn't even have the energy to resent his former lover. Being married to his father was punishment enough.

The thought of icy, aloof Charlotte, who at one time he had considered to be the epitome of beauty, brought back to mind the hellion he'd just encountered. Luz Alana Heith-Benzan could not be more different than the woman he'd fancied himself in love with once. Evan had been drawn to Charlotte's vulnerability. She'd brought out his protective instincts. She'd always seemed too delicate for the world, and he'd wanted to shield her. Luz Alana, on the contrary, stood strong and tall even when it seemed clear to Evan that she too needed a defender. A woman doing business on her own in a world that constantly repudiated them had to carry more than a few battle scars, but she was unwavering. The difference was, of course, that Charlotte was happy to be taken care of and Luz Alana would not have a man as her savior.

A golden Amazon pulsing with purpose. The rum heiress had certainly elicited a reaction from him, not to protect her perhaps, but to safeguard. To ensure she struck where she aimed, that she accomplished what she intended. But as intriguing as she was, Evan's own challenges were not going to solve themselves. He was here to sell some whisky and, hopefully after tonight, obtain the last piece he needed to enact his father's undoing. He could not allow a pretty face and tempting rump to deviate him from the mission.

"It appears there will be a ball to celebrate the duke's birthday," he finally told Raghav.

Evan's disgust rose as he read over the accompanying note asking that he incur the costs of the event. To this request, the Duke of Annan had added a reminder that he'd had multiple offers for the purchase of the Braeburn but had kindly declined them, for Evan's sake. "I have been bestowed the honor of paying for most it."

Raghav leaned in to read off the paper in Evan's hand and made a sound of revulsion. "Your father is an atrocious human being."

"Which is why I need this plan to work," he murmured, feeling more determined than ever to do whatever it took to break free from his father once and for all.

"Indeed," Raghav conceded, then pointed to a tiny barrel

adorned with a variety of tropical silk flowers. "What shall I do about this?"

Evan's eyes drifted to the bottles of dark amber liquid next to his own water of life. He had to admit the dark blue and silver letters on her bottles contrasted well with his own green and gold. Something rather alarming bloomed inside him as he recalled that pert nose and strong chin staring him down, telling him she was living proof Scots and Dominicans could learn to get along.

Regret was not a feeling Evan indulged, but in that moment he wished his life and his plans allowed for the chance to find out for himself what Dominicans and Scots could do when they engaged in...relations.

"Get the table for her, please," he told Raghav with finality. Attempting to explain what it was about this woman that had made him so conciliatory would require he think over things he simply had no time for. "And don't expect me here this evening. I have to look in on my sisters and make sure Adalyn knows she can't stay with me." There was no way his widowed sister was going to stay in a flat with three bachelors, but she was reckless enough to expect that very thing.

Raghav quirked an eyebrow at that. "I would love to see how your sister takes to being told what to do."

"I am cursed with strong-willed women." His vision filled once again with that unflinching chocolate gaze and the delightfully raspy voice berating him for touching her rum. Before he could bite his tongue the words were out of his mouth. "Find out what you can about the rum maker. It sounded like she could use some help."

"Are you offering to be her champion?" Raghav asked, annoyingly delighted by Evan's newfound heroism. "Now I am truly looking forward to learning more about this rum heiress. I'm so impressed with her work already." The corners of his friend's lips turned up.

"I help people," Evan said peevishly.

Raghav nodded in acknowledgment, a seriously irritating smile on his lips. "You are a very generous man, but you're not usually distracted by a pretty face when you are in your business pursuits." That was his best friend's polite way of saying that Evan could be a ruthless bastard who would mow anyone down when he was after something.

All true, but he still wanted to extend a hand. He was serious about the fraternité spirit. His lips turned up on their own volition when he remembered what she'd told him what he could do with his brotherly love.

"I am serious, Raghav. Just let her know if she has any more trouble we can help her."

"All right. Come see me at the office when you're done with Adalyn. You'll need a drink and some more affable company… after."

Maybe it would do him good to search out a way to release some of this tension. The office Raghav was referring to was none other than Le Bureau, the most exclusive brothel in Paris, where they had spent a few evenings since their arrival in the city. If you desired it, Le Bureau would provide it, for a price. Raghav had been availing himself of the company of a couple of very amenable young men, and Evan couldn't deny he had grown to appreciate the ease of getting what he needed without complications. He liked exchanges where everyone knew what was expected of them. Evan's father's penchant for setting the rules of a game and unilaterally changing them while everyone else ran around trying to fulfill his whims had helped him develop a true loathing for surprises. At places like Le Bureau, everyone knew their role and behaved accordingly.

"Fine," he finally agreed, picking up his cane and hat. "You're a terrible influence."

"Yet here you are engaged in a business partnership with such a reprobate. Sédar has a special program tonight," Raghav explained pleasantly, as if he were talking about a literary salon. "Live coitus, apparently. As per the request of some distinguished exhibitors." Raghav lifted a shoulder in a uniquely Gallic expression. "When in Paris…"

The mention of a live coitus show was as good a time as any to end a conversation. With a tip of his hat, Evan turned toward the exit. It was getting late, and if he was to make his appointment, he had to make haste. Despite himself he took a fountain pen from his pocket and quickly scribbled a note. He handed it to Raghav before departing.

"Make sure she gets this."

Who the *she* was didn't need to be voiced out loud.

Evan climbed the steps to the now-familiar private mansion on avenue Montaigne, marveling that it was only six months ago he'd been summoned to this address for the first time. Since then, he'd come here a dozen times to plot and plan. He'd known they'd been getting closer, and he hoped that tonight he'd finally have in his hands what he needed to set everything in motion. The last piece of the puzzle that would result in his father's undoing. The thought was oddly calming. After all, Evan had been preparing for this end since the first night he'd come to this place…when he'd been made aware of a secret that cast his father's past misdeeds into a new and far more sinister light.

What he and his coconspirator intended to do would not come without consequences. The ones for Evan were clear and irreversible, and beyond those there was no way to predict how his father would react when his secret was brought to light. Which was why no one, not Raghav nor Murdoch nor his sisters, had any idea with whom he had been working. He *had* revealed to them that he was growing closer to some proof showing his mother had left a will, but they didn't know the hows or whys.

The moment he stepped up to the black door, his host's butler appeared on the threshold ushering him in.

"Bonsoir, monsieur. He is waiting for you." Mr. Pasquet was an imposing man, with the height and presence one expected in a butler of a grand home. His skin was a deep brown that reminded Evan of ebony. It was impossible to pinpoint his age—not a young man, but certainly not old. His hair was very short, and he always dressed impeccably.

Being the son of a duke meant Evan had lived surrounded by opulence all his life, but the wealth and elegance in his family's homes felt dated. Almost obsolete. Too much gold leaf and frescoes, wall hangings with the faces of ancestors he'd rather not think about.

This home was elegant, to be sure, but it felt modern. Almost involuntarily, his eyes went to a large painting on the wall. It was of a boy looking out a window, his torso erect, as he clutched the sill. He was smiling brightly, as though his eyes had finally landed on the person he'd been waiting at the window for. The figure seemed to jump out of the canvas. His delight at whatever he saw was hard to turn away from. When he'd inquired about the artist, Evan had been informed the painter was José Ferraz de Almeida Júnior, a Brazilian who'd trained at the École des Beaux-Arts.

Not far from that one was a landscape of a valley sunset with colors that fascinated Evan. There were cliffs made of red rock and green hills under a vast pink-and-purple sky. He'd been so distracted admiring it he almost crashed into the carved double doors which led to the studio where Evan usually conferred with the master of the house.

"Entrez." Evan stiffened when he heard the baritone through the closed doors. He braced himself as Pasquet pushed them open. These meetings could be unpredictable. More than once Evan's temper had slipped from his control.

"Welcome, brother." Evan knew to at least expect that taunting greeting, and yet it still caught him by surprise. He found it disorienting to be confronted with the type of authoritative demeanor he typically commanded in this sort of exchange. Equally disorienting was encountering a face so undeniably similar to his and yet unknown for most of his life. Evan's size was notable. Even in Scotland, where Highlanders were known for their considerable height and strength, he stood out. Iain— his older brother, now five years dead—had taken after their mother, as did his sisters. Lean and fine-boned where Evan was built like his father. So, apparently, was the other brother he'd never known existed, who tonight lounged in one of the room's plush armchairs.

Apollo César Sinclair Robles, the son of a woman the Duke of Annan had married when he'd been nothing more than the second son of a duke hunting for a fortune in the Americas. Evan knew what that was like, the drive to secure a future. Except his father, instead of working, chose to marry a young heiress in Cartagena. When she died in childbirth, he'd abandoned the child and fled to back to Scotland with his newfound wealth. The son survived, and was raised by an aunt, his mother's older sister. She, in turn, left the boy her sizable fortune, which Apollo would now use to destroy the man who had abandoned him on the day of his birth. The man who hadn't even had the decency to give the wife he'd let die in her childbed a proper burial.

Evan hoped to be there when it happened.

"Evening." Evan offered Apollo a nod and went to procure a drink. His older brother liked to play games, calling urgent meetings, then taking his time delivering the news, but Evan didn't have patience for it tonight. "What do you have?" he asked, taking the armchair across from Apollo.

Without saying a word, the other man walked to his desk and picked up what looked like a bank-vault box. He noticed Apollo was not making light of what they were discussing tonight. He usually provoked Evan with something salacious or prodded until they came close to blows. It was like putting two tigers in a cage, but tonight he was subdued. He seemed almost somber when he sat down and gently set the box in front of Evan.

He didn't recognize it, was certain he'd never seen it. And yet something about the way that Apollo was looking at him, his eyes serious, made Evan's skin prickle with apprehension.

"This was your mother's," Apollo said stonily, and Evan's stomach soured. "The lock was removed by me. We had to look inside to make sure it contained what we'd been after."

"How did you find it?" Evan croaked.

"It took a lot of doing. I didn't want to tell you unless we knew the lead was good. One of my men located it." In the last year Evan had learned that his brother had many men working for him, and quite a number of them did not exactly observe the rule of law. "He tracked down the name of the woman who had attended to your mother at that sanatorium." Five years before Catriona Sinclair's death, the duke had had her put in a sanatorium, claiming she was a danger to herself and her family. Neither Evan nor any of his siblings had been allowed to visit her. She'd died there alone.

"After a lot of doing, we found an address for the attendant in Stirling. She passed away a few months ago, but she'd left the box with her daughter." Apollo looked quite pleased with himself, and though his usual bravado was tempered somewhat, his eyebrows were arched in an expression Evan had seen in the mirror many times. Even after all these months Evan found himself taken aback by this man who looked so much like him. His brother's brown skin and curlier hair were the only two things that were really different from his own. Otherwise, they could've been twins.

"How did you get her to hand it over?"

"She parted with it once we told her we were working for you, and after we put a few guineas in her purse. It's in there," Apollo told him ominously.

Suddenly, Evan felt unsteady, unprepared. He'd been hoping

they could find his mother's will, but he had never expected a box. In the seven years since her death, he'd held on to his anger toward his father like a lifeline. He'd pushed down every reminder of the woman who'd birthed him. He told himself he didn't deserve to dwell on those tender memories when he'd failed to save her.

He tightened his fingers on the lid to stop the shaking as the contents were revealed. There was an opal bracelet and an emerald necklace he recognized, along with several rings. One he hadn't seen since he was a boy. His mother's aquamarine ring. It had been a gift from his grandmother, and Catriona had always said she would give it to him or Iain, whichever of the two was first to marry. But when Evan announced his intention to marry Charlotte, Catriona had never offered it.

Not that Charlotte would have been content with a simple aquamarine and a few small diamonds. She'd been very particular about the jeweler and stones she preferred.

He removed the jewelry carefully, setting each piece on the table beside him, and returned to uncover two small envelopes. The sight of his mother's elegant looping handwriting made his throat close for a moment. He breathed through his nose, reading his sisters' names on one of the envelopes and his and Iain's on the other. He set those aside to be examined more closely when he was alone. The only thing left was a small bundle of folded papers.

"The will."

Apollo nodded, but his expression changed. "Yes, but Evan—" something about the warning in his voice made Evan snap his gaze back to his brother "—there's a complication."

"A *complication*?" He scanned the words on the pages quickly, his heart hammering. There was no satisfaction in this. Winning like this was not winning. The thought of his mother alone in that place knowing no one would come for her gnawed at him. No, this was no victory, but he would make his father pay.

He made himself focus on the paper in his hands, his anger rising with every word he read. To Beatrice and Adalyn she'd left dowries they'd never received. To Iain she'd left the town house in Heriot Row and the estate in Dundee, which he would have received at the time of his marriage. The same properties their father had borrowed against so many times they were currently in the process of being repossessed by the bank. Before going on he made himself reach for the tumbler of whisky Apollo had placed in front on him and took a searing gulp. The liquid sat in his stomach like sludge. The final wish of his mother was for the Braeburn to go to Evan. Despite his dark mood, his pulse raced as he read, and then the complication became clear. The house, the land and the distillery would go to him on the occasion of his marriage…as a wedding gift.

"A wedding gift?" he asked, biting off a curse.

"That's what it says," Apollo retorted, with a hint of a sardonic smile on his lips Evan would've dearly loved to swipe off. His mother had always been obsessed with her children marrying. It was one of those things Evan could never understand. Her own union to his father was so troubled. And yet, she maintained the hope that they would find love. Bitterness flooded his mouth at the thought of what his mother would've thought of the duke's new wife.

"The duke can't refute the contents of that will." Apollo's assurances pulled Evan out of his ruminations and brought him back to the problem at hand. His brother sipped from his own whisky and shrugged. "It's not ideal, but the document is verifiable and legal. The duke has to give you the distillery once you get married."

Wrung out, Evan slumped back in the leather armchair as he tried to make sense of what this meant. The distillery could be his…if he married. Evan could not think of anything less appealing than the prospect of tying himself to someone, even if it was temporary. But he would still do it, whatever it took. This was not merely about finally claiming what was rightfully his. The distillery was his future. It would be his livelihood. Especially after Apollo made his existence known and assumed his place as heir apparent.

Not that the Duke of Annan had anything but debts for his successor.

"We began the process of acquiring the last of it this morning," Apollo voiced into Evan's stunned silence. It took a second for him to realize what his brother had said, but once he did, he turned his full attention on Apollo. His brother, with Evan's help, had over the past six months identified every debt their father had accrued and had systematically bought them out. Every penny the duke had borrowed, he now owed to his sons.

"How long?"

Apollo lifted a shoulder, a cold glimmer in his eyes. "Ten days, perhaps a fortnight," he said and smiled darkly. "Depends on how shambolic our father left things."

"We have two weeks, then," Evan scoffed. Their father had the tendency of grabbing for money without much regard to where and under what conditions he signed off. It had taken a dozen solicitors and accountants to untangle the mess he'd made.

"Be ready in one," Apollo said dryly. "There is still the matter of when and where we will make our father aware of our little partnership."

A shiver coursed through Evan at his brother's sinister tone. Evan had absolutely no qualms about publicly humiliating their father; on the contrary, he would relish every second of it. Various scenarios had been discussed, but they could not set a time until the will had been found. Evan patted the invitation from the duke in his jacket pocket. "I've just been invited to the duke's yearly birthday ball to take place next month in Edinburgh."

Apollo's grin was sharp as the blade of a knife. "Mine must have gotten lost in the post," he said caustically. "What kind of sons would we be if we did not help our father celebrate?" Every word out of the man's mouth dripped with malice.

It would be an unholy mess. Utter and complete humiliation for the duke.

"We must be there, of course," Evan said as a frisson of anticipation licked up his spine.

"I suggest you sort out your marital situation by then. It will go infinitely better if we do it all at the same time."

Evan nodded, without missing the warning in his brother's voice. Apollo had fulfilled his end of the deal, finding the proof Evan needed to get the Braeburn out of his father's hands. Evan would, in return, assist his brother in claiming his place as the heir to the dukedom of Annan.

"I'll be ready."

Three

Paris was a long way from Hispaniola, Luz mused as she took in the lively scene at Le Grand Véfour. Antonio, a cousin of Aurora's who had been living in Paris for a few years, had brought them there, claiming it was the place to see and be seen. And there certainly was lots to see; at almost midnight the place was bustling with people.

Luz sank into the red velvet banquette as she took in the scene. The expansive dining room was flanked with rows of round tables, filled with diners all dressed in the latest fashions. The walls were embellished with elaborate white molding, done in the wedding-cake style. Paintings of Bourgogne landscapes displayed on baroque gold frames lined the walls. That, paired with the mouthwatering aroma of butter and garlic wafting from the sizzling platters the servers carried around the room, made for a true feast for the senses. It was Paris, after all, and here absolutely nothing was considered too much when it came to indulgence. This was not a place for those pursuing moderation, and after the year she'd had and the travails she was sure awaited her, Luz would partake as much as she could.

"We have champagne." Manuela's delighted voice pulled Luz

from her reverie and back to her friends. "I do love these chaperone-free adventures," her friend announced happily.

"Amaranta's going to stop letting you do whatever you please one of these days, Manu." Aurora was the most reluctant of the group when it came to mischief—at least the kind that didn't involve more political causes. Still, she took the glass of champagne Manuela handed her and gulped it down thirstily.

"Never. She wants us to enjoy ourselves!" Manuela asserted, and though their cousin Amaranta was quite lenient as a chaperone, these evening adventures were certainly pushing her boundaries.

Luz just shook her head at her beautiful friend. For the evening, Manuela had selected an emerald green gown which enhanced all her best attributes. The fabric had been selected for her by Charles Frederick Worth himself, and the jewel color contrasted against Manu's deeply brown skin was stunning. Her friend could be fanciful and a bit naive when it came to the people she cared for, but she knew the power of her beauty, and she wielded it with ruthless precision. Tonight Manuela was out for blood.

The plan was to dine first and then walk to Le Bureau, the most notorious—and luxurious—brothel in Paris for what was being billed as a *special program* in honor of the exposition. Amaranta, as lenient as she was, would never approve of evenings at brothels. Which was why Manuela suggested they curate the report of their intended entertainments for the night. According to her, what Amaranta did not know would not hurt her. Luz tended to agree and had happily smiled and nodded along when Manu informed Amaranta that after dinner they'd take in a performance of Jules Massenet's *Esclarmonde* at the Théâtre Lyrique.

In truth, Le Bureau was of interest to Luz not for its scandalous reputation but because it was owned and operated by Sédar and Seynabou Cisse-Kelly, a pair of Irish Senegalese siblings, who were extremely good people to know if one was in the business of selling spirits. Tonight she intended to introduce herself to Seynabou, who Antonio assured her would connect her to the right people and perhaps become a buyer herself. Luz was optimistic about the possibility. One thing she'd seen again and again in the time she'd worked with a salesforce made up of only women in Santo Domingo was that women in trade were unmatched in their resourcefulness and could be magnificent allies.

She no longer could count on formal channels to keep her business afloat. A person could only have so many doors slammed in their face before they gave up the illusion that what worked for some could also work for them. Men would not deal with her—nothing surprising there—so she would have to carve her own path going forward, and she would not accomplish that by having tea with society ladies.

"Antonio, did Luz tell you about her encounter today?"

"Manu," Luz warned as her friend offered her a feline grin. "There is nothing to say." She lied even as her stomach swooped at the mention of her clash with the Scot distiller. The distiller who had not been present tonight at the judging. She *had* looked for him, she'd berated herself for it, but she had let her gaze stray more than once looking for a tall figure with sable hair.

"*Nothing* to say? About the Great Scot?"

Aurora snorted at the name Manuela had given the man. Luz knew better than to encourage her and bit back a smile.

"He was positively taken with our Leona."

"Taken?" Luz scoffed, then turned her attention to Antonio, who had his hands propped on his chin as if he was settling in for a bedtime story. "The man was a nuisance." An exceedingly attractive nuisance, but a nuisance, nonetheless. "He almost ruined my display," she explained.

"It seemed he saw the error of his ways," Aurora reminded Luz. And he had done that, or at least finally recognized that one table was not enough for both of them to properly feature their spirits. When she'd arrived at the reception that evening, she'd found two smaller tables side by side where the one they'd argued over had been. On one all her bottles had been artfully placed, almost exactly as she'd initially arranged them. The Scot's whisky bottles—*Braeburn*, she'd learned—stood on the other.

She'd been annoyingly pleased when she'd found a note on heavy paper, pinned under the Dama Juana.

I hope this manages to keep an impending diplomacy incident at bay...at least for now.
-ES

He thought he was clever, and she really ought not to have been as charmed as she was by the note. But he *had* fixed their problem and found a way to get them both what they wanted.

"You didn't back down, and that's what matters," Aurora continued, bringing Luz out of her reverie. "And you did magnificently at the judging tonight, querida."

"And looked wonderful doing it," Manuela added, making Luz blush. She caught a reflection of herself in a mirror on the wall opposite them. She did love this midnight blue gown. Having only recently come out of mourning, she hadn't worn anything this sumptuous—or exposed—in an age. She took in the cap sleeves threaded with silver that gave the illusion of constellations. The plunging bodice which frankly revealed almost too much. She was dressed to make a statement this evening, even if she wasn't yet certain what in particular she wanted to communicate. Even if she'd chosen the dress while a certain distiller, and the possibility of seeing him again, had been plaguing her mind.

"Glasses raised, mesdemoiselles," Antonio quipped, mercifully distracting Luz.

"To our rum Leona. Congratulations on winning the selection," Manuela declared, a little louder than necessary, causing a sea of heads to turn in their direction.

"Salud," Luz echoed, puffing up with pride. There had been almost one hundred spirits in the judging, and only twenty were selected for an award. It was all the sweeter to have seen her rum be selected for a gold medal this evening after so many weeks of setbacks. Tonight's success was a timely reminder for her that if she managed to get Caña Brava into the hands of the right people, she would succeed. She knew what she had. It was just a matter of others catching up to that. And this rum maker was not giving up without a fight.

"Ay no, Luz," Manuela grumbled, hand flapping in her direction. "That's not the countenance I expect to see on a woman who is about to conquer Parisian nightlife." Manuela liked to appear to the world like she was selfish and vain, but her friend was one of the most observant people she knew. Manuela was attuned to the people she loved: she'd probably seen the fretting written all over Luz's face.

Luz shook her head, not wanting to bring the mood of the table down with her, and instead veered right into the one thing she ought not be thinking about. "Don't mind me. I was just wondering why after all the commotion this afternoon, the Scot could not bother to make an appearance."

"He made up for it," Manuela retorted as she topped everyone's glass with more champagne.

Luz made a face.

"The man probably had one of his helpers get the table. It's not like he found the timber and carved the thing on the spot."

"He didn't have to do it and he did, and that's not nothing," Aurora retorted, which Luz could not exactly deny. "And his business partner was quite dashing." That was said with a speaking glance directed in Antonio's direction.

"I'll concede Mr. Kapadia *was* delightful," Luz admitted before applying herself to the plate of escargots that had been placed in front of her. The snails' texture reminded her of the conch dishes that were so popular at home. But even if she hadn't been used to the chewiness, the garlic and butter sauce they were smothered in was reason enough to try them. She listened to the others distractedly as she pried one off the shell with a tiny fork.

"Kapadia was very curious about you," Antonio informed the table, and Luz almost catapulted her little gray snail into the table across from them.

"What do you mean, *curious*?" she asked diffidently before popping the escargot into her mouth, hoping the chewy mollusk would keep her from any outbursts.

"He mentioned that you'd—" Antonio cleared his throat as he obviously tried to keep his lips from turning up into a smile "—that you'd piqued Mr. Sinclair's interest."

Sinclair.

It suited him. Luz's foolish heart gave a little hop at the revelation, and she valiantly refrained from asking what the other letter in his initials stood for.

"He also asked about your business, and I told him that you were here with the hopes of bringing your rum to European markets." Antonio stopped to take a sip from his glass of champagne, and Luz had to bite her tongue to keep from asking him to get on with it. "They are based in Edinburgh, and I mentioned you intend to settle there. I hope that's all right."

"It's fine," she assured him when he started biting his lip. Antonio had a propensity of regaling third parties with long-winded biographical accounts of his associates. By now, Kapadia was probably intimately acquainted with her life's story.

"He asked me to extend an offer to assist you in any way you required once you arrive in Scotland."

"Oh?" The heat on her face and her racing heart were likely surprise at the unexpected kindness. Nothing to do with E. Sinclair and his sinful smile.

"That's a generous offer," Aurora observed.

"Indeed." Manu nodded. "That Scot might be a useful man to know, given the situation with Childers."

Luz's stomach twisted at the mere mention of her elusive trustee. That afternoon they'd arrived at their town house in the Place des Vosges, only to find a letter from Mr. Bruce, the solicitor who had been handling her inheritance. The man informed her that Percy Childers had refused her request to release the funds of her inheritance. She despised being in this position and once again wished her father had been more forthcoming with her on affairs that affected her future. That he had at least confided in her that he was reluctant to leave the finances in her control. That way she would have at least been prepared for this battle. Another one she'd have to fight on her own.

Sinclair and his self-assured, commanding face appeared in her mind. Perhaps, if all else failed with Childers, he could be a last resort.

"He'll be at Le Bureau tonight," Antonio said, an eyebrow raised salaciously.

"Sinclair will be there?" The question flew out of her mouth before she had any chance of stopping herself.

"Monsieur Kapadia only mentioned *he* would be attending the special program this evening."

Sinclair got under her skin in all the wrong ways, but his business partner seemed a good sort. She was already intending to search out the owner of Le Bureau; she'd just add properly introducing herself to Mr. Kapadia to her endeavors for the evening.

Manuela had made Luz promise to enjoy herself tonight, and she still planned to, once she'd taken care of more important matters.

"I just want to note that I am not in favor of this outing," Aurora complained, turning everyone's attention toward her. "There may be people we know there. There are hundreds of Mexicans here for the exposition as well as Venezuelans and Dominicans. Frankly, the last thing I want is to run into the same sanctimonious bores I left Veracruz to get away from."

There was an astonishing number of attendants from the

Americas at the exposition. Thousands arrived from the thirteen countries which were hosting pavilions, and many others were there as guests or to do business. Just the day before, Luz had conversed with a physician from Guayaquil, Ecuador, who had delayed his return home after finishing his studies at La Sorbonne to be part of his country's delegation. Paris was a thrilling place to be, but she understood Aurora's trepidation.

Manuela made an unhappy sound as she took a bite of steak tartare. "If they're also enjoying the establishment's entertainment, what moral high ground do they have to judge us for doing the same?"

"Some of us are trying to practice medicine in an already very difficult terrain and need our reputation to be taken seriously, Manuela."

Manuela's mouth lifted in the sneer which usually meant she was about to say something utterly disreputable, and Luz braced for it. "And some of us are trying to ruin our reputations so we can be left in peace, Aurora."

"Don't be too hard on her, Manu. She likes to be careful," Luz said as she leaned to squeeze Aurora's hand. Luz took in Aurora's tense shoulders and found that she understood her better now than she ever had. It wasn't that Aurora couldn't let her guard down. It was that as a woman—a Black woman at that—Aurora was confronted with naysayers at every step. It made one feel like the only way to live was perennially battle ready. Manuela, who could never stay angry for more than a minute, slumped in her chair and put an arm over Aurora's shoulders.

"Fine, I'll behave. Unless of course the opportunity presents itself to do a little damage," she said, holding her index and thumb with a sliver of space between them, then pointed her coupe at Luz. "Luz Alana could be outright catastrophic in that gown."

Luz ran a hand over the embroidery along the edge of her bodice and smiled. This interlude was likely her last time to indulge and misbehave before she bid goodbye to her carefree past and settled in for a life of endless responsibilities. If she was destined for spinsterhood, she would only arrive there after this brief detour. And when images of a certain handsome face with a lazy smile and intoxicating honey-colored eyes began parading in her mind, she brushed them aside. She had bigger game to hunt.

Luz stood and picked up her beaded reticule, signaling to the others it was time to press onward. Le Bureau awaited.

"Paris, beware! This pride is on the prowl."

Four

"A wedding gift," Evan's cousin Murdoch noted apprehensively for the third time in as many minutes.

"Yes," Evan answered as he ran his hands over his face. They were in a carriage on their way to meet Raghav at Le Bureau. After Apollo's revelations, he was indeed in need of a distraction. Once again, his mind—as it had all day—drifted back to the rum heiress, and he wondered how she had fared at the reception tonight.

"And you're sure this proof you obtained is legitimate?" Murdoch's aggrieved tone pulled Evan from his recollection of the beauty.

"I'm sure," he said, in an attempt to smooth the scowl on the other man's face. "The documents are legitimate." Apollo's men had been able to obtain the name of the attorney who had drawn up the will. Funny thing about that attorney. When Apollo's men had tracked him down, they'd discovered he'd been killed on his way home from his London office only six months after Evan's own mother's death. Evan couldn't help but wonder if the duke had that man's blood on his hands too.

"It's all in the papers she left. Grandfather left the Braeburn to her in trust, and its management only passed to my father because he claimed there was no will."

Murdoch made a noncommittal sound as he digested the information. He understood where his cousin's frustration was coming from. This was the first time in their entire lives that Evan had kept a secret from him. Not since the moment they'd met at ten years old when Murdoch's father—Evan's uncle—had returned from Jamaica with a wife and three children. Catriona Sinclair, despite her husband's disapproval, had made sure Evan and his siblings grew close with their cousins, and Evan and Murdoch had embraced each other with the unbounded enthusiasm that only two rambunctious boys can have. Since then, Murdoch had been Evan's confidant for everything. It was not easy keeping Apollo's existence from his cousin, but this was something Evan had to do alone. Murdoch would likely disagree and say this was just Evan's need to martyr himself for the sins of his father. Perhaps in part it was, but he would not let this touch anyone he loved.

"Mother always thought there was something odd about that." There was no love lost between Murdoch's mother, Odessa, and the duke. She'd despised the way he'd treated Catriona.

"She also left me one of Grandmother's rings," Evan told Murdoch, who grunted as if he'd punched him in the stomach. Their grandmother, who'd had humble beginnings, was not the distant, cold matriarch that was so common in the Scottish peerage. She'd doted on *all* her grandchildren with equal fervor. She'd been the one to encourage Evan to take part in the whisky business when he'd expressed curiosity on a long-ago visit to the Braeburn.

Evan's mother had been loving too, but her health, especially her nerves, was fragile, and his father exploited that. Hers was a blind love. In her eyes her husband could do no wrong, and the Duke of Annan abused that devotion in every manner he could, until he had no use for his wife. Then he'd forsaken her to a fate

Evan wouldn't wish on his worst enemy... No, that wasn't true. What he wished on his father was far worse than that.

Evan's musings were interrupted when their carriage came to a stop in front of Le Bureau. Murdoch sent him a questioning look as they reached the bloodred doors.

"Your father is not going to take this lightly. He does not like to lose."

Evan only nodded as they waited for one of the two large men standing on either side of the doors to allow them in. The duke did not like to lose, but the plans Apollo and Evan had would not exactly offer him many choices.

"Why not wait? Once you become duke it will all go to you."

Evan scoffed at that. "Come on, cousin. That could take twenty years." And there was also the minor detail of Evan no longer being the heir apparent. "I can't run that risk. The distillery is the only holding of my father's that not mired in debt. It's only a matter of time before he sells it. And you know it's about far more than that. My father stole this from me."

Murdoch grimaced before clapping Evan's shoulder. "Sounds like we're in the market for a bride, then," Murdoch announced as they entered the expansive front room of Le Bureau. That was his cousin's way: he would never lie to Evan or spare him a harsh truth, but at the end of the day, he would be at his side.

"Am I supposed to find a wife here?" Evan stood next to Murdoch, scanning the room with the practiced ease of those who had learned to hunt together. A brothel was probably not the maiden market his mother had envisioned when she planned for his wedding gift. But there was very little left of Catriona's dreams for her children, Evan thought bitterly.

"At least you can count on the negotiation process being transparent."

Evan laughed at that, though the mention of a woman with canny negotiation skills brought Luz Alana Heith-Benzan back to mind. He could not deny the prospect of a wedding night with her *was* extremely tempting. Though, he could not imagine she'd be amenable to being his—or any man's—temporary bride.

And it *would* be temporary. Evan's life could not accommodate a real marriage—not that any of the women of his class would want to be cleaved to him once he lost his title and became Edinburgh's biggest scandal in a decade. No, what he wanted was to be left in peace to make his whisky. Once things with Apollo were finalized, the only plan Evan had was to spend his days at the Braeburn and hopefully make right some of his father's wrongs.

"Mm." Evan snapped his head up at the sound of appreciation coming from his cousin; given where they were, it could only mean one thing. "If the offerings tonight are all as enticing as the jewel currently talking to Raghav, we may be en route to Gretna Green at first light."

The room was large and very crowded, and it took Evan a few seconds to see who his cousin was referring to. Once he recovered from the shock of finding Luz Alana at a brothel at least one hour past midnight, his eyes drank her in.

She was dressed in silver and deep blue tonight, her skin glowing against the satiny fabric of her bodice. Her hair, which he'd seen up earlier today, cascaded around her shoulders in dark brown ringlets. She and Raghav were roughly the same height and she had her head very close to his in order to hear what he was saying. Whatever it was must have been amusing, because her face split open in a delighted smile, and suddenly the idea of being tied to a woman didn't seem quite so confining.

Finding her here was not something he would've anticipated, and yet there she was. *And why was she here?*

"Did you listen to a single word I said, Evan?" Murdoch's aggravated tone directed his attention back to his cousin and away from the vision in blue and silver stealing his focus.

"I know her," he rasped. His throat felt rusty, and there were strange things happening inside him. Like the impulse to go place himself between her head and Raghav's. Pluck the man right off the ground and put some distance between him and the heiress. Ten or fifteen feet would do.

"You stopped talking," Murdoch murmured. Right, he'd been in the middle of a sentence. Perhaps Apollo's news had worn on his nerves more than he thought.

"She makes rum. From the Dominican Republic. Her father was Scots." Or at least he assumed the man was no longer of this world, unless Scottish fathers had significantly relaxed their position on what their unmarried daughters were free to do.

"Hispaniola," Murdoch muttered with interest. "Is she married?"

"I assume not," he said, pulse kicking up at the question.

"Perhaps we should join Raghav?" Murdoch suggested, and Evan felt a moment's hesitation. Quite suddenly, going up to the rum maker felt monumentally important. Something he ought to prepare himself for.

"Are you scared of her?" Murdoch's amusement was starting to grate.

Evan rolled his eyes and started toward her, but in that same moment, Luz walked purposefully in the opposite direction. By the time they'd reached Raghav she was out of sight.

"Where did she go?" Evan asked with such force that Raghav took a step back.

"Good evening to you too, Lord Darnick."

"Raghav," Evan warned, "I'm not in the mood for games." He knew affecting his more commanding voice with his friend would be moot. He did not scare as easily as the rest of the population.

"Tell me how the meeting with your mysterious partner went first." Raghav was still smiling, but Evan knew he was not asking for sport. If he got this out of the way quickly, he could go and find his heiress.

"I have the will," he whispered. Raghav's eyes widened, and

for a second Evan feared the man would start clapping, but Evan's expression seemed to dampen his excitement.

"But…" his business partner prompted reluctantly.

"He has to get married," Murdoch declared happily, apparently now fully on board with this harebrained idea.

"I don't follow."

"My mother's instructions were for the distillery to be put in my name as a wedding gift," Evan answered through gritted teeth, eyes still roaming around the room. Where could she have gone?

"Oh my," Raghav muttered, his eyes impossibly wide.

With every person he told, the reality—and urgency—of his situation became more inescapable. He wished he could just kill his father and be done with it, but that would not be as satisfying as seeing the man ensnared and entrapped by his own greed.

"Precisely. Which is why it's imperative that we locate that beauty that just escaped us." Evan heaved a sigh at Murdoch's incredibly loud voice. By the end of the night everyone in Paris would know about his predicament.

"Miss Heith-Benzan?" Raghav frowned in the direction Luz Alana had departed. "Why?"

"Did you learn more about her?" He attempted to allay the desperation in his voice, but there was no helping it.

"Not much," Raghav hedged, but Evan knew better. The man could've easily left whisky distilling to be a spy at the Home Office—not that he would ever even consider working for the British Crown. If anything, Raghav's trouble was that once he got people talking, he couldn't seem to get them to stop.

"Tell me," he insisted, and Raghav threw both hands up in defeat.

"All right," he whispered, looking around. "I really don't like to divulge a lady's secret, especially one who makes rum of that quality."

Evan's mouth tightened. He wanted to be the one tasting her rum.

"Just tell us what she said," he grumbled, eliciting a speaking glance from his cousin and a derisive one from his friend.

"Well, this I heard from Antonio, the very comely gentleman who accompanied her and her two friends tonight at the reception." Raghav's cheeks pinked at the mention of Luz Alana's companion, then his lips turned up. "They call themselves Las Leonas. It's rather adorable, and it means—"

"We can deduce. Please get on with it," Evan urged. Though he *was* charmed at the idea of that hellion likening herself and her friends to a pride of lionesses.

"She's only here for the summer months."

"She came alone?" Evan interrupted. "No husband, father?"

Raghav shook his head. "She's here with her friends, but it seems like she's had to cut the trip short." Was she going back to Hispaniola so soon?

"Apparently she's establishing herself in Edinburgh in the next couple of weeks or so."

"That's convenient," Evan heard Murdoch exclaim from under the water his brain seemed to be suddenly submerged in. It had been so long since he'd craved like this. The distillery… that was retribution. It was getting what was his. But this was pure need. Need was a risky emotion.

"Establishing herself in Edinburgh…permanently?"

Raghav nodded. "Yes, according to Antonio, she's having some trouble with the trustee to her inheritance."

"That sounds dire." It could mean anything really, and likely none of it good.

"Quite," Raghav concurred, looking around again. "I didn't get many details, but from what Antonio said, she's departing to Scotland forthwith. She's asked me if I'd be willing to provide her some guidance once we're all back in Edinburgh."

He liked the idea of her asking anyone other than him for

help even less than he liked the thought of Raghav tasting her rum. What was the matter with him?

"She came to a brothel to ask you for help?"

Raghav's grin deepened. "She's here to do business," he said, then seemed to realize how that could be interpreted and fluttered his hands. "Not that kind of business. Her friends wanted to see Le Bureau, and she'd heard about Seynabou. She's going to attempt to sell her some of her rum." Raghav's smile was in full force now, and Evan felt his own lips turn up.

"She's bold," he said, not bothering to hide his appreciation of her tenaciousness.

"And that's where she's gone. I pointed Seynabou out for her. She's offered to gift me one of her rum casks as a thank-you."

"I see a lot of possibility here," mused Murdoch. He was likely teasing, but Evan was truly beginning to think that he was being presented with an opportunity he'd be a fool to ignore.

"Did she say *when* she would give you the cask?" Evan asked, head swiveling around the room looking for his lioness.

Raghav frowned at that. "No, I was going to call on her tomorrow and settle the details. In fact, if we could get our hands on a few of her casks, that would make for a phenomenal batch of Special Reserve. The bourbon ones we used on the last are stellar, but this rum is like nothing I've ever tasted."

Evan caught a glimpse of blue and silver go through a set of curtains on the far side of the room and turned in that direction. Perhaps a brothel was indeed the ideal place to secure a temporary wife.

"Where have you been?" Manuela asked dramatically as Luz came upon them in one of the many sitting rooms on the ground floor of Le Bureau.

"I was formally introducing myself to Mr. Kapadia," she explained, leaning to pluck a glass of champagne from a tray carried by a very attractive young man dressed in a burgundy jacket with lavish golden embroidery on the lapels. "I was thanking him for his offer to assist me when I arrive in Edinburgh." Things with Childers would likely only get worse and she was not too proud to take a hand if it was extended to her, for Clarita's sake. If it came attached to a certain arrogant, too-handsome, too-tall, insolent Scottish arse, so be it.

Manuela made an impatient noise which was a mix between a huff and grumble. "No more work tonight. We are supposed to be enjoying ourselves. You are *allowed* to, Luz Alana. We're in a place built for pleasure. *Indulge*, Leona, for once."

She opened her mouth to argue, to recriminate Manuela for not taking her situation seriously, then deflated. Her friend was right. She should be snatching the moments of joy she was given. She couldn't remember when she'd last taken a day for herself. It wasn't just her father's death either; she thought about the distillery and ways to improve the business constantly. Conceiving ways to get her ideas past the gauntlet of objectors she found at every turn. Even with her father's support things had been difficult. It was more of the same, except now she had no champion.

Let yourself have this night, Luz. It will all be waiting in the morning.

"What mayhem have you organized for us?" she asked, proffering a white flag. She would still keep an eye out for Seynabou Cisse-Kelly, but she would try to have a good time. Manuela leaned to kiss Luz's cheek and waved a hand in the air as if offering the entire establishment to her.

The famous brothel, at least when it came to the decor, certainly lived up to its reputation as the most lavish in Paris. From the glittering crystal chandeliers to what seemed like miles of bloodred velvet, the place evoked indulgence. And it was certainly popular; there were patrons everywhere. Ladies and gentlemen sipping champagne while canoodling on plush settees or behind one of the curtained-off nooks around the room.

"There is much to do this evening. Antonio said there are even live shows."

"Absolutely not," Aurora snapped.

"You're a physician," Manuela interjected. "A scholar of the human anatomy. Think of this as research." Aurora's snort made it clear she would do nothing of the sort.

"Consider me a *no* for any kind of live entertainment," Aurora said with finality, just as Antonio approached them.

"Ah, my Leonas!" he exclaimed, his handsome face the very picture of hedonist delight.

"Our gentleman has returned," Manuela trilled and immediately hooked her arm in his. "Antonio and I are heading to the upper floor, where I'm told there is an array of Sapphic pursuits this evening."

"You're incorrigible," Aurora balked without heat.

"A lost cause," Manuela confirmed giddily.

"I *have* secured a table at the grotto if you'd like to get some refreshments." Their escort pointed to the far end of the large space, his eyes widening when he saw a beautiful woman in a bright yellow dress walk through a set of curtains. "That's Seynabou," he whispered to Luz, who instantly perked up.

She winced internally, aware she'd be breaking her promise to Manuela only seconds after she'd made it, but she could not miss the chance to talk to the proprietor of Le Bureau. This place was teeming with the upper crust of…everywhere, really. She must at least hand her card to the woman.

"I'm sorry. I promise this is the last time." She shot a regretful look at Manu, who threw her hands up in defeat.

"Go." Her friend shooed her in the direction where Seynabou had disappeared.

"I'll wait here," offered Aurora, a little too eagerly. Probably desperate to avoid anything involving witnessing people in sexual congress.

"I don't advise that we split up," Antonio warned. "Maybe you and Aurora can go together while Manu and I…" He trailed off as Manuela rubbed her hands and squealed.

"Excellent. Debauchery in pairs is the best kind of debauchery," Luz quipped as she pulled Aurora along. After securing a fortifying glass of champagne for her friend, they made their way to the set of curtains through which a dozen patrons had already disappeared.

"Are you sure this is all right?" Aurora asked, gripping Luz's hand so tightly she was certain she heard something crack.

"We'll be perfectly fine, Aurora," Luz assured her friend as they made their way briskly across the room. "We'll only stay until I am able to approach Madame Cisse-Kelly," she said, reminding Aurora that this was not merely a frivolity. If there was anything one could always appeal to, it was Aurora's doggedness. Persistence was a language her friend was quite proficient in.

"There." Luz pointed at two chairs near the back of the room. "Let's sit." There was a pair of unoccupied seats behind them, and they'd have a better view of the small salon. "I'll keep an eye out for her, and as soon as I see an opportunity I'll go introduce myself."

They got settled into their plush chairs while Luz let her eyes roam around the room, but Seynabou was not in any of the four rows of seats arranged in a semi-circle in front of the stage. It would be hard to miss the woman with that bright yellow dress. Luz was so distracted by the surroundings she missed the sounds of distress coming from Aurora. When she finally turned to her friend she found her frantically waving a hand toward the rounded stage.

"Oh dear," she whispered calmly, not wanting to add to her friend's escalating horror. She tried to surmise exactly what she was seeing. A peculiar piece of furniture that looked to Luz like one of Aurora's surgeon chairs being wheeled out onto the stage. But she doubted they were about to witness a medical procedure.

"I think this is one of the live performances," Aurora whimpered. She was a bit wild-eyed, which for her was tantamount to fully fledged panic.

"Perhaps," Luz demurred, hoping her nerves would not get the best of her. For all that she pretended to be cavalier about all this, she'd never even seen a man fully in the nude. She'd seen workers in the fields back home take off their shirts when the heat became too much, yes, but this was in a very different context. And now she was about to watch one making love to a woman right in front of her.

She was about to suggest they escape when the lights in the room lowered, and Seynabou herself walked out on stage.

"Should we leave?" Aurora's voice was so tight Luz was surprised she could get a word out at all. Walking out on a person you are trying to ingratiate yourself with the moment she took the stage was not the best way to make a first impression.

"I don't want to cause a commotion," Luz hedged, as calmly as she could manage under the circumstances. "Let's wait until she's done speaking, then we can go." Aurora made a sound of pained agreement.

Seynabou was striking. Her skin was almost the same shade as Luz's, but her hair was a fiery russet. She had it down, which was provocative in itself, and it fell in waves against the sunflower-yellow fabric of her dress. Luz's French was quite rusty, and she had to listen closely in order to catch the meaning of what the woman was saying. She was so focused on her task she didn't notice the newcomer who sat in the chair behind her.

"Mademoiselle Caña Brava. Imagine finding you here."

Five

"Shouldn't you have a chaperone?" Evan asked with a casual air, as his eyes painstakingly traced the line that went from the nape of her neck to the curve of her shoulder.

"Maybe, but I don't. What about it?" He had to fight to keep a straight face when she turned around, those brown eyes full of venom.

"Just wondering what a respectable young woman would be doing in the audience of such compromising entertainment." He goaded her, already fully off task and not particularly concerned about it. If one was contemplating an arranged marriage to destroy a duke, it ought to involve some amusement.

"I'm here for the same reason everyone else is." Luz Alana harrumphed, making a show of smoothing her skirts before continuing. "What are *you* here for? Lessons?"

Evan barked out a surprised laugh that got him shushed by a patron on the right side of the theater. He'd been so focused on the beauty in front of him he hadn't noticed the woman in a very minimal amount of silk who'd walked onto the stage followed by a man in shirtsleeves and breeches. The male performer sank into the chair and positioned himself so he was leaning back with his thighs spread.

"Looks like Bertie let them use his Love Chair. I've not seen it before, but the rumor is he uses it to pleasure two women at once." Evan forced his voice to sound as if he was commenting on the wallpaper.

Luz's companion let out a tortured whimper at his observation.

"Just ignore him, Aurora. He's inventing all this to torture me. Why in the world would anyone call themselves *Bertie*?"

"Bertie is His Royal Highness Prince Edward." He was rewarded with a growl for his efforts. "He's a regular patron here at Le Bureau. Ah, no more talking. Seems like they're about to get started."

Luz Alana hissed at him, and Evan had to bite the inside of his cheek as he turned his attention to the stage. The woman performer was now straddling her companion's thighs. He, in turn, was busy lowering the top part of her garment, giving the audience a better view and himself better access to her breasts.

Unbidden, an image of Luz Alana stole into Evan's mind. Of her astride his lap in nothing but a bit of red satin. Her generous breasts just inches from his mouth. Her wild curls cascading over her neck and shoulders, a flush of pink staining her caramel skin. He'd take one of those curls and use it to tug her closer. Pull down the fabric until those lush mounds were exposed to him, and then he'd taste her. He'd pluck one nipple and suckle it until it hardened between his lips, then take the other and do the same. He'd let his hands explore until he reached the wetness between her thighs. He imagined the lusty sounds she'd make in that throaty voice of hers as he dipped his fingers into her heat.

She'd beg him for more, and he'd give her everything she desired.

"Are you quite all right?" Her irritated voice snatched him out of his filthy fantasy. He was hard as stone and certain he must've made some kind of distressed noise because Luz was looking at him like he was completely mad.

"I'm very well, thank you," he said too brightly. But like the hardheaded prick he was, he went right back to needling her. "What's your opinion on the lady's breasts? I like them a bit heftier myself, but small and perky are quite all right, if you like to keep one hand free."

Loud moans and slapping of skin were forthcoming from the stage by now, and their detrimental effect on Luz's friend's nerves was obvious. The poor woman was miserable. With a quiet "Luz, I can't," she fled from the theater.

Luz Alana stood, still looking longingly at the stage, likely trying to catch a glimpse of Seynabou. He had to admire her boldness *and* her loyalty. She came into the theater to accomplish something but would not abandon her friend in order to do so.

"I could introduce you to Miss Cisse-Kelly," he offered, to which she responded with a scoff.

"Right, in exchange for what? A grope?" She managed to sound extremely puritanical for a woman sitting merely feet from an admirably enthusiastic fellatio performance.

"I promise, that's not what I had in mind." She shot him a murderous look from under hooded eyes, and suddenly he wanted whatever it was she was holding in. He craved to see this woman magnificently unleashed. "On second thought, if you're offering, I'd be more than happy—"

"Pendejo!"

That got the attention of one of the large men the Cisse-Kellys dispersed around their establishment. With impressive alacrity, both he and Luz Alana found themselves being dispatched from the small theater and out into a low-lit room.

Luz Alana's cheeks were splotched with crimson, as was her neck, and she was mumbling a barrage of words in Spanish—most of which he was almost certain were threats aimed at his person. In this small space built for secrets and pleasure, it was hard to remember he was in pursuit of a business arrangement. Not when the swell of her bosom kept clouding his thoughts.

This woman could be the key to Evan's future, and all he wanted was to take her mouth.

A reasonable man would get on a train to Edinburgh in the morning, where he'd have a dozen debutantes stumbling over themselves at the chance of marrying the Earl of Darnick. But reasonable men rarely ventured after treasures, and Luz Alana Heith-Benzan was much too intriguing to walk away from.

"A row at the exposition for our first meeting, and now we've been booted out of a live fellatio performance," the bastard drawled, while Luz struggled to bring her temper to heel. "I'm curious to see where a third encounter with you will lead, Miss Caña Brava."

"You know that's not my name," she snapped. She'd tried to maintain her composure, especially after Mr. Kapadia had offered her some help, but this man had a gift for getting under her skin. As things stood now she was a sweaty, heavy-breathing mess, with her back pressed to a wall while he was fresh and crisp as lettuce.

Cabrón.

"Luz Alana."

The way he said her name was *indecent*. She felt every syllable reverberate through her. The man was, frankly, too virile, too attractive, too everything. He had her nerves in absolute shambles.

"*Light* and *beauty*. Fitting."

She knew he was probably having fun with her, getting her flustered for sport. Still her breath hitched when his gaze locked on her mouth as she ran her tongue over her dried lips.

Vamos, Luz Alana. Controlate.

"Miss Heith-Benzan, to you, sir," she said haughtily, and his eyes crinkled like he found her infinitely delightful. "What do you want?"

"To make you a proposition."

"Are you making some kind of point regarding my being at an establishment like this?" she demanded, both hands on her waist, not caring that her irritation was on full display. "Is that it? You think you can say anything you like because women who frequent brothels don't deserve respect?"

His expression changed for a second, as if she'd caught him off guard, but before she could wield another recrimination, he was back to that lazy grin that flustered her so.

He took one step closer to her, and every muscle in her body clenched almost painfully.

"I assure you my opinions on what warrants respect have nothing to do with where a grown adult decides to spend their time." He was so close now, and there was *so much* of him. Shoulders that looked as though they weathered any storm. His fine evening jacket was a perfect fit, and it strained as he moved. "In fact..." He brought his head down and pinned those hazelnut eyes on hers. "I tend to find that the qualities which polite society deems admirable differ quite drastically from what *ought* to be called so." They were so close she could see flecks of gold in his irises. Luz fought the urge to press in closer. She should say something, but nothing, not a single word, could pass the knot in her throat.

When he spoke again, the teasing tone from before had completely evaporated. "I also don't presume to know what the, uh..." he cleared his throat "...unattached, independent modern woman does in her leisure time." By now the playfulness was gone from his voice. "*Are you* unattached?"

She did not like the way her skin tightened at the question. This was an excellent moment to walk away, to turn on her heels and run out of this hidden corner. Instead, for some unfathomable reason, she replied.

"Not that it is remotely your business, but yes, I am completely and *quite happily* unattached."

"That's good, very good." His voice had suddenly gone smoky, making all the air leave her lungs at once. The effect he had on her could not possibly be good for her health. This much agitation was not sustainable.

"I don't know what games you're playing at, Braeburn," she told him, rising to her full height, though her nose barely reached his bearded chin.

He was too tall, damn him.

"If you're implying that I am a spinster, you don't have to tiptoe around it. I am very proud of that fact. I have no desire to marry." She paused, remembering the situation with her inheritance, and for a second a cold panic gripped her.

No, she wouldn't think about that. Childers would come around. *He had to.*

"I cherish my independence. It's the only weapon I have." The admission slipped out of her mouth before she could stop it. Horrified, she felt the prickle of tears in her eyes. She could not remember the last time she'd felt this inadequate, this exposed.

No, that was a lie. She recalled it perfectly. It was the day she'd overheard two of her father's friends talking about her. More like laughing at the idea any man could want to "take her on." What would anyone do with an "opinionated, combative hellion" whose only virtue was "her mystifying gift for business"?

"It's Sinclair." Evan's deep voice brought her out of that horrible memory, and she focused back on him, somewhat confused.

"Pardon?"

"My name is James Evanston Sinclair," he told her in a soft voice she hadn't heard from him yet. "Evan to my friends. And my proposition was regarding your casks."

Evanston. Evan. That was the *E* in *ES*, then. It suited him. She silently said his name and almost smiled as it occurred to her that it sounded the same in Spanish.

"Casks," she repeated as she returned her gaze to his expectant stare.

"Casks," he confirmed so very pleasantly, making her feel warm and soft, when only a minute ago she'd been ready to swipe that sardonic smile from his face. Luz didn't think she'd ever had so many opposing feelings at once. From moment to moment she went from wanting to murder him to fighting the urge to climb all the way up to that arrogant, hard face and kiss him senseless.

"My partner, Mr. Kapadia, said that he sampled your rum and would like to use your casks to proof our next batch of Braeburn Special Reserve. I thought I'd offer you a deal. Casks for facilitating an audience with Miss Cisse-Kelly."

"I see." The one time someone had actually come to her for business since she'd set foot in France and she'd made an utter fool of herself...in a brothel.

He kept those hypnotizing eyes pinned on her, an unnerving and relentless examination. She felt that undivided, focused attention down to the tip of her toes. She was rooted in place, could not make herself move.

"Raghav is quite taken with the rum," he mused in that smooth, addling voice of his. Heat ran up her spine like tendrils of fire. "He said it was good." He used the word *good* like he had his doubts on whether Mr. Kapadia understood its meaning. "Not as excellent as the Braeburn, of course. But pleasing to the palate." That damned smirk was back, and she shivered from the way those rolled *R*s scraped over her skin. "For a rum."

For a rum? Este comemierda.

She opened her mouth with every intention of giving him detailed instructions about what he could do with his opinions on her rum, but then Sinclair—Evan—derailed her again by leaning closer, until his enormous hand was pressed to the wall over her head. He reached into his jacket and pulled out a leather-bound flask as she trembled from head to toe. His handsome face had a boyish expression that made an image of him waving a white flag at her come to mind. But she was not foolish enough to relax under that friendly stare. This was not a man to play games with.

"Dram?" he offered. She shook her head.

"No, thank you."

He quirked an eyebrow as he took a sip. "You don't want to know what the competition tastes like, then?"

She scoffed, rolling her eyes.

"Competition would imply we're in the same category."

He barked out a laugh, and again the sound reverberated through her like rolling thunder. That playful regard spurred her on, urging her to meet the unspoken challenge. It didn't feel like mockery anymore, but like a very tempting invitation.

"I've got my own." Luz lifted the right side of her skirt and fished for the flask pressed to her thigh. She grinned as he choked on a mouthful of whisky when he lowered his gaze to where her hand had gone.

"That's convenient," he said hoarsely, sounding impressed.

"I have a pistol on the other leg."

That brought on a coughing fit. She unscrewed the slim bottle in her hands, extremely pleased with herself.

"Slàinte mhath," she said, tipping the flask in his direction, and she watched his jaw tighten, nostrils flaring. She sipped slowly, eyes fastened on him, and from one second to the next his lazy repose turned into something far more predatory.

A hunter ready to pounce.

"And I thought you were dangerous in Spanish." His brogue was more pronounced now. Every word sinking into her bones like that first drop of rum on the tongue. Scalding and sweet. Luz should've heeded the danger there, but instead she drank deeply, never taking her eyes off him. When she was done she ran her tongue over her bottom lip, then offered Evan her flask.

"Would you like to try the top selection for sugar cane— distilled spirits?"

He didn't answer, only moved closer. Heat bloomed inside

her from the way he looked at her. Hunger—unfiltered, undistilled, burning hunger. As if he intended to swallow her whole.

Keep your head, Luz Alana. Lionesses are not meant to be prey.

"I'll taste yours if you taste mine."

Air could barely make it out of her lungs as his eyes raked over her. She felt his gaze on her skin like a flurry of heated caresses. He was testing her, letting her see he desired her. Taunting her to see if she'd crumble.

Luz handed Evan her flask, and she took his in exchange. She tipped her head, letting the smoky liquid flood her mouth, then watched him drink—mesmerized by the way his throat moved as he swallowed her rum. Once he'd finished, he sniffed the opening of her flask.

"Very complex. I didn't expect the wood notes. What is it?"

"It's the casks. Dominican mahogany." She was enjoying the game now.

"Ah, the ones you'll be giving me tomorrow when I secure your meeting with Seynabou." She sniffed the air, and he grinned.

"So." He eyed the flask in her hand. "What's the verdict, Mademoiselle Caña Brava?"

With Evanston Sinclair, it was hard to know if he was teasing her or if she was supposed to be in on the joke. A million butterflies fluttered in her stomach just the same. "Good peat, prominent caramel notes. It's decent," she declared. He guffawed, and suddenly she was laughing too.

"The Braeburn—" *Goodness, those Rs again!* "—is more than decent, beauty. It's the top selection for grain-distilled spirits." She couldn't argue with that. Like Caña Brava, his whisky had ended the night a winner.

"Not as good as the Gran Reserva." She took back her rum and secured it against her thigh. She would not react to the way his eyes followed the movements of her hand. "But good."

"I'm glad the judges disagreed with you, then." His smile was cool, but the fire behind that amber stare still burned bright.

"I'm not who needs to like your whisky. Don't you have a betrothed who can provide the besotted feminine adulation you seem to desperately need?"

He angled his head down, so their mouths were only inches apart.

"Are you proposing, Luz Alana?"

It wasn't a question; it was a challenge.

"May I remind you I have a pistol strapped to my thigh," she warned, and his shoulders shook with laughter. "If you believe I won't shoot because I am a woman, I suggest you reconsider." The threat would have sounded far more severe if she wasn't fighting the urge to press her nose or, worse, her mouth to that dip at the base of his neck. He smelled like tobacco, leather and the peat of the drink that had passed his lips, and why did she keep obsessing about the man's mouth?

"I never knew imminent bodily harm could be this…riveting. Can I see it?"

Could he see what?

Her mind was swimming. Words barely registering. His voice was in large part to blame for her quandary. Silvery and intoxicating. Melting her to the core. That paired with his size and his perfectly shaped lips: it was an assault on the senses.

"You are quite the discovery, Miss Heith-Benzan." He leaned in, his firm hand branding her lower back. She pushed up, certain this was the most reckless thing she'd done to date, but in that moment, she couldn't muster up the ability to care. Luz was well aware what this would look like if anyone walked in on them, and she also knew nothing could pull her back from this precipice.

"Let's have a taste, love," he coaxed, fingers gently brushing her cheek. Every word out of his mouth was like a flame burning down her good sense. Her belly fluttered, and her nipples hardened as they brushed his jacket. The kiss was imminent, and she would let the world burn to get it. She held in a gasp as he brought her closer to him, crushing them together.

There would be consequences to this, she was sure, but still she closed her eyes expectantly.

"Alana," he murmured as he ran the pad of his thumb over her bottom lip. Such a light, gentle touch, from such a hard man. She ached with need, her mind wiped clean of anything else. Centuries of anticipation couldn't have prepared her for the moment when he covered her mouth with his. She opened for him and he tasted her, delicately, just a flick of his tongue, and she melted for him. Evan anchored her to him with a strong arm around her waist, and then he went to work on her mouth. He explored her like his sole mission in life was to cherish every inch of her he could reach. She kissed him back, eagerly, mouth open, tongue timidly meeting his at first, then bolder when a sound of pleasure escaped him.

Why had no one told her kissing could be like this?

"Luz Alana, are you still in here?" Luz almost wept with frustration when Aurora's voice pierced through their heated silence.

For a large man, Evanston Sinclair could move fast. He gracefully backed away, leaving her space to turn toward her friend's voice, her heart caught in her throat, and her body protesting the loss of his warmth.

"I'm coming for my casks tomorrow, Luz Alana."

A statement of fact, not a question.

"Cask. Only one. You overestimate your negotiation skills, Evan," she said over her shoulder as she stepped out into the alcove outside the small theater. "But if you do secure a meeting with Miss Cisse-Kelly, I could be convinced to part with more."

"I will deliver on my promise, Miss Heith-Benzan." The man's voice was debilitating. "And just so you know, I am nowhere near done with that mouth of yours. I am beginning to see that perhaps it was an error underestimating *your* many skills."

She didn't turn to look at him when he called after her so he wouldn't catch a glimpse of the satisfied smile on her lips.

Six

It was jarring to be walking in the shadow of such an enormous amount of steel, especially so early in the morning. The size of Eiffel's tower was beyond anything Evan had ever seen, and that was quite a statement considering the gravity-defying bridges the railways had built throughout Scotland. But those bridges had a function. This gargantuan web of metal was built solely to be admired.

It was so acutely... *French*.

Evan tended to prefer things that served a purpose. It wasn't that he couldn't appreciate a beautiful painting or a sumptuously manicured garden, but he tended to gravitate to objects that were pleasing and functional. As a child he'd been fascinated by a cabinet in his grandfather's study. It was a beautiful piece of craftsmanship with elaborate carvings, and inside it was a puzzle. Whenever Evan visited, he'd spend hours opening drawers and pulling on levers attempting to unravel it. There was something infinitely captivating about an object that drew you in for its exquisiteness but kept your interest because of what it could do.

Like the infinitely tempting rum heiress he was about to pay a visit to.

"Oi!" Raghav's unusually coarse cry told Evan he'd probably drifted off again. He'd been doing that all morning. "What exactly is your plan with Miss Heith-Benzan?" There was a tinge of impatience in Raghav's voice. This was not the first time he'd asked the question, and Evan was yet to come up with an answer.

The truth was, he didn't have one thus far. Luz Alana was herself a puzzle, and a beautiful one at that. Evan had walked away from that kiss with a yawning hunger he hadn't felt in… well, ever. She was so vivid, so deliciously ardent. When she felt something strongly she simply could not hide it. Not about her rum or his kisses. It was addictive.

"I'd like to learn more about her. I do think this could be beneficial for both of us." It was true Evan wasn't yet certain how *she* would benefit in the arrangement he had in mind, but that's why he needed to see her again. He wanted to know more about this errant trustee and glean how receptive Luz Alana would be to an offer of help to resolve that matter.

"Learn more." Raghav laughed. "Wasn't that what you supposedly did last night?"

"I did ask for a taste of the rum." *Among other things.*

"Evan," Raghav said, voice heavy with censure, "she is in a very vulnerable position. I want the distillery out of your father's hands, you know I do, but I won't be a party to seeing her used." All humor had gone from his friend's voice.

Evan didn't argue; Raghav was not being unfair. He was usually willing to go to extremes when it came to getting back at his father. "You were the one who so helpfully pointed out she was in need of some assistance, and specifically of the kind I could be of help with."

Raghav remained unmoved. "Not if it meant getting her mixed up in whatever you are up to with your mysterious ally." And that was one of the things that Evan respected most about the man: there were lines he would not cross, not for love or money. For Raghav the ends absolutely did not justify the means.

"Evan." Raghav's voice had an edge now.

"I want to help her," Evan admitted. "She is tenacious, and she is bold. She deserves a chance to set up her business without every prejudiced sod from here to Aberdeen interfering with her." He thought about the way she'd stood up to him yesterday. At the Palace and then at Le Bureau. She was magnificent, intrepid...and he loathed the idea of her being defeated before she'd even begun.

"Her rum is good too," Raghav added, somewhat mollified.

Evan made a noise of agreement. "Better than good. It's the best damn thing I've had outside of my own whisky," he said truthfully. Both of them had been in this business long enough to appreciate when they came upon something remarkable, and Luz Alana Heith-Benzan made excellent rum.

Anyone could concoct something decent with the right materials and equipment, but achieving complexity—that was far more elusive. Spirits were like people: what you put into them at every stage made a crucial difference as it matured. What he'd tasted last night had astonishing depth. Its flavor had caught Evan completely off guard and left a lingering sweetness in his mouth long after he'd tasted it.

Much like the woman who made it.

"All we're doing is procuring some casks, confirming she received Seynabou's message and perhaps formally offering her some assistance getting settled once we're all back in Scotland." He proffered this in a light tone, attempting to smooth out his friend's deeply furrowed brow.

"I hope that's the extent of it, Evan. Truly, your father is not a man who takes lightly to being toyed with. I don't like the idea of having her involved in whatever standoff is to come."

That was true enough, but if Evan's plan went accordingly, by the time the Duke of Annan realized his time was up, he would not be in any position to retaliate.

"The lifts are finally operating," Raghav said at length, tipping his head back to take in the steel beast above them. It seemed he'd had his fill of discussing Evan's eternal feud with his father. "Murdoch said they're taking five thousand people up there every day."

The French had accomplished something truly astonishing. They had claimed the Exposition Universelle would be a gathering of cultures and nations like the world had never seen, and they had delivered on that promise. In the two weeks since he'd arrived Evan had experienced a very different city than the one he'd visited many times before. Paris had always had a life and rhythm of its own. But now with millions of people descending here at once from what seemed to be every corner of the world, the place was incandescent.

"There it is." Raghav pointed to the small building just beyond the base of the tower that housed the pavilion for the Dominican Republic. "We can't stay for long. Dairoku is expecting us in an hour."

Evan nodded, taking in the structure, which was about a fifth of the size of the one they'd built for the British exhibit. It was made in a neocolonial style, with beautiful wood carvings along a wraparound porch, painted in white with moldings a cheerful sky blue. Large windows framed each side of the door. Evan noticed they did not have glass, which allowed some of the aromas to waft outside. Even from where he stood, still a few yards from the entrance, he could smell the vanilla, tobacco and timber being displayed.

"This business should not take long." As he strode in purposefully behind Raghav, it occurred to him that he'd thought the same thing the night before, and that had not gone at all as planned. His eyes took a moment to adjust to the darker room, which meant he heard her before his eyes could find her. The moment they did, he understood that his earlier assurances to Raghav and to himself were not as nearly as steadfast as he'd believed.

"Sir, I have already informed you, I am the distiller."

The mere sound of her voice primed Evan like a soldier poised for battle. His body knew the reaction for what it was. Lust. Attraction. Nothing surprising there either. She was lovely. Full red lips, and those strong cheekbones with their smattering of freckles. Her figure that even with the sober clothing she wore today could not hide the curves and lushness of her. There was quite a lot to appreciate in Luz Alana Heith-Benzan, and his body responded to it. But it wasn't the lust that troubled him; that he could handle well enough. The danger was the itch right under his skin to be the man who protected her from whatever and whoever had caused that strain in the words she'd just uttered. The peril was in the possessiveness slithering up his back and spreading into his limbs like manacles.

That was much more treacherous territory.

"It's Bridgewood," Raghav said with distaste. Evan took a closer look and indeed saw the very unsavory character who happened to operate a dozen luxury hotels across Europe. He was a nuisance and a desperate sycophant to anyone who he perceived as an advantageous acquaintance. Heirs to dukedoms fit into that category.

"I find it hard to believe that any self-respecting spirit maker has sent a woman as their representative. Are they not interested in finding buyers?" Bridgewood's voice became more insolent with every syllable, while Luz Alana's countenance remained the very image of placidity. It was as if the more irate the man got the more she fought to appear oblivious to it. But Evan was looking very closely, and he saw that Bridgewood's badgering was getting to her. Nothing glaringly obvious, just a slight wobble in her chin, a sharp intake of breath. She was fighting to not let the man see her fall apart.

Emotion came upon him swiftly, and a noise very much akin to a warning growl escaped him. The sound made her look up. For a moment her pained composure was replaced by surprise and then—just for a second—something that looked like genuine pleasure. Her full lips tipped up, brown eyes brightening as their gazes locked, then she looked away. Another man would recoil at the slight, but it only made her that much more appealing to Evan. With a woman like this, he'd have to earn every smile, every soft word. Nothing would ever be granted easily, making every inch of ground gained all the more gratifying.

"Mr. Sinclair," she sighed as the man in front of her prattled on.

"Mister?" Raghav asked in a whisper, the word awash in delighted curiosity.

"There wasn't time to cover my courtesy title last night." His answer elicited a low and devilish laugh from Raghav.

"All right, I trust you know what you're doing." He sounded like he didn't believe that in the slightest. "I will go greet Antonio while you continue to misrepresent yourself."

Evan rolled his eyes but let Raghav go without argument, because the truth was that he almost wished he could keep his title a secret awhile longer. His position in the peerage cast a long shadow, corroding every relationship in his life. To Luz Alana he was just a fellow distiller. He wasn't ready to shatter that notion.

"Whether the rum is good isn't relevant. I do not do business with women," Bridgewood declared as Evan reached the table.

"Sir, I assure you the rum will taste just as delicious when sold by a woman," she appealed to the insufferable man in that unflagging, friendly tone. He could see from the lines around her mouth the enormous restraint it took to not tell the man to go to hell. He loathed seeing her be put through this.

"She's right, Bridgewood," he said as he clapped the man on the shoulder, prompting him to pull back from the table and turn away from Luz Alana. "The rum is excellent…the best I've tasted," he added, holding her gaze for a second longer than what was appropriate.

"Darnick, I would've thought you only drank whisky," the man said with forced politeness, and Evan could feel Luz Alana's gaze boring into him.

"I like to learn about the competition," Evan said, and winked at Luz Alana, who was looking at him suspiciously.

"*Darnick?* I thought your surname was Sinclair," she asked, her expression doggedly neutral.

"Darnick is a...family name," he explained vaguely, while Bridgewood sent him a speaking glance. Evan locked eyes with the man, daring him to say a word. "What do you say, Bridgewood? Are you going to secure the best rum at the exposition for your hotels? I met with César Ritz's barman this morning and told him he couldn't leave Paris without some Caña Brava to serve at the Savoy." The Swiss hotelier had just taken the helm of the iconic London hotel, and everyone in the city was keeping an eye on every move he made. "You're not going to let the Swiss outshine you in your own city?" Evan had to suppress a smile at the man's affronted expression. He'd known Bridgewood had a fragile enough ego to fall for this kind of juvenile taunt.

"I will take a dozen cases. Have them sent to this direction," Bridgewood declared at length, handing Luz Alana a business card.

The rum heiress sent Evan a bewildered look. "Yes, of course." Her voice was laced with just a touch of breathlessness that Evan found distractingly enticing. "Though, I could offer you a better price if you buy it by the cask. A cask is about two hundred liters." When she saw Bridgewood hesitate she spoke up again, this time not bothering to disguise her excitement. "The casks are a special reserve, for sale only at the exposition," she added, eliciting an interested look from the hotelier. The man flushed, clearly displeased with a woman daring to push him, but too intrigued to turn her down.

She was born for this. A true lioness.

Bridgewood turned to Evan seeking approval. He had the unattractive habit of painstakingly mimicking the upper classes in dress, speech, even in what he drank. To his credit, he'd at least built a career out of it. Evan nodded, granting the man the permission he seemed to require before making the purchase.

"Oh, all right," Bridgewood huffed, as if it was his own money he was spending and not the fortune of his employers. "To be delivered by tomorrow. I leave for London in three days' time and want all the inventory on the train with me. Payment will be made on delivery." He gave Evan a clipped nod and headed out of the pavilion without so much as a glance in Luz Alana's direction. Evan watched with disdain as the man left, then he turned back to Luz Alana.

"Mr. Sinclair, three times in two days. I may be forced to reach the conclusion that your only occupation in Paris is turning up wherever I am." Those lips were as luscious and tempting this morning as they'd been last night. And that smart mouth was frankly intoxicating.

"This is the thanks I get for making a sale for you." He was provoking her, and was rewarded with a delicious little growl.

"My rum sold itself," she retorted with absolute certainty in her voice. She believed in her rum, and the Bridgewoods of the world could never change that.

"I expected at least a thank-you," he intoned, and she scoffed. "Something along the lines of... *Thank you, Evan. Not only are you devastatingly handsome but also a brilliant salesman.*"

She laughed at him. Head thrown back as if every word he'd said was deliciously absurd. As far as aphrodisiacs went, self-assurance in a woman was unusual, and yet...

God, but he enjoyed this woman.

"I had the situation in hand, or at least was attempting to," she said, her voice more serious now, subdued. It was a crime for a woman with this much fire to be dimmed like this. If it wouldn't jeopardize the sale she'd made, he'd bring Bridgewood back here and make him apologize to her. Kiss her feet. He hated seeing those shadows behind her eyes.

"Now that we've agreed on our impressive execution of that sale, I will be taking the casks I was promised. Two dozen should be enough." As he'd hoped, her brown stare immediately lit on him. Her morose expression replaced with that provocative irritation he seemed to bring out in her.

"Two dozen?"

Yes, he preferred this fiery hellion much better to the wary woman from seconds ago.

"First—" she assumed a pose he could only call combative and pointed a finger up in the air "—I *never* promised. I said I would *consider* it, if you got me in contact with Miss Cisse-Kelly." His hands itched to reach for her. To drink in all that passion with a deep, languorous kiss.

"I spoke to them. If an invitation hasn't yet arrived, you'll be hearing from Miss Cisse-Kelly's secretary by the end of the day." Seynabou and her brother had been curious. It wasn't every day that an earl asked a brothel owner for a favor. He was not a man to ask for concessions in general. Being beholden to others was not something he enjoyed, but seeing the woman in front of him flush with pleasure was well worth it.

"Thank you. Truly." Her face softened as she continued. "I will honor my offer to Mr. Kapadia and you." Her cheeks flushed with pink, and he wondered if, like him, she was recalling the details of their last conversation pertaining to casks. "I do still need to *sell* the rum before I can empty the casks. I have not been very successful on that end. The one you just assisted me with is the first sale I've had all day." Damn it all, he should've trounced Bridgewood and forced him to buy even more. At this rate, he'd soon be the proud owner of all the Dominican rum in Paris.

"Then it seems I will have to claim my casks in Edinburgh," he told her, his voice hoarse.

For a moment they just stared at each other. That same electric current that had passed between them the night before, pulsing in the space around them.

"On second thought, I do have something I could give you today."

"Where could you have possibly hidden a two-hundred-liter cask of rum?"

"Give me a second." The hint of mischief in her voice reminded Evan this was a woman who walked around Paris with a pistol and a flask of rum under her skirts. His cock pulsed at the idea of laying her on a bed wearing only those.

"Here we are." Her muffled voice brought him out of his lustful thoughts. When he lifted his gaze to where she'd been standing, he found himself in the presence of an utterly delicious, plump, heart-shaped backside.

He was fruitlessly attempting to will his blood flow to head in a different direction when she popped back up.

"For you," she said, beaming at him as she thrust two miniature casks in his direction.

The two could not be much bigger than a gallon jug.

"*These* are my casks?" She looked devilish, and Evan had to bite down on his cheek not to dissolve into a fit of giggles. "Aren't these the ones you had at the display yesterday?"

"You seemed so taken with them," she told him with absolute solemnity, even as she visibly fought for composure. Delighted mischief shining in those beautiful eyes. She was laughing at him…again.

At that very moment Evan concluded that he could apply his days exclusively to studying the many moods of Luz Alana Heith-Benzan and be utterly riveted by every single one of them. If only he was the kind of man who could possess a ray of sunshine like this and not smother it in darkness.

"I see Miss Heith-Benzan has run circles around you once again," Raghav drolled as he sauntered up to them, eyeing

the tiny cask in Evan's hand. "Most unimpressive, Sinclair."
He leaned in to take Luz Alana's gloved hand. "Miss Heith–
Benzan, you look radiant today. Is this from Jeanne Paquin?"
he asked about her light yellow dress. That immediately elicited
a pleased smile from his cask nemesis. And even though Evan
knew Raghav was this charming to everyone, he could barely
keep himself from nudging the man out of the way.

"Please call me Luz Alana." She sent a luminous smile in
Raghav's direction. Evan's stomach twisted painfully. "It is not
Paquin, but you have a remarkably good eye." She winked in
approval as she ran a hand over the row of buttons on the front
of her bodice. "It's one of my cousin Delia Marie's creations."

She was wearing the same cameo brooch she'd had yesterday.
The stone was one he'd never seen before: the color was a crystalline blue with cloudy swirls of white. Like she had a piece of
the sky pinned to her chest.

His clothes suddenly felt tight, and his skin prickled.

"She is very talented, and you are a fantastic model for her
creations," Raghav said, eliciting another blinding smile. The
prickling relocated to the back of Evan's neck. Had someone
covered the blasted windows? This discomfort had to be from
the heat.

"Raghav, don't you have a meeting to go to?" He growled,
and two pairs of eyes stared at him like he'd grown a second
head.

"*We* are supposed to go meet some Japanese buyers," Raghav
retorted.

"Japanese buyers?" Luz Alana asked with obvious interest.
"You're meeting with them now?"

"That's right," Evan said cautiously, but she was already moving out from behind the table to stand between him and Raghav,
the bright, alluring smile from earlier fully back in place. She
was just a tad shameless when it came to her business. One more

item in the list of things he found deeply irritating in everyone but her.

"Gentlemen, I have a proposition for you." She flashed rows of perfect white teeth at them. "I will be happy to give you a couple of my two-hundred-liter casks, as a gift, of course, in the spirit of fellowship and camaraderie of the exposition." She was nothing but sweetness now.

"I thought we had agreed to that already." Evan could not trust himself with more than that as she prepared to deliver her coup de grâce.

"As I mentioned earlier, I do have to sell the rum in order to empty the casks. Fortunately, we seem to have a solution right in front of us." She leaned down to grab an enormous leather bag and heaved it onto the table, then extended a hand toward the exit. "I would be honored to accompany you to your meeting with the Japanese buyer."

She was blatantly blackmailing them, and if they were not surrounded by people, Evan would've dragged her to a dark corner and had her right then. "Did you just extort an invitation to meet with our buyers, Miss Heith-Benzan?"

"Absolutely," she conceded happily. "And there's no need for that kind of formality among associates. Call me Luz Alana, please, Evan."

Raghav lost his battle and let out a bark of laughter.

"My, how things change in a matter of seconds," he said as she regaled them with another cloying smile.

"We are here to do business, Mr. Sinclair." She angled her head to the side, looking positively angelic. "Mutual aid is vital for all of our success at the exposition, as you so wisely advised me just yesterday."

"*Mutual aid,*" he echoed, and she nodded with a brash grin on her perfect mouth.

"Luz Alana makes a compelling case, Evan," Raghav said—

or rather wheezed, as the man was turning an appalling shade of purple. "Fraternité and all that."

"Exactly." She clapped with enthusiasm and started moving around the room. "I only require a few seconds, and I shall be ready for our meeting."

"We are not suitable chaperones for an unmarried young woman," Evan added solely for the purpose of hearing what outlandish thing would fly out of her mouth.

She did not disappoint.

"Mr. Sinclair, you must stop worrying about my chaperones," she said, her voice still sweet as honey. "But if you are so worried for *your* virtue, I'm sure we can find someone to help protect you from my wily ways."

"*My* virtue." He called after her, but she was already crossing the room to talk to a man at another table.

"She's got you reduced to parroting her words, old man. I never thought I'd live to see it," Raghav observed unhelpfully, just as their companion joined them again.

"Gentlemen, shall we?" It seemed flagrant behavior gave Luz Alana a particular glow. She looked bloody radiant as she brushed past them.

"We don't want to make you late for your buyers," Evan grumbled as he chased after her.

Seven

Evan Sinclair was bewildering.

The man went from overbearing to disarmingly heroic from one moment to the next. Not to mention charming. Distractingly, dizzyingly charming. It was no small feat keeping her wits about her in his presence. Women probably crumbled at the mere sight of that dashing smile.

Luz hoped she could resist that onslaught of tempting smiles and spine-tingling winks. She absolutely had to stay on task with Evan Sinclair, because one thing was clear: he was a very good man to know. After only an hour, she'd left the Japanese pavilion with a lucrative contract to supply a few of the families in the Kazoku—the Japanese aristocracy—with Caña Brava. As irritating as it was to admit, she'd accomplished more with his help in one morning than she'd done on her own in the month she'd been in Paris.

"Why didn't you let Dairoku sample the Dama Juana?" he asked her as they made their way out of the pavilion and on to the crowded street on the fairgrounds. She whipped her head up in surprise. A flicker of warmth ran through her at his recalling the name of the spirit.

Then he ruined it with his high-handedness. "Which I still haven't been allowed to try, by the way."

"Are you a buyer, Mr. Sinclair? You're worse than Clarita." The man was absolutely maddening.

"Do you take pleasure responding to my questions with another question?"

Luz could only laugh in response, but he continued.

"And shall I assume Clarita is your friend from last night?"

"Clarita's my sister. She's ten," she told him pointedly. Raghav snickered at her taunt, but Evan's countenance remained impassive.

"There are two of you? How did your island stay above water with a pair of Heith-Benzan sisters storming about?"

"You're far less amusing than you think," she said as soberly as she could manage.

"And yet I keep making you laugh."

"*At* you, not *with* you," she retorted. His lips twitched, and his eyes were bright with humor. He looked younger when he smiled, and so handsome—devastatingly so.

He didn't comment immediately, and they walked in companionable silence for another minute before Evan spoke again.

"You were very good in there. Dairoku was impressed too." He almost sounded surly. As if the words had left his mouth without his consent. But they didn't sound insincere. The man truly kept her emotions swinging on a pendulum.

"Thank you," she said shortly, unsure of how to respond. It had been a long time since she'd been offered any validation for her work. She'd gotten the medal last night, but that was for the rum. Not her work. *Her* efforts. It was pathetic that such a simple gesture had her almost in tears, but she was parched for some recognition from someone other than her friends.

Joyful laughter rang through the air, and Luz noticed a group of children playing in the fountain underneath Gustave Eiffel's tower. They were dressed in the smart, colorful frocks so typical of French children. One little girl of about six years was being chased by another, both shrieking with absolute delight. Their braids had come undone but neither seemed to notice. Luz thought of Clarita, of how little time she'd had to be a child since they'd left the island, to play with other children.

"It's true about Dairoku." Evan's voice jolted her. "He is shrewd and extremely selective of who he does business with." He paused when she glanced at him. He seemed to be weighing his words. "I would've thought you'd take advantage of the opportunity and present him with all the spirits you are producing."

She should've known he would not leave that alone.

She sighed inwardly, searching for a response. Because she couldn't say the true reason: that she'd finally had a successful day and she didn't have the strength to have the Dama Juana, which she'd created with such love and enthusiasm, be dismissed as undesirable. She'd thought about it, of course. She'd brought the smaller box with two cordials she'd created and the Dama Juana. But even after Dairoku shared with her that his great-aunt had been the largest sake maker in Japan for forty years, and that the older woman's empire was so large she had her own fleet of ships, Luz Alana hadn't been brave enough to offer Dairoku anything beside the rum.

"I forgot them," she lied.

Evan made a noise that sounded a lot like *I don't believe that for a second*, but he let it go. "I'm afraid I must excuse myself, Luz Alana," Raghav said, startling her. She'd almost forgotten the man was right behind them. "I have a previous engagement. I'm sure Sinclair would be happy to escort you back the rest of the way." He sent Evan a look that would've made a lesser man stand at attention.

"I don't need an escort," she hedged, reaching for her bag, which Evan had refused to let her carry out of the meeting with Dairoku.

"I will leave you both to resolve this," Raghav said before

he rushed off, leaving her and Evan to stare at each other as people brushed past. Neither of them said anything for a long moment, but after a third person almost knocked her over, she extended a hand.

"Thank you, Mr. Sinclair," she told him. "I appreciate the help you offered me today." He reached for her hand and gripped it as though he meant to keep her there.

After this she'd have no reason to see him again. Not in Paris, and in Scotland he likely would be busy. Something inside her screamed to say anything, do anything to keep him there for bit longer. She knew the urge for what it was.

She desired him. Beyond that undeniable fact, she liked how he looked at her. As if he could see right through the mask of confidence and optimism she so painstakingly donned and the mess of doubt and exhaustion that lay behind it didn't put him off one bit. She forced herself to recall what she'd always thought of a man's attentions: *they were never worth the cost of her freedom.* She steeled herself against her racing heart, the warmth blooming inside her from his touch. This was a mirage, she told herself. *This will leave you empty-handed and with a mouth full of sand.*

She pried her lips open to say something blandly polite and final, to say a goodbye. He spoke first.

"Would you—" He looked unsure. A self-conscious smile appeared on his lips, and Luz wondered if she'd have to catalog Evan Sinclair's smiles by their degree of transcendence. "Are you hungry?"

"Hungry?" She said the word as if it was a foreign concept even as butterflies took flight inside her. She should leave this as it was. Not risk making things awkward with the one person who'd offered her help. It had been such a triumph of a day so far. She should take this victory and be on her way; instead she stood there wondering why he hadn't mentioned the kiss.

"I'd have to get back in an hour. I promised my sister I'd take her to Cairo Street," she offered in answer, and he gave her a smile that transformed his entire face.

It was quite simple, really. She didn't have the strength to walk away from him.

Not yet.

"Very well, I promise to return you intact and on time."

On time, perhaps. *Intact* was not even a remote possibility.

Eight

"*I keep a table at a small brasserie just on avenue de Suffren.*" Evan pointed toward the gate which was assigned only to exhibitors. "We will be seated immediately."

"You *keep* a table?" She raised an eyebrow in question.

"It's a small place, a family restaurant, and normally I come in after the lunch rush," he explained.

She nodded distractedly, then added, "I'm not passing judgment."

"It's all right if you were. There is much to judge when it comes to myself and my family." He spoke the words nonchalantly, as though he fully expected her to have drawn conclusions about him. And she'd certainly started to, but he kept stumping her with his bewildering honesty. "My father takes much pride in our family's long history of wealth and what he refers to as position." He practically spat the words. There was a harshness in him she had not seen before. "I don't pretend it has not benefited me greatly, but much to my father's chagrin I make it my duty to remind him of just how we happened upon that position."

Those last words he uttered with such complete derision, she imagined a healthy dose of it was directed at himself. One thing was certain: there was no love lost between Evan and his father.

"My father was from a wealthy Scottish family. His political views, on the role of Scotland in the transatlantic slave trade in particular, made him very unpopular with his kin, you see." She surprised herself by sharing this intimacy with a virtual stranger. *A stranger who has done more for you in a day than your father's associates.*

"Ah," Evan said in apparent understanding.

"I never met any of them," she clarified. "We never went to Scotland with him. They never came to see us. In the end, he lived in Hispaniola longer than in Scotland." Her father had always talked about his homeland with a mix of longing and regret.

She looked up to find Evan patiently waiting for her to continue. "His grandmother left him a generous inheritance, and with that money he left for the Caribbean with the intention of investing in business ventures. That's how he met my mother. He was the primary investor for the distillery."

"I figured that your family had owned the distillery for generations—" He stopped abruptly as if he realized what he'd alluded to.

This was as good a time as any to test those particular waters. She'd trained herself to do this in those two years she'd lived in Switzerland. Just face it head-on and say the words.

"You can say it." She used the practiced, easy tone she'd perfected over the years. She looked straight at him too. Made sure he saw the calm in her face. She didn't hide from the truth, and she didn't let anyone who did get very close to her. "If my family had owned the distillery for generations they likely would've been slavers." His cheeks reddened slightly at that, but she continued. "My father was never personally involved in the slave trade, but his family's fortune was certainly due to it, at least in part." She affected a perfunctory lift of her shoulder before she continued to the next part. "As do many of the wealthy families in Scotland—all of Great Britain, for that matter."

She did not quite say *Yours included*, but she didn't have to. To his credit, his gaze never wavered from hers. He let that truth sit between them and did not offer a single excuse or attempt in any way to dismiss what she'd said. "On my mother's side, I am only the third generation that has been able to own land. It's a point of pride for us that every bottle of Caña Brava has been made by the hands of free people."

He stopped abruptly, and Luz braced for it. The list of the many ways the colonies had benefited from having the Brits and the Spaniards ravage their people and their land. How they should be grateful for the language and the religion imposed on them. How fortunate they were to be allowed on British soil despite their…inadequacy. Even as she steeled her spine and wondered if she'd just ruined the one chance she had to receive any kind of help in Edinburgh, she realized the thing she was most sorry for was that she wouldn't be able to remember this afternoon with a smile.

Seconds passed and he'd yet to say a word. He hadn't let go of her arm—in fact he'd coiled it more firmly around his—which made it so they were pressed together like bookends.

"I will see about getting you a few more meetings with some of the Braeburn's buyers," he said in an astonishingly blasé tone and began to walk again. This time it was her who was tempted to stop in the middle of the walkway. She wanted to force him to turn around and look at her, but he continued in that brisk, assured stride. When he spoke he kept his gaze straight ahead. "You are correct, yours is a legacy to be proud of. Mine, on the other hand, only warrants being razed to the ground."

Only then did he turn to her, and there was something haunted and wild in that honey-colored gaze. It struck her that despite his candor she was likely seeing the real Evan for the first time, and this was a man with his share of demons. She opened her mouth to say something. *Thank you*, perhaps, or *You took my insulting your ancestors quite well*. But he didn't let her.

"Here we are," he told her, pointing to what looked like an establishment that attracted a working-class clientele. She peered in through the window and only saw a few wooden tables packed into a very small dining room.

"It looks closed," she said, glancing at the door.

"It usually is at this time," he confirmed. "But Monsieur and Madame Fournier will have something for us." He knocked on the door three times, and after only a moment, a small plump woman with a jovial face and smooth bronzed skin opened the door for him.

"Ah, Monsieur Écosse," she welcomed Evan with a familiarity that confirmed he was indeed a regular costumer. He greeted their hostess in turn with equal enthusiasm and introduced Luz to Madame Fournier.

"Bonsoir, mademosielle," the woman said warmly as she ushered them in.

"Bonsoir, madame," Luz whispered as she took in the cozy interior of the restaurant. It was even smaller than it appeared from outside.

"Vin blanc pour vous?"

Evan nodded, then turned to Luz. "Would you like a glass of wine?"

"Yes, please," she said, then caught herself. "Vin blanc pour moi aussi. Merci."

They were promptly served their wine and offered the plats du jour while Evan playfully responded to their hostess's questions. Madame Fournier's English was passable, and Evan's French could barely get him through placing a lunch order, but it was clear they were old hats at figuring out a way to understand each other.

Luz was once again...charmed.

"She calls you *Mr. Scotland*," she said, amused, once they were alone.

"I rather like the sound of it in French," he confessed.

When he'd told her that he kept a table, she had not envisioned this, a tiny family restaurant, with four tables, operated by a Vietnamese woman and her French husband. She'd expected chandeliers, frescoes, lushly covered banquettes. Not this intimate, unassuming room that smelled like good food and freshly oiled wood. It was a place she would probably not consider if she were on her own. But Evan with his fine clothes and his refined air seemed right at home here.

"Tell me more about your land in Santo Domingo," he prompted, jerking her out of her musings. "What's it like?" He was leaning in, close enough now that she could smell the dust and sweat from a day walking in the fairgrounds, and just beneath that tobacco and something warmer. Sandalwood, perhaps. She'd never liked the scent of sandalwood, but on him... she finally understood why it was a popular scent. She straightened as she considered what to say about her home. That life seemed so far away.

"It's called Las Tres Rosas." He nodded in response, leaning back in his chair. "In the twenties, when the island was fully under Haitian rule, President Boyer put out a notice that he would give land to any freed men who came from the United States." She was momentarily distracted when he took a sip of his wine, watching his throat move as he swallowed. It seemed everything the man did diverted her attention. "My mother's father heard about it, he ventured to Hispaniola and claimed some land for himself." She ran her finger on a divot in the wood as she recalled her family's story. "He'd been living in Mexico for a couple of years after making the journey to freedom from Tennessee. His wife died only a year after they arrived in Hispaniola, but he had his two daughters with him. They were given a hundred acres on the eastern tip of the island in the region of Higüey. Part of the land is right on the coast. He built a house only about a mile from the beach. He named it Las Tres

Rosas for the three roses in his life. My grandmother Sylvia, my mother, Clarise, and my aunt Catherine. That's where I always lived, other than my two years at finishing school, that is." After her father died, the farm, the house, the distillery—all of it had felt oppressive, like the memories would smother her. But now, with a little distance, she could think about it fondly again. She could recall the good bits of her life there without that searing pain.

"Sounds like a lovely place."

"It's paradise," she said simply.

"And how did Caña Brava happen?" She shifted in her seat under his attention. He had a way of looking at her that made her wonder if he could read her thoughts.

"Higüey had very good land for growing sugar cane, and distilling is in my family's blood. It started with my great-grandfather in Tennessee. He made bourbon." For his master, but that was not the story. This story was about what her family had done with their talents, not about the people who exploited them. "He passed all his secrets to his only son, my grandfather, and *he* put them to use making rum. He started small, only producing a few casks a year, but it was so good it became very popular in the area. It was my mother who had the idea of expanding production, but she had a very particular idea of how to do it. She wanted every person who worked in making the rum to have a stake in it. Beyond their salary, they received dividends from the sales."

Evan seemed genuinely perplexed by that. "Your family shared the profits with the workers," he said slowly, as though trying to grasp the concept.

"Yes." She nodded, and again that flicker of pride sparked inside her. She'd been so bogged down in trying to make connections here, she'd forgotten the history and tradition that she was carrying forward. What it meant to keep her family's legacy alive. "It didn't make our family rich, but I think it's what makes our rum different. Every person that works on Caña Brava feels ownership in it. I think that comes out in the product."

Her mother had once explained that the reason their home was comfortable but not opulent was because her great-grand-father had reviled the stark differences between how the main house lived in comparison to everyone else. Luz's family made sure they didn't have so much that it took away from others having what they needed. "For everyone to have enough, we cannot have so much. That's what my mother always said."

"Ah." Evan's response pierced the silence between them and shifted her attention to the food that had arrived while she talked about her family. Madame Fournier had placed two small bowls of soup on the table before slipping away without notice. It was fragrant and smelled of ginger, star anise and something spicy. Aromas that were familiar but combined in a way that was new to her.

"This is wonderful," she said as she raised a spoonful to her mouth. The flavors exploded on her tongue. She focused on her food for a time, enjoying the soul-nourishing goodness of it. When she finally looked up, she found Evan observing her.

"You like the food." He looked very pleased with himself, and she nodded, spying a few crumbs on his neatly trimmed beard.

"You have—" She ran a finger over the spot on her own chin where he needed to clean up.

"The downside of looking roguish and mysterious is that I sometimes will wear my food," he said, managing arrogance and charming self-mockery at once. He patted his face with a napkin but didn't quite manage it. She reached for him with hers. The moment her hand touched that strong jaw, the air around them thickened into something that ran through her like an electric current.

Impulsive, unplanned touching of Evanston Sinclair was not advisable. She pulled back as if she'd been shocked, though his eyes stayed on her with that same hungry, predatory look he'd given her at Le Bureau. She panicked and opened her mouth.

"Tell me about where you make the Braeburn," she prompted, a little desperately.

He kept that heated brown gaze on her for a moment. "My mother's father bought the land…" he looked up as if trying to recall a detail that had suddenly escaped "…oh, about forty years ago. He didn't come from money, my grandfather, but he made a lot of it with the railways. The Braeburn he bought to make a statement. Almost ten thousand acres in the Highlands." He paused again, and she could sense a discomfort there. As if he didn't want to go further, but after another moment he spoke again. "He left it to my mother when he passed. She and my uncle were his only children; my uncle got his other holdings, and my mother got the Braeburn. The family who previously owned it had been making whisky for generations, but my grandfather kept the distillery dormant while he was alive. My maternal great-great-grandmother was a distiller in her own right—she operated a shebeen out of her home that clothed and fed a generation of Buchanans."

He grinned at the sound of surprise that escaped her lips. Luz's dad had told her about the shebeens, unlicensed drinking houses all over Scotland that were usually operated by widows. It was not something she would've thought a gentleman would confess having a family connection to. Much less sound proud of it.

"The Scots like to forget it was our women who made our whisky what it is," he said with a lift of his shoulder. "I was close to my grandmother, and she told me about that side of our family. I was always interested in it, and—" He stopped, and it looked to her like he was about to say something, then thought better of it. She was surprised at the disappointment she felt to know he'd held something back. "I took it upon myself to revive the distillery about ten years ago," he explained, but something was different. The brightness from earlier had been replaced by the brittleness she'd seen when he'd mentioned his father. It un-nerved her to see him like that.

"Did your mother leave it to you?" she asked, and his face turned even more grave.

"Not quite," he said, with a stark smile. There was a story there, surely, and she almost asked, then decided to let it go. He clearly didn't want to talk about it, not with her.

"You're also carrying on a family legacy, then," she said, not quite sure why it seemed important to establish that kinship between them.

"I guess I am." He looked at her with surprise, like it had not occurred to him there was a significance to that. His brow fur-rowed, and his teeth snagged his bottom lip as he sat with what she'd said. Right then, Madame Fournier arrived with plates of mouthwatering braised beef with thinly sliced fried potatoes and buttered green beans.

"This is absolutely divine," she told their hostess, and when the woman had gone back to the kitchen, she turned to Evan. "Thank you for this."

He shook his head as if there was nothing that warranted that, but she felt extremely grateful to this man for giving her such a pleasant day. Her plans for a summer of adventures in Paris kept being derailed by the many stumbles she'd taken with her business dealings. If she had a moment to herself, she spent it agonizing about her errant trustee or her failed business meet-ings. Even food, which was usually one of the things she most enjoyed when traveling, had been an afterthought. All the stress had her stomach in knots most of the time, but today she was ravenous. This simple meal was one of the most enjoyable she'd had in Paris.

"What's the name of it? The land where you make your whisky."

"Braeburn," he said with a laugh. "And the house is Braeburn Hall. We're not very creative with our names."

"Braeburn Hall," she mused. "Your very own Pemberley,"

she teased, and he threw his head back with a laugh. It was becoming a bad habit, this craving for Evan Sinclair's mirth.

"Good God," he groaned as if the mere mention of the estate belonging to Jane Austen's beloved romantic hero was an affront to decency and good sense. "It's been seventy years. Are people ever going to stop talking about that cad, Darcy?"

"Men might. I doubt women will," she said with feigned regret, as she chewed another perfect bite of crispy potatoes. "I'm afraid you will have to continue to endure being measured against an unattainable paradigm of male virtue."

"The man barely spoke ten words to the woman in the entire book." Evan made a rude sound, and now *she* was the one barking with laughter.

"You seem to know an awful lot about *Pride and Prejudice* for someone who views it with such distaste." His cheeks flushed, and he looked so alluring she had to focus on her food to keep from sighing.

"Of course I've read it," he groused, but she had a feeling the peevishness was more for her amusement now. "It's practically a matter of survival for any man preparing to endure a London season." He sounded so utterly flustered by the whole thing she found herself grinning again. Her face hurt from it, like spending a day with Evan had put muscles into use that had remained idle for too long.

"I am sure your efforts were appreciated," she told him, envisioning the distiller charming his way through London ballrooms with his impassioned censure of Fitzwilliam Darcy. Unbidden, a prickle of jealousy niggled at her, a thorn in her side. But Luz was no debutante, and Evan was certainly no beau.

"Is Austen popular in the Caribbean?" he asked before taking his own bite of food. His eyes were on her, alight with curiosity.

"She was quite popular in my finishing school, but that was Switzerland. In the Americas we have our own love stories. There are quite a few women authors writing them."

"Will you ever go back?" he asked, surprising her.

"I haven't thought that far," she confessed. "After my father's death, I was focused on finishing the plan he'd had for expanding the distillery." And on her own hopes of possibly building something that was just her own. "I suppose I'll have to eventually, but there's a lot I need to accomplish before that," she said, at length. "Today's sale and the meeting with Mr. Dairoku was a good step in that direction. Thank you."

"You must stop doing that," he told her, visibly uncomfortable from the praise. "Besides, it was a business agreement," he said, with a tone of finality.

"You could've said no or taken it back."

"I don't go back on my word. Never." She believed him. "Your composure today was admirable. I didn't expect you to be so…poised."

"I can't afford to be unprepared," she said with equal candor. "Men don't usually take me seriously. Whenever I find myself in a position to be listened to, I must capitalize on it."

"That's admirable." Direct and honest, always. She truly did not know what to make of Evanston Sinclair. But she *was* proud of how she'd handled herself today.

"Do you have a plan for when you get to Edinburgh?" he asked, just as a lovely cup of berries was placed in front of her. Their meal was coming to an end, and she found she was sorry for it. She popped a plump raspberry in her mouth, and a whimper escaped her as the sweet juice of the fruit burst forward. She looked up to find his eyes tracking the movement on her face as if he were attempting to memorize every inch of her visage. The sound that came out of Evan made her think of a badly wounded bear.

"I like berries," she said in apology. He kept staring at her mouth. She could feel the heat of it like a caress.

"And they like you. The fruit has tinted your lips a very appealing red." The gravel in his voice brought on a shiver. Luz was not one to be swept away by a man's sweet words. She was much too cautious of what they weren't saying, of their intentions, to let a compliment go to her head, but with Evan everything seemed to strike right at the heart of a place she hadn't known existed. For a moment she forgot what he'd asked her.

"To answer your question, I don't have any business associates in Scotland. I was hoping I'd make some advantageous connections here, but I may not have much more time…" She hesitated, not sure how much to say regarding her situation with Childers. "I have to resolve some issues pertaining to the funds I'll use to set my business in Edinburgh."

His brows furrowed and his jaw moved like he was working out what to ask. "What exactly is the problem with the trust?"

He was prying, asking her personal things, but thus far no one seemed to be able to help her with Childers, and he was clearly connected. Perhaps he'd at least offer some advice.

"My father left an inheritance in trust for me, but when he set it up I was just a girl. A child, really, and so it's quite well protected. The only way I can access it is through the trustee or through my spouse in the event that I marry. Since I am unmarried, I am at the mercy of the trustee who is not complying with my request that he release the funds to me."

His expression changed then, almost like he didn't want her to notice his interest.

"And you don't have profits coming from the distillery to keep your finances afloat?" The way he spoke it was more than mere curiosity—almost as if he was confirming facts in an inquiry.

"Not really. I gave most of the shares back to the employees before I left. Clarita and I now own only ten percent. But my hope is that I can expand the business—not just growing the rum's distribution but introducing other products as well."

"Like the Dama Juana," he said, and she smiled at his careful pronunciation.

"Yes, but Dama Juana is just one thing. I also have a couple of cordials that I'd like to market specifically to women." He perked up at that, eyeing her with interest. It was truly sad how little the man had to do to make her feel appreciated. It was sadder still how desperately she soaked it up. "I hope that there's interest in buying products that are made without exploiting the workers."

"If you're so invested in growing the profits, why did you give up your shares?" He was clearly fishing for something, but she could not for the life of her surmise what that could be.

"My personal enrichment is not the only thing that matters," she explained, expecting a comment about her idealistic views and poor business sense. None came. "Caña Brava was always meant to be an endeavor that benefited the collective, not just my family."

He looked ready to ask more questions, but a throat cleared in the back, and Evan's head snapped in the direction it came from. An older gentleman was standing a few feet away, clearly trying to attract their attention.

"It seems the Fourniers need to get things ready for the evening meal."

Luz didn't think she imagined the tinge of disappointment in his voice at having their conversation cut short. Or maybe she was attributing her own feelings to him. "I do have to get back," she said, and her shoulders instantly felt heavier than they'd been a moment ago. She checked her pocket watch and saw that she only had twenty minutes before she was to meet Clarita, Amaranta and the Leonas. "My sister will be waiting for me soon."

"Yes," he said, pushing his chair back and standing. She pulled her coin purse from her bag, and he held a hand up. "Please, it's taken care of."

"All right." She knew when to admit defeat. She let him pull out her chair, and when he placed a firm, possessive hand on the small of her back and led her out of the brasserie, she went along with that too. The heat of his touch reached the very core of her and she let herself quietly enjoy the contact until they neared the entry to the fairgrounds. Only then did she turn to him again, this time to finally part ways.

"I—" She lifted her face at the same instant he lowered his, and quite suddenly their mouths were a mere breath away.

"One kiss at a brothel can be brushed off, Luz Alana" he warned as he brought her closer. "A second…"

His lips were so close, and she didn't want to talk. She didn't want him dragging reason into this moment. She wanted the kiss, burned for it. She wanted him to take her mouth like he had last night—rough and hot—and make her *feel*. But the man would not budge.

He wanted her to ask.

"What happens after a second one?" Was that breathless, reedy voice hers?

He walked them into a corner hidden from view. He looked composed enough, his dark gray suit impeccable, but his eyes— they singed her.

"What happens is that I come back for a third one." He pressed his lips to the spot right below her ear, mouthing the words against her skin. "And a fourth one."

"Oh," she squeaked as his teeth grazed against her, and still the blasted man would not kiss her. So she did the only sensible thing. She tugged on his very neatly tied four-in-hand and crashed her mouth against his. She smiled with satisfaction when he responded with a growl and lifted her against the wall of the alley. All she could do was hold on. The door to the Fourniers' restaurant was mere feet away. Anyone could walk by and see, and she could not make herself care. She'd been nothing but sensible in these last two years; she'd been sensible her whole life. Always pressing on and doing what had to be done. The future of Caña Brava, of her family's legacy, of Clarita were hers to secure. And that was an inescapable, absolute truth. Her responsibilities owned her, but this kiss, this moment was hers.

Kiss the wrong man for the right reasons.

Luz did. Tasting Evanston Sinclair was her reward. She was anchored to him. One of his hands firmly on her hip, the other clasped at the base of her neck as he plundered her. His tongue gliding against hers in a wicked, dark caress, and she responded in earnest.

The first time Luz had been tentative, shy, letting him guide her. Now she applied to her own exploration. She let her hands drift up until they met on the back of his head. It was like being locked with a warm wall of granite. His body was hard, but so alive. His massive thigh pushed between her legs, eliciting a gasp that she could barely recognize as her own. Every sound of hers seemed to spur him on, stoke the flames of his passion. She was suspended in this kiss, as if gravity herself had given up trying to keep the two of them tethered to the ground. She floated in his embrace, the only thing grounding her were those powerful hands and the rough scratch of his beard as he pressed his lips to hers again and again. Forcefully, possessively claiming. Like her mouth was his and he'd had enough of allowing her to think any different.

That first kiss at Le Bureau had been a soft breeze, but this… was a storm. He ravished her with drugging, urgent kisses.

"You," Evan said, and he sounded dazed. Luz waited for him to finish, but he just shook his head, pinned her with that wild gaze and took her mouth again.

A door opened loudly, forcing them to pull apart, but Evan moved briskly so that she was completely shielded by him. His big body concealing her from prying eyes. She stiffened in his arms as her mind cleared and she realized just how openly she'd let the man take her. He must have noticed her distress, and he made a soothing sound and planted a soft kiss to her temple.

"We'll go in a second," he told her and pressed another ticklish kiss to her heated skin.

His hands drifted to her chest; when she looked down he was running his finger along the edge of her mother's brooch.

"What stone is this? I've never seen anything like it."

"It's larimar. They've only found it in Hispaniola. I like to wear it because the colors remind of the Caribbean Sea." Would she confess all her secrets to the man?

"It's beautiful." His voice was so soft, and his body so hard. She caught herself before she could start wishing for things she could not have.

"You don't have to walk back with me," she told him, suddenly needing to create some distance. Struggling to maintain control as she was pulled into waters that she could not possibly navigate. He shook his head, softly rubbing his thumb to her cheek.

"I will walk you back," he declared, in a tone which allowed absolutely no room for discussion. And when he pulled on her hand and led her back to the fairgrounds, Luz wished with all her heart that this could be more than a stolen afternoon.

Nine

Twice now he'd kissed her while he was supposed to be assessing this business about the will and the distillery. It was madness, all of it. But now he knew he would make her the offer. An offer of marriage could be as beneficial for her as it was for him. An arrangement that would solve both their predicaments. He had not liked what she'd said regarding the trustee. It had taken an enormous amount of control not to pry for the blackguard's name and send his lawyers after him. He'd seen women left destitute under circumstances like this and, heaven help him, he could not walk away from this. From her.

"I can see myself the rest of the way," Luz Alana said as they neared the pavilion. Her soft voice dragged Evan out of the disorder that kiss had made of his mind.

"What are you doing this evening?" he asked her bluntly.

She frowned at the question. "I'm going to the soirée the Mexican delegation is hosting at their pavilion." She gave him another one of those curious looks. "After I finish with Clarita, I will go to our town house to get ready."

Evan was still considering a course of action when a choir of voices called Luz Alana's name. They stopped just a few yards from the Dominican pavilion and almost ran into three women and a child. One he recognized from Le Bureau. Another looked a few years older than Luz Alana, and was holding the hand of a young girl. If Evan hadn't known Luz Alana had a sister he would've guessed it on sight. She had her older sister's nose and round cheeks and identical soulful brown eyes.

"Oof, Clarita," Luz Alana cried as the child threw herself in her sister's arms. "Have you had a nice day, sweetheart?" she asked, kissing the top of the girl's head.

"We played in the fountain," Clarita said excitedly, then pointed at the very wet hem of her skirts.

"The only sensible thing to do on a warm day," Luz Alana said and beamed at her sister. She seemed genuinely pleased with the news. Most guardians would rebuke the child for supposedly unladylike behavior and remind her the proper ways a young lady should behave, but not this lioness.

"Sweetheart, this is Mr. Evanston Sinclair." She raised a hand toward him, but her eyes were a little guarded now. He found himself yearning for the open, smiling looks he'd been regaled with in the brasserie. "This is my sister, Clarita, and my cousin Amaranta Marquez Puello. Aurora you met last night." She blushed at the mention of their encounter at Le Bureau, and heat washed over Evan. "Aurora is the very first woman licensed to practice medicine in Mexico," she informed him, her voice full of pride.

"And this is Manuela." Luz Alana gestured to the beauty with russet curls, standing on the other side of Amaranta. "She's an artist, and two of her paintings will be shown at the Paris Salon."

Manuela bowed, offering him a very wicked smile. "Mr. Sinclair, three times in two days. If this was Venezuela, you'd be inquiring about a dowry by now."

Oh, this one he would have to watch out for.

"Manu," Luz Alana warned, which only made her friend's smile deepen.

He bowed in courtesy. "A very impressive group, indeed," he said sincerely. They were all beautiful and clearly accomplished. But he could not take his eyes off Luz Alana.

"Does your beard itch?" Clarita asked, making him laugh.

Evan scratched his chin. "Not usually, but I do have to care for it."

"How?" she asked and crossed her arms in front of her in an identical imitation of her older sister.

"Clarise Luz, where are your manners?" Luz Alana attempted to rebuke the child, but the force of it was dampened by the woman's indulgent tone. This little girl was clearly adored by these women, and she knew it.

"It's all right," he told Luz Alana, who didn't look very upset. He turned back to Clarita, who was waiting rather impatiently for his answer. "I—or my valet, rather," he admitted, "trims it with very small scissors, and then he rubs bay oil in it."

"Do you comb it?"

He couldn't help his grin. "Every day."

This seemed to satisfy her. Evan looked at the three other women, and noticed they were all sending concerned glances at a paper now in Luz's hand.

"You talk like my da."

"I am Scottish, like him," Evan answered without prompting, one eye on Luz Alana as she read.

"We're going to live there, in Edinburgh," Clarita said and then looked up at her sister again, as if needing confirmation.

"That's right, we'll be there soon," Luz Alana said distractedly, gaze fixed on the note.

"Do you know any children there?" Clarita asked, cracking Evan's heart in two.

"I do. My sister has twins. One girl and one boy. They're eleven," he told her, and she seemed to mull this over.

"I'm ten. Maybe we can go meet them? The children." The

yearning in her small face disarmed Evan. The Heith-Benzan women seemed to be set on ruining him today.

"Not today, darling. Perhaps once we're in Edinburgh we can meet Mr. Sinclair's niece and nephew," Luz Alana hedged, valiantly attempting to smile, but Evan could see that whatever she'd read in that letter was not good news. "We have to go to Cairo Street." Her voice shook when she spoke, and it was all Evan could do not to ask what was wrong.

"Can he come with us?" Clarita appealed, turning to him. "Luz Alana is going to buy me a picture book about the Valley of the Kings." Evan could see Luz Alana fighting tears, but after a moment she got herself back in control.

"What did it say?" Amaranta murmured.

Luz only shook her head. Aurora's face darkened with fury, and Manuela's crumpled while Clarita asked Evan about the twins. But by the time the child turned around, the women were all looking down at their young charge as if everything was right in the world.

A pride of lionesses, indeed: whatever trouble was brewing, they would not worry the child with it. Evan could barely contain the need to intervene. To destroy whatever made this fierce woman look so scared.

"Clarita, sweetheart, we have to go. I need to respond to the letter before the telegram office closes in thirty minutes."

"If that's going to Edinburgh, I can have it couriered for you," he blurted out. "We have a clerk at the British pavilion that takes telegrams to the main office. That one's open until the evening." Sounding casual was an impossibility at the moment.

She hesitated.

"Please," he insisted. "Let me help."

"Do you know any men we can send after a wayward trustee?" Manuela asked, eliciting a barrage of exasperated-sounding Spanish words from the three other women.

"What?" the artist asked innocently. "We can certainly use the help."

Luz Alana sent Manuela a withering look that would've sent a lesser woman—or man—running for cover. But Manuela was made of stronger mettle. Luz Alana turned to Evan then. Her face, which had been open and relaxed when they'd dined, now tight with worry. He could almost see the long shadow of the albatross hovering over her.

"But maybe he can marry you, and then you don't have to ask that man to help you!"

Every head in their small group turned in Clarita's direction with a speed that would've been comical if the situation was not what it was.

"Mi amor," Luz Alana said, her voice tired, "why do you think I need to get married? We don't need anyone to help us."

"But you said," Clarita told her sister, her small face brimming with worry. Evan ached to take both of them in his arms, do away with everything casting this darkness over them.

"Mi niña—" Luz Alana engulfed her sister in a fierce embrace, her eyes filled with unshed tears "—you don't have to worry about any of that. It will be all right. *We* will be all right. Trust me, esta bien?" Luz Alana whipped her head in Evan's direction as if only now recalling he'd been a witness to this very private moment.

"Thank you, for everything, Mr. Sinclair."

He was no longer Evan, and he'd never hated his family's name more than at that moment. She offered him a resolute stare and a firm handshake. The complicit spark in her eyes was gone now, and what remained was the flinty stare of someone who had the weight of the world pressing down on her. She walked away from him with her head held high, a woman who would do what she must.

No explanations, no cowering, no tears.

Raghav found him some time later, after he'd watched the small pride head in the direction of the Cairo Street exhibit.

"You look grim," his friend said, and Evan grunted.

"Here, this was left for you at the pavilion," Raghav said, pulling a blue envelope from his jacket.

Apollo.

Evan opened it, still unsettled from the scene with Luz Alana. The message was, per usual, short and to the point.

It's done. The duke's birthday will be the talk of the town this year.
ACSR

Evan folded the note and slid it into his pocket, his eyes fixed on someone's lost kite, fluttering in the wind.

"Who do we know in the Mexican delegation?" he asked as they started to walk. "I need an invitation to the soirée they're hosting tonight."

Ten

"Any luck?" Manuela asked as she glanced around the main room in the Mexican pavilion, which for the evening had been transformed into a tropical garden.

"None," Luz told her friends, joining them in the corner of the ballroom they'd commandeered. The letter from her solicitor in Edinburgh had gone a long way to suffuse any lingering illusions she had about prolonging whatever it was she'd been doing with Evan that afternoon. She'd had a moment of real panic after reading that Percy Childers had doubled down on his refusal to advance her any funds and instead had requested an audience with Mr. Bruce to "discuss" the solicitor's involvement. As trustee of the inheritance, Childers could release the lawyer and find someone who was more amenable to his scheming. Which could potentially be catastrophic. Childers had set a date ten days away, and Mr. Bruce strongly advised Luz to make herself available to attend. It had been a timely reminder that she had absolutely no time to waste on distractions of the male variety—no matter how bone-melting their kisses.

The departure to Scotland was now imminent, and tonight was her last chance to secure a shipping partner with a route to the Caribbean. Among the guests were a number of trades-men, including several who operated between the Caribbean and Europe. She'd attempted to speak with some of the gentle-men she knew either owned steamships or had distributors in England and Scotland, and she'd been rebuffed, ignored and in one instance...laughed at. She'd hoped the fortune from ear-lier in the day would continue this evening, but it seemed her streak had run out.

"Valencia wouldn't even talk to me," she muttered, slumped against the wall. She hated the feeling of tears stinging her eyes. "You'd think I was asking them to drink my blood," she cried as she scanned the room again, searching for any potential busi-ness contacts she had not yet approached.

"If you asked them that, they'd probably take the card," Au-rora scoffed, with her *Men are absolute basura* scowl.

"I still think you should've taken the Great Scot's offer to help, Leona." Manu had been harping on that point from the mo-ment they'd left the man at the fairgrounds. And she'd wanted to, when he'd practically pled that she allow him to help her; she'd desperately wanted to say yes. But she'd muddied the wa-ters with the man far too much. With Seynabou Cisse-Kelly and Dairoku, she'd at least been able to trade the favor for some rum casks. But she had no more casks to give—as they were all full of the spirit—and she would not keep accepting favors from Evan. Not if she expected him to take her and her business seriously.

With a sigh, she turned her attention to the dance floor in an effort to at least pretend she was enjoying herself. There was greenery everywhere, large potted fan palms and yucca trees, all brought from Mexico for the exposition. The orchestra, which was currently playing a danza by Juan Morel Campos, was on a raised dais at the far end of the improvised ballroom. Behind them on the wall was an enormous circular arrangement of ferns, red dahlias and white orchids, lushly displaying the colors of the Mexican flag. The candlelight gave the affair a seductive feel,

and Luz almost wished she hadn't chucked her fan behind a potted palm. A dance or two might help improve her mood. Her
beautiful saffron gown, with its delicate lace overlay and provocative décolletage was going to utter waste. Thinking about
dancing only served to bring Evanston Sinclair to the forefront of
her mind. The way he gripped her hips as they kissed, how well
they fit together. *Stop obsessing about the man, Luz Alana.* With
effort, she turned her attention to a couple on the dance floor.

Luz recognized one of the women who'd come over on the
ship with them. Her family owned half the coast of Costa Rica,
apparently, and she was dancing with a tall, imposing man. He
would've attracted attention merely due to his size, but he was
handsome too. He was a graceful dancer, gliding his partner
around the room with ease. While the beautifully dressed woman's focus was fully on her dancing partner, his was elsewhere;
the man's eyes searched the room as though he was looking for
someone. Something about his expression was so familiar. Perhaps he'd also been on their ship?

"Who is that?" Unsurprisingly, the answer came from Manuela.

"You don't remember Magdalena Alcazar? You were there
when she talked our ears off about her Arabian horses." Luz's
mouth twitched as she kept her eyes on Magdalena's partner. He
had that same commanding, slightly dangerous presence as Evan.

Making everything about that blasted man was becoming a compulsion.

"I meant her dancing companion."

"Oh, you mean *el heredero.*" Aurora scoffed as she glared at the
gentleman in question. "God's gift to women, or so one would
think with the way the entitled pendejo walks around."

Both Luz and Manuela turned to their friend in surprise. This
kind of outburst was very unusual for her.

"He asked Aurora to dance, or more like let her know what
an honor it would be for her to dance with him," Manu said
through a fit of giggles. Aurora scowled.

Luz was about to ask again for the man's name but was interrupted by Manuela's gasp.

"The Duke and Duchess of Sundridge," an usher bellowed before an elegant couple descended the stairs to the dance floor. The woman certainly had bearing. The only word Luz Alana could come up with was *statuesque*. Tall, with bronzed skin, jet-black hair and violet eyes. Luz Alana could see why Manu was captivated.

"They certainly know how to make an entrance. Do you know her?" Even Aurora seemed somewhat stunned by the Duchess of Sundridge.

"I…" Their friend hesitated, still at a loss for words. "She was at Le Bureau. In the upstairs area," Manu said in a faraway voice. The upstairs that offered a variety of *Sapphic pursuits*.

"Did you talk?" Luz Alana inquired.

Manu shrugged, uncharacteristically shy. "There was an exchange," she answered vaguely. At that moment, the duchess reached the edge of the dancing area, her head held high as she surveyed her surroundings. The very portrait of urbane aristocracy.

"Is that her husband?" They'd announced him as the duke.

"It's her stepson," Antonio said quietly as he joined their trio. "He's only a couple of years younger than she. She's Chilean. Father's American, ungodly wealthy. Silver mines." Well, that explained the belt entirely covered in onyx the woman was wearing.

"When the duke died she changed her residence from London to Paris. The new duke and his stepmother share the same…" Antonio loved a dramatic pause "…preferences."

At that moment the woman's gaze landed on them—well, more precisely on Manuela, who seemed to bloom under the older woman's attention. The duchess did not even attempt to be discreet in her examination of their friend.

"Well, this is an interesting development," Aurora muttered

as their friend exchanged several more heated looks with the duchess. Luz was about to concur with the sentiment when Antonio spoke. "Alerta, Luz Alana. Llego tu escoces."

Luz's whole body reacted to his words. For a moment she felt slightly disoriented. Almost afraid to look where he was pointing.

Aurora made a pained sound. "We might as well head home now, Antonio. These two will be useless the rest of the night."

"Very funny, and please stop calling him *my* Scot." She chastised even as her stomach churned with excitement and a not a small amount of nausea.

She could feel his presence before she laid eyes on him. And then there he was, at the top of the stairs, irrefutable in that blunt elegance of his. He looked dashing in his formal wear, with a pretty blonde on his arm. She fought the wave of jealousy that flashed through her as she took the woman in. She was dressed in a lovely pink gown that was unassuming yet seemed to complement all her attributes—and she was staring up at Evan like he'd hung the moon. She'd let the man play her for a fool, and now here he was, with another woman. He'd probably come here just to rub it in her face.

As they approached the steps, Evan's companion pointed at one of the enormous flower arrangements on the far side of the ballroom with an awe-filled expression. He looked down at her with such naked affection that all the air went out of Luz's lungs at once. She was still struggling to get herself under control when their names were announced and then she truly feared she would be sick.

"The Earl of Darnick and Lady—" The blood rushing to her ears didn't let her hear the rest of the usher's announcement.

"Earl?" Luz heard her three friends whisper in unison.

"He can't be married, can he? Did you know about the..." Manuela made a gesture with her hand and bowed, which Luz assumed meant *Earl*, but she only shook her head in response.

Earl.

The word continued to ring in her head until she felt light-headed. Luz decided the best course of action was to remove herself from the room before she did or said something she would absolutely regret. She knew she should move her feet, exit the premises, but something about the way he was looking around, searching, scanning the room kept her rooted in place. Then his eyes found her, and his expression transformed into something quite different. He took her in with such unguarded pleasure that for a few seconds she felt her heartbeat in her whole body.

How bloody dare he?

"I have to go," she told her friends as she pushed into the crowd of people.

"But he's coming over here," Aurora exclaimed as Luz escaped.

"That's not the effect one wants to have on his future bride," Murdoch commented unhelpfully, while Evan considered what to do about the murderous look Luz Alana had shot his way before disappearing into the crowd.

"Is that your rum heiress?" Adalyn asked, gaze fixed on Luz Alana's retreating form.

"She's not *mine*," he protested, still tracking her as she moved around the room.

"Are your eyes aware of that fact? Because they were ready to pop out of your skull the moment they descended on her."

Murdoch snorted, while Evan continued to ignore his sister's taunts. "She's exquisite, Evan. Not everyone can wear saffron, but she looks absolutely majestic."

"She does." That he could not deny. She was the most beautiful woman in the room. Her dress, as the one she'd worn at Le Bureau, displayed every one of her many attributes to perfection. He'd noticed that she did not favor the elaborate ruffles and cascading tulle so many of the society ladies wore. Luz

Alana's style was more understated. Embroidery, perhaps a bit of embellishment on the hems and sleeves, but not much more. It was in the colors that she did not hold back: a tropical, fiery flower among a sea of wan pastels.

"I'm going to go look for her," he said impatiently.

"Excellent," piped Adalyn with a clap of her hands. "What shall we do? What is the plan?"

Murdoch, that sod, guffawed at Addie's enthusiasm as if they were about to pull off a caper.

"*Your* plan should involve enjoying yourself with Murdoch this evening. I will go speak with Miss Heith-Benzan." Just then he found her on the edge of the ballroom. She was speaking—or at least attempting to—with a man, and in her hand she had a small card which she was trying to hand him, but instead of taking it, he turned his back on her and walked away. Fury filled Evan as he watched her face crumble.

"That bastard," Evan growled, itching for a fight.

"Oh no! How rude," Adalyn gasped behind him.

"Excuse me," he said, already walking toward Luz Alana, who had left the little piece of paper on the floor of the ballroom and gone to hide behind the fronds of a stunningly large plant. Whoever that heel was, he would find him and make him kiss her fucking feet. He picked up the paper and saw that it was her business card. He recognized the embossed seal from her rum bottles, and below it was her name and title.

Caña Brava Rum & Spirits
Luz Alana Heith-Benzan
Distiller

Despite his irritation at the man and his concern for her, he had to smile at her gall. The woman was trying to do business at a ball. Before he could talk himself out of it, he turned on his heel and stalked across the room to the refreshments table where that bastard was holding court. He clapped the man's shoulders and roughly pulled him away from his little party.

"Oi," the man barked, and on a closer inspection Evan recognized him as the owner of a fairly large London shipping firm. She'd likely been trying to inquire about a shipping contract and the man couldn't even show her some decency.

"Come with me," Evan growled, gripping the bloke's upper arm.

"What do you think you're doing, man?" he whined while Evan dragged him across the room.

"It is Lord Darnick to you, you fucking pustule," he spat out, as the shipper's face instantly blanched.

"Lord?" he asked, and Evan's mood darkened further. The magic word always seemed to work best on the absolutely worst people. "Where are you taking me?"

"To apologize to the lady you just disrespected in front of everyone." That elicited an affronted balk, and Evan tightened his hand into a punishing grip. "You've no idea how much I would relish taking out every one of my many frustrations on you."

"But she's a——"

"Take my advice and shut up, before you lose every tooth in your head." The man had quit struggling and was now looking at him with genuine fear. At least his self-preservation instincts seemed in working order, even if his decency was sorely lacking.

Evan didn't get too close once he reached Luz Alana, not wanting to startle her. She had her back to the ballroom, the lines of her shoulders tense, head bowed. Something dark and cold moved in him at the sight of her distress. He would commit all matter of violence for this woman tonight if it would help wash away the misery radiating from her.

"Apologize," he ordered the man. She stiffened when she heard his voice but would not turn to face him yet. His only view at the moment was the back of that flaming dress and a cluster of flowers on her hair of the same color.

"Miss Heith-Benzan, I've someone here who would like to speak to you."

"Go away," she said miserably. Evan shoved the man forward.

"My apologies for earlier, miss," the man said shakily, and her head finally popped up.

"What did you do?" She was looking—glaring—at Evan while the other man continued to proffer mea culpas and scrambled to pull a card out of his pocket.

"What's your name?" Evan barked.

"Johnston, William Johnston." Evan bared his teeth at the man who looked like he was on the verge of tears. Not so fucking brash now, was he?

"Mr. Johnston has reconsidered the way in which he conducts himself with you." Johnston's face paled, but the man managed to nod.

"I'd be happy to assist you with your shipments, Miss…"

"Heith-Benzan," Evan snarled, and the man shook like a leaf. Luz sent him an unfriendly look, then nodded at the shipping merchant, a fresh card in her hand.

"If you are truly interested in speaking about a shipping contract for my rum, I would gladly contact you in the morning." She looked down at the card the man was offering but did not take it. "I don't want you to do it if he's forcing you." Her voice shook slightly, and Evan wished he'd just taken the man outside and thrashed him.

"His Lordship has made me aware that you have a legitimate business." Evan could only narrow his eyes at the shipper's lies.

"His Lordship did, did he?" she said, thoroughly unimpressed, and sent Evan what could only be considered a withering look. "I'll take you up on your offer, then, Mr. Johnston," she said with a polite nod and plucked the card from between his fingers. The man turned to Evan, likely to slather him with insincere compliments.

"Get out of my sight before I make good on my threats." The man removed himself with impressive alacrity. Evan never took his eyes off Luz Alana, who looked ready to strangle him.

"Am I supposed to be impressed by what you just did?" Her arms were crossed under her breasts, which pushed them up and out. Between that and the sweet little growl in her voice, his cock throbbed in his trousers. Her eyes were another story. Evan was quite certain that if one could incinerate a man with their glare, he'd be a pile of ashes.

"And here I thought I was helping a fellow distiller."

She scoffed at that. He threw his hands up in defeat, aware that he'd somehow cocked things up...again.

"Let's start over." She only narrowed her eyes at his suggestion. "I should've asked you first before intervening. I just loathed seeing him ignore you like that." She thawed minimally at the apology.

"Yes, you should have." He could tell she was considering what else to say, but after a moment only bit her bottom lip.

"You ran from me. I've been looking for you since I arrived," he finally said.

"And I was *avoiding* you since you arrived." Now he was the one biting his lip, but only to keep from grinning. There was likely something very wrong with him, but he found the way she let him know exactly how she felt extremely arousing.

"And here I was thinking we'd made strides this afternoon. You certainly seemed to be warming up to me when I..." She growled at that, and stepped up closer to him, likely so she could insult him without having to yell. His cock throbbed again.

"Do you lie to all your friends about who you are?" she demanded. "It didn't occur to you to mention that you're an earl the first or second time we met?" He'd received a variety of reactions from women the moment they learned about his title over the years, though fury was a new one. No fawning or adulation from this woman.

"It's more of a third-meeting thing, really," he said jokingly. She scowled, unamused by his attempt at humor. "Besides, my title wasn't exactly relevant during our previous interactions.

My father is a duke, and so I am an earl." He knew he sounded like a heel, but he abhorred ever speaking about his connection to that blasted title.

"Arrogante pendejo."

He caught the word *arrogant* and was quite certain whatever else she said was not apt for the surge of arousal that coursed through him.

"I am fully aware I'm not supposed to enjoy the verbal abuse," he said, coming a bit closer while she sent him vicious looks. "But whenever you speak Spanish I become thoroughly galvanized with the idea of ravishing you in a dark corner."

"Dominican Spanish," she corrected.

"Tell me more." She looked poised to give him an earful and he was positively riveted.

"It's the same as Scots English," she explained. "It's not your tongue, it was forced on you, and like your whisky you've blended it into something that's your own. Anyone who hears a Scotsman speak recognizes the sound. We've made this language that was imposed on us ours too. When I speak, West Africa is on my tongue, Taino is on my tongue. Castilians have *their* Spanish, and we have our own."

She was a bit winded by the time she finished, and he found that his own breathing was coming faster. Seeing the world through Luz Alana's eyes was an utterly transformative experience.

"Is this what it's like to be a man? Constantly out of breath from being allowed to speak your mind without being interrupted?" He wasn't certain she'd meant to say that out loud, but he could not help the delighted laugh that escaped him.

"You are the most alluring thing in all of Paris, as is your *Dominican* Spanish. I particularly enjoy hearing it against my ear when I kiss you."

"You're a swine, did you know that?"

"I've been made aware of this particular attribute of mine,

yes." He truly did want to ravish her. Sit her on his lap and have his way with her while she blistered his ears in her Dominican Spanish.

"Still not funny," she said. He was about to make another joke when her eyes fixed on something over his shoulder and her face fell. "I would think your lady would not take kindly to you speaking with women in hidden corners."

His *lady*? What on earth was she on about… Wait.

"You mean my sister?" he asked as realization dawned on him.

"Your sister," she repeated, her eyes narrowed into slits.

"You don't have a very high opinion of me, if you'd think I go around kissing other women when I have a wife." He was a bit offended by that. Despite his attempt at humor, he had felt close to her today. It bothered him that she thought him capable of that. *When have you ever cared what impression people have of your integrity?*

"And you're doing a splendid job of supporting my very accurate assessment, *Earl of Darnick*."

"I should've told you," he admitted.

"Yes, you should have." God, but he liked this woman. She tipped her chin in the direction of the ballroom. "Your sister, then?"

"Yes. Adalyn is the younger of my two sisters," he said, pointing at the pair who were unabashedly watching Evan's conversation while they danced around the room. "Beatrice, my other sister, is in Paris too, but she's not here tonight. My whole bloody family is in town at the moment."

Luz Alana's mouth quirked up at his grousing. "Don't you need to get back to her?" she asked.

"She's fine," he assured her. He was getting impatient. She was still not close enough, and he was yet to touch her. "She's dancing with my cousin Murdoch."

"Your cousin who was born in Jamaica." He was ridiculously touched by her remembering that detail.

"That's right." He gently pulled on her gloved hand. "Don't go," he urged, and despite the remaining traces of menace in her gaze, she came out from behind that damn palm, finally letting him get a full view of her.

Beautiful seemed like such a useless, absurd word in the face of what he had in front of him. It was like saying a diamond was but a pretty piece of cut glass. Just the sight of her made him feel famished and replete all at once.

"Dance with me." His voice was gravel, roughened by all the words scratching at his throat.

"I don't like dancing. My corset is too tight. I can barely breathe when I'm standing still," she said, churlish even as her body swayed to the music. Her scent was intoxicating, vanilla and something floral, orange blossom perhaps.

"Now who's the one lying?" he teased as he gathered her to him.

"I'm telling the absolute truth. This blasted thing is like a gauntlet." Nothing had ever been more appealing to him than Luz Alana Heith-Benzan's bottom lip pushed out in a surly pout.

"We must find a way to end the evil reign of corsets, then."

"The person who discovers an alternative will have the devotion of women everywhere," she assured him as they stepped onto the dance floor. The moment they did, a new piece of music started, causing her eyes to flash with recognition and pleasure.

"You like Strauss?" he asked as he moved them around the room.

She opened her eyes at his question, then her expression changed to amusement. "This is not Strauss. This is Juventino Rosas. He's a Mexican composer." She said it with a hint of challenge, as if expecting him to dispute the possibility of such a thing as a Mexican composing a waltz.

"What's it called?" he asked, and her face opened like a spring flower. The brilliance of it stunned him. He'd pleased her, and he very much wanted to do it again.

"'Sobre las Olas,'" she said. "'Over the Waves.'" His hand tightened on her lower back, bringing her to him, and then he put his mouth to her ear.

"Is this your favorite composer?"

She pursed her lips as they danced, head canted to the side, as if he'd asked a very serious question.

"I like this, but my favorite pieces are the danzas. It's music that was created in the Caribbean, and it feels and sounds like home. There is a composer, born in Puerto Rico, whose father was Dominican, Juan Morel Campos. He might be my favorite." He absorbed the information, curious about this music that felt to her like the tropics.

"Tell me something else in your Spanish," he cajoled, and she let out a husky titter that coiled around his bones like rings of fire.

"Te gusta provocarme," she whispered.

"Are you provoking me, or am I provoking you, Luz Alana?"

"I am wondering that myself, Evan," she told him cheekily, effortlessly flowing to the music. She was a beautiful dancer, her feet moving gracefully, hips swaying in perfect rhythm as she perched in his arms. He was not fond of ballrooms, but he could dance with this woman all night.

"Was that bastard Johnston the reason you were hiding in a corner?"

The question had an instant effect, and that fire in her eyes burned out as quickly as it had roared to life.

"I didn't expect it to be this hard," she confessed. "I never assumed it would be *simple* to do business here on my own, but I drastically underestimated how unwilling people would be to even speak with me." Her small hands tightened on him as she spoke. He could feel the distress in her. He wanted to make it all go away. "I have to leave for Edinburgh sooner than I'd thought, in just a few days, really, and I will leave only with the sales you helped me with." Her upper lip wobbled, and rage ensnared him. "They will never take me seriously."

He stopped in the middle of the floor and brought his hand under her chin, nudging until she looked at him.

"I take you seriously, Luz Alana." Blood rushed to his temples as he opened his mouth, practically shaking from how much he needed this woman to believe him.

"*You* want to kiss me," she rebutted.

"I do," he confessed, and her lips parted expectantly. This wildness inside him was no condition in which to make life-changing decisions. But now he had to do this, and soon. "I also respect how much passion you have for your business."

"I can assure you that you're in the minority."

"Maybe you haven't had the right audience," he hedged. "You were brilliant with Dairoku. He sent me a note after we left him thanking me for bringing you to our meeting."

"That only worked because you vetted me," she countered, and he couldn't exactly deny that. "Everyone wants to do business with you, Evan. You're an earl, for God's sake. You don't know what it's like for me. You walk into rooms like you expect the sea to part, and everyone acts accordingly. I can't get anyone to give me the time of day."

"You're right," he conceded. "I don't know what it's like for you, and I…" He couldn't do it here, not in front of all these people. It had to be somewhere when they could be alone together. Where they could talk like they had earlier, honestly. As equals. "Would you like to get some fresh air?"

Eleven

―――――――――――――

"Are you intending to get me drunk with that bottle of champagne?" Luz asked as she watched Evan nab a bottle from one of the tables before whisking her out into the gardens behind the pavilion.

"I thought I'd bring something to entice you."

"Is that how earls operate? Steal champagne to woo unsuspecting ladies into dark corners?"

Without a word he tugged her to him until there was only a breath of space between them. Their bodies were not quite touching, but she could feel the heat of him warming her from the tips of her toes to the top of her head.

"Does this usually work on women?" She had no intention of letting him know the effect he had on her.

"I believe," he whispered, as his hand on her back did away with what little space was left between them, "it may be working on you."

She felt that *you* in her core, turning her insides molten. This was a very dangerous game to play with the only person who had been willing to help her. She was dancing on flames tonight, and she could not seem to stop. How could she when

he'd brought her that bastard Johnston, like a gladiator presenting his queen with the head of her enemy?

There was absolutely no keeping her wits about her with this man.

"Why did you bring me here?" she rasped as he grazed her
forehead with soft kisses.

"I'm taking you to the top of the tower," he informed her
placidly, and she could feel his lips forming the words on her
skin. The effect was so hypnotizing it took her a moment to
digest what he'd told her.

"You're what?" she said, finally pulling herself out of the fog
she'd been in. "It's closed," she pointed out, and he proffered
her a lazy smile that was as sinful as it was sweet.

"It's closed for the public, Luz Alana. *I* am not the public."
The sardonic tone of his voice really should infuriate her. But
there was an eagerness in his eyes that disarmed her. He wasn't
whisking her away, he was inviting her to go on an adventure
with him, just like he'd done this morning.

"It's terribly inappropriate," she said weakly, as the thought
occurred to her this would likely be her last chance to go up
the tower. Amaranta had taken Clarita up after their jaunt to
Cairo Street, but Luz and the Leonas had had to get dressed for
the soirée. It would be romantic to go up tonight, and reckless.
But this was Paris, and the man was so very tempting. Evan Sinclair—no, Lord Darnick—and a bottle of champagne. Just the
two of them at the top of the world.

It could be a memory to sustain her on the endless lonely nights ahead.

"Oh, all right," she huffed. He grinned that wolfish grin that
made her knees weak and grazed a soft kiss on her cheek. The
velvety bristle of his beard made her shiver.

"I thought that Remington with the mother-of-pearl handle
you have strapped to your thigh could serve as chaperone," he
drawled against her ear.

She bit back her own wolfish grin and lifted a shoulder. "As
long as we're both aware of the possible risks…to you."

"Oh, I am very aware that you are very dangerous." His eyes were glittering with hungry intensity. "Luz Alana, I want to offer you a business partnership," he finally said, surprising her. "A way for you to get situated in Scotland and access my many distribution networks in Europe and beyond. I would like to assist you in gaining access to your inheritance as well."

"My inheritance?" she asked, perplexed. "How can you help with that?"

"Simple. We get married."

If he had not been holding her up, Luz would've crumbled to the ground.

"Is this a joke?" she asked, suddenly very angry. Had she misjudged this man completely? Because Evan Sinclair so far had proved to be many things, but she did not think him cruel.

"On the contrary." And he did not sound at all like he was joking. In fact, she had not seen him look more intent. "I assure you I've never been more serious about anything in my life," he told her, and even through the barrage of emotions and thoughts whirling through her brain, she believed him.

"I don't understand." Or at least she couldn't possibly be understanding correctly. "We only met each other yesterday."

Had it really only been one day?

"And in that time, we've both learned that we are running out of time to sort our particular situations," he said, confusing her further. "You have to obtain control of your inheritance, and a, uh, complication has come to light in my own affairs."

"What kind of complication?" she asked as she watched something like fury flash through his face.

"The land where I have my distillery is under my father's control." She could see it was costing him to maintain his temper. "I can only get the Braeburn out of my father's hands if I get married." His tone was even enough, but this clearly meant a great deal to Evan. From what he'd told her at the Fourni-

ers', she knew the distillery was more than just a business en-
terprise for him.

"But won't it pass to you when you're duke?" Something she
couldn't quite identify passed over his face, but he only shook
his head.

"I can't count on anything when it comes to my father, and
while the distillery should be rightfully mine..." Any trace of
humor and lightness evaporated almost instantly. His entire demeanor transformed whenever he talked about his father. "He
won't let me have it until I force his hand. He's in a fair amount
of financial trouble, and I can't risk him selling it out from under
me. If I have to get married to save my business, that's what I'll
do. I thought you might feel the same."

Luz felt as though she had floated away, that she was observing herself having this utterly mad conversation from three feet
above.

"Why aren't you in financial trouble if your father is?" She'd
heard of many aristocrats who had descended into ruin in the
past fifty years. It wasn't as easy to amass those fortunes now
that they didn't have free labor across the Atlantic.

"My business has nothing to do with my father or the holdings of the dukedom." There was something that sounded very
much like pride in his voice. "I am not..." he paused, pursing his
lips, and for a second she thought he would stop talking entirely
"...I was not meant to be the heir apparent. My brother Iain was
the oldest, and when he died it passed to me." He cleared his
throat again as if the conversation made him uncomfortable. It
almost seemed as if he wasn't at ease discussing his own standing in his family line. "The distillery is the only reliable source
of revenue in all of my father's holdings, and he doesn't want to
give me the control."

"I'm sorry about your brother," she said sincerely. He nodded
tersely, his jaw clenching for a moment, and when he finally
spoke his voice was unwavering.

"Thank you."

His gaze flickered away from her, and she noticed him take in a sharp breath. Luz was familiar with that particular gesture. That moment when grief cuts through you unexpectedly and the pain feels so fresh, the wound so deep, you can hardly get air in your lungs. This man had experienced too much loss in his life, and in that, at least, they had a kinship.

"If he has the dukedom and the land, why can't he liquidate that to ease his financial burdens?"

The question seemed to lighten his mood, and he offered her an appreciative smile before answering. "Very good, Luz Alana," he said. His praise wrapping around her like a velvet embrace. "He can't touch most of it. You see, my grandfather, my father's father, was—well, I wouldn't call him an abolitionist, but he was supportive of the cause. When he could no longer finance his efforts with his allowance, he began to sell some of the dukedom's holdings. My great-grandfather was enraged by this and decided to put most of the assets of the duchy in trust. The Duke of Annan can live in the residences, and his duchess can wear the jewels, but anything my father could easily liquidate is locked up tightly."

"Your great-grandfather punished his own son because he was supporting the abolitionists." Luz said it out loud, in an effort to absorb that level of malice.

"He did," Evan said in that same terse, overly contained tone he used whenever his father was the topic of conversation. "My father resents it enormously. Even if he can still borrow against the holdings, which he has." A bitter laugh escaped his lips, and Luz shivered at what she saw on his face. "He still hates that he can't do what he pleases because his own father had *some* morals."

"What exactly do you have in mind?" She could hardly believe she was considering this.

"We marry, I make your trustee redundant and pass the control of your inheritance to you. As a married man, I can demand

that my father honor my mother's wishes and pass the ownership of the Braeburn to me. I'd be happy to give you a divorce
once it's all settled."

That last bit should not sting as much as it did.

"You get what you want, and I get what I want. It's the perfect solution."

"You speak like marriage is easily reversible." She knew that
the laws had changed when it came to women's property, but
divorce was entirely different.

"Nothing is irreversible if you're willing to pay, Luz Alana."

"Spoken like a man born into power and wealth."

To his credit, he blushed.

"Doesn't mean it's not true," he said, lifting a shoulder in the
universal gesture for *I don't make the rules, I just benefit from them.*

Legally she would be able to keep whatever she brought into
the marriage—like the town house her father had purchased in
Edinburgh, her rum and her inheritance—which was really all
that mattered to her. Well, there was more to it. He *could* help
her; he already was. She also wanted him, and as his wife, perhaps...

Not now, Leona. Business first.

"Fair enough," she conceded, trying to get terms established
before her attraction for Evan Sinclair took over making decisions for her. "And you'll forfeit all claim on my trust or any
other assets I bring to the marriage?"

"I'm a wealthy man, Luz Alana. I don't need your inheritance.
My father won't let me have the distillery because it's the only
way he can keep pulling my strings, and so he can continue to
extort money from me to fund his extravagances."

"Will your father approve of you marrying me?" she inquired,
not voicing the reason for the question. But she didn't have to:
they both knew why she asked.

He flashed her a grin that was as sharp as the blade of a knife.
"The only people who need to approve of my choice in mar-

riage are you and I." It was not the answer to the question she'd asked, but his father was not exactly her problem.

"It's an ideal solution," he insisted as he moved closer. "We're both dedicated to our businesses, neither of us want the ties of a spouse's expectations or the messy complications of love. And yet..." He tilted his head down, until their faces were close enough she had only to angle her body an inch farther and they'd be kissing again. Whatever he saw in her face deepened his knowing smile. It wasn't that predatory one from before or the sharp baring of teeth he sported when talking about his father: this one was a honeytrap. Dangerous in its sweetness. He cleared his throat, still intently looking at her. "And clearly there is enough physical attraction between us that there would be additional benefits to our arrangement."

She slid to the side, needing to not be so close to the man's mouth. "I have to think about this."

"Most women who are offered marriage by an earl would jump at the chance."

"Would you offer marriage to most women, my lord?" she asked sweetly.

The look he gave her carried with it enough electricity to light the tower. "I swore I never would, and yet here I am offering it to you."

And despite knowing it was purely transactional, her foolish heart raced as he reached to tuck an errant curl behind her ear. "Come on, darling. The observation deck awaits us."

"Just be careful, as you step out," Evan instructed as he gently pulled her out of the lift.

"The air is so much colder up here," Luz said as a shiver ran up her spine. He stopped in midstep at her comment.

"Of course, you're chilled," he replied, already starting to remove his jacket. She protested weakly as he leaned over to place it over her shoulders, and again she shivered. But this time it was for a very different reason.

She could still not believe she was here.

Once Evan had managed to convince him with a bribe, the lift operator had boarded them on the contraption and begun the ascent. It had taken about twenty minutes to get to the top, and they had been quite nerve-racking. Luz had ridden the Giessbach Funicular when she'd lived in Switzerland, but it was on rail tracks; this felt like she was being swept up straight into the sky. Evan had been marvelous. Patient and gentle when she would fret, entertaining her with a humorous story about his first ride in a New York lift a few years before. Then he'd asked about her experiences in finishing school. By the time she'd regaled him with a few anecdotes featuring the Leonas, the operator was announcing they were about to arrive.

"It's like being in a birdcage," she observed as they walked to the edge of the platform where a metal screen wrapped around the top of the tower. A few feet away Evan finally uncorked the bottle of champagne, the popping sound abnormally loud in the thin air. The Leonas would not believe it when she told them. The jaunt to the tower was inconceivably the most sensible part of the evening thus far.

"Champagne, mademoiselle?" he asked in that brogue-laced French of his as he sauntered toward her. The wind had blown his hair from its earlier confinement; with his sable curls and that beard he looked utterly disreputable.

A gentleman pirate.

She stretched out her hand to take the bottle he offered. Their fingers brushed, and Luz swore the electrification of the tower was running through her. She took a drink and as the bubbles exploded on her tongue, she felt giddy with the thrill of this night.

"If you look closely, you can make out some of the buildings below," he said, coming to stand behind her. He placed the bottle on the ledge in front of them and used a free hand to point at something to the left and below. The other one he wrapped securely around her waist.

"That's Trocadero." His warm breath made her shiver, but the heat of his body covered her like a blanket. "And those are the boats on the Seine. You see them?"

Every time she felt his lips grazing her skin, she shook. Tiny tremors that made her think of the ripples a stone makes when tossed into calm waters. She wanted to turn around and ask him to kiss her, but she also wanted another minute like this, pretending that this was real. That a beautiful man had just asked to marry her and whisked her to the top of the Eiffel Tower to celebrate. It scared her how much she wanted that. How much she wanted him. Evanston Sinclair had seeped into her blood like fast-acting poison.

"If you could have anything when you arrived in Edinburgh, what would it be?"

"Why are you asking me that?" The question surprised her. It wasn't that she didn't have answers at the ready. It seemed all she'd done in the last few weeks was worry about those very things.

"Because I think what you need, Luz Alana, is an ally."

How did one even respond to something like that? But she guessed if they were going to follow through with this, being more forthcoming could not hurt.

"Getting this situation with my trust sorted, for one. Then selling the remainder of the Caña Brava at a good price. Getting Clarita situated with a good governess." She opened her mouth to share the last thing that she wished for but then clamped it shut. There were many things she dreamed of, but that was not one she was ready to have crushed by the world as implausible or silly.

"How about your Dama Juana and the cordials?" he asked, snatching that little flickering flame of a dream straight from the most guarded corner of her heart. She was relieved not to be facing him because even in the shadow he'd likely see what that question did to her. She sank back, pressing tightly into him, and let free the things that she'd kept even from her father.

"I'd love to push forward with the cordials. I didn't get very far before my father died, but I'd started selling the Dama Juana back home." He made a sound of interest, and she could feel his head bob up and down. "Through women vendors."

"That's very shrewd." His voice was full of approval. "Women have always been at the heart of selling spirits. Like my great-great-grandmother with her shebeen. Even this champagne we're drinking—we have the widow Clicquot to thank for devising it." It had been a surprise when he'd proudly spoken about his family's humble beginnings at lunch, but knowing now the man was an earl...it was probably best to divert her attention back to business.

"Yes, in Santo Domingo street commerce is very much dominated by women vendors. As it is in most places, really." Even here in Paris, there were hundreds of women street merchants, and in places like Le Bureau, the workers made a small commission on every bottle they sold a customer. Women made for a powerful salesforce. "We trained dozens of vendors on sales and how to keep their accounts. In exchange for installing small stalls for them, we asked that they place our bottles of rum where they could be seen by passersby. There was a significant increase in sales."

He made a sound of approval at that and brushed a kiss to her forehead. "You are a born businesswoman. I may need you to help me with my own sales strategy."

She tried to listen for traces of mockery in his voice. She couldn't detect any. Just genuine praise for her work. She made herself continue talking before she could dwell too much on the way her pulse was racing.

"The cordials we only tested with a few of our more successful saleswomen, but they did very well. I think if we can find the right packaging created especially for women customers… Something that will appeal to the modern woman could have potential."

Evan didn't say anything for a long moment, and that insidious self-doubt began to creep in. Her father had dismissed her ideas for the cordials every time she'd brought them up, until she stopped sharing them.

"Liquor with women as consumers in mind from the first step…could be an untapped market." Her throat closed from that simple but unequivocal validation. "You are right about the packaging too. You could perhaps commission an illustrator to make some art for you." He squeezed her tight and brushed a kiss to her temple. "It's a good idea. What are the flavors for the cordials?"

"Lime and pineapple," she said after a long moment. "They were my great-grandmother's recipes. My mother always talked about doing something with them, but she never got around to it. I want to do it for her, and for me. I like the idea of building a business that serves women first."

"I think you should have the chance to at least try," he said in a husky voice, and without any warming turned her around until their fronts were mashed together. There were only a few lights above them illuminating the tower, but this close she could see his face clearly. "You are a fascinating woman to know, Luz Alana Heith-Benzan." He said it like she was a riddle he didn't quite understand but was determined to decipher. She didn't know if the prospect of that thrilled or terrified her, but then he bent down until his lips were brushing hers, and that became her sole focus.

"Should we seal our deal with a kiss?" he asked so quietly he was practically mouthing the words against her lips.

"There is no deal yet," she reminded him breathlessly.

"Hmm, then perhaps this is where I should unleash my persuasive skills on you."

If this was what it felt like when he was holding back, Luz feared greatly for her self-control.

"Your lips." The two words contained volumes. "From the first moment I saw you, I've been mad with the thought of hearing my name escaping from them on a sigh or in a piercing scream." He was dotting kisses along her neck now, his teeth lightly scratching the sensitive skin. Every place he touched reverberated through her. Every sensation magnified. "The things I want to do to you, to make you cry from pleasure."

"Please," she moaned, not even sure what she was asking for, as he teased her with more butterfly-soft kisses. It was jarring to be pressed against such a solid, unyielding body and feel such tender caresses at the same time.

"What do you want, mo cridhe?" He used his thumb to tilt her head and placed open-mouthed, wet kisses on her collarbone, on the swell of her breasts. His hardness was a brand pressed against her, making her gasp. She had the most wicked urge to touch it, trace her fingers along it. Grip it, fill her hand with it. She'd never been like this with a man, and she could now see why chaperones were insisted upon. She heard her breaths coming faster, felt her lips tingling, and still he would not kiss her. She groaned in frustration as he brushed his damn whiskers along her cheek and let out a husky, wicked laugh.

"Need something?" The man was *insufferable.*

"Kiss me, Evan," she demanded. He made a sound of delighted approval and did exactly what she asked. He invaded her mouth with dizzying skill. His thumb pushing her mouth open as he plundered her. All she could do was hold on.

How can one feel gently cradled and utterly ravished at once?

"Can I touch you here?" One of his hands pressed at the apex of her thighs, right where she ached.

"Yes," she moaned, eliciting a predatory sound from him.

His big palm glided up the inside of her thigh, leaving traces of fire on her skin. When he reached her garter, he grinned against her lips.

"It delights me to no end to know you carry a gun under your dress," he told her before taking her bottom lip between his teeth. Her heart pounded with breathtaking force, and her head swam, but nothing could've prepared her for the secret, light touch that followed his words.

"So wet. I am going mad with wanting to taste you," he groaned as he cupped her in his hand. It felt like her heart was pulsing there, right in his palm.

"Evan," she begged as his hands explored, fingers spreading her.

"Mmm, has anyone touched you here?" he asked, his voice like sin, pressed to her ear.

"No." She shook her head and gritted her teeth at the overwhelming sensations coursing through her.

He growled again before taking her mouth as his fingers shattered her. His stroked her clitoris with devastating precision. Every nerve in her body was pulsing.

"Open your eyes, darling," he told her as he circled his fingers at her core. "Look at the stars while I give you this."

She cried out when her orgasm crashed into her, and he took her mouth again. Luz kept her eyes open as pleasure enveloped her, and it felt like the night was a dark velvet blanket giving them cover.

She whimpered as the last tremors racked through her. She could feel his hardness against her, insistent. But he was solely focused on her, whispering soothing words in Gaelic as he smoothed her skirts, and then kissed her again. She was still searching for words when he finally spoke.

"I think this arrangement could be very beneficial, indeed," he said, and in an instant the bone-deep warmth she'd been feeling was replaced by a horrible chill.

"Right," she bit out, hiding her eyes from him, stiff in his arms. He had ruined the moment, but he was right to keep her head out of the clouds. If she was to do this, she needed to remember where she stood with Evan Sinclair.

"Luz Alana, look at me," he coaxed, but the lift operator's voice pierced through the haze and after one chaste kiss on her lips, Evan pulled away on a sigh.

Something changed between them as they entered the lift again, and the closeness and heat from before evaporated, leaving them both lost in their own thoughts. Luz mulled over the proposal Evan had made and whether it would be a good idea to enter into a marriage with a man she could see herself falling desperately in love with. She could be practical, get her money back and her business going, and have a man in her bed who she desired and who seemed to at least respect her independence. He was not offering her what he could not give her, and he expected her to do the same.

This could work. You will *get your heart broken, but it could work.*

The lift shook Luz as it docked at the base of the tower, and Evan reached for her hand to steady her. "Thank you," she said, accepting his help.

"It was nothing," he demurred as if he hadn't just taken her on a private excursion up the Eiffel Tower on a whim. He sounded distracted, probably reconsidering his offer, she thought.

"Is the address at the Place des Vosges the best place to find you?" he asked as they walked back in the direction of the pavilion. God, she'd never told the Leonas she was leaving the soirée. She really needed to get back.

"Yes."

"I'll send for word tomorrow," he told her before stepping away. "Your pride is here."

Luz turned to see Aurora and Antonio step out through an opening among the hedges. They waved to her, and she lifted a hand, feeling unprepared for the time with Evan to end. "I must go." She was glad to at least sound normal.

Evan smiled at her in a way that made her belly dip and her skin prickle. He slid his hands into the pockets of his trousers again, and that's when she realized she was still wearing his jacket over her shoulders. She slid it off and stepped closer to hand it him. "Thank you for letting me use it." Their hands brushed as he reached for it, and she felt that shocking thrill of his touch again.

"Think about my offer, Luz Alana."

She opened her mouth to demur, to ask for more time, but Aurora and Antonio were already upon her. By the time she turned to bid Evan a good evening, he was gone.

Twelve

"*Are you sure this is what you want?*" *Aurora asked Luz* as they walked up the street to Evan's mansion flat. Her friends had both asked her that very question a dozen times in the last two days, and she still didn't think she had what they would consider a satisfying answer. After what felt like a thousand conversations about Evan's proposal and every potential pitfall if she agreed to marry, she finally felt prepared to face him.

"It's the best choice I have at the moment." It was the only answer she could offer that would not require they dissect the situation again, and he was expecting her. "Without my inheritance, I barely have enough to get settled in Scotland and live comfortably for a year while I get the business set up. That's not a viable option, and I'm not letting Childers continue to hold my inheritance hostage." Not when she had hundreds of workers counting on her securing more buyers. When she had her sister depending on her. Not when her own dreams were at stake.

"Do you trust him?" asked Manuela, who had made her own marriage deal for the sake of her family. Luz was not one to indulge in self-delusion. She knew the risk she was taking, tying herself to a man who could make himself a nuisance in her life forever if he chose to.

"She doesn't have to trust him," Aurora answered before Luz could. "That's why she's making him sign papers agreeing not to touch her money."

"It's only temporary," Luz added, mostly as a reminder for herself. "He *will* give me a divorce if I wish for one."

"*Do* you wish for one?" Manuela asked, always seeing further than anyone else.

"It's not love." And it wasn't, even if lust was certainly there. "It's a mutually beneficial business arrangement."

"But you want him," Aurora stated.

"I do," she admitted, not bothering to offer any explanations. What was the point of lying?

"Then you're already faring better than most marriages in the aristocracy, Leona." Manu gave her an affectionate swat. "You still haven't told us if you trust him."

Luz considered her friend's words as she tightly clutched the leather binder holding the agreement a lawyer had drafted. She wasn't foolish enough to enter the arrangement without putting into place some legal protections. Manuela had procured the assistance of her friend the Duchess of Sundridge, and the woman had promptly produced an American solicitor who she assured Luz would draw up a contract that would effectively pinion Evan out of any claims on her inheritance and—as much as was legally permissible—her person. Luz and Aurora had spent most of yesterday in the seventeenth-arrondissement offices of Mr. Crouch being plied with legalese and such a thorough line of questioning, Luz was certain the man now had better command of her life than she did herself. The contract was, according to the mustachioed solicitor, the legal equivalent of a heavily guarded fortress.

As far as her trust in him was concerned, Aurora was correct. If Evan agreed to sign the contract, she wouldn't need to trust him. Not really.

And though she was covered by the legal protections, that hadn't really been the point of Manuela's question. There was a difference between wanting something and it already being a fact. Did she trust Evan, even without the assurance of the contract? She found that she did. Which likely made her a fool. It didn't make it any less true.

"I believe he'll help me if I help him. It's a transaction."

"But there has been…" Aurora paused dramatically, and Luz rolled her eyes "…intimacy."

"A moderate amount," she prevaricated even as heat flooded her face. That unnerving shiver she felt any time she recalled the feel of his beard against the swell of her breasts while his fingers explored her, that had been… Not the time to recall that particular dalliance.

"Oh my, look at that flush on her cheeks! I'd wager the Great Scot has plundered and quite possibly pillaged," Manu exclaimed with glee. Luz groaned.

"Oh my," Aurora whispered, closely examining the expression on Luz's face. "Have you *faite le coït*?"

"Saying it in French only makes it sound more vulgar, Aurora." Manuela's voice was like a foghorn. "However, as your best friends in the world, it *is* imperative we are instructed on just how much of the earl you've…rendezvoused with?"

"Is that even a word, and could you two take a respite from the French innuendo?" Luz begged, biting back a laugh.

"Does everyone in the Jardin des Tuileries need to be made aware of her personal affairs, Manuela?"

Manuela only laughed at Aurora's admonition. "Talking is absolutely not required," Manu said happily. "We can make it a game of charades. What are we contemplating here, platanote or platanito?" She accompanied this by holding her hands ups, palms facing each other about a foot apart, then closed the space to about three inches.

That was when Aurora reached her limit.

"Manuela, would you stop?" she exclaimed, audibly horrified. Which was curious since she'd been the one to commence this line of inquiry. "I have absolutely no interest in hearing any details about the man's genitals."

Manuela fluttered her hand in a dismissive gesture.

Why had she thought having these two accompany her was a wise idea?

"I am asking purely for clinical purposes," Aurora informed them with the disapproval of a schoolmarm dealing with unruly children. Manu rolled her eyes, her hands thankfully now clasped behind her back. "I have about thirty-six hours to procure a cervical cap for you, and I'd like to know if you require one."

Luz could not be in the same room with Evan without feeling like her clothes were set to incinerate right off her body.

Yes, it was best to be armed with all means necessary.

"Gracias, amiga, I'd appreciate that greatly," she said sincerely. Lying to herself about what she would or would not be doing in her marriage bed was one thing. Not taking the appropriate precautions to prevent a pregnancy was entirely another. Jane Austen might've thought preparation foolish, but Luz was not a genteel English lady of leisure. She was a Dominican rum distiller who would have control over every aspect of her life she could.

"I do want to talk about the wedding night. Because despite her unforgivable crassness, Manu did raise a topic of some heft."

It took Luz a moment to deduce the comment was dripping with double entendre. "Aurora, that is beneath you!"

"That is likely one of the positions Lord Darnick will require of you." Aurora was now practically crying from laughter.

"I adore the direction this conversation has taken." Manuela clapped, and Luz gave up trying to be serious. "You must take that pink negligee I got at Cadolle's shop. The Great Scot will tear it off you."

"It's not a real marriage, Manu," Luz declared, unsure for whose benefit she was making the assertion. "I don't need wedding-night frippery."

"Some of the best copulation to be had happens between people who aren't really married, querida." Manuela winked saucily. Luz wished more than anything she could take a page from her friend's book and let things wash over her. That she could live in the present without allowing the uncertainty in her future strip away all possible enjoyment.

Unbidden, the image of herself tipping a bottle of champagne to her mouth as the wind whipped around her at the top of the tower came to mind. She'd been more spontaneous in the few days since she'd met Evanston Sinclair than she had been since her father had died. She'd thought that side of her was lost—dead and buried with her parents. Snuffed out by the weight of all the things she was now responsible for. With Evan, she'd found it. She wanted to be more like that free-spirited Luz. But that Luz had not been on her own that night at the tower: she'd been leaning on a hard body, with strong arms anchoring her in place. A body that would not be hers to keep when this was over.

"That's it," Aurora announced, pointing at a house on the rue de Rivoli. Luz's stomach did a somersault. It was nerves, and right underneath that was anticipation. Apparently, she was hiding it more poorly than she thought, because soon she had Manu's arm around her waist and Aurora's tight grip on her shoulder.

"He can't get any of your inheritance. This is a reasonable, if slightly melodramatic, solution to your problem," Aurora said in a valiant attempt to bolster her.

Manu, in one of those moments of shattering acuity, leaned

in and whispered in her ear. "It's perfectly fine to want this for more than just your inheritance, querida."

Luz only shook her head, swallowing down her useless denial.

"You deserve to have a man who looks at you like he did the night of the soirée."

"That's just lust," Luz insisted.

Manuela made a noise of frustration and then spoke again in an uncharacteristically impatient tone. "Men like Darnick always have choices, Leona. It would be in your best interest not to forget that *you* are his."

Luz's head was still ringing with her friend's words when she raised the door knocker to negotiate her marriage of convenience with the Earl of Darnick.

"Let me see if I have this right," Raghav drawled as he pierced a bite of kipper with this fork. "You've asked Luz Alana to marry you, she's said yes, and you plan to elope to Scotland leaving me to deal with the rest of the exposition alone."

Murdoch, who was also sitting at the table, shook his head. "Given that, according to my cousin, this is strictly a business negotiation, it's imperative to be precise about the details." Evan rolled his eyes at Murdoch's taunting. "He did extend an offer of marriage to Miss Heith-Benzan. However, when he sent a carriage yesterday to her residence, she instructed the footman to relay upon the Earl of Darnick that she would convey herself to his home when she was ready."

Raghav made an alarming choking noise while Evan glared at his cousin.

"The more I learn about Luz Alana the more I like her," Evan's business partner said when he finally was able to speak.

Evan had the same problem. He hadn't seen her in the two days since the soirée, and his mind—as busy as it was—kept returning to the rum heiress. The last two mornings he'd roused from a fitful slumber to a raging cockstand and lingering dreams of a golden beauty astride his hips, moaning her pleasure in Spanish. *Dominican* Spanish, he corrected himself, and his lips turned up at the memory of the heiress's explanation of what was on her tongue whenever she spoke in her native language.

With great effort, Evan redirected his attention back to his table companions.

"It's an ideal solution. I need a wife to obtain the distillery. She needs a husband to gain control of her inheritance. Highly convenient for both of us." He knew his casual tone was not fooling either of the two men, but the alternative was to confess he'd talked himself out of going to Luz Alana's town house three times just that morning, and he did not need their ribbing on top of everything.

"Are you sure that's all there is?" Raghav asked with aggravating perspicuity.

"What else could there possibly be?"

"Oh come off it, Evan," Murdoch said with a laugh. "I saw the way you looked at her at the soirée. For God's sake, man, you were acting like a sodding bloodhound. You nearly pissed a circle around her once you got her in your sights."

"Sod off." Evan could not muster much heat in his denial, since Murdoch's assessment was not very far from the truth. There was something in Luz Alana that called to a visceral part of himself Evan scarcely understood. He was not a savior; he never had been, not even with Charlotte. But for all the self-sufficiency Luz Alana exuded, there was this air of forlornness in her that he found irresistible. That night at the tower, it had been nearly impossible to walk away from her. Evan was still mulling over that when a cacophony of yelps and howls shattered the last of his hopes at a peaceful morning.

"What is this I hear about a betrothal?"

Evan emitted a pained groan at the sound of his sister Beatrice's booming voice. That could only mean that Adalyn and her pack of feral dachshunds were not far behind.

"Did you do this?" he asked, glaring at Murdoch.

"I went for a ride in the Bois de Boulgone with Gerard at sunrise," Murdoch offered innocently, eyes shining with repressed mirth.

"This is why I didn't tell you—" Evan didn't finish his sentence because in the next second he was set upon by his two sisters, a toddler and three extremely energetic sausage-shaped dogs.

"Bea, Addy, have a heart, I've barely touched my cup of coffee."

"We'll be very gentle with your nerves, brother," Beatrice assured him as she placed her hat on an armchair, then handed him his thirteen-month-old niece before walking around the table proffering kisses, while Addy fed her demonic canines his bacon.

"She is so lovely, Evan," Adalyn contributed, as if the few glimpses she'd had of Luz Alana were sufficient to make a full assessment of her. This was the kind of meddling that Evan usually quashed the moment his sisters attempted to interfere in his private affairs.

The curious thing was that this time, he actually wanted to know what Addy thought of Luz. He suspected Adalyn, with her women's rights crusades and rebellious spirit, would get on with Luz Alana. He envisioned them all in a cozy room, fire roaring in the hearth, Adalyn playing some of those Caribbean composers Luz Alana loved on the pianoforte, dancing, laughter…absurd things that would never happen because he wasn't *marrying* Luz Alana Heith-Benzan, he was entering into a business arrangement.

"Oh my, are these reveries happening often?" Bea's feigned concern rudely pulled Evan out of his thoughts.

"Chronically." That from his soon-to-be-former best friend.

"Do you not have anything better to do?" he asked his newly arrived guests, taking a seat in one of the smaller chairs, since Beatrice had claimed the one that belonged to the master of the house.

"Better than hearing about your proposing to a woman who you met days ago?" This time the astonishment was not feigned.

"A very beautiful woman," Murdoch interjected, with a slick smile that made Evan want to punch his cousin right in the mouth.

"Papa knew her family." Beatrice let that piece of information land in the middle of the room as she tore a piece off a croissant. *Papa* was her husband's father. Their own progenitor required no such endearments. "I asked him about it at breakfast, since Murdoch said she was from the Caribbean."

"How many breakfasts have you had, Beatrice?"

If his sister could slice through flesh with her eyes, she'd be the best surgeon in Scotland. "I am *gestating*, James Evanston, and attempting to keep myself nourished as I grow another of Gerard's enormous bairns is no easy feat." They all laughed at her put-upon expression as she bit into the pastry. "As I was saying, you remember Papa was a solicitor in Barbados for some time." Her smile widened in that way that Evan remembered only too well from their childhood. It was usually the preamble to someone getting splashed with cold water or having a frog tossed on their lap. "He knew her father, Lachlan Heith was his name, a good man according to him." That was high praise if it came from the ambassador. The man was as honorable as any Evan had ever met. He was a fearless critic of the vestiges of colonialism in the West Indies and a staunch abolitionist. He had almost lost his diplomatic career for it.

And he'd known Luz Alana's father. He smiled remembering her lesson on Dominican–Scottish relations from their first meeting.

"What else did the ambassador say?"

His sister smiled shyly.

"Did your rum heiress tell you she was the granddaughter of a baron? Her father was the youngest son of the Baron of Gaile."

"*That* I did not know." Evan was surprised at the flash of disappointment. She hadn't trusted him enough to mention that. Which was ridiculous and hypocritical given everything *he'd* kept—and would continue to keep—from her. But perhaps Luz Alana's approach was the wiser one. Only offer up information as was required.

Beatrice made a sound of approval as she chewed her croissant. "It seems he broke with his family in his early twenties and left for the Caribbean."

"The plot thickens," Murdoch intoned, which Evan ignored.

"Has she talked about the rest of her family?" Addy inquired as she sat with her retinue of yapping dogs. Adalyn had always yearned for a big, loving family. When she was small, she'd beg their mother to leave her in Murdoch's home for weeks at a time. Unfortunately, there would be no Heith clan forthcoming.

"She's talked about their business model, which is highly unusual," he told his sisters in an effort to steer the conversation into safer waters.

"The workers own shares in the distillery," Raghav explained. He'd been fascinated by the idea when Evan relayed it to him.

"Yes." He enjoyed talking about her. Liked even more to see other people recognize how magnificent Luz Alana was. "The workers get dividends from the distillery's revenues on top of their compensation."

"That's certainly different," Beatrice said.

"She only has a ten percent interest remaining, shared with a younger sister. She returned her father's shares before she left Santo Domingo, which is partly why she needs help. But the more pressing matter is her inheritance. Her father left it in a trust she cannot access, and she needs the funds to start her business in Scotland."

"And how are you to help her with that?" Addy's eyebrows immediately shot up with interest.

"Upon her marriage, her husband would automatically become the administrator. I've agreed to release all the funds to her once we've wed."

"She's putting a lot of trust in your hands," Beatrice said with an approving tone Evan did not want to investigate too closely.

"You'd find her plans for her business expansion interesting, Addy," he redirected...once again. "She wants to make cordials from tropical fruits and develop the product especially for women. She wants the production process and the sales to all be done by women too." Evan suppressed a smile when his sister's eyes lit up. "She experimented in the Dominican Republic by training street merchants to sell her rum, and it did very well. She wants to do that in Scotland with the cordials."

"I would love to hear more about it." Addy had that hungry glean she got when she identified her newest pursuit.

"I commend the extremes you're going to in order to help a perfect stranger, brother. But unless you've transformed into an entirely different person in the month since you left Edinburgh, I know there must be something you're getting out of this deal."

Beatrice had him there.

"You mean besides a wealthy heiress that looks like a goddess?" Raghav said in that tone he used when he was preparing to trample on every single one of Evan's nerves.

"You are well aware that I don't plan to touch her inheritance."

"But a loveless marriage, Evan. I don't want that for you."

Adalyn had given up everything to escape that fate. When their father had informed her that at nineteen she'd have to wed a prosperous viscount, who was not only almost three decades older but whose previous three wives had died in mysterious circumstances, Addy had refused. Knowing she'd be disowned, she'd eloped with one of the compatriots she knew from her many political associations. She'd been happy for a time, and then the man had died of consumption only two years after their marriage. Since then she'd lived off the income she received from their grandfather's inheritance and the assistance Evan provided.

No, his sister, who lived faithfully by her ideals, would not want him to compromise.

Suddenly he felt a little defensive on Luz Alana's part. What Adalyn had done hadn't been easy. She had given up everything, but when she eloped with William, she'd had her own money—not a fortune, but enough to live on comfortably—and she'd had Evan and Beatrice. Luz Alana only had herself, plus a sister to look after.

His niece was having a wonderful time attempting to tear Evan's beard off by the root, so he stood up and placed her on his shoulders where her chubby arms couldn't reach his face. The baby made piercing sounds of delight as Evan searched for the best way to relay this part to his sisters. After a long moment he gave up and decided to just come out and say it.

"I was going to come see you both after I'd heard from Luz Alana, but you're here," he said, coming to stand by the mantel facing the settee his sisters had commandeered.

He was confronted with a matching set of frowns.

"First, I need you both to understand there are questions I cannot answer at the moment, for good reasons." Murdoch groaned, and Raghav scoffed. Evan pointedly ignored both of them. "I've been working with…" he paused, the words *our brother* on the tip of his tongue "…an associate to find mother's will." Both his sisters gasped at that. This was something the three of them had talked about many times over the years. Iain, who tended to believe their father blindly, had not shared their suspicion that the duke had lied about their mother's wishes.

"An associate?" Beatrice asked suspiciously.

"Yes," Evan said shortly, gently passing the baby back to her mother. "Wait for me here."

"Evan," his sisters cried in unison.

"I've got something for each of you in my study." Evan made

haste and procured the pieces of jewelry that had been in the box. The will he left in the safe.

When he returned, he found four adults, one baby and three dogs staring expectantly at him.

"These were in a box with it," he said, handing his sisters the bracelet and necklace their mother had left for them. His heart was hammering in his throat as he reached for the baby again.

"Where?" asked Addy, with tears in her eyes.

"We were able to track down the nursemaid that took care of her in the sanatorium." He relayed the details he knew—like the money and land they were both meant to inherit but his father never honored, along with the conditions of his own inheritance of the Braeburn—interspersed with more questions from his sisters that he couldn't answer.

"We cannot let father know we have the will for a few weeks. I will make sure that you get everything that mother left to you, but the timing is imperative." His sisters only nodded with that unwavering trust they had in him.

"A wedding gift," Beatrice murmured, her countenance contemplative. "Could you try to get around that? If it's in the will that it'll go to you..."

"I could, but Father could contest it for years. I have consulted my solicitor here, and he assures me this is the most effective way to get it back from him. If I can satisfy the one condition for it to come to me, then he can't deny it." Not that Evan had time for other routes, not when Apollo was set to descend on Edinburgh like a cyclone in less than a fortnight.

"And you've told your lady this?" There was no ignoring the frisson of pleasure that crawled up his spine at hearing the word *your.*

"She knows," he said, also not enjoying the slightly wild sensation that came upon him whenever the subject of Luz Alana made its appearance. He would need to work on those reactions soon. "There is no Prince Charming in this story, and blessedly,

Miss Heith-Benzan does not fancy one. She wants a business partner, not a doting husband."

"And when is all this meant to unfold?" Beatrice asked, always with her eye on the target. Evan did look forward to sharing this particular detail.

"I thought I would surprise our dear father at his birthday celebration, given that I'm expected to pay for it."

His sister's smile was dangerous.

"Finally, a reason to attend that yearly spectacle of self-indulgence. He will be *furious*." Beatrice looked positively bloodthirsty.

"He will be more than that," Evan assured them. "There are other things that I cannot share right now, which will likely become public." Adalyn seemed startled, but Beatrice had that cold, mutinous look she usually only reserved for their father.

"Bea, there will be a scandal."

Beatrice dismissed his warning. "Don't worry on my account," she said with a shrug. "Gerard's family is much too necessary to the ton for him to ever worry about them, and you know I would love nothing more than to see our father lose that all-important regard of the peerage."

When Beatrice told her father she would marry Gerard, the grandson of a tradesman whose family had risen to prominence out of sheer perseverance and grit, he'd forbidden the marriage. Then, when he realized the fortune she'd be marrying into, he agreed to give his blessing *if* she gave up her dowry. In addition to requesting a generous compensation from Gerard's family.

No, he hadn't feared either of his sisters objecting to their father's destruction.

"So where will this wedding be?" Murdoch asked, breaking the tension. Evan kept an eye on his sisters, who were clearly still digesting, their attention on the heirlooms from their mother.

"I was thinking Braeburn Hall," he said, moderating his voice. The images of Luz Alana walking through the heather to reach him, of her standing on the little cliff-side chapel at the estate, filled his head all the same.

"That's an interesting location choice for a wedding that is, as you've informed us, purely a formality." Beatrice could be so smug.

"What is so interesting about me choosing our family countryseat to elope, Beatrice?"

"Absolutely nothing, unless you take into consideration it's the place you love most in the world and have poured your life into for the last decade. And you're choosing it to be the place where you marry when you could do it quite literally anywhere once you cross the border."

"Thank you for that, Murdoch," Evan said through gritted teeth.

"And you're willing to wage a war with Father, and let's not overlook *marrying*, which you swore never to do after Charlotte," Adalyn chimed in unhelpfully.

"Are you all quite done?" Evan asked, unclenching his jaw. "I need to marry for the *distillery*, and I need to go to the Braeburn before I make Father aware of the will. I must take certain precautions. We all know how vindictive and reckless he can be when he doesn't get his way." That reminder swiftly wiped away the mocking smiles directed at him. These people knew what the Duke of Annan was capable of.

"Things won't be easy for her in Edinburgh. She won't be welcome in many parlors," Evan said, directing the conversation to what had been weighing on his mind for the last two days.

"She's likely very aware of that," Murdoch supplied in the same eerily calm manner he always approached the bigotry of their home city.

"She likely won't want to be in many of them," Beatrice noted, and Evan was fairly certain his sister was right. Still, he didn't want that for her. He rarely mixed in society these days: he was focused on his business, and businesspeople were who he consorted with, but maybe Luz Alana expected more. Then again, perhaps after they each had what they wanted, she'd want nothing to do with him or his ilk. He couldn't blame her if that was the case.

"We will help," Beatrice assured him.

A brisk knock on the door broke the taut silence in the parlor.

"My lord, a Miss Heith-Benzan is here to see you." Evan's head snapped up at attention.

The reaction to that news was immediate and absolute. His whole body thrummed with awareness that went as deep as muscle and bone. He was too excited, too eager. He felt...frenzied. He had the baby sleeping on him and suddenly had no clue what to do with his arms, his legs.

Evan opened his mouth, but nothing came out. He heard a sound of gratified knowledge from behind him, and then Beatrice's voice broke through the pandemonium that was his mind.

"Oh yes, this is clearly devoid of all emotion."

Thirteen

Luz thought she'd entered the Parisian home of the Earl of Darnick prepared for almost anything. One thing she did not anticipate was being confronted with the sight of Evan Sinclair, holding a sleeping child in his arms, in a room full of his family and very long small dogs.

"My apologies," Evan told her as he walked over to the pregnant woman in the room and handed her the baby. Luz had not met his older sister, but she could see the resemblance instantly. The sable hair and those piratical eyebrows. "I've been ambushed by my relations, who seem to perennially disregard any and all rules on when to call at people's homes."

She clutched to her leather binder for dear life as she searched for something to say. Then people started coming forward, and she understood why Evan had utilized the word *ambushed*.

"It is such a pleasure to make your acquaintance, Luz Alana. I am Beatrice, his older sister." The woman brought Luz in for a one-armed hug and bussed her cheek while she held on to the child with the other.

"Lady Beatrice," Luz said awkwardly, and Evan's sister waved her hand around as if Luz had just committed a sin.

"Please call me Beatrice or Bea." She grinned as she dealt with the wiggling child in her arms before giving up and setting her on the floor. The baby propelled away with astonishing speed and sat up to play with the pack of small sausage dogs.

"Evan told me you have younger sister," Beatrice said with what appeared to be genuine interest.

He'd been talking about her to his family, then. It was moot to try to control the warm glow in her belly. When she glanced at Evan—whose cheeks were now an intense pink—he only rubbed a hand over his face.

"Yes. Clarita," Luz responded a bit unsteadily.

"Fiona," Beatrice said, pointing at the baby who was now chasing the dogs around, "is my youngest, for now." She patted her belly with a smile. "Katherine and Colin are eleven and will be thrilled to have a new cousin."

"Don't monopolize her, Bea," said the other woman in the room, who Luz recognized from the soirée.

"I'm Adalyn. I saw you the other night but was not able to say hello properly."

"Very nice to meet you, Adalyn." Luz obliged and moved to press her cheek to Adalyn's. The moment their faces met, one of the small dogs rushed up, tilted its conical head up at them and started barking madly. "éclair! Stop harassing our guest," Adalyn moaned, adding to the cacophony, while Luz hid a smile behind her hand.

"She is not *our* guest," growled Evan, who seemed to have finally had enough. "She is *my* guest, and if you could all please remove yourselves from my parlor I would be much obliged." He turned to Luz then, and he looked so handsome and utterly harried that her heart skipped a beat. "My apologies for my family and their absolute lack of manners."

"How is saying hello contrary to observing manners?" Beatrice inquired unrepentantly.

She liked this woman.

"I could return later," Luz suggested and moved to hand the binder to Evan. Perhaps it was best just to leave the contract and have him read it first. She was much too enamored with this new side of Evan to be in the right state of mind for a negotiation.

"That will not be necessary," Evan announced with the voice she assumed he learned at earl-in-training school. "*They* will leave, and *you* will stay." That pronouncement was followed by a withering glance at his relations, who, while uncowed by his display of temper, did at least initiate some movement.

"Oh, all right. We will be properly introduced on the train home, then," Beatrice said as she picked up her bonnet from an armchair.

The train home?

"Next time I see you, I'd love to hear about your cordials idea. It sounds marvelous." Adalyn beamed at Luz as her brother gently but firmly pushed her out of the room. The two men in the group had stayed behind, stopping to greet Luz before exiting after the sisters.

"Miss Heith-Benzan." Raghav kissed her gloved hand and winked. "Go easy on my business partner."

"There's no chance of that," Luz retorted, making the man laugh. She liked Raghav and, what was more, respected the way she'd seen him conduct himself at the different events they'd been at together for the exposition. It spoke well of Evan that he associated with men like Mr. Kapadia.

Next was Evan's cousin, who she'd also seen at a distance at the soirée.

"Murdoch Buchanan. Very pleased to finally make your acquaintance, Miss Heith-Benzan."

"Mr. Buchanan." She greeted him with a bow, and he waved the formality off.

"Murdoch, please." The man was aggressively handsome. Dark brown skin and high cheekbones that gave him an imperial air. Tall and powerful. Maybe it was a trait that came from Evan's maternal family. "I've heard a lot about you from my cousin."

"All good things, I hope."

"Nothing but the most fervent praises." The man's smile was devastating, and he wielded that weapon freely and effectively. A rogue, to be sure. Luz could only imagine the mischief the cousins got up to together.

"I thought you had business at the exposition, Murdoch," Evan said tightly, as he clasped his cousin by the shoulders.

Murdoch laughed but obligingly stepped out of the room.

"I will see you later, Miss Heith-Benzan," he called as Evan shut the door soundly in his face.

Luz's mouth twitched as Evan leaned heavily against the door and turned his eyes heavenward as though seeking serenity.

"My apologies," he finally said, and again Luz found herself bewildered by all the emotions Evan Sinclair could churn in her in a matter of minutes.

"No need," she said frankly, then because she had to confirm, she asked, "Did your sister name her dog Éclair?"

Poor Evan only shook his head from side to side.

"The other two are Aubergine and Sauerkraut."

Luz lost her battle with a fit of giggles, then stopped when she realized there was a pet-naming discrepancy.

"Sauerkraut?"

He finally lowered those amber eyes to her, and for a moment she could not catch her breath.

"We suggested Frankfurter, but she thought it was a mite morbid."

They both laughed at that until an easy silence fell between them.

"It's nice that you're close with your family." She sounded forlorn, but she could not help it.

"They're a nuisance," he told her, voice redolent with affection.

"I liked them," she admitted, and she had. They reminded her of the Leonas. Of the relentless ribbing and fierce loyalty of her friends. She was glad to know Evan had that. He pushed off the double doors, his gaze on her as if he was detecting something he'd missed before. He took a few steps until he was only a foot away, then pointed at the binder still in her hands.

"Are you prepared to negotiate the terms of our agreement?"

Disappointment sank through her when he redirected the conversation away from his family.

"You told your sisters about me." He didn't react but for a slight nod.

"I did. Beatrice's husband has great relations with Edinburgh merchants. She can be of help to you. And Addy's very involved in women's rights and supports efforts to organize vendors and such. She might be a useful connection for you, if you decide to move forward with your cordials."

That would be useful, and helpful.

Then why was she disappointed with the explanation? *Because you wanted him to tell his sisters about you for no other reason than because he could not help it.*

"Yes, thank you." They both lingered there until Evan seemed to snap out of it and pointed to a door on the side of the room.

"Let's go to my study. We can talk there."

The study was different than the other room. More elegant and masculine with its leather furniture and scent of tobacco. It was not filled with light and the smell of bacon or the remnants of dogs and babies. It was a room for serious conversation, and in a way Luz was glad he'd brought her there. They seated themselves across from each other on plush leather wing chairs. She felt like she was being swallowed by hers, while Evan seemed to cover every inch of the one he was perched on, lounging in it like a king on his throne.

"That's for me?" he asked, pointing at the binder she was still clutching.

"Yes." She handed the parcel to him and decided to just get

it over with. "It's an agreement I had a solicitor draft on my behalf." He nodded, perusing the papers. "It would prevent you from having any claim on my inheritance, the house my father left me in Edinburgh, or any profits from my distillery or any future businesses."

He raised an eyebrow but didn't comment. His beard was newly trimmed. It reminded her of the fastidiously landscaped gardens at Versailles. Not a whisker out of place. Her hands itched to touch it; that night at the tower it had surprised her how soft it felt under her hands. She could smell the oil he used on it from here, bay and allspice. Not scents she associated with Scotland or Paris—no, that was a fragrance of the tropics. She itched to know why Evan Sinclair had a predilection for it.

"Your terms seem reasonable," he finally said, setting that steadfast leonine gaze on her.

"You agree to all my conditions?" Luz could not eliminate the suspicion from her voice, but Evan only smiled at her.

"As long as you agree to mine."

There it was. She'd known he hadn't been forthcoming of all he expected from her. At least he hadn't waited until after they were married.

"I'm not giving you an heir."

"A *what*?" He sounded genuinely flummoxed, eyes practically bulging out of his head. The reaction was so visceral she was grateful he had not been drinking anything or he would've sprayed her with it.

"Why on earth would you think I'd require ye give me a bairn?" Judging from how acute his brogue had become, he truly was surprised.

All right. She would not be expected to produce children, but the thought wasn't *that* absurd.

"Why wouldn't I surmise that you'd require an heir, *Lord Darnick*? It's not as if your lot isn't obsessed with lineage and passing on all your land and ill-gotten gains to the next generation." She was suddenly annoyed, and a little hurt, that the thought of a child with her seemed so distasteful. Which was doubly irritating, given she absolutely did not want children with this man or *anyone*. She had one child to raise already, and that was all the responsibility she wanted when it came to progeny.

A muscle fluttered in his cheek as if he was clenching his teeth, but when he spoke he was perfectly placid.

"If there is one thing you don't ever have to worry about, it is my desire to perpetuate anything having to do with my family's lineage." A shiver ran down her spine as she held his stony gaze. It was unsettling to have those eyes she now associated with warm, pleasurable things filled with such intense loathing.

"If you don't require children, then what are your conditions?"

He surveyed her slowly, languorously, a sweeping glance over her eyes, a moment on her lips, slid down to her neck, then back up again.

"I would ask that you reside in my home when we arrive in Edinburgh. It will be better for both of us to maintain appearances. A couple of months should be sufficient." He was sprawled on the wing chair now, thighs spread, chin resting on his hand as he looked at her from that hypnotizing, half-lidded gaze. A powerful, beautiful specimen, dangerous even in repose. "Once we arrive in Edinburgh, things will move quickly. We will be married by then, of course."

The shock those words provoked. Flames roared to life inside her.

"We shall be married in Scotland." She sounded breathless. She was more than that: this conversation had her flapping in the wind.

"It would take too long to do here. Getting the permission would take weeks. I have to be in Scotland before then, and you also have time constraints. Once we cross the border into Scotland, all you need to be is a resident. I live there and you own property," he explained, then averted his eyes. He focused on something over her shoulder. "I thought we'd go to Braeburn and marry there. It's a day of travel. Just a few hours from Edinburgh."

"Why not just marry in Edinburgh?" she asked, and she saw the flutter in his cheek she now associated with Evan being asked to answer things he'd rather not.

"I thought it would be good for us to have a few days to get to know each other."

Her body could no longer control itself if Evan was in the room, she thought, pressing a hand to the pounding behind her sternum. "How long do I need to wait before I can ask for a divorce?" she made herself ask.

When he looked at her, his gaze was sardonic, self-mocking, and something in her ached at having caused it.

"Don't anticipate it should take more than three months. As I said, we will take care of your trust immediately. I will need several weeks to get things in order before I can have the distillery's ownership reverted to me."

"But isn't it a wedding gift? Wouldn't your father, learning of your marriage, automatically be alerted to start the process?"

He smiled, but it was sinister.

"It's not quite as simple as that, but it won't take long." He had the demeanor of one who readying for bloody battle. "I will have a retinue of lawyers working to get everything in place to pass the ownership to me. In the meantime, you'll need an office and a solicitor to help getting Caña Brava legally established. Perhaps some help assessing the viability of the cordials venture. I'll facilitate all of that."

She wanted to reach for that offer like a lifeline, to snatch it and not let go. "I appreciate the sentiment, but I'd rather take care of my affairs on my own."

He pinned her in his sights for a second, then surprised her with a sharp, icy laugh.

"Whatever suits you," he said with cutting indifference. "If you ever require my help, you are only to ask. These are my conditions, Luz Alana. That we marry at Braeburn, and that you live in my home for the first ninety days. Your sister and your cousin are welcome, of course." That last bit he managed to inject some warmth to. "Otherwise, you will be free to do as you like."

"Can I live in my house on Heriot Row after the ninety days?" He shot her one of those long, scrutinizing looks.

"If that's what you desire. I plan to move my residence permanently to the Braeburn once things with the deed are settled. You can continue to live in my town house on Queen Street or use yours. It's up to you."

Another of those benign smiles that made her want to scream.

Dread swirled in her at the prospect of that house she'd never seen. The idea of being there on her own with just Clarita and Amaranta felt...desolate.

"Any more requests from you, Luz Alana?" He set the papers aside, clearly done with her.

"I have two of them."

"So many requirements." He was amusing himself by teasing her, and she didn't like this side of him, brittle and impervious.

"This is not the kind of arrangement one goes into without setting some parameters." He nodded in concession and gestured for her to go on, which made her temper flare. She forced her face into a neutral expression when she finally spoke.

"I ask that you don't keep information from me, as you did regarding your title. I don't like to be kept in the dark." She was expecting another cold look or a chilly smile, but for a second he seemed...wary? It was gone in a flash and quickly replaced by that now-familiar—and infuriating—sardonic expression.

"I did not lie, I just didn't reveal a certain part of myself. I can't say that I'm very attached to the title. It has very little to do with who I am."

She could only gape at him.

"You are telling me that being born into the British nobility, one of the most ruthless, violent and powerful systems to have ever existed, has no bearing whatsoever on who you are?"

He opened his mouth to say something, then apparently reconsidered.

"Fair," he conceded. "I can promise that anything that I am at liberty to say, I will relay to you."

She retorted with an anticlimactic "Thank you."

"And your last request?"

What she intended to ask next had not been part of the plan she'd arrived here with, but suddenly she could not hold it in. The question made her blood churn and her guts twist, but she'd gotten this far, and she would not waver now. Luz clasped her hands on her lap and forced herself to lift her eyes to his face. She'd been attracted to men before; she could recognize when one was interested in her in that way. She'd even reciprocated with a spark of interest now and then. But she'd never felt so aware of another person before. If Evan was in the room, her body hummed with the need to get closer to him. Her skin pulsed and tingled in places, days after he'd touched them.

She wanted more of that, of him. Luz had no interest in entanglements that intruded on her life or her plans. Of affairs that could hinder her ability to be a proper guardian to Clarita and a good steward to her family's legacy. But she craved what Evan made her feel. And she *was* marrying the man.

"Luz Alana?" Her name on his lips made a delicious shiver crawl up her spine.

"I'd like for us to—"

He raised an eyebrow in question, and she swallowed thickly, certain there were flames dancing over her face.

Vamos, Leona. Pide lo quieres.

"I'd like for us to be physically intimate while we are residing together." She didn't look away, she didn't blink, she didn't *breathe*. "I like when you touch me, and I want you to share my bed."

Fourteen

Later on, Evan would marvel at how much composure he exhibited that morning. With her incendiary request still ringing in his ears he had to force himself to hold on to the armrest, in fear he might launch himself at her like a rabid beast. He was still fighting the urge when she spoke again, in the same tone one inquired how the other person took their tea.

"Only if that is agreeable to you, of course. I would not want you to feel obligated."

"Agreeable," he finally murmured, recalling Raghav's taunts at Luz Alana's adeptness to reducing him to parroting her words.

The woman did have an astonishing knack for rendering him speechless.

"Yes, if you are amenable to it, I would like us to, uh…copulate." His lips twitched at the way her voice squeaked on the last word. Evan could not remember the last time he'd been this amused and aroused at once.

"I see."

And he did see…now. Luz Alana was as eager as he was. He looked down at her lap where she was wringing her hands, then at her eyes, which were molten, needy.

Her face was flushed with red, those enticing pink lips slightly open. Evan's higher self struggled to maintain control, reminding him there were details to work out. That he had to call for his solicitor, arrange for his private train car to be readied. That he needed to sort all manner of arrangements for their departure from Paris. All of it swirled like water down a drain. The only thing that mattered was getting his hands on her.

"Come here," he rasped, but she didn't move.

"I didn't mean for us to start copulating now!" she cried, then covered her face.

Evan had to bite his tongue.

"Luz Alana, sweetheart, if you don't want things to become frenzied..." he had to adjust himself before his prick burst through the placket of his trousers "...you must stop wielding that word in my direction."

After a couple of breaths, she finally came out from behind her hands and was biting her bottom lip so alluringly Evan hung on to his control by a thread.

"Luz," he said with a bit more force, making her jump, and he watched her pupils dilate. "I asked you to come here."

"Where?"

His cock seemed to be attuned to her breathing, because every time a little puff of air escaped her lips it pulsed in his trousers. "Here." He pointed to the V of his thighs. "I'd like you to sit here, and then I'm going to touch you, like you asked." She licked her lips, and he had to grit his teeth to keep from spending like a schoolboy. "You know what I've been curious about since that night at Le Bureau?"

She responded with a sharp shake of her head.

"How those beautiful breasts would feel in my hand."

Another shaky little gasp.

"Would you like that?" His voice was gravel now. "To have my hand palming your breasts, tweaking one of those sweet little tips, while I take your mouth. Make you moan for me."

He reached for her.

Luz looked slightly panicked as she took his hand, but after a moment of silent consideration, she went to him. They both scurried with her skirts until her round bottom was snuggly nested in his groin.

"Good girl," he praised as she slowly drove him mad with the delicious friction of her rump on his cock. "I'm going to kiss you now." She nodded, eagerly pressing herself to him. He was already halfway to ruination, and it was barely noon.

He brought her head down and kissed her soundly. This time her tongue met his with unabashed hunger. She twisted her body, striving for more closeness, and opened to him like this shared breath was the only thing keeping her alive. Luz Alana nipped at his lip, then lapped at it, as she ran her fingers through his beard. Fingernails softly grazing his skin. She explored him like she'd been holding back and she finally could get her fill.

It was electrifying. With effort he broke the kiss to whisper against her mouth.

"You want me in your bed, Luz Alana?" He sounded winded, out of control. "You want me to spread your thighs and enter you until you're full to the brim with me."

"Evan." Those little tight gasps. He wanted to absorb every single one.

"Is that what you want?" he asked, suddenly desperate to hear her say it. "My fingers inside you, flicking that little pearl that had you screaming for me at the tower." She was trying to crawl farther onto his lap, now seemingly as desperate as he felt. He gripped her by the waist and lifted her until she was straddling him.

"Yes," she said, her voice a taut thread, ready to snap. "That is what I want."

He made himself take in a breath, as whatever it was that held him together was being ruthlessly ripped at the seams by this woman.

"Unbutton your jacket for me," he demanded as his hands slid under her skirts.

She shivered at the contact of his skin on hers, but she didn't retreat. His lioness would have what she wanted.

"I'd like to taste your breasts, Luz Alana. Has anyone done that for you? Swirled their tongue around your nipple, sucked it into their mouth?" She gave a little shake of her head and hid her face against his neck.

So damn sweet.

His hand found her heat as she pressed tender little kisses on his skin. Gently he coaxed her from her hiding place and brought her face up, so he could look at her. He wanted to see her reactions. He'd been entranced that night at the tower with the way her eyes fluttered closed when he touched her. How her mouth made a perfect O right before she climaxed for him. He wanted to see it again. He slid the pad of his finger over the furrow of her. The folds hot and slick, and his mouth flooded with saliva at the thought of tasting her sweetness. He circled the bundle of nerves, and she froze, mouth falling open on a gasp.

"So hot for me already, sweetheart," he praised before bending his head to mouth a breast through the layers of fabric. He bit down softly, eliciting a lusty little moan. "Come on, love. Let me see them."

She made quick work of the buttons of her bodice, as well as the chemise under it, as his hands taunted and teased her. He dipped two fingers in her, and she rocked into that touch as she labored to reveal more of herself to him.

He was gripping her left thigh to bring her closer to him when he noticed.

"No pistol today?" he asked, unable to suppress his amusement.

"I wasn't sure how things would go today," she explained. Evan made a distracted noise at her explanation, much too riveted by all the luscious golden-brown skin in front of him. "I didn't want to be tempted to shoot you." Preoccupied as he was with unlatching her corset, it took a moment for the words to register.

When he lifted his eyes to hers, he found such an impish glint in them that he felt his body flood with something very akin to joy.

"You are delectable," he said simply, too short of words and too full of precarious emotions to risk saying more. He cupped her breasts, loving the scorching heft of them. He lapped at a nipple with his tongue, circling the tight nub as she writhed under him. "I love how you move."

She cried and moaned at every filthy thing he whispered in her ear.

"More, please," she cried softly, and he obliged. His fingers found that secret knot hidden in her soft folds, and he flicked it, just as he flicked her nipple with his tongue.

"Yes, love, come for me," he urged and brought her down for a kiss as he slid into that tight heat. Fast, vigorous circles with the pads of his fingers until he felt the tremors of her thighs; her hands, which had been loosely hanging on his shoulders, gripped him tight as she thrust into his touch frantically, eyes closed and head thrown back in pure bliss. Needing more of her, he lifted his head and mouthed the base of her throat.

The taste of her, he would never get enough.

Evan kept coaxing more tremors from her until she slumped against him. He petted her softly, curving his hand to her bottom. He was painfully hard, but he didn't remember the last time he'd been this satisfied. Luz was still breathing harshly against his neck when he turned to press a kiss to her mouth.

"This was not how I planned things to go," she muttered in a languid voice that truly did liken her to a lioness in repose.

"I'd love to hear what you thought would transpire after you volleyed the word *copulate* in my direction."

"That's a fair point." She laughed huskily and shook her head. She looked utterly debauched, her breasts glistening from his attention, and he should address the matter of his cockstand before he was permanently injured. He just could not make himself move.

"Don't I need to do something about this?" she said, pressing herself to his afflicted organ.

"Not today," he said tightly before tucking an errant curl behind her ear. "But rest assured, I will be availing myself of that copulatory clause."

She laughed, and it was crystalline and clear. A sound so carefree, Evan could hardly believe he'd been the cause of it.

"Are we really doing this?" she asked, her voice shaking ever so slightly. He could not forget the risks this woman was taking for him. He could not let her down.

"I am agreeable to all your terms, Miss Heith-Benzan," he told her very seriously.

She considered him for a second as she moved to prop herself up and, rubbing his cock with her rump in the process, elicited a pained hiss.

"What if I want to?" Every muscle in Evan's body seized at once.

"If you want to what?" he asked very carefully.

"What if I want to take care of this now?" She caressed his girth in her hands awkwardly, but her flushed, beautiful face was a study in determination. "Provided we can have a conversation about contraceptives, I think this is the perfect time to get copulation out of the way." She said the words casually as she drove him mad with a tight, steady stroke.

"I take precautions," he admitted, and she nodded approvingly.

Evan breathed through his nose, attempting to stop himself from rutting into her hand like an animal. Their foreheads were pressed together now, and their tongues tangling again.

He couldn't stop kissing her. Which was so odd, because kissing had never been something he thought about very much. But with her, it was a delight, an indulgence.

"Have you done this before?" He pulled back, so they could look at each other.

"No." She shook her head, eyes squeezed shut. That moment of shyness, combined with the way she was touching him, had quite an effect on Evan. His heart could explode at any moment.

"Are you sure you want do it now? With me?" It had to be asked. He tried very hard not to subscribe to the hypocritical morals of his kind. He didn't bed virgins as a matter of principle, but the thought of being the first man to ever be inside this woman rocked him to his core.

She finally opened her eyes, and they had that spark in them he'd begun to recognize as the Luz Alana *come what may* look.

"I want to." She looked upward as if searching for guidance, her hand now lying limply on his throbbing cock. The eager bastard would have to wait until he'd made sure this woman was prepared for what he was about to unleash on her. "I do want you, and I'd like it to be somewhat in my control."

"Once we do this, we'll have to marry," he warned.

"I thought we'd settled that." Her brows furrowed adorably, and he had to bring her down for a kiss.

"We did," he said, light-headed. He was in a truly sorry state. She was supposed to be the inexperienced virgin, and yet he was the one gasping for breath.

"I don't see a reason to wait until the wedding," she argued, and he'd clearly taken a wrong turn in this conversation if she thought he needed to be convinced. "This isn't a conventional marriage, it's a temporary arrangement, and I..." straight white teeth caught her plump bottom lip for a moment "...I want to."

If she only knew he was already past being able to deny her anything.

"All right," he said tightly, feeling every ounce of blood in his body rushing down to his groin.

"What kind of precautions do you take?" she asked, like a true businesswoman, getting all her terms settled before she forged ahead.

"I take papaya-seed lozenges."

She seemed surprised by that.

"That's a common contraceptive in the Caribbean," she mused. "I didn't know it was used here."

"It isn't," he admitted. "My aunt Odessa, Murdoch's mother, handed us each a bottle of them before we went to university with strict instructions to take two a day and still use French letters so we didn't come home poxed. She's been providing us with them ever since." She made a sound of approval at his explanation.

"I look forward to meeting your aunt."

"You'd like her." And she will love you, he thought, but didn't dare say it. "I think she gets the lozenges from an apothecary in London that's owned by the Duchess of Linley."

Luz Alana's eyes lit at that. "I know who she is. She's from Hispaniola!" She wiggled her rump when she was pleased, and nearly caused him to disgrace himself.

He pushed their foreheads together and breathed for a moment.

"I promise to make this good for you," he told her as his heart raced.

"I know," she whispered, lips brushing his. So close to him. No one had ever gotten closer. He bit his tongue to hold back the rest of what wanted to come out of his mouth. Reckless promises, unreasonable vows that he could never keep. But oh, how he wanted to be the man this woman deserved.

He couldn't be, but he *would* make this good for her. Without a word he pushed up to standing with her still wrapped around him, eliciting a surprised squeal. He responded by sucking lightly on one of those bare nipples that were driving him mad and started moving.

"Evan, put me down," she demanded, even as she wrapped those strong thighs around his waist.

"I plan to, as soon as I get you in my bedchamber." He walked blindly toward the door connected to his private rooms. "It's next to this one. Once I have you there," he said against her ear, while he turned the doorknob and strode in, "I plan to take every inch of clothes off your delectable body and have my way with you."

He put her down in the middle of the room and stepped back to admire her.

"Here we are, Luz Alana." He sounded winded. He felt like he was floating.

"Here we are," she repeated, now a little shyer than she'd been in the other room, but she didn't look away. Once this woman decided she'd do something, she faced it head-on.

"I want this," she said simply but very firmly. She started unbuttoning the rest of her chemise, but he shook his head and moved toward her.

"I'll undress you."

Luz felt like she was in a dream. A fevered, hot, dizzying dream. She knew this was not smart. That it was likely a huge mistake to do this now, but she was crawling out of her skin with need. The way he touched her. He made her feel sated and ravenous all at once.

She wanted more of him, always. Constantly more. Maybe if they did this, if she had him, she'd feel more under control.

Evan made quick work of her clothes with the practiced expertise of a man who'd disrobed his fair share of women. He was quiet as he unbuttoned first her skirts, then smoothly pulled back her bodice. He kissed the back of her neck as he reached around and undid the last hooks of her corset. Luz couldn't hold in the sigh of relief that escaped her when she was finally free from the blasted thing.

"Better?" he asked so quietly she almost missed the question. It was hard to focus with his hands on her like that.

"I hate those things."

He shook his head, causing his beard to graze her cheek. It was a toe-curling, electric sensation with her skin oversensitized like this. She shivered at the thought of that scruff on her belly, between her thighs.

"Poor darlings," he crooned as he palmed her breasts and kneaded them gently. "I'll have to tend to them later." Every word out of the man's mouth seemed to be directly connected to whatever it was that held one's joints together.

He walked around her until he was facing her, impossibly large. It was a massive room, with high ceilings and furniture scaled to accommodate a man of Evan's size, but he still seemed to occupy the entire space. He was fully dressed still, slightly disheveled, but composed as he gracefully went down to his knees in front of her. Luz could not say that she'd ever given much thought to the circumstances of her first time with a man.

As a girl, she'd dreamed of having a soul mate who loved her like her parents did each other. But then her mother had died and she'd witnessed the desolate, unending despair of her father's grief, and that illusion had lost a little bit of its luster. Then she'd lost him too, and the dreams she'd had for herself had been set aside. Only her responsibilities and her obligations propelled her forward.

Clarita's future, Caña Brava, the cordials, Scotland—all of it was hers, yes, but also her family's. Even this marriage was for them. The arrangement that would permit her to fulfill the dream that her mother and grandfather had started. But this man on his knees for her. His clever hands, his hot, hungry mouth giving her pleasure she scarcely knew was possible… This was just hers.

"Put your hands on my shoulders, m'eudail," he asked as he unlaced her kid boots.

"Step out." She did so, smiling at how thick his brogue was now, making the *out* sound like *oot*. Once the shoes and stockings were off, he gripped her ankles and ran his palms up her calves, behind her knees, until he reached the flask she always had fastened to her thigh and grinned up at her.

"No pistol but rum, then?" he asked, eyes bright.

"I fully anticipated you would drive me to drink, Evan," she griped, and he barked out a delighted laugh as he tossed the flask on the bed.

"Luz Alana." Every time he said her name like that, as if it was an undeniable truth, something fizzed under her skin. He sat back on his heels for a moment, just looking, the humor from a second ago replaced by something she could only call predatory heat.

"I've dreamed of this," he said as he pressed his nose to the undergarment covering her mound of curls. "May I?"

She could only nod. With excruciating gentleness he slid the linen garment down and off and pushed her chemise up to her waist. His face was a study in concentration as he took her in. He licked his lips like a boy in front of a table laden with his favorite sweets.

"Take this off, sweetheart," he said, letting go of the linen bunched around her waist. She pulled the last of her clothes over her head without any inhibition now. Desperate to know what it was that she and Evan would do in this room. She had heard about the mechanics of the act from Aurora, had already felt so many pleasurable things at his hands, but her blood rose to a boil for what was coming.

Evan ran his thumb over the seam where her folds met, and without hesitation licked in. His tongue parted her, and the shock of that wet, heated, velvet touch on her most intimate place made her cry out.

"Mm," he moaned as he lapped at her, using his thumbs to hold her open. "Sweet as honey. Put your leg over my shoulder, love," he murmured against her skin before swiping along the center of her. With a firm grip he guided her until she was half straddling his face. "That's it." A rumbling noise escaped him. "Sometime very soon, I'd like to spend a day just doing this." With his thumb he lifted the hood that concealed her clitoris, then swirled his tongue on that vulnerable skin, then sucked.

"There she is," he cooed as if he'd found a perfect pearl in an oyster. He swiped the flat of his tongue on it, and her vision blurred, her legs felt unsteady as he ate at her. There was no other word for the way he suckled and licked. Nosing her mound of curls like he wanted to inhale her. He would pull back, as if to assess any place he'd missed. Spreading her for his view, and then he'd go back in for more. Evan gorged himself on Luz until she was keening, rocking into that secret, dark caress, mindless as she chased the climax he was expertly bringing her to.

"I'm—" She gasped as a wave of blinding pleasure crashed into her. Her mind emptied of everything that wasn't that hot mouth and those clever hands on her making her shatter. A weak whisper escaped her when she was too sensitive, and Evan pulled off slowly. He didn't stop touching her. He traced open-mouthed kisses to her skin that felt like flames licking at her belly, her navel, her breasts, until his mouth was on hers again. She could taste herself on him, and she was lost, lost to this moment.

"Can I have you?" he asked, already moving them to the bed.

She almost made a joke about needing to be returned to her shelf when he was done, then thought better of it. She'd be forced to deal with reality eventually; no need to bring it into the bed with them.

Evan made a pained sound as he laid her on the bed, then braced his hands on each side of her head, looming over her as he watched her with alarming intensity. He was still fully dressed. His elegant blue-gray morning suit in shambles from his exertions.

"I want to see you," she asked, not caring how it sounded,

and he smiled a new kind of smile. One that made his whisky eyes look molten, not just with that sensuous heat but with something much more unsettling. She nearly had to look away.

"I can do that," he said, sounding a little too pleased with himself.

He stood from the bed and disposed of his clothes like a madman, his tie and cufflinks landing across the room while Luz propped herself on her elbows to better witness the unveiling. With every piece of clothing that was torn off, her eagerness grew.

He was much too beautiful. His chest was sculpted with muscle, and a swirl of sable hair ran from between his pectorals in a train down to the placket of his trousers.

"See something you like?" He eyed her with that arrogant glint that made her belly flip.

"Quite a few things, as a matter of fact." She *was* admiring him, and she didn't mind him knowing. There was a lot to appreciate when it came to Evan Sinclair's body. With his eyes locked on hers, he pushed down his trousers.

"Copulation is imminent, Luz Alana," he warned as he stood there before her like a flesh-and-blood, libidinous god. Wickedly virile, his erection jutted from a nest of curls.

Her heart hammered in her chest, hard, so hard she felt the pulsing in her whole body. She *was* nervous and a little scared. Not of the pain that she'd been warned about: she could survive that. Surviving Evan Sinclair was a whole other matter.

"I'm waiting, Sinclair," she said defiantly, impressed at the steadiness of her voice.

His nostrils flared as his eyes took her in, slowly, so agonizingly slowly… Then he pounced. He covered her with that wall of sinew and heat. Their limbs sliding together in a silky friction. He kissed her for a long, breathless moment as his hands roamed over her skin. He palmed her belly, cupped her breasts, then surprised her by taking a nipple between his teeth, making her arch against him. She felt his rough palm descend, searching for her again. Then he was there, with that expert, knowing touch.

He lifted his head and looked at her as his fingers glided inside her.

"So tight." His speech had become staccato, as if his control was slipping.

"It might hurt a little," he said with astonishing tenderness.

His slid down her body until he was back at the apex of her thighs. He spread her with his fingers and glanced up at her.

"So pink and pretty," he whispered reverently as he grazed her labia with the pad of his thumb, making her buck up from the shock. "Like a flower." She closed her eyes, a mixture of embarrassment and searing heat overwhelming her.

"Do you know how beautiful you are?" he asked her, and she shook her head, her handle on words slipping with every second. He clicked his tongue in disapproval and continued that maddening, delicious caress.

"Open your eyes, love. Burn me with those scorching brown eyes." She did, and was confronted with his own heated gaze.

"I'm going to taste you now." Her breath hitched and he made a sound of approval. She didn't speak, just let him work, now anticipating what she knew he could make her feel. Instantly her body responded, heart racing as he brushed the flat of his tongue against her clitoris in a focused and unrelenting assault. Within seconds she felt her climax swirling in her again, but he moved away just before it could crest.

She cried in frustration, and he laughed with devilish satisfaction.

"The next time you come, I'll be deep inside you."

"Promises, promises," she taunted breathlessly. "I'm ready, Evan, please." She scissored her legs, skin prickling as he leaned over and grabbed a small bottle from the bed, then coated his member in a viscous liquid.

"Almond oil," he said, just as the scent reached her. "It makes it easier." That attention to her comfort disarmed her. For a man that loved to say how uncaring he was, Evan Sinclair was an awfully considerate and attentive lover.

"Look at me, mo chridhe. I want to see your face as we do this." She felt his hardness kiss the entrance of her body and sucked in a breath bracing for him to push inside. Evan Sinclair would not be rushed. He slid into her body with agonizing control. Shallow thrusts until she could accommodate him. It was the most tender of invasions.

"So sweet, so good," he groaned, then leaned in for a kiss.

"Evan," she gasped. He pushed the hair out of her eyes, his eyes intent on her. Looking for signs of distress, she thought.

"I'm fine. I want more." Something feral flashed in his eyes at her words, and he sheathed himself deeper. It felt so big, almost too much, but he slid in with excruciating moderation. There was a moment of searing pain, which he kissed her through, his tongue gliding with hers as their bodies fused together—until they were locked completely, and still she wanted more.

"Tell me how I feel inside you," he asked, his voice raw.

What could she say? *Possessed, whole, cherished*? Any of those answers would be too intimate, too much like she believed this was real.

"So full," she gasped, as he looked at her with a searching intensity that made her want to hide. "More," she pleaded, arching against him. He gave her what she asked for, surging into her.

"Is this what you need?" She opened her mouth, unsure what would escape her, but soon he was taking her so thoroughly that all thought fled from her mind. The only thing that mattered was reaching for the climax crawling up her limbs. The sounds created by Evan's body colliding against hers in that perfect, exquisite rhythm made her think of swimming in the ocean on days the water was restless.

Agua brava.

Furious water, an undertow that could lift you up and wash you away. That would never leave you quite in the same place it found you. That returned you slightly—but irrevocably—different. So that at night when you lay in your dry bed, you still felt the memory of that wave moving inside you.

Still inside her, Evan moved his hands and pressed his thumb to the knot of nerves right where their bodies were fused together, and Luz didn't think again. She felt the walls inside her spasm, which elicited a wounded sound from Evan, who redoubled his thrusts. Her body and her mind careened into a bone-melting climax.

Evan dropped his head against her shoulder, puffing labored breaths to her warmed skin. She smiled as she mentally assessed the aches in her limbs, the soreness on the inside of her thighs, the slight burn on the spots his beard bristled her skin. She felt… altered and a slew of other things that were best not to look at too closely.

"You are a constant assault on my plans, Luz Alana," he said with a groan as he carefully left her body. His tenderness as he did so felt achingly intimate; the absence of him shocking. Then he arranged their position until she was lying on his chest. She made a sound that was something between protest and apology. Then he pressed a kiss to her temple and tipped her head up to look at him.

"How do you feel?" What was that in his eyes? Concern? Hope?

Why did she want to know?

"Good," she said brightly. "Wonderful, thank you. This was…" her voice trailed off as she scoured her brain for words that suited "…ideal."

He stared at her with that steadfast regard, as if he looked intently enough he'd manage to extract the words that she would not say. She looked away, hiding her face on his formidable chest.

"We will have to make travel plans," she mumbled against his skin.

"I will take care of it," he said, his hands gliding on her skin. She believed he would. She'd learn to rely on him. To count on his presence, and then he'd be gone. She loathed how much the prospect already ached.

"Is it too uncouth to have a nip of rum before noon?" she asked in a self-mocking tone, feeling unsteady. Wondering how she would find her way back to shore once her time with Evan Sinclair was done.

"I may need a nip of something myself," he confessed wryly and moved to pluck the flask from where it had landed at the foot of the bed.

She unscrewed the top and offered him a drink after taking a sip. He took it from her with a rueful grin and shook his head.

"You are one of a kind, Luz Alana Heith-Benzan." He sounded...perplexed. And she truly had to stop dissecting everything the man said.

She had to reestablish the terms here, affirm what they were doing. With effort, she forced herself to pull away from him. By the time she could face him again she was almost certain her face was not displaying every single one of her muddled emotions.

"Thank you for the lovely interlude, which I suggest we revisit, but I would like to get on with formalizing things. The business with my trustee is becoming rather urgent, and I can't delay the departure for Edinburgh much longer."

Just like that, his expression shuttered. He nodded and sat up, the silence between them oppressive, a living thing pressing against her.

"I am glad the interstice was to your satisfaction," he said icily as he left the bed. "I will use the dressing room." He picked up her clothes and laid them very carefully on the bed. "The en suite is there." He pointed to a closed door without looking at her.

"When you're dressed come back to the study. I will need some information to arrange our travel."

Without a backward glance he walked naked into another room, leaving Luz to grapple on her own with the wretchedness of doing the right thing.

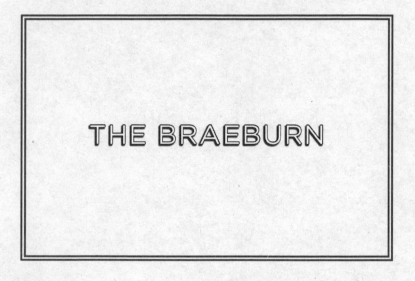

THE BRAEBURN

Fifteen

"*This is impressive,*" *his betrothed commented wanly as* she looked around his private train car. It had been an ordeal to ready everything for their departure. He'd hardly seen Luz but for a few hours the day before when they'd come to supervise her rum casks being appropriately stowed in the train for the journey to Calais and then a cargo ship to Leith. Miraculously—and thanks to an exorbitant amount of francs and pounds—they'd managed to get their affairs in order and on the train out of Paris only three days after they'd signed their contractual agreement.

Things had been strained between them since Evan's thorny reaction to Luz Alana's cavalier attitude after they'd made love. But she seemed to be taking things in stride and today was as pleasant as she'd ever been.

She was behaving in a marvelously civilized manner. He was the problem. He should've been elated that the woman who he was to spend the next three months tied to, desired to have him in her bed with absolutely no other expectations than to enjoy each other and amicably part ways when the time came. The mere thought of it put him in an absolutely foul mood. So foul in fact that in the last two days he'd been told by Murdoch,

Raghav and his sisters to get his head out of his arse before they convinced Luz Alana to cut her losses.

"My grandfather owned a good portion of the railways at one time." The car was lavishly decorated in mahogany and damask. No Second Empire fringe and gold but dark greens and blues. To his taste, which was a bit more on the subdued side of things. They would not be sleeping in the train tonight. Evan had arranged for the traveling party—and it was a large one—to stay at an inn in Calais from where they'd take the ferry to Dover the next morning. In the end they'd required four private cars instead of the two he'd hired to accommodate his two sisters, Bea's three children, Murdoch, Luz's sister and cousin as well as the two of them. The only two missing were Manuela and Aurora, who would travel to Edinburgh in a few weeks once Luz Alana was settled.

"Will we take this same one into Scotland?"

"No, the family's cars will be waiting for us in Dover, and those will take us up to Montrose."

Luz Alana's eyes widened at the mention of the arrival in Scotland while Evan nervously fisted his hand around the ring in his trouser pocket. He ran the pad of his finger over the aquamarine stone and cringed internally. Maybe she wouldn't like it or would think it was too simple. He should've bought her something new, something that didn't have the significance this ring had. He didn't need to give her a ring at all given the circumstances of their arrangement. But the moment she'd left his flat he'd thought of nothing else but seeing his mother's ring on her finger. He could not stop muddying the waters with this woman.

"Is Clarita settling in?"

Why was he stalling? This was merely a formality.

"She's very happy to have other children to travel with." Luz always brightened when the conversation turned to her sister, which in turn made him want to ensure the child was treated like a empress. "Thank you for setting up a time for them to meet yesterday. She was anxious, and it helped to spend time with the twins before we left."

"Of course." He nodded, maddeningly polite, as an oppressive silence descended between them. *Just give her the damn ring.* He'd prevaricated when he'd collected her that morning. He'd failed to do it in the carriage, he'd waffled as they'd gone to the cargo cars to *once again* inspect her rum was stowed properly. Here he was, still unable to do something that ought to be a simple part of this ruse they were undertaking.

"Is something wrong?" she asked, a brittle smile on her lips. She was wary of him because he'd behaved like a damn child after he'd bedded her, and now he was making it worse with all this brooding.

"I have something to give you," Evan finally said as he closed the distance between them and pulled the ring out of his pocket.

"Oh," she gasped as he took her gloved hand and pulled on it until he was touching her delicate fingers. The now-familiar snap of electricity crackled when their fingers met and with new-found urgency he slid his mother's ring onto her finger. "You didn't have to," she told him even as she lifted the hand to look at it more closely. The platinum band, with its oval cabochon-cut aquamarine surrounded by a cluster of thirty-four tiny diamonds, looked like a small flower on her finger.

"You are my betrothed," he told her in matter of explanation, with a voice that sounded like he'd swallowed fistfuls of sand.

"It's beautiful." She sounded odd, but he could not make out the expression on her face. "Aquamarine," she said softly, looking it over. "It's my favorite stone." She looked up then, eyes bright with something he did not dare examine. "The same color as the ocean in the Caribbean. Like the larimar."

The words all stuck in his throat.

"It was my mother's," he finally managed. She looked almost stricken. She opened her mouth, and he braced for her to say they must keep things impersonal, that he was blurring the lines she'd so carefully laid down. But she only smiled and moved to kiss him on the cheek.

"I'll take care of it while it's in my possession."

A knife to the heart. Evan thought himself immune to cutting words, and yet this woman's thoughtful consideration had pierced him to the core.

They stood there in that dismal quiet until he could not take it anymore, and he pulled her to him.

"Oh hell, Luz Alana, I've made a shambles of this." She let him engulf her in his arms, looking up at him with those dark eyes and an even darker expression.

"Are we friends again?" She looked furious, even as she pressed close.

I don't want to be your friend. I want to be your sentinel, your squire, the body that covers yours every night.

"We were never friends, Luz Alana."

Her eyes narrowed into slits at his querulous remark.

"We're something bigger than that. We're coconspirators. We each hold the other's future in our hands." One of those little surprised gasps escaped her lips, and he gave up all pretense. He covered her mouth with his and fed his gnawing hunger.

"Don't make me wait again," she rebuked, clasping her hands around his shoulders. She opened to him, tongue caressing his with deftness. No shyness, no demure pretense.

Not his lioness.

He feasted on her mouth, hands roaming down to that generous rump to squeeze. She yelped, and they smiled against each other's mouths.

"I want you," he said, between fevered kisses, on her jaw, her neck. As always, the latest ladies' fashions presented themselves as barricades between himself and this woman's skin. "I could take you right there." He looked to the plush damask-covered chaise, making her balk. He refrained from tearing open her bodice, but he was tempted. "I'd lift your skirts and slip inside."

She moaned in between deep, lush kisses. "I can't stop thinking about the way you hold me. That tight, exquisite heat."

"We can't," she said weakly, even as she exposed more of her throat for him to kiss. "Not while we're with your family. It will send the wrong message."

That dampened his fervor, and he pulled away to look at her. Her mouth was a vivid pink and bruised from his kisses. He imagined seeing those pillowy rosy lips stretched as she pleasured him.

"Evan, are you even listening to me?"

He shook his head like a wet dog, addled by the things he wanted to do to this woman.

"Don't worry about my family," he reassured her. "You'll learn to pretend they're not there, like I do," he said meaningfully, and she laughed, eyes bright with amusement.

"Do you mean to wait until we're in Edinburgh?" he protested. "We can leave them in Calais and they'll figure out a way home."

He was only half jesting.

"I'm serious, Evan. It's just a few days. I don't want to give them the wrong impression. This is meant to be *temporary*."

It nettled, but it was the truth.

"I don't want to make things any harder later. Adalyn and I have already begun to talk about possibilities with the cordial business. Beatrice offered to help secure tutors for Clarita and introduce me to some of her friends. Things are moving so fast." She was being sensible and he was behaving like his cock had absolute reign over his mind and body.

"We have to be prudent," she said against his lips, and it was truly pathetic how relieved he was that she wasn't pulling away completely.

He kissed her, then let her go with a sigh.

"I *am* being prudent," he retorted with absolute sincerity. "If I was doing what I actually want, you'd be horizontal on that chaise with me buried inside you, not talking about my blasted relatives."

"Evan!" she gasped, but there was as much desire there as outrage.

"You're probably right," he groaned. "God knows my family has absolutely no decorum. They will likely be barging in here any minute like a pack of sodding rhinos."

She grinned at that, and he caught the quick glance she shot at the ring on her finger. They smiled idiotically at each other until Evan's prediction materialized into an extremely bothersome reality.

"We've been wondering where you were!" exclaimed a fresh-faced Adalyn as she entered the small parlor with her pack of barking throw pillows.

"Where else could we possibly be, Adalyn?" Evan asked in exasperation, while Luz Alana sent him a look that clearly said *This is exactly what I was referring to.* "We are on a moving train." His sister ignored him and made her way to Luz Alana.

As annoyed as he was, he liked how much his sister and Luz Alana got on. "Oh, Evan—" Addy looked at him, eyes brimming with tears "—you gave her Mama's ring." Luz Alana bravely allowed Adalyn to tug on her limb as she examined the ring.

"It fits you perfectly, and it *suits* you."

His pretend bride-to-be nodded stiffly. Adalyn knew they were not actually engaged, which made her putting on that show much more irritating. Despite what she'd been through, his sister still believed she could will the things she wanted into being. If only that were true.

"Thank you," Luz said a little too brightly, then swiftly directed Adalyn's attention to less treacherous waters. "Did you want to look at the cordial recipes? I have my great-grandmother's journal here," she offered. Adalyn practically shrieked with enthusiasm, and the two of them ducked into the private bedchamber to retrieve the book. Evan would've sulked over the interruption, but Beatrice trampled in with her retinue of children, plus Clarita, Amaranta and Murdoch in tow.

In a matter of seconds there were Scots, Dominicans and Jamaicans sitting or lounging on seemingly every surface of the train car.

"Luz, mira, this spider can eat a goat in one gulp!" Clarita called from where she sat on the floor, holding up a book open to a page where there indeed was an illustration of a gigantic furry spider crawling up a palm frond with a live goat between one of its pincers.

"I don't know if those are based on real creatures." She shot a glare at Evan, who had presented her younger sister with the book that morning. The volume was supposed to be an "illustrated history of the wonderful and curious things of nature," but so far Luz had been forced to behold depictions of steamship-sized, man-eating octopi and a creature that looked like a mix between a whale and a boar.

Evan, who was in his usual predator-in-repose sprawl on an armchair opposite Murdoch, nodded encouragingly at Clarita. He'd sat on the opposite side of the room to Luz, which she supposed was his way of heeding her request they refrain from any intimacy while in the company of his family. Except barely thirty minutes into the truce she'd imposed, she was ready to put an end to it.

The man was like a fever that she could not break, and what was worse, she was not certain she wanted to. Her eyes lingered on him for a moment, halting on his powerful thighs, one of which at the moment was bouncing a delighted baby Fiona. She let her gaze roam higher to his snowy-white shirt, which Luz knew hid sculpted muscle and that silky swirl of sable hair. Her heart raced as she recalled the way Evan had loomed over her when they'd made love. Ravenous for her. She heard a hitch of breath come from his direction and turned to find him staring at her with such naked lust that when he winked at her heat pooled between her legs. She had to force herself to look away.

An amused laugh from Amaranta pulled Luz's attention back to Adalyn, who was sitting next to her on the small settee.

"Sorry," she said, embarrassed. "Where were we?"

"I think these could be very popular, Luz Alana," Adalyn said, pointing at Luz's grandmother's notes for a pineapple cordial, which involved soaking the rinds and core of the pineapple and cinnamon sticks in a mixture of rum and sugar. There would also be syrups without alcohol which Luz hoped would allow them to appeal to a wider market.

"I'm also considering experimenting with adverts that are aimed at ladies," Luz added, glad to see that Adalyn could appreciate her vision. "My friend Manuela found some street advertisements in Paris. There is a new style of illustration using very floral and feminine designs. Many Parisians are using them to sell their liqueurs and confections. She knows a few artists she thinks could make some sketches for us."

"Something easily identified." Adalyn nodded, contemplating Luz's ideas. "I adore it and love even more the thought of women in Hispaniola and Scotland and beyond all working to make a product that was created for women to be consumed by women."

"Yes, that," Luz said, unable to hide her excitement.

"My mother may be a useful collaborator, Luz," Murdoch said from his perch next to Evan. "She's very connected to West Indians tradespeople in Scotland and England."

"That would be wonderful. I'm looking forward to meeting Mrs. Buchanan."

"You must never call her that," Murdoch informed her with a laugh.

"Oh," Luz said, confused, and looked to Evan, who was smiling in that fond way he did when his family—other than his father—was the topic of conversation.

"She is Aunt Odessa to all of us," he told her.

"She becomes very peevish if we call her anything else," Beatrice's daughter Katherine piped up from her examination of a frightening sea creature with horns and a forked tongue.

"I shall abide by that rule, then," Luz assured the group, a warmth spreading inside her. Maybe she and Clarita could make a home in Edinburgh.

"Luz Alana, we must think about setting up an office. Perhaps even one that could have a small storefront."

"She will have an office in my building, Adalyn," Evan decreed in that high-handed way he had sometimes.

"I most certainly will not," cried Luz stubbornly, nipping that idea in the bud. As much as the thought of having him close appealed to her, it would be torture to see him daily once things between them were done. She didn't think she could bear it.

"I own half a city block in Leith. You can have an entire floor where I keep my offices," he retorted with equal bullheadedness.

"I saw a smaller building for sale on Princes Street, not too far from Jenners." Adalyn looked between the two of them with amusement.

"Oh?" Luz had heard of Jenners, the famous Edinburgh department store. "It's but a five-minute walk from your town house, brother." Addy's tone was conciliatory, but Luz appreciated that she was not letting Evan dictate what they would do.

The Earl of Darnick was not pleased at having his wishes contradicted. He'd have to live with it.

"The bonded warehouses are in Leith," he grumbled. "You will have to inconvenience yourself with seeing me every now and then." He didn't seem angry exactly, more like a boy who'd had his dreams of cake for supper dashed.

Luz had to bite her lip to keep from grinning.

"Pouting won't work on me, Evan Sinclair."

"Men are tedious," Clarita said with a shake of her head, eliciting a laugh from everyone.

"Your great-grandmother created all of these?" Adalyn asked as she carefully flipped through the delicate pages of the journal. She ran her fingers gently over the notes scribbled on the margins, and the hand-drawn illustrations that usually accompanied the name of a fruit or herb and its use.

"She did. She learned to make the liquors and tinctures from her mother as a young girl and became known for it. The master of her plantation asked that she make them for his family, but she would never write down the recipes for them. She told them she could only do them from memory, but in truth she had a very meticulous process. She just didn't want them to have her secrets. When she got her freedom, she began to sell them in the market. When he heard, her old master came to her and offered to buy them, but she refused." When she finished talking, she could feel every eye in the room on her.

"What was her name?" Evan asked. He was sitting up and looking at her very intently.

"Aida." Luz smiled when Amaranta responded pronouncing the name as it was spoken in Spanish.

"Aida's Cordials," Adalyn mused. "I think that sounds perfect. Oh," she said, eyes widening as if remembering something significant, while Luz caught her breath at the idea of a business that carried her great-grandmother's name. "Evan, you must convince the rear admiral to attend Father's birthday. This is just the kind of thing he would be interested in." Evan stiffened at her sister's request. For a moment he seemed almost scared. Adalyn didn't seem to notice. "The rear admiral is an old friend of the family's, more of our mother's, but he's in charge of acquiring all provisions for the Royal Navy, and I think he'd place an order of Caña Brava and your Dama Juana without much convincing, and the fruit syrups too." That did sound promising, but Evan's reaction to the mention of the man was definitely off.

"He hasn't attended since mother passed," Evan said, in the tone of someone who had already said this very thing multiple times and had been ignored. "Besides, I don't know if Luz Alana will want to attend the ball." His tone was amiable enough, but his eyes still had that alarmed look to them. Adalyn eyes widened at the way her brother said the last word.

"What ball?" Luz pressed.

"My father throws himself a lavish party every year, which we are all forced to attend," Evan explained, without meeting her gaze. Was he embarrassed to take her to the ball? Did he intend to leave her at home for the three months they were to live together?

"And I could meet the rear admiral there?" she asked, to which Adalyn nodded very reluctantly.

"He used to attend annually, but thanks to Charlotte he's snubbed it for years."

Luz, who'd had one eye on Evan, saw the change in his demeanor the instant Adalyn mentioned this Charlotte. Where he'd seemed forbidding at the mention of the rear admiral and the ball, he was absolutely panicked now.

"Who is Charlotte?" she asked cautiously, her gaze roundly on Evan. He seemed genuinely dismayed at the question.

"Oh no." Adalyn's face fell as if she'd just realized she'd committed an unforgivable mistake.

"She's our father's second wife, the duchess. The rear admiral is her uncle," Evan informed Luz in an overly calm voice. That was clearly not all she was, given the sudden tension in the room. Murdoch looked ready to bolt out of his chair, and Adalyn was holding back tears. Then there was Evan: his face was stony, icily staring at something in the distance.

Luz's stomach churned with dread. Whatever it was she would not like it. Clarita broke the tension with one of her favorite questions.

"Did she die?"

"Clarise Luz," Luz tried to rebuke her sister, but Evan spoke.

"Charlotte and I were to be married." His voice was so carefully moderated, so intentionally calm, it made the hair on the back of Luz's neck stand on end. "She broke the engagement and married my father instead. Six months after my mother died."

"Oh." Clarita sounded as confused as Luz felt.

Was this the reason for their arrangement? A way for Evan to get back at his father because he'd stolen his betrothed? Was that why he hadn't mentioned the ball? He likely didn't want to give the woman the impression that Luz had any significance in his life.

And what if it was? It shouldn't matter. She should not care what his reasons were.

She hated that she felt as though her chest was caving in, air refusing to enter her lungs. She'd lied to herself. Every time she'd told herself she was in control of what was happening. That she understood the consequences of what she'd agreed to. She ran a hand over her face, and the ring he'd just given her brushed her mouth. Her stomach turned, misery pooling in her gut like lead.

Had he given it to her first? Was this Charlotte's discarded ring?

She stood up too quickly, head swimming as if she'd popped out of the water after staying under too long. Disoriented, slightly sick and unsteady. She didn't want to look at him.

"Luz," Evan said, standing up, but she ignored him. She felt so ridiculous. Foolish.

"If you'll excuse me," she said as calmly as she could. "I've—" She couldn't finish, just clamped her mouth shut and made her way to the door.

"Luz, amor," Amaranta called, placing the book on the table as if about to rise. Luz put a hand out, shaking her head.

"No, te preocupes, stay with Clarita. It's just a bit of motion sickness," she lied. "I just need a rest."

Evan followed her to the door while the others painstakingly avoided looking in their direction.

"I'd like to be alone," she said as she fought for control.

"I didn't tell you because—" He was right behind her, just inches from her back. That solid presence which only an hour ago had felt like the harbor she yearned for now seemed hazardous.

She'd been an imbecile, establishing boundaries as if he cared for her, when all along he'd been trying to attract another's attention.

"I don't require an explanation, Mr. Sinclair. Your affairs are yours, and mine are my own." He flinched, and she dearly wished it offered even a modicum of satisfaction. She wished she could take everything back because this hurt too much.

"I want to marry when we cross the border, and I don't want family with us." He stiffened as soon as the words were out of her mouth. In his eyes she could see the questions, but he didn't ask them. "This is already complicated enough. We should just get it over with so that when we arrive in Edinburgh we can get this business sorted." She shook her head as her throat clogged. With her stomach in knots she slid the ring he'd given her off her hand. He flinched when she tried to give it to him. He was too close, and she needed air.

"Luz Alana, please don't. The ring is yours—"

She shook her head, hard, and pressed it into his open hand.

"This isn't mine. I don't need this to hold up my end of our bargain. If you'll excuse me," she whispered before pushing open the door.

The last thing she heard as she walked out of the room was Adalyn's soft but resounding rebuke.

"Evan, why didn't you tell her?"

Sixteen

"*May I speak with Luz?*" *Evan asked Amaranta, who* didn't look particularly happy with him, although she hid it better than his fiancée—who had not so much as looked his way at dinner. Having endured life with his father's perennial displeasure with his children, Evan thought himself immune to disapproving looks or icy silences. Four hours of Luz Alana looking through him as if he was invisible had soundly shattered that notion. After the third time he asked her a question and she replied with a terse one-word answer, he had been ready to tear his hair out.

That and dealing with a weepy, remorseful Adalyn had him at the very limit of his patience. He had no idea what Luz Alana was thinking, other than she clearly didn't want to see or talk to him. And that she didn't want family present when they married. The request should not have bothered him as much as it did. It was merely a formality.

Nothing related to Luz Alana is a formality.

And damn it, Evan didn't mention the ball because, frankly, he didn't want her anywhere near his father. Didn't want the Duke of Annan making her a scapegoat for his anger just because she happened to be standing next to Evan when he and Apollo brought his world crashing down. But he should've known she'd be hurt to hear he was planning to attend without her. That at the very least she'd feel slighted. He couldn't blame her for being cross about hearing about Charlotte the way she had. All of it was his doing.

He'd felt absolutely wretched when she'd handed him the ring, eyes full of hurt. He still had it in his pocket, hadn't been able to place it back in the safe in the bedchamber.

Now here he was at her door in their inn at Calais, prepared to say whatever he had to in order to make her happy again. She'd been so aloof and distant from everyone at the table but for her sister. She'd reminded him of a butterfly in a cocoon then. Carefully protecting herself from the dangers outside. Guarding her papery wings from the things that would tear her apart.

And Evan's secrets had been the blades she'd had to hide from.

"She's not here," Amaranta said defiantly.

"What do you mean, she's not here?"

"I thought she'd gone off to talk to you," she told him, now looking a bit more concerned.

"No," he said, surprised at Amaranta's tone. "I haven't seen her since dinner." Luz Alana's cousin considered this for a moment, but before she could answer, Clarita stepped into the small sitting room.

"You should check the docks."

"The docks?"

"She's likely making sure the rum is stowed properly in the ferry. She worries about it a lot." Clarita spoke with alarming sobriety. "If I'm sorted, the rum is the other thing she would make sure was safe for the night. She did the same thing at Le Havre."

"She's been on a knife's edge about the cargo," Amaranta concurred. "Until she's reached her final destination, she will be excessive in her care."

"She's gone to the dockyards on her own, at almost ten in the evening?" Modulating his voice so as not to frighten the child in his presence was a battle. "The docks are not a place for a lady during the day, much less in the dead of night!"

Amaranta sent him a warning look when Clarita's face darkened with worry. He was making things worse. "Why didn't she tell me?" he asked, despite knowing what the answer would be. "I would've taken her."

"Luz Alana doesn't believe she has anyone to do these things for or with her, and I can't say I see that changing based on today."

Amaranta's words struck true, and regret flooded Evan. "I'm going to find her."

He was pinned with a dour look. "She won't appreciate you coming to fetch her like she's an errant child," Amaranta said without prevarication. Whatever she saw on Evan's countenance softened her somewhat, though not by much. "Perhaps by the time you get to her, you'll devise a plan to make her feel as though help has arrived and not that she's being collected. Good night, my lord," she said before softly but firmly closing the door in his face.

Evan pondered that last directive from Amaranta for a moment, before spinning on his heels and heading for the stairs. With every step his worry for Luz Alana's safety was replaced with annoyance. Of all the reckless things to do! Evan could understand her being angry at him, but placing herself in harm's way only to make a point was completely unnecessary. After a hasty stop in his rooms to acquire his pistol and blade, he scribbled a message to be delivered to Murdoch in the event he was not back with Luz Alana by midnight.

By the time the fiacre driver dropped Evan on a well-lit corner at the top of a cobblestone street, he'd worked himself into a proper rage. He walked at a purposeful clip, staying under the light of the electrified streetlamps. The area, which during the day bustled with longshoremen and sailors, was practically deserted. He was dressed too elegantly to be walking alone in an area like this so late at night. Evan almost wished one of the men likely lurking in the shadows would start some trouble, just to have an excuse to purge the sickening worry that seemed to worsen with every step he took with a round of fisticuffs. He was halfway to the water and still didn't see any sign of Luz Alana. If anything happened to the stubborn, insufferable woman… No, he couldn't think about that.

By the time he reached the street where the spirits were being kept, he could feel rivulets of sweat running down his back. And that's when he heard it: a shriek and then an eruption of sound. He couldn't know for sure if what he'd heard were sounds of distress, but he was certain it was Luz Alana. He took off at a run, his heart in his throat as ice seeped into his bones. The only thought in his head, as he hurried toward the knot of people huddled at the opening of an alleyway, was that he'd gut anyone who'd laid a finger on her. As he reached the source of the noise he saw movement within a cluster of bodies huddled by a streetlamp, and then he spotted her. She was standing in the periphery of the group, head bowed as if trying to get a better look at something. At a distance she didn't seem to be in distress—and then she laughed.

Luz Alana didn't giggle in a girlish manner or emit graceful, delicate sounds when she found something amusing: she rumbled with it. And that intoxicating rolling thunder, when it reached him, made him stumble, his elegant formal shoes slipping on the wet cobblestones.

And what in the devil was the woman doing? Was she *carousing* with a group of sailors?

"Luz Alana Heith-Benzan, are ye trying to put me in the ground?" Evan bellowed at his betrothed, who was now happily pointing at a plank four men seemed to be using as table to play…dominoes?

The moment she heard his voice the smile slid from her lips

and her expression shuttered. It was like catching a sliver of a perfect blue sky, only to have it obscured by gray clouds.

He was the gray cloud.

"What are you doing here, Evan?" She was still dressed in the emerald green walking suit he'd threatened to tear off her that afternoon after he'd given her the ring. Instinctively his eyes went to her hand, regret twisting in his gut again.

"I am here to ensure that you don't get yourself killed. What in the world do you think you're doing traipsing around the Calais dockyards?"

"I spent my childhood helping my parents oversee rum shipments. I can handle myself perfectly fine." She thrust her chin in his direction. The men—who at least had the sense not to provoke him—were all gawking at them. They all had weathered brown skin and appeared to be seamen. They were also standing much too close to her.

"Luz Alana—" it was a miracle he managed to get the words out with his jaw as tightly clenched as it was "—you are *dangerously* close to obliterating the very last thread holding my temper together."

"Then go," she said with pugnacious finality.

"For God's sake, woman! You couldn't have told me you wanted to come here?"

One of the men stepped closer, as if to whisper something to her, and Evan's fists clenched.

He took a couple of menacing steps forward in the hope that they could see he was in an extraordinarily volatile mood. "I suggest you allocate a few yards between yourselves and my woman," he barked. Thankfully, the men heeded his warning, but they stayed to watch, leaving him and Luz Alana to face each other with an audience.

"Do you mind? You interrupted the game." She waved a hand at the two who were still holding up the plank with their knees, eyeing him and his betrothed with interest.

Evan pinched the bridge of his nose and exhaled slowly in an unfruitful attempt to summon even a shred of serenity. This was what Luz Alana reduced him to: prayer and hyperventilation. At length, he looked at her and was confronted with a very unfriendly pair of chocolate brown eyes, but right beneath that anger was such clear hurt, he almost wanted to look away.

"If you wanted to come and see the rum, I could've brought you."

She scoffed. "My rum is not your concern, Evan." He kept getting distracted by her mouth. She'd been biting at it through dinner, and it was still pink and puffy, just like when he kissed her. "There are three things I need to always be safe. My sister, my grandmother's recipes and my rum. It's all I have." He flinched at the crushing certainty in her words. She truly felt that alone. He wanted to refute that, but he knew she wouldn't believe him. He hadn't given her much reason to.

"If you've inspected the rum, then what are you doing lingering out here?" he asked, temper flaring again. "You must know this is not safe, Luz Alana. Sailors are not proper company for a young woman." He sounded like a bloody arsehole.

"*Cuban* sailors," she corrected with such studied composure Evan sensed something beyond her irritation with him was amiss. The sailors in question had moved on with their evening, probably once they realized there would be no melodramatic conclusion. "And I was here because they invited me to sit with them after your guard denied me entry to the warehouse."

He thought what he'd been feeling was rage, then what she said registered and he almost shook with anger. How much more humiliation would this woman have to endure because of him?

"He did what?"

"He didn't believe the rum being stored there was mine." She said the words with such excruciating calm. By the time she finished Evan was certain he'd turned to stone.

"Luz Alana," he said, reaching for her, but she moved away.

The warehouse did not belong to him. One of the Scotch distillers he was friendly with offered it to him. He should've asked more questions about who the man employed.

"No, I don't need your apologies."

It wasn't as if he didn't realize this went on all the time. He'd seen Murdoch and Raghav experience snubs and outright humiliation on more occasions than he could count. Which had led him to impulsively initiate more than one scuffle in the past. There were dozens of places he wouldn't step foot in because they'd harassed Murdoch or mistreated Raghav. Over time, he'd come to understand that it was not for him to determine how these incidents were approached. Responding with aggression or civility was not his decision. That belonged to the person experiencing the slight, the offense.

His role was to bear witness to it and help when and if he was asked.

None of that knowledge seemed to be working now. He wanted to break things. He wanted to inflict violence, hurt the person who had hurt her.

"If you're to survive the next ninety days with me, you must learn to let this kind of thing go," Luz Alana said, snatching him out of his thoughts.

"Whoever it was, they will be sacked," he told her, which only seemed to infuriate her further.

"And then what? You give him a real reason to hate people who look like me?"

She was right, of course, but Evan needed for *someone* to pay for this. Some punishment to be exacted on the person who had done this to her. Then he remembered why she'd been out here alone in the first place.

"I don't know how to fix this," he confessed, and she laughed bitterly.

"You *can't* fix this." Her eyes were bleak. "There are certain people whose prejudices cannot be budged, not even by the Earl of Darnick."

That stung. The bitter truth usually did.

"I don't want to dwell on this, Evan." She sounded exhausted. "Self-righteous outrage is not a luxury I can afford."

There were so many things he wanted to say and do, but they were all for his own benefit. His pride was smarting because this woman who he'd come to respect, to care for in the span of only a few days had been mistreated, and he was helpless to make it better. Nothing he had could protect her from this.

After a long moment, when he felt more under control he reached for her hand, and to his surprise she took it. She looked done in, and despite how much he wanted to place the blame on that damn guard, he knew he was partly, if not entirely, to blame. She'd come here on her own because of him.

"Let me take you to see the rum," he pled, and he almost wept with relief when she allowed him to tuck her into his side before making his way to the door of the warehouse.

"Is that him?"

The guard's eyes widened as he saw them approach, the sneer he'd had on his face when she'd previously spoken to him now replaced by alarm. Evan kept her hand in his as they walked. He was vibrating with animosity.

"Evan," she warned, but his eyes were locked on the man who, from the terrified look on his face, by now seemed well aware of his previous mistake. Luz felt absolutely no pleasure from any of it.

When they finally reached the door, Evan let go of her hand only so he could get within threatening distance of the guard. He had to be in his middle age. From his size and demeanor Luz could surmise he'd likely been intimidating in his prime, but he was softer now and certainly no match for Evan, who towered over him by at least five or six inches.

"Know that the only reason you will keep your job and what's left of your teeth is because of my fiancée's kindness." The other man only nodded. "Do you have the keys to get inside?" Evan growled, making the guard shake like a leaf.

"Aye, my lord, but not for this main door." He fished a ring with two keys from one pocket and handed it to Evan. "This one opens the side door. I got one chap on each of them. You want me to show ye?"

Evan took the keys and fished a handful of coins from his pocket, then made a pronouncement in that commanding tone. "Come back in thirty minutes, not a second later, or so help me I will knock your bloody block off, no matter what the lady says." Evan blew air through his nostrils with such force he reminded her of an angry bull.

The guard was out of sight with astonishing quickness. As irritated as she was by all this, a wave of heat still surged through her body. It was hard not to react at that mighty display of fury on her behalf.

"I wish you would've let me fire him," he grumbled. She could only laugh at how put off he was.

"Are you truly implying that I have any say in what you do, Lord Darnick?"

Something hot flashed in his eyes at how she'd lingered on *Lord Darnick*. The look he gave her was…incinerating. He raked that whisky-colored gaze over every inch of her body as he leaned on the door. Just when the heat on her face was becoming unbearable, he reached for her hand.

"Come with me."

He pushed open the door and waved his hand for her to walk through it. "Go on. Inspect that all is in order." Everything about this moment felt wrong. Luz wished that this afternoon had never happened. She walked farther into the large room and noticed that it was almost completely empty, and the only casks she could see were of Caña Brava.

"Where are yours?" she asked, but he didn't answer.

The barrels were lined up in rows of six, propped up on wooden pallets. Each one was tall enough to reach her midthigh. The space was meticulously clean. She was so deeply in her own thoughts as she took stock of her rum that she almost didn't hear Evan's question.

"Are you satisfied with the conditions?" he asked again, and though he still sounded terse, the irritation from before seemed to have gone out of him. After a pause he added, "I have the whisky in the other side of the warehouse since we have the furnace going in this one."

Furnace? That was why it was so hot in there.

"Is the room warm enough?"

"What?" she asked, looking around until she found the two boilers in the corner.

"You said you were worried the colder temperatures would alter the taste of the rum. I had them turn on the boilers in here."

She *had* said that. She'd expressed her concern offhandedly as they'd looked at the casks being loaded into the train in Paris. She had not expected Evan to do anything about it, much less arrange for a heated warehouse.

She didn't know what to say, and worse, she was feeling positive things for him again, when she'd finally managed to rein herself in. But there was no stopping the overwhelming wave of gratitude and relief at having someone take care of things for once.

"You didn't have to do that." She crossed her arms across her chest for good measure. She was, after all, furious with him.

"You were concerned about it, so I took care of it," he bit off, visibly flustered.

"That's interesting, because if I recall I also expressed concerns over you keeping secrets from me, and you didn't seem to heed that request. When did you plan to let me know about your father's ball which you don't seem to think I'm fit to at-

tend?" He'd been ready for this. He took her recriminations un-
blinkingly. For some reason his stoicism only made her angrier.
"Or that you were engaged to be married to your father's wife,
Evan?" Her voice felt too loud in the quiet room.

Evan looked at her for a moment, his head askance, as if trying to assess if it was worth it to respond. He was standing a few
feet away, and he was very still. She wished he'd come closer.

"If anyone is not fit for purpose, it is my family. My father is
an odious man." He rubbed his face as he did when he was frustrated. "I didn't want to expose you to his vitriol." She didn't
think he was lying to her, but the way he held himself, that
wasn't all of it. "And Charlotte isn't exactly a secret." Perhaps
he *was* trying to infuriate her.

"Then why didn't you tell me the truth?" His eyes darkened at her words, and a flicker of uneasiness passed through
his countenance.

"What truth is that, Luz Alana?"

She saw his hands fist in his pockets, his body rigid with tension, and for a moment she thought she could feel the string between them being pulled so tightly it was near snapping. She
was too attached already, behaving like a spurned woman when
Evan Sinclair had made her no promises beyond assistance with
her inheritance.

"It doesn't matter," she finally said, leaning against the barrels. They too were a support, but not like the body of the man
standing just a few feet from her.

"Now you're the one lying," he replied, and she could feel
the animosity rising in him.

"I don't know what you're talking about, and it's not a lie. *It
doesn't matter.* If this entire arrangement is a ploy to get back at
your father for stealing the love of your life," she said and lifted
a shoulder, pleased with the steadiness of her voice, "that's nothing I need to concern myself with."

"That's your conclusion, then, that this is a plot to soothe my bruised pride?" The line of his mouth was taut, and she could see he was at the very brink of his patience. She pushed him again.

"I couldn't say, Lord Darnick. I don't know very much about you." She was being reckless now. "I hope your efforts are well received by your lady."

She was tired of this day, of feeling let down by Evan but still wanting him. She was tired of worrying about things she could not control.

Evan closed the distance between them. When he reached for her, she moved out of the way, scared that if she fell into his arms she'd fall apart.

"I'm sorry," he said, pulling her to him. "I'm sorry I didn't mention the ball. I'm sorry that I didn't tell you about Charlotte." He whispered the words so softly against her temple, like one did to a child that needed calming.

"Do you love her?" she asked, despite knowing she didn't want to hear the answer. He made a pained sound in response, and she felt him shake his head against hers.

"I don't think I ever loved her, not really. I don't think I knew what love was. I'm sorry," he repeated, holding her tight, and she felt tremors coursing through him too. She'd suspected she was half in love with him the moment he slid that ring on her finger. But this, hearing, *feeling* Evan hold himself accountable only served to confirm it.

"You don't need to apologize," she demurred, gulping down tears as she tightened her arms on his back.

"I do," he whispered into her hair, as he rocked her like she was a child.

It made no sense. Her friends embraced her all the time; she held Clarita constantly. Then why did it feel like this was the first time she'd been comforted in years? Why did this man's touch manage to quench the parched places in her that nothing ever seemed to allay?

After a moment he lowered one of his arms, and she kept

her face hidden in his chest as he fumbled with something in his pocket. Then he took her hand and wordlessly slid the ring onto her finger.

"Will you wear this again?" She didn't have the energy to deny him. "And I'd like for us to go to the Braeburn for a few days, even if we don't have family. Please."

She could float away but for the grounding force of his touch. But he would not be there to hold her up forever. Everything about this man was ephemeral. Her survival depended on never forgetting that truth.

"All right." It wasn't that she didn't want to go; it was that she wanted it too much. Pretending things with him were real would only hurt more once he was gone.

Seventeen

"*Your hair looks lovely, my lady,*" exclaimed Mrs. Crawford, who was assisting Luz ready for dinner since she'd not brought a lady's maid.

Lady Darnick. That was who she was now.

In the end, they had been married at a clerk's office merely steps from the Montrose railway station, travel-worn and in the clothes they'd had on since the day before. Luz, who did not take to the constant vibrations of British trains, had walked somewhat unsteadily the few hundred yards to the clerk's office from the platform. So tired she could've fallen where she stood, with Evan rumpled and brooding by her side. The entire affair had been exactly the cursory, slapdash fracas one would expect when two people were marrying strictly for convenience.

Evan heeded her request to marry without friends or family present, and so they'd parted ways with the rest of their travel companions before arriving at their destination, the railway stop for Braeburn Hall. Murdoch had remained in London, and at Carlisle Beatrice had boarded a train to Dumfries for a short stay at Gerard's family country house with Clarita, Amaranta, Adalyn and the rest of her brood in tow.

Luz had begun to regret her request before they'd even descended from the train.

They had not been completely on their own at the ceremony—if one could call it that. Mr. and Mrs. Crawford, the married couple who served as butler and housekeeper at Braeburn Hall, had been waiting for them at the Montrose station when they arrived. The two received them with a basket of refreshments Luz's nausea didn't allow her to eat and a posy of heather and ivory tea roses she held on to for dear life for the few minutes it took for the clerk to join her and Evan in matrimony. Evan, whom she'd barely uttered a dozen words to since Calais, had been very serious as he recited his vows.

And after, the two of them made their way to Braeburn Hall in a cabriolet which her new husband drove himself. The day had been sunny, and from her perch she'd been able to see the landscape as they approached Evan's estate. The place was enchanting. The house was more like a twenty-bedroom castle done in the Scottish baronial style. The freestone structure was surrounded by turrets and large bay windows. It was an impressive sight of gray and white flanked by a dense pine forest with the sea to the east of the home. Lovely in that stark, haunting way of this land. She could see a change in Evan the moment they entered his lands. Almost instantly his shoulders relaxed, his demeanor lightened somehow.

That was, until the moment they'd come back from a short walk on the grounds and a footman had run out of the house with an urgent correspondence. Evan had opened the blue envelope and had rushed inside the house, promising to see her at dinnertime. Not exactly the wedding day of her dreams. Not that she indulged in that kind of fantasy.

She'd believed him when he'd said that he didn't love Charlotte. And yet, she could not make herself stop ruminating over it. Wondering if when he'd recited the vows for the clerk, he'd wished it was *Charlotte* beside him and not Luz. There had been something bleak about him as he stood in front of her that afternoon. And he'd been so quiet after. Lost in his thoughts as he showed her around, as if only his body was there but his mind was a million miles away. Despite the truce they'd reached that night at the warehouse, Evan had respected her request and been the perfect gentleman on their journey. No stolen kisses, no flirtatious banter. He'd heeded her requests so faithfully she'd all but given up on any more intimacy. Which made the wedding gift he'd sent to her bedchamber all the more confusing.

She'd come to get dressed for dinner to find a large glossy white box containing lace and silk undergarments. Not just any undergarments—the man had acquired a contraption that appeared to be a corset which had been cut in half. Instead of extending from the breasts down to her hips, it sat right above her rib cage. It was lovely and far more comfortable than any corset she'd worn. It was done in pale pink satin and a creamy Sevillian lace along the hem, with a luxurious silky material for the lining. The best part of it was that she could breathe while wearing it. Despite herself, she smiled remembering the card she'd found in a box from Herminie Cadolle's boutique.

This should reduce the suffocating devices forced upon all that beautiful and supple flesh. I'd ask that you think of me when you wear it, but I know how much you abhor undergarments.
-E

Evanston Sinclair was confounding.

"Shall we move on to the gown, my lady?" Mrs. Crawford softly pulled Luz out of her musings.

"Yes, I'm sorry." She smiled ruefully and walked over to look at herself in the standing mirror.

"This is a very peculiar corset, my lady," Mrs. Crawford muttered, nonplussed by the strip of brown skin visible at her midsection.

Luz made a sound that of agreement as she pulled on the chemise the housekeeper handed her. It did look odd, but Luz rather liked it. A warm, fluttery feeling passed through her at the idea of Evan peeling away her clothes and finding her in the garment he'd gotten for her. Perhaps this was his way of letting her know he wanted her in his bed.

"How did you come to work here, Mrs. Crawford?" Luz asked, in an effort to distract herself from her own thoughts. Although, in truth, she was rather curious about the woman. She clearly adored Evan and seemed to take in stride the fact that the laird had arrived with no prior warning with a fian-cée from the Caribbean. Though that was likely due—at least in part—to *Mr. Crawford* being a tall, handsome Trinidadian.

"His lordship's mother, the duchess, hired us," she said as she tied Luz's petticoats. "Mr. Crawford and I had been working at an inn near Fife and saw the advert for a couple to be house-keeper and butler. We didn't have much experience in look-ing after a grand house like this one, but the duchess gave us a chance. We've been here for almost twenty years now."

"And you stayed on after she passed away," Luz said, and the woman's face immediately turned somber. She seemed to weigh her words but ultimately only nodded. And they were soon dis-tracted by the efforts of getting Luz into her gown, with all the buttons, hooks and lacings.

"There," Mrs. Crawford said, a little winded from all the pulling and pushing. "Master Evan has done very well indeed," the woman declared as she admired Luz. Her face flushed at the words, but she had to admit that despite the circumstances, she at least appeared a bride in a sky-blue tulle gown with green crystals sewn to appear as ivy along the waist line, sleeve caps and hem. The frothy skirt swayed when she moved. "Now the jewels," Mrs. Crawford announced and grabbed the pair of tear-shaped emerald earrings from the table.

"That first year was trying," the woman finally said in response to Luz's question. "The duke didn't want any of the staff her grace had hired to stay. We all thought we'd be sacked, but Master Evan wouldn't hear of it." Luz frowned as Mrs. Crawford continued. "He told his father he'd take over all the expenses for the estate and pay all our wages, and he's kept that promise." There was true affection and pride in her words. "His Lordship's not made it easy for Master Evan. It's a testament to his love for this place that he hasn't given up on it. But he promised his mother he'd care for it, and he hasn't let his father push him out."

Luz had noticed the moment they'd arrived at Braeburn Hall the way the house staff behaved toward their laird. Evan was fiercely loved here. She knew the difference between true respect and deference awarded out of fear. These people adored Evan, and his fondness for them was just as evident. He knew the name of every person they'd encountered on their walk, asked after their children, seemed to know their ages and talents. It had been touching to see it, and now she understood that regard was well earned.

Despite what she'd surmised about his intentions, this wasn't just about getting back at his father. Evan genuinely loved this land.

"What was the late duchess like?"

Mrs. Crawford's countenance showed a mixture of affection and regret as she fussed with Luz's hair.

"She was a good mistress." There wasn't a trace of falsehood in the woman's words, but Luz sensed there was a caveat there. "She was fragile in her temperament, and she had a weakness for her husband." Mrs. Crawford seemed to struggle with how much more to say, but Luz could tell she was determined to apprise Luz of some truths regarding her new husband's family. "Master Iain, their firstborn, was a good soul, but he was like the duchess, and he was no match for the duke. It was left to Master Evan to stand up to his father, and it's made them bitter enemies. He carries a heavy load, Master Evan does." The older woman let the words hang in the air for a moment, but when she looked at Luz again, she was smiling. "And still, he minds after every one of us here. When our son Robbie said he wanted to be an engineer, Master Evan got him an apprentice-ship with Mr. Murdoch in Edinburgh. He just started a junior engineer position this January!" Mrs. Crawford's homely face flushed with pride.

"He must care about your family a great deal," Luz said through the constriction in her throat. But Mrs. Crawford shook her head, as though Luz had completely missed the point. "That's how he is with everyone here, my lady. He's helped most every family here in some way. That's why I was glad to see him with you today. Miss Charlotte—" her mouth twisted as if she'd bit-ten into a lemon at the mention of the woman "—or I should say *the duchess,* he didn't look at her the way he looks at you."

"Oh?" That brought Luz up short, a distressing fluttering robbing her of her speech. She did not dare ask Mrs. Crawford what she meant. That was information she did not need, but Luz was no match for the woman's loquaciousness.

"I've prayed for him to find a lady who sees just how good he is. That cares for him the way he deserves." Her eyes were brimming with tears now, and Luz was torn between running screaming from the room or joining her. "And I saw at the cer-emony today that you do." The housekeeper gave a self-con-scious, watery laugh, shaking her head. "Mr. Crawford warned me not to come up here and talk your head off." Luz smiled at that, but the older woman had more to say. "But we both wanted to make sure you were all right. When we wed, it was just the two of us. My family did not—"

This time she did hold her tongue, though she smiled up at Luz. "It's not important. Hugh and I have been happy for thirty years, and I wish you and Master Evan the same."

It was a stab to the heart, so painful Luz thought she'd double over with the impact the words had on her.

"Thank you," she said, her voice strained.

"My apologies, my lady. I forgot myself." Mrs. Crawford wiped her eyes.

"It's all right. I enjoyed hearing about Lord Evan's family." What she wanted was to ask more questions about Charlotte. What she looked like. What it was that Mrs. Crawford had seen in Evan's eyes during the ceremony. But that way lay madness.

She had to focus on getting through what would surely be an excruciating dinner full of awkward looks and stunted silences. Then she'd come back to her bedchamber and sulk.

"There is no dinner gong, but you can come down when you're ready," the woman told her, reaching for the doorknob. "If there's nothing else?"

Luz shook her head, and then her eye caught the leather-bound volume she'd laid on a spindly table holding up a vase of ranunculus.

"Would you do me a favor?"

"Of course, my lady."

Luz picked up the small volume and handed it to an expectant Mrs. Crawford before she could change her mind. "Could you please leave this in Lord Darnick's bedchamber?"

The woman raised an eyebrow, but in a surprising moment of restraint didn't question the request. "Of course, my lady," the older woman said obligingly. "I will let Master Evan know you're ready for dinner." She turned just as she pulled the door open. "I don't mean to be too forward, but that door right by your mirror…"

Luz turned her head in the direction the housekeeper indicated. "Yes?"

"It connects your chamber with Master Evan's."

That was delivered with a glint in her eyes that made Luz's face heat.

"Of course," she said, flustered.

"We're very pleased to have you as the mistress of Braeburn Hall."

"Thank you," Luz murmured, breathing very slowly as she watched the older woman leave, wishing she had Amaranta or Clarita here as a shield from the resounding proximity of Evan Sinclair's bed.

Eighteen

Evan had been prowling his room like a caged tiger for what seemed like hours. He could not sit through another meal of them both chewing and swallowing without speaking a single word. He'd been avoiding the truth about what was happening with him from the moment he'd laid eyes on Luz Alana. He had plenty of excuses as to why he'd pursued her, but when he'd stood in front of her and recited those vows, he could no longer deny what he wanted.

It was as ridiculous as it was undeniable: he was in love with his temporary wife. And now he was hiding from her like a damned coward.

He'd brought her here, to the place that meant more to him than anything in the world, and he'd squirreled himself away in his study so he didn't have to face the fact that in a week's time, she'd altered everything he thought he wanted for himself. The prospect of a life of solitude making whisky didn't make sense anymore. He wished he could set himself on a different course than the one he was on, but now it was too late. He could not go back on what he had promised Apollo, and he would lose her for it.

A knock on the door offered a reprieve from his thoughts and he rushed to open it. He found Mrs. Crawford holding a small book in her hands, seeming awfully pleased with herself.

"Her Ladyship asked me to give you this. She's ready for dinner," the older woman said, handing him the leather-bound tome. "And if you don't mind my saying, sir—"

"Of course not." Evan managed to suppress any trace of sarcasm. Mrs. Crawford habitually apologized for being too forward, right before she dove into his personal affairs.

"You should go to her." Her expression was not the usual easy one Evan secretly called her *loving rebuke* expression. Margaret Crawford was deadly serious. "Our wedding day is something women look forward to our entire lives, and having no one there with you..." Her lip wobbled at whatever she was recalling. "It's wretched. No matter what she tells you, no woman wants to be on her own on her wedding night."

Damn it all, she was right.

"Thank you, Mrs. Crawford," he told the woman, who was looking at him inquisitively. "I'll go see her now," he offered.

"You care for her." It was not a question. With effort he cleared his throat, but nothing came out. "She cares for you too. I can already see it changing you. You've been carrying much too heavy a load on your own, and I think you finally found someone to make it lighter," Mrs. Crawford added after a moment, a hopeful smile on her lips, before turning toward the stairs.

He closed his door with the older woman's words ringing in his head and opened the small volume. It was poems, in Spanish. He carefully leafed through it and noticed that there were handwritten notes inserted between certain pages. He took them out and realized she'd translated some of the poems into English for him. He scanned a few verses, his eyes snagging on a couple of lines. *Song of Autumn in the Springtime by Rubén Darío*, she'd written, in her loopy, elegant cursive.

She gnawed at the very heart of me,
that's what she strove to do...
love's flame for me she was,
and she could make each embrace, each kiss,
a synthesis on eternity.

With the book still in his hand, Evan started moving. He pulled open the door connecting their rooms with such force he was surprised he didn't take if off the hinges. He made his way into her room with such haste he crashed into her.

She fell into his arms, and he kept her there. It felt as though it had been years since he'd held her.

They both spoke at once, "I'm sorry for not coming sooner" colliding with "I was going down to dinner."

"Your dress." Not just her dress but all of her was breathtaking.

"What about it?" she asked, in that surly manner of hers. He bit back a smile and took a moment to admire her.

"It's beautiful. You're beautiful." Her eyes had been downcast, her focus on something at her feet, but after a moment, she glanced up at him. Her breath caught at whatever she encountered on his face. He imagined he must look stunned, unsteady. But when she spoke it was not to titter at his compliment.

"Did you finish reading all your correspondence?" she asked, her chin jutted up pugnaciously, but he could see the question in her eyes. Who did she think he was corresponding with?

"Does the duchess require your presence in Edinburgh?" Her eyes blazed with a possessive glint that should not have been as arousing as it was. He took a step toward her.

"I don't have any business with duchesses, Luz Alana."

She harrumphed, pink lips pursed. He had to fight the urge to take that mouth and apply himself to demonstrating which woman it was that plagued his thoughts from the moment he rose until sleep took him.

The letter that arrived had been from Apollo, of course. Evan had asked that he look into Luz Alana's mysterious trustee. It turned out Percy Childers was a scoundrel with a dreadful reputation who had acquired an alarming amount of gambling debts. There was even a rumor the man might've been involved in his own father's death. He would not worry her with any of that. His men would find this Childers and impress upon him that he was not to toy with the wife of the Earl of Darnick.

He'd sent his brother a note thanking him for the information and requesting they change the plan to confront their father at the ball. He asked if they could return to their initial plan to do it at the duke's club. If Luz Alana wanted to attend the ball, he would take her, but he worried that her presence there might give his father the wrong idea of her involvement in the scheme. He would not betray the promise he made Apollo, but he would not put Luz Alana at risk either.

"Why am I here, Evan?" Her face crumpled, and she turned away from him, walking over to a gilt console table and leaning her hands on it.

"I asked that we marry in Edinburgh," she said, still facing away from him. "But you've brought me here only to leave me on my own. I don't belong here, Evan."

That statement pained him the most. It did not matter what he'd told his sisters or Murdoch. He'd brought Luz Alana to Braeburn because this was the one place in the world he felt at peace, and he'd wanted the memory of her here with him.

"I'm sorry I left you alone," he told her as he closed the distance between them. She scoffed, but when he stood behind her, his front flanking her back, she didn't move away. He placed his hand over hers, twining their fingers together, searching for a connection. "I don't want to quarrel."

He wanted to give her something sweet to remember from this thing that would end terribly for them both.

"Well, I do," she said, but when he turned her toward him,

she acquiesced. With a finger he tipped her chin up, and that brown gaze was full of yearning.

He wasn't strong enough to not take what she was offering either.

"I think we could both think of a better way to spend our wedding night," he suggested as desire surged through him.

"Dinner is ready. What will the servants think?" she said feebly as he gathered her in his arms, fed up with words and pained silences.

"Sod dinner," he said with a grunt, making her laugh, then gasp, when he picked her up and sat her on the table.

"These gratuitous displays of strength are beneath you," she grumbled, cheeks flushed with a very appealing pink. Just like that, the mood had turned playful, seductive.

"I think you like it." He leaned in to place a tame kiss at the base of her throat. Her breath hitched a little, making her chest heave.

"*I* think you're an imperious ass." She delivered the insult with a cheeky smile kicking up her lips. Lust roared in him like a bonfire, with crackling, sparking flames.

Evan had never thought himself a romantic, and he certainly was not parsimonious when it came to lovers. If a woman wanted his company and he shared the sentiment, he was more than glad to indulge as long as the arrangement suited them both. *Monogamy* had not been a part of his vocabulary for years, not to mention *commitment* or *permanency*. Even with Charlotte he'd never been possessive, but something feral gnawed at him when he leaned back to admire his bride.

She was…luminous. Fierce and fragile all at once, a complicated woman. One that he desperately wished he could deserve.

"You are the most beautiful thing I've ever seen," he whispered as she watched him through half-lidded eyes, leaning back on her hands so that her breasts pushed out invitingly. He had to lean in but a few inches and he could capture some of that lush flesh between his teeth. His mouth watered, cock already hardening in his trousers.

The plunge of her dress gave him just enough of a glimpse of her breasts to make his mouth run dry. Then he remembered.

"I left you a gift," he said as she tightened her legs around his waist, bringing him closer.

She nodded primly, then pressed her lips right to his ear.

"I'm wearing it."

He breathed through the impulse to tear the dress to tatters. He never knew, *never knew* he could burn with desire like this. That the mere thought of something he'd bought for her against her skin would turn him wild with lust. *Luz Alana Sinclair-Heith.* He didn't dare say it out loud, in case he startled her with an ownership that did not belong to him.

But he could think it.

"How do I take this off?" he asked, well aware that deciphering the sophisticated and bewildering engineering of women's fashions was beyond him in that moment.

She only smiled, pressing those bountiful breasts to his chest.

"Undo the ribbon in the back," she instructed, and he did so with alacrity, pulling on the sides until he could push down the bodice. His breath caught and his vision swam for a moment when he finally peeled away enough layers.

Mine.

"Do you like it?" he asked, voice rough as he moved to cup her breasts in his hands.

"Mm," she mumbled, pushing into his touch. "I do. Evan…" Her voice was reedy, heavy with need, and something in him responded to that call as if his soul finally recognized its reason for being. With his thumb he pushed down the lace covering her. When he revealed the dark brown tip of her breast he bent down and sucked it into his mouth, familiar already with the taste of the cocoa butter she used on her skin. He swirled his tongue around the nipple, flicked it until she cried out, spine arching. He played with her, pulling skin into his mouth until it reddened, then doing it again. He wanted to mark her, he wanted to inhale her, devour her.

You make me yearn to be known, and I don't know how to do that.

He went to kiss her, but his bride was faster, capturing his bottom lip between her teeth and licking into his mouth. She took as much as she gave, and he reveled in all of it. All he could do was fall to his knees.

He pushed up her skirts until they were a cloud of tulle around her waist. He glanced up and found her gazing down at him eagerly. With his eyes locked with hers, he ran his thumb along the seam of her, feeling the wetness of her arousal.

"My bride," he breathed, making her gasp. "What do you want, mo cridhe?" He wanted to hear her say it. Wanted to, if only here in this place, in this way, uncompromisingly give her exactly what she asked for.

"What you did before," she said, eyes closed now. He clicked his tongue, lapping the tight nub of nerves, and she bucked as if shocked.

"Eyes open." She looked at him through slits, unamused by his demands. "Ask for what you want, Luz Alana."

"Your mouth…" She trailed off as he rubbed gentle circles on her clitoris, just a caress. "What you do…to make me climax."

He pressed up so his shoulders kept her open to him, and he descended on her like a ravenous beast. She gripped the back of his head as he feasted on her, the sounds he made echoing in the room. He slurped her up, drinking everything she gave him—always parched for her. He grazed his teeth against sensitive skin there, and she moaned, a deep guttural sound. When he pulled up the hood to expose that bundle of nerves and sucked her roughly, she screamed his name, her legs trembling against him, until her climax crested.

"I need to," he said, voice low and rough, "I have to be inside you."

He moved up her body, pushing down his trousers without caring if he tore them to pieces in the process. Their mouths were locked together, tongues wrestling. She wrapped her legs around his waist and canted her hips as he pressed inside. They both gasped as he sought to seat himself, deep, deeper inside her.

"This is…" he muttered, unable to voice what was urging to leave his lips.

This is what I needed. The only thing that matters. The only place things make sense.

"The way you take me in. Perfect." Evan drove into her body with barely restrained desperation. "I can't get enough." He punctuated every word with a hard thrust.

"I need more," she begged, her head thrown back as she moved to meet him, mindlessly reaching for her climax again.

"Take what you need," he grunted as he walked them to the bed, still buried inside her. He only made it to the edge, and then she was astride him. "Use me, love," he said as he gripped her hips. She leaned forward, planting her palms on his chest, and rocked into him. She was glorious, her breasts swaying as she chased her pleasure. He reached to pinch a nipple, and her mouth fell open in a silent cry.

"You love this," he said as his hands worked her.

"Evan," she yelled hoarsely as she stiffened on top of him, her channel spasming around him. Soon he was sinking into his own orgasm, limbs aflame as blinding pleasure exploded inside him. He heard himself cry out as her fingers dug into his skin.

Every time with this woman he felt made anew. Like every sin had been atoned for. Washed clean of everything that had been. He knew better than to believe that, but how he wished it were true.

"I think you tore my new favorite corset," she muttered testily against his mouth, and he throbbed with contentment. They'd managed to clean up somewhat and were now lying in bed together.

Dinner, in the end, had been brought to them on trays which were discreetly delivered to his bedchamber while Luz Alana hid under the covers. They ate and talked, sharing a plate of cold chicken, fruit, cheese and bread. Not exactly a wedding feast, but once again a simple meal with this woman proved to be more gratifying than any he could think of.

"I'll buy you a dozen," he told her between kisses.

"But I liked this one."

"I'll buy every single one Madame Cadolle has in her shop," he said, handing her the bottle of champagne they'd been sharing, drinking straight from the bottle. Luz raised it to her mouth and shot him a sideways glance before drinking deeply.

"If you think I'm going to say you shouldn't indulge me, you're very mistaken," she enlightened him between sips, making him chuckle. A new thing he did, thanks to Luz Alana.

Once she was finished with the champagne, she moved and sat between his legs, pressed as tightly against him as she could.

"This is not how I envisioned my wedding night, but I don't know if I'd change any of it. It's been oddly perfect." She handed him the bottle, looking up at him with a rueful expression, not knowing she'd just ripped his heart right out of his chest. He obliged by taking a drink before placing it on the wide edge of the headboard.

"You are well loved here," she said, still looking at him, a bit curiously now. Searching for his reaction to her words. It wasn't a question, exactly, but he was certain there was a very particular answer she was after.

"I stay away for weeks, sometimes months at a time, and the only way I can ensure that the distillery and the land are well cared for is by caring for the people that look after it."

She shot him a disbelieving look, then settled back against his chest.

"I'd believe the distillery is the sole reason for your dedication for the land if Mrs. Crawford hadn't made a point of regaling me with a long list of reasons why her Master Evan is an absolute saint."

He let out a pained groan.

"It was very sweet," Luz said, laughing. "Despite your efforts to seem heartless, it's clear your family and those in your employment care a great deal for you. That's admirable."

He made a sound of dismissal, feeling very uncomfortable with the conversation.

"I hardly think treating people with civility merits admiration."

"Fair enough," she conceded. "Although in my experience, simply behaving civilly rarely elicits genuine affection and respect."

"You have a lot of experience with civil men, then," he teased, but she seemed to take him seriously.

"My father was like that. Though he had his shortcomings, he always tried to be fair."

"I thought you had a good relationship with your father," Evan said, surprised.

"I did. He was a good man, but he was overprotective and more old-fashioned than he liked to admit. When he died we were already reaching a point where what he wanted for me was very different than what I wanted for myself. He never said it outright, that he preferred I marry and give up my involvement in Caña Brava, but given the conditions of his will, I wonder." She paused there, her face grave, as she ran a finger over the linen sheets that covered them. "After he passed away, I found out that he'd already selected his general manager to take over the distillery when he retired."

"Is that why you let go of your shares?"

She didn't answer, instead torturing him by steadily running her hands over his thighs. She made a sound of appreciation as she reached the wider, more muscular parts.

"You seem particularly drawn to this area of my body." He liked when she touched him possessively. As though taking stock of her belongings.

"They're like Greek columns!" she cried in feigned alarm. "The Parthenon has less heft hoisting it up. You're nearly too virile, frankly." She sounded utterly affronted, making him laugh. "And yes, it was in part why I returned the shares." She spoke very quietly. "You're the only person I've said this to. Not even the Leonas know."

Evan scarcely knew what to say, much less how to grapple with what was happening inside him.

"Guzman, that's the person running Caña Brava now, is a good man," she continued. "He was practically born on the land. His father was one of the cutters. In truth, he deserved the position. It was just that my father never told me what he intended to do. He decided to give away what I thought I'd been working for without telling me. And I wonder if it was because he didn't trust me, or because he assumed I'd eventually come to my senses and settle down to domesticity." She sounded so outraged at the very idea anyone could think such a thing. Evan decided in that moment he'd do whatever it took so that Luz Alana could pursue whatever it was she wanted without ever wondering if she was enough.

"I've barely known you two weeks." *God, how could it be only that long?* "And I am certain suggesting domesticity to you is the surest way to put me on the receiving end of that pistol you always carry around."

Her shoulders shook with mirth, and after a moment she laid her head on his shoulder.

"That assessment is not very far from the truth."

Evan sighed, considering his own conflicted feelings regarding his own parents—especially his mother.

"My mother was fragile," he heard himself say. "But despite how much my father exploited that, I think in the end she loved him more than she loved us."

"Maybe she had no choice. Women's lives can be a series of daunting choices. Our freedom or our peace, our safety or our pride. Every day we negotiate these things." He grunted at the power of her words and shifted so that more of her was laying on him. He liked her weight there. "It's easy to judge our morality or call us weak, but when the world is controlled by men who see us as dispensable, our survival depends on learning to discern between the battles we can win and which ones we can't afford to lose."

He thought of how quiet his mother became when his father was in a rage, as if she wanted to disappear, and he wondered what horrors she'd had to endure when she was alone with him. He remembered Charlotte, who had five younger sisters and a father who was a drunk and a wastrel: perhaps her choice to marry a duke had been about more than vanity.

Perhaps the woman next to him saw this world and its realities a lot more clearly than he did.

"Maybe," he echoed, lost in his memories. "I used to stand up to him, when he was cruel to my sisters, when he pushed my brother Iain too harshly. But he never punished me, he just treated them worse and let me know it was my fault." This was something he'd never shared with anyone. It was the reason he didn't want her anywhere near his father. "I'd beg him to hit me instead, but he knew that seeing them pay for my rebellion was the best way to wound me."

She turned around then, quietly, slowly, as though he was a skittish wild thing that would run off if she got too close.

"That's horrible. I'm so sorry," she said, wrapping her legs around him as if to shield him with her smaller, softer body from the harshness of his past.

"He sent my mother to the asylum after I confronted him

about my sister Adalyn. He wanted to marry her to this disgusting peer. The rumor was the man beat his first wife relentlessly, so I helped Addy elope. He was furious, mainly that my mother, for once, took my side." He remembered that night, his mother's shaky, small voice as she asked her husband to understand, the duke's fury when she didn't blindly take his side as usual. "A month later he shipped her off to an asylum in the Orkneys."

"Oh, Evan." She pressed kisses to his chest, mouth open, as she spoke soothing words. He didn't deserve her comfort, and yet he was too damn wrecked to push her away.

"What happens when we get to Edinburgh?" she asked, her face turned up to him so that her lush mouth was alluringly presented to him for a kiss. "Even earls who repudiate their standing have certain responsibilities."

Was that longing in her eyes? Did he dare tell her that all he wanted once they arrived in Edinburgh was for her to stay?

"Let's forget about Edinburgh for now." He bent down to kiss her shoulder, the curve of her neck, as she sighed with pleasure. Luz ran the tip of her finger from his temple to his jaw, scratching through his beard as she went.

"I didn't think I fancied these."

He pulled her to him so her heat was pressed to his arousal.

"Have I changed your mind?" he asked before dipping down to capture a nipple between his teeth.

"I am very close to being convinced," she confessed hotly, as he tipped them until he was looming over her.

"I must apply myself to it, then," he said before pressing inside her again, and then neither of them had anything to say for a very long while.

He'd allow himself the next two days with her, and once they arrived in Edinburgh he would do whatever he had to in order to protect Luz from the plans he had with Apollo. He would not let his choices touch her. Even if it meant making an enemy of his brother.

Nineteen

"*Mr. Clark said you have the new Stein and Argyle* stills," Luz Alana called with excitement from where she stood next to one of the copper pot stills he'd had installed last spring. After breakfast she'd asked to return to the distillery as she had more questions for the Braeburn's master blender. She'd been fascinated by Paul Clark, an American Evan had hired away from a bourbon distillery a few years earlier on a trip across the Atlantic.

"Clark can tell you a lot more about them than I can. He came up with the design."

"Lord Darnick is fearless," Clark said with humor, and Luz Alana responded with a smile that lit up the older man's usually serious face. Evan could not blame him for being smitten with her. So far everyone who'd crossed paths with the new Lady Darnick had fallen just a little under her spell. She'd been magnificent to behold, here in her element. Her eyes shining with unbridled curiosity at every new thing she discovered. Evan couldn't remember ever being happier.

On the heels of that came the reminder of the telegram he'd received from Apollo just that morning. In a few words his brother had let him know unequivocally that he would not alter the plans they'd made. The duke would be unmasked at the ball, and no one must know of his existence…or there would be consequences.

Will you betray me too, brother?

Those had been the last words in Apollo's message, and they'd served their purpose, reminded Evan that he had obligations. That going back on his word and putting his own wants first would only prove that like his father, he was selfish and self-serving. Once he told the truth to Luz Alana he would lose her, but if he turned his back on his brother he feared he'd lose his soul.

You have her now. That must be enough.

This morning she was attired in what she'd called a *working summer dress*, which her cousin had designed especially for her. It was made of a light material that she informed him allowed her to stay cool in the oppressive humidity of the tropics. It was a pale yellow with a wide skirt that carried no bustle, the bodice done without any frills or embellishments other than a panel of lace covering her upper chest. A row of mother-of-pearl buttons went from the base of her throat all the way down to her waist. On any other woman it would've looked homely, but the color made her bronzed skin glow, and it accentuated her lush curves. Errant chocolate and honey curls framed her face over her straw bonnet. He could hardly keep his eyes off her.

"Evan, come," she said, waving her hands. "Can you take me up so I can look inside?"

It'd been like this since their wedding night. It was as if Luz Alana had opened a door to him which had previously been closed, and from those glimpses he'd gotten of this freer, infinitely curious creature, he knew it would not take very much for him to be irrevocably lost to her.

You are lost already.

"We'll be late for our outing." Evan pushed off the doorframe he'd been leaning against and went to her, his pulse quickening with anticipation as he got close enough to touch her. His bride, Luz Alana Heith-Benzan. *Sinclair-Heith* now, he reminded himself as something wild burst inside him.

"Mrs. Crawford has everything ready for the ride out to the beach," he coaxed, then grinned as her eyes widened at the mention of their plans for the day. "I've a basket replete with berries for you."

"Raspberries too?" she inquired, letting him pull her to him until he had her by the waist.

"Loads," he whispered, mouth pressed to the sensitive patch of skin below her ear he'd recently discovered.

"Evan," she protested with apparent embarrassment, but he heard a slight intake of air he'd grown familiar with in the last couple of weeks. "Mr. Clark is right here."

"Mr. Clark has five grandchildren," he told her as he caught a glimpse of the man in question moving farther away from them to go check on one of the stills. "He is well aware of what people typically engage in on their honeymoon and is probably as puzzled as I am as to why we're not currently in bed. We are doing a very poor job of behaving as newlyweds." She trembled when his lips grazed over the lace covering her collarbone.

"It's fairly warm. Perhaps the beach would be a good idea," she pronounced in a low, lusty tone that went straight to his groin.

"Yes," he agreed eagerly. "I need to get you away from here for the day. You are much too popular with the staff." She laughed at his feigned annoyance. In truth he loved seeing her get on with everyone in the house. It took quite an effort not to let his imagination run wild with images of them walking hand in hand in the gardens years from now.

"My charm is irresistible," she told him as they reached the curricle.

"It is to me," he said truthfully.

"If only the distillers and tradesmen in Paris had been of the same opinion." She tried to sound as if she was only jesting, but he saw the shadows in her eyes as he helped her onto the conveyance. Once he'd secured the baskets of food and climbed up next to her, he pulled her to him by the waist. He startled her enough that her bottom ended deliciously pressed to his groin.

"You are exceedingly tempting," he told her, and in response, she wiggled her rump so that it brushed deliciously against his now very hard cock. He gritted his teeth in aroused agony but kept her pressed to him. "If my current state doesn't make that clear, let me say it. You are more than charming. In fact, you are supremely enticing, and my main concern now is that half of the staff here is enamored with you. *I* can't get enough of you, and I suspect neither can they, if all the besotted smiles are anything to go by. I don't think I'd ever seen Clark's teeth until you arrived here, for God's sake." She made a little sound of protest, but before she turned away he saw the happy twinkle in her eyes.

"Where are you taking me, Lord Darnick?" she asked, face turned up to the sun as he set them on the path to their destination.

"You'll have to wait and see." She huffed without any true heat and kept turning her head this way and that. It was a while before she spoke again.

"The mountains here are so different to Switzerland." The wistfulness in her voice made Evan look away from the road toward the hills covered in heather that his bride was pointing to in the distance.

He made an inquiring sound, curious of what she meant by that. "They're so rugged and blunt," she explained. She squinted adorably, as though she were attempting to decipher the precise difference she saw but could not quite articulate. At length she turned to him. "There's wildness to them," she said finally. "Like they were built for giants to lounge on." She relayed this discovery with such seriousness, he almost leaned in and kissed her.

"Furniture for giants," he summed up. "Which would make the Alps what?"

"Giant fairy castles," she said brightly. He did kiss her then, a quick and sultry thing, needing to taste the brine of the sea air on her skin.

"We house giants with clubs, and the Swiss are lodging fairies, then?" he teased, his gaze lingering on her for a moment too long.

"Eyes ahead, Lord Darnick," she rebuked playfully. "And I didn't know what else to call it," she admitted, hands up, palms out. "They're beautiful, but a little rough, like they were built to be traveled. The Alps are so pristine, like they're meant to be admired but not touched."

"How are the mountains in Santo Domingo?" he asked, curious to hear how the two places that made her compared to each other.

"Small," she quipped, and he laughed again. "But we don't need them when we have such overwhelming beauty in other ways. Mangrove forests, waterfalls and bays that will take your breath away. It really wouldn't be fair to the rest of the world if we also had impressive mountain ranges." He could hear the pride in her voice. She missed her island.

"Would you ever go back?"

She considered his question for a long moment, and when she answered she didn't look at him.

"When I left I didn't think I would. It was difficult being there without my mother and father. Without the distillery. Now with the cordials and the Dama Juana, I have a reason to return, something to build that's my own, a new kind of bridge between my two homes." He thought about his father and the destruction he'd left behind.

And here was this woman, dauntlessly creating new roads for herself.

"Here we are," he said a bit hoarsely as he maneuvered the horses into the clearing where he'd leave the curricle.

"The beach is just down there." He pointed at the path between a thick swath of tall beach grass leading to the water. "It will take us a few minutes to walk down there, but it's completely private."

"This is lovely," she said. "Everything is so expansive." She spread her arms wide and lifted her face up to the sky. She made his heart leap.

"The estate had belonged to the Earl of Kinsell for generations," he told her. "The ninth earl's gambling habits eventually bankrupted him, and my grandfather purchased the land which included miles of coast and golf links." She made a noise of understanding, her focus still on the horizon. He expected to see judgment in her eyes when she turned to him but instead was confronted with a cheeky smile.

"We will see how your private beach compares to mine."

"I didn't know this was a competition," he ribbed as he helped her down.

"Oh, it isn't," she assured him. "We may not win in the majestic-mountain category, but from what I've seen so far, our beaches soundly defeat yours in white sandiness and swimability," she declared with a completely straight face.

"Swimability." A bark of laughter escaped his lips as she grinned at him.

"Come here, m'eudial," he whispered, and without hesitation she put her arms around his neck and pushed up to bring their mouths together. He licked into her with the endless hunger he always had for her. Their tongues slid together as he tasted her sweetness. He nipped and stroked until she was panting in his arms.

"We'd better stop." He nodded, pulling back reluctantly, then perked up when he remembered what was waiting for them.

"Let's go down, love. I've got a surprise for you."

"I don't like surprises, Evan," she warned as she bent to grab one of the baskets filled with food.

"You didn't like me either and we both know the miracles my charm and virility have done on that front." She flapped her hands around trying to whack him in the arm.

"You are insufferably vain," she told him, the smile on her lips betraying her words, and a wellspring of tenderness lit him to the marrow of his bones.

"Evan!" Luz screamed as she tossed her boots, fisted the hems of her skirts and ran to the water as fast as she could. Her bonnet would've flown off her head but for the silk ribbon tied to her neck. The beach bank went on forever here, the wet sand extending for what looked like miles before one reached the small waves gently lapping at it.

In the Caribbean the water reached land hungrily. A fierce, passionate embrace. Here it was a slower, more sedate joining. The sand was cool on her feet, and dark, not white and fluffy like she was used to, but there was still that briny air that stuck to your face and the sound of water, air and sand comingling incessantly.

She was home.

Luz's euphoria lasted right until she reached the water and the burning iciness of it stole her breath. She laughed through her gasps as the frigid spray she'd kicked up slashed her face.

"I thought you were going to turn into a mermaid and swim away," Evan teased, catching up to her. His smile was different here, those sharp edges gone, replaced by laugh lines that crinkled his eyes and made him look younger and so comely it made her ache somewhere deep inside.

God, she wanted this man. Wanted him with an intensity that scared her. More than wanted, she…loved him.

Unbidden—mortifyingly—a sob escaped her throat, and her vision blurred from tears.

"The water is so cold," she blubbered as Evan gathered her to him, peppering kisses on every surface of her face.

"Ah, mo cridhe, I should've told you. It's icy even in the summer." He spoke to her in a soothing voice he used on her sometimes.

"It's all right," she assured him, feeling silly now, even as her feet went numb in the frosty waves lapping at them. "And it is beautiful here."

It *was* stunning.

So vast and green, and yet stark all at once. And so far away from the home she knew. Another sob tore out of her throat, and before she knew it he'd swept her up in his arms, her cold feet dangling in the air.

"Enough of toying with hypothermia. Let's get you to dry land." Instead of demanding he put her down, Luz pressed her face to the crook of his neck and inhaled that now-familiar and comforting scent of sandalwood. "The tent is not quite as lavish as our bedchamber at Braeburn Hall, but it'll do for a lazy morning, I hope." Her chest tightened at the casual manner in which he referred to their bedchamber.

The descent from this would be dark and terrible.

"Here we are." Luz lifted her head to get a good look. She'd only gotten a glimpse of it before she'd ran off like a lunatic toward the water.

"Is this for us?"

"For you," he corrected, then gently put her down so she could walk the rest of the way.

"How did you get all this here?" she asked, amazed.

The canopy had to be twenty feet wide. The floor under the tent was covered in rugs and carpets, and there were cushions of all shapes and sizes. Along one side of it was a table with jugs of water and what looked like lemonade at one end, and a stack of small plates, linen napkins and cutlery at the other. There was even a small crystal vase with white irises and pink roses. Evan walked over and placed the two baskets of food they'd brought with them at the center of the table, then turned back to her.

"You said you missed days on the beach." He sounded casual enough, but she saw two small red circles appear on the apple of his cheeks as he walked over to her.

He was nervous. Unsure if she'd like what he'd prepared for

her. He was all flushed and reminded Luz of her da when he'd stayed out for too long in the Caribbean sun.

"You did all this for *me*?" The words fell out of her mouth before she could stop them.

"I had a lot of help," he confessed. How could it be that the man was even more dangerous when he showed this bashful side? "Mrs. Crawford recruited half of the staff to carry all this down here at dawn. Which means you are obligated to love it, for the poor woman's sake. One of the footmen nearly maimed himself when she insisted only the marble-top sideboard would do."

She laughed at his attempt at expressing concern for the footman's tent-related injuries.

"I will be certain to express my gratitude to Mrs. Crawford. Thank you."

"I may require a more forthright expression of that sentiment," he announced as he put his arms around her. She would miss this most of all, feeling cocooned in his solid embrace. "I want to know, does the beach meet some of your very high standards? Iciness aside, of course."

Luz Alana let herself be rocked by Evan as she looked out. She'd been to other beaches in Europe. Nice and the Amalfi Coast, but they didn't look quite like this.

"Hm," she mused, searching for the right words. "There are rocky beaches in Hispaniola too, but everything is surrounded by palm trees. And there's so much life around the water. The tropics were created to envelop, to cradle. The water itself is like a warm hug. That might not make a lot of sense." She cringed at her rambling, but he made an encouraging noise which she recognized as his *Tell me more*.

"The tropics are lush and vivid, and there's this place which is rugged and a bit sparse but no less beautiful. I can already see myself falling in love with her." His hold on her became slightly stronger then. "In some ways it's better that it is so different. I don't ever have to feel like I'm replacing it."

"You belong here," he told her. She turned in his arms, sinking into the feel of him, and soon she was being picked up and placed gently in the nest of pillows on the rugs. He covered her with his strong body, his shirt was unbuttoned at the neck—he was much more casual in his dress at Braeburn—and she could see the trail of hair on his chest that went down to his...

"Won't the servants come?" she asked, reminding him and herself they were exposed out here.

"Not if they want to keep their hides," he muttered against her neck, but after a moment pulled back with a sigh. "Although, we probably should consume some of the food Mrs. Crawford packed for us. She becomes peevish when we don't properly appreciate her efforts."

He attempted to appear exasperated, but there was too much fondness in his voice for it to be effective.

In deference to the housekeeper, she obediently began to look through one of the baskets as she collected her emotions. That's when she saw the small poetry book she'd gifted him on their wedding night tucked into one of the baskets.

"You brought it!"

He nodded, very soberly. "I want you to read for me. We never got around to it on our wedding night." His voice was heavy with meaning, and it made her skin prickle with gooseflesh recalling what had prevented them from reading that evening. "As long as you understand that I will not be responsible for all the shocking things I may be tempted to do to you when you recite to me."

"I think the threat may have had the opposite effect you desired," she teased, leaning back on her hands, the little book on her lap.

He pounced then, peppering her with open-mouthed kisses and lurid promises as his hands moved over seemingly every ticklish part of her body.

"On the contrary, it was exactly the reaction I was hoping

for," he told her before jumping up to the table, athletic and graceful while she fought to work air back into her lungs.

"I was promised raspberries," she chided, making him laugh. Luz moved the cushions so she was propped up on them and turned her head to watch him move. Well, more like admire.

A man that well-made warranted contemplation.

He'd discarded the open waistcoat he'd been wearing and was now in shirtsleeves and light gray trousers that hugged those powerful thighs and muscular backside.

"Hold this for me, sweetheart," he said as he went to one knee and handed her a small tray he must have produced from one of the baskets. He'd carefully placed the food on one side and a glass of lemonade on the other.

There was something utterly decadent about a big man like this being domestic. Luz was certain Evan did not make a habit of serving others, and yet he didn't just seem at ease with it; the satisfied little smile on his lips as he took pains to make her comfortable told her he was enjoying it. Once the tray was secured on the ground he lay back down next to her.

He plucked two berries from a small dish and put one against her mouth. Luz's heart beat wildly as she opened her mouth and he popped it between her lips. She caught his finger between her lips, grinning around the trapped digit.

"If you keep doing things like that," he said as his eyes darkened with lust, "I'm going to assume you're trying to seduce me, wife."

The air went out of her lungs at the word. He'd never used it, and the impact of it left her winded. This man was hers, even if it was just for this day; he was her husband. Mio, she thought of those sparkling amber eyes and that strong, mobile mouth.

Mio. Mio.

Not forever, not like she wanted, but that heartache was for another day.

"Let's see what we can find," she said a little too brightly, as she flipped through the pages. Luz laughed when she saw where she'd landed.

"This is a perfect choice," she said, running a hand over the page, turning the book toward him so he could see. "'Foolish Men,'" Luz proclaimed primly.

"Hm." Evan turned his head to the side, squinting at her, like a confused wolf. "Insults don't make for very effective seduction, a thasgaidh. Unless of course you tell me how reprehensibly large my cock is and how bloody talented I am at making you come for me." The words made heat bloom in her core. "Those insults are quite welcome."

"You're extremely crass." Luz didn't even attempt to hide her smile. They both knew she found his filthy overtures infuriatingly arousing. "It's the title of the poem. It was written by Sor Juana Inés de la Cruz, who was a Mexican nun," she informed him, and he regaled her with that lupine smile again.

"That sounds ominous, although I can't say I blame her for the themes she chose to expound on."

"This is serious, Evan. She wrote this more than two hundred years ago." This was usually the type of conversation that resulted in her being chastised for her irreverence and unladylike ways. None were forthcoming from her husband. "She was a rebel, and her opinions on the place of women in society were radical."

"I assume she was not popular in her time, then," he commented without any judgment.

"She's not popular now," she said pointedly, to which he responded with an arch of his brow.

"I hope that my admiration and..." he said as he gave her an extremely lascivious look "...appreciation for opinionated women hailing from the tropics grants me some mercy."

"Don't be so sure, Sinclair," she shot back, biting back a grin. "Are you ready?"

"Loins have been girded."

He was unfairly handsome and much too clever for his own good, even when he was being an utter cad. Luz cleared his throat and read the first few verses in Spanish.

"That was quite forceful, but I fear you could be whirling insults at me and I wouldn't mind if they sound like that." His eyes were like embers now. "You are enticing in any language, but in Spanish you are magnificently beddable."

"You're taking the wind out of the sails of my battle cry, Evan!" Luz complained, and the scoundrel laughed. "I was supposed to deliver this poem in a thoroughly bellicose tone, and it's very hard to do so when you're looking at me like that and saying I'm 'magnificently beddable.'"

"I am honest to fault."

"You're insufferable." She read the rest of the poem, translating as she went, relaying the scathing commentary on the oppression of women and the ruthlessness of men.

When she was done, they both stayed quiet for a moment, and when Evan spoke he was very serious.

"I can't imagine a woman being brave enough to write that and not getting pummeled from every direction." He sounded genuinely regretful.

"One becomes quite bruised from merely concurring with what she espoused," Luz said, echoing the sentiment.

His lips turned up, but he was not smiling. In fact, his countenance held absolutely no humor in it. "Men have made a world where only we can thrive. Everyone else is in a fight for survival."

"White men, you mean," she countered.

"By and large," he responded with a sigh.

"Read me something else," he requested, taking his hands from under his head and using one to bring her down for a quick kiss. She flipped through the small book knowing what she was searching for.

"The author of this one is a man, Salvador Diaz Mirón. He's from Veracruz, the same city as Aurora. 'Desire,'" she exclaimed when she found it. "That's the title," she said, anticipating a filthy comment. Evan didn't disappoint.

"Mm, do say more," he encouraged, his hands massaging circles very, *very* low on her back.

"Stop groping me. It's distracting," she protested without much heat, and he gave her one of those toe-curling, extremely suggestive laughs.

Yo quisiera ser agua y que en mis olas,
que en mis olas vinieras a bañarte,
para poder, como lo sueño a solas,
¡a un mismo tiempo por doquier besarte!

By the third stanza and the fifth pained groan from Evan, Luz realized picking an erotic poem to read while sitting on the man's lap was perhaps not the best choice.

"What did that one mean?" he asked as his hands, which were now decidedly on her rump, tightened in a very pleasurable way. She squirmed, making him hiss and push up against her.

"It says," she said, struggling for focus, *"I'd like to be the waters in which you come and bathe."* He grunted again, and this time his left hand swiftly slid under her dress. She pushed into his touch, instinctively craving that shocking pleasure she knew was near.

"Finish the poem, darling," he demanded as his other hand worked to undo the buttons of her dress.

She never got to.

"Luz Alana," he whispered into her hair as he gathered her in his arms, the poem and the book forgotten as they tangled themselves in each other. "The way you please me, mo cridhe."

She wanted this forever. So much it started feeling more important than what she'd come to Scotland to do, and all of it terrified her. But she didn't have to let go yet.

Not until Edinburgh.

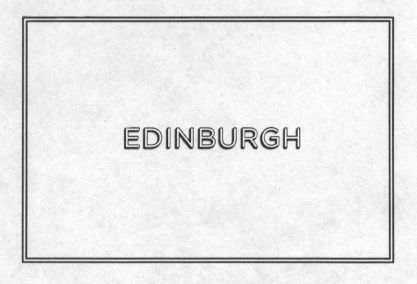

EDINBURGH

Twenty

It was done, Luz thought as she stepped out of Mr. Bruce's office. It was barely nine o'clock, and she was walking to the already-familiar St. Andrew Square with full control of her inheritance. This morning—after ten days of countless visits to Mr. Bruce's office, an initial planned audience with Percy Childers at which the man never showed his face, and poring over what seemed like a mountain of papers—Evan had signed the control of Clarita's trust over to her and ordered the final release of funds of her own bequest. She had everything she'd told herself she needed to start her life in Edinburgh.

Evan had gone above and beyond what he'd promised her. He'd met with Mr. Bruce and her trustee alone, ultimately making sure Childers lost any grasp he had on her inheritance. And he'd harnessed every one of his contacts to help Luz establish herself once they left Braeburn Hall. It had not been an easy feat. Percy Childers made himself a nuisance at every step, even going to the lengths of threatening Mr. Bruce's person if he didn't help him hold on to the purse strings of Luz's inheritance. But Evan had been relentless, and as of today, the nightmare was over.

Her rum-importing business was being constituted, and the

initial steps for launching Aida's Cordials were in place. Two days ago, with the first release of funds, she'd begun the process of purchasing the first shipment of limes and pineapples for her cordial production. In a few weeks, the first batch of raw materials would set sail from the port of Santo Domingo to Edinburgh.

Johnston had followed through after their encounter at the soirée and would do the transport for her on this occasion. The next day she was scheduled to visit the site of a bottling plant in Leith she was leasing. Things were in motion. Caña Brava would soon be able to be shipped anywhere in Europe, and Aida's Cordials was no longer just a kernel of a dream.

Her head and heart were full to the brim with all the tasks she needed to complete. Really, she should be elated to have accomplished so much already. Instead she was walking with dread weighing down her limbs with what was to come.

The Duke of Annan's ball was tomorrow night. Evan no longer seemed reluctant about her attending, although since they'd come back from the Braeburn it was hard for her to know what he was thinking. She'd barely seen him in the past few days as he endeavored to make all the legal arrangements necessary to ensure his father could not deny him the deed to the distillery. He'd told her he would make that demand at the ball the next evening, and then their obligations to each other would be over.

Just as they'd agreed.

Just as she'd told herself hundreds of times that she wanted.

Then why did she feel like her heart was breaking?

She looked up at Evan and saw that he was just as lost in thought as she'd been a moment ago. They'd been like this for days now. Sitting next to each other, but their minds somewhere else. It was bizarre. She'd given herself to Evan in every way imaginable in the two weeks since their marriage. She'd never felt closer, more open, to anyone than she had with this man. At times it felt like he knew what she needed, what she wanted, better than she did herself. And yet, she could not make herself tell him how she felt. It was absurd, when in their bed she was completely uninhibited in demanding what she desired. She had never felt freer than when she was in his arms, but there was a chasm between them that she could not bridge.

Every day he seemed to drift away a little more, and dozens of times she'd almost asked if it was something she'd done. But she would not behave like a lovesick girl. She would not open herself up for rejection. She knew how things would go. He'd attempt to let her down easy and would ever so kindly tell her he had no interest in a wife and that permanency was not the deal they'd made.

She couldn't bear it.

"I did not like what Mr. Bruce said about Childers," Evan said moodily, rousing her out of her thoughts.

When they'd arrived at his office that morning, Mr. Bruce had informed them that Childers had been to see him again, making threats. Her former trustee had not taken to being confronted with an unexpected husband, and since he could not threaten an earl, he'd been bothering Mr. Bruce instead. He'd even sent Luz an unhinged letter, demanding to be reinstated. She hadn't mentioned it to Evan, not wanting to fan the flames of his ire toward her former trustee, he had enough to worry about. And the man was clearly delusional. Luz just wanted to put the entire thing behind her.

"There's nothing he can do now that you've released the funds to me. He's redundant, and he knows it," she said in an effort to smooth the scowl on this face. As they reached their carriage, she took a moment to admire the crest on the door. Not that of the Sinclair family but the one belonging to the Braeburn.

"He's a bloody nuisance. If you would just let me send one of my men to—"

"Evan, you will not have the man thrashed." Despite herself she found her husband's eagerness to defend her endearing.

"We can revisit this later," he muttered, clearly not ready to put an end to the possibility of having Childers trounced. "I've a meeting with my own solicitor now, but the topic is most certainly not closed," Evan said as he helped her into the carriage. When he stepped back instead of following her in, Luz realized he was not accompanying her.

"You're not coming to the train with me?" she asked with as much indifference as she could manage when all her emotions seemed to be reaching their boiling point. Manuela and Aurora were arriving in Edinburgh from Paris. They would be at the ball with her and stay for a few weeks to help her settle—and to pick up the pieces of her shattered heart from every corner of the city.

"No." He shook his head, eyes hidden from her. "I need to finalize some of the loose ends regarding my mother's will. It's only up the street from here." He pointed to a gray building on the other side of the square. "Won't Amaranta come with you?"

She flinched at his tone. As if she was an errant child he'd found someone else to mind. How could it be that merely hours ago, when she'd woken up in his arms, she'd felt like Evan could reach to the deepest part of her?

She looked down at him from her perch in the carriage and tried but failed to read whatever it was that he wasn't saying. "She is. Thank you for all you've done, Evan," she finally said through the knot in her throat. He made a pained sound and ducked his head.

Tell me that you'll come with me. Tell me why you've been hiding from me, she pleaded in unutterable misery into the suffocating silence.

One of Luz's uncles was a rice producer in Cotuí, right in the center of the island. Once, he'd taken her and her cousins to the fields with him. In preparation to step on the sodden paddies, she'd tied the hem of her dress at her knees and put on rubber boots. Her uncle had even given her and her cousins sturdy sticks they could use to keep their balance. Their party had barely got a few feet in when one of her cousins lost a boot in the mire and had to go back, and Luz didn't fare much better. This was what she felt like now. She thought she'd been prepared, that she'd come into this arrangement with the tools she needed to walk straight through the other side. But instead, here she was trampling through a muddy mess that she was desperately ill-equipped to navigate.

"Nothing to thank me for. Simply honoring my side of the bargain." He tapped the side of the carriage a couple of times, and immediately the coachman set the conveyance in motion. "I'll see you at home," he called before tipping his hat and walking away in the opposite direction.

Luz kept her eyes on him as he strode away with that forceful gait of his. Then, just as he reached the corner, she saw him stop by the side of a carriage and get in. There was a crest on the door, but she could not make out any details. Luz felt ill as she lost him from sight. He'd lied to her. She'd known it in the way his jaw clenched, how he could not look at her. He wasn't going to see his solicitor. And what of it? Evan didn't have to explain himself to her. He didn't owe her anything.

Through eyes hot with unshed tears Luz applied herself to taking in Princes Street, wide and bustling before her, and wondered if anywhere inside those shops she'd find sandalwood soap to remind her of him when she could no longer press her nose to the crook of her husband's neck.

"I told you I'd come here after I was done with Luz," Evan groused as he stepped into the study of his half brother's newly acquired Charlotte Square home.

"And I told you I had urgent business to discuss with you," Apollo announced as they sat across from each other. Evan had walked away from Luz Alana with his stomach in knots and needed some time to clear his head. But Apollo's carriage had been waiting for him only yards from Bruce's door.

"So?" Evan asked in exasperation.

"Everything is settled. Our lawyers sent over everything." Apollo waved a hand over the pile of papers on his desk. If the duke only knew that his sons had been plotting his demise for weeks only a few minutes from Annan House...

He'd know soon enough.

Evan riffled through the papers. He and Apollo now owned every note, every loan, every debt of their father's. The man had hawked everything that was not nailed down to the point that any holdings of the duchy not tied up in the trust and everything Evan's mother had left, with the exception of the distillery, were essentially in the hands of lenders. The entire thing was an unholy mess, and it had taken months and a small army of lawyers and private investigators procuring notes from gambling halls and pawnbrokers all over Scotland before they could even start. Half of the tenants' lands had been on the verge of being foreclosed by the banks. They'd already spent a fortune pulling properties from the brink and paying off what seemed like every unscrupulous banker in the British Isles. And now they owned their father.

At least on paper, a fact they would press upon the Duke of Annan tomorrow night at his birthday ball. The moment Evan had been working for months to achieve, the justice he'd hoped for years he could exact on his father.

"Do you think he'll try to garner support from other peers to dispute that I'm his legitimate son?" Apollo's expression was impassive, but in the time they'd been working together, Evan had learned to recognize the very rare occasions when his brother seemed unsure.

"He wouldn't willingly admit that he'd put himself in a position to ask for help." The Duke of Annan would never open himself to anyone questioning him. Evan would bet anything on that.

"But he owed money to half of Scotland," Apollo refuted, and Evan shrugged.

"He owed *bankers* and *burghers* money. He would never let on to any of the men of his club that he's up to his eyeballs in debt. If any of them got wind of his true situation, he'd borrow even more money to throw a lavish party just to make a point."

Apollo made a rude sound, obviously exasperated. As much as the man was a genius at planning and scheming, he still had trouble understanding the maddening inconsistencies of how their father's mind worked. Evan, on the other hand, had spent his life witnessing the depths of the duke's revolting behavior. He looked at his brother for a moment as he perused the papers that they'd both looked at over and over, and he prepared for what he'd actually come to do today. To do what could no longer wait.

In the almost two weeks since Apollo had sent him that note tantamount to emotional blackmail, Evan had tried to focus on the two things that he'd promised: helping his brother expose their father and making sure Luz Alana gained control of her inheritance. He had considered forbidding her to go to the ball; then he recalled that his bride would likely shoot him in the leg for suggesting that he could tell her what to do. He also could not let her walk into the duke's house tomorrow without knowing what was happening, and if that made Apollo his enemy, so be it.

"That is not the demeanor I expect from a man who is on the cusp of tasting the ambrosia of revenge," Apollo drawled in that half-amused tone he always had.

"I'm not in the mood for your humor, Apollo." Evan slumped into the armchair opposite his brother and put his head in his hands. The other man clicked his tongue.

"Are you having second thoughts again?" This time the humor in his voice was gone. Apollo's tone was not accusatory, not exactly, but Evan knew there was only one right response to that question.

"This is not about me having second thoughts, it is about other people not getting hurt in the process."

She is worth whatever the consequences.

"Out with it, little brother," Apollo demanded, waving his hand in the space between them. "You are dampening my celebratory mood, and I can't say I appreciate it." Other than Luz Alana, his half brother seemed to be the only person that didn't take his assurances at face value.

Apollo's devil-may-care affectations tended to irritate Evan during the best of times, but today, when he felt like his world was on the cusp of collapsing, it was infuriating.

"Stop calling me *little brother,*" Evan bit out, to which his brother responded with an amiable baring of teeth. "I won't keep this from Luz Alana anymore." His tone was defiant, and Apollo in turn raised an eyebrow in apparent surprise. "I don't want my wife walking into that ball without any idea of what we're doing. I am telling her tonight." Every time he used the words *my wife*, something tight and angry seemed to unspool inside him, even in this moment when misery seemed to coat him.

His words were followed by a resounding silence. It took Evan a moment to realize that Apollo was not roaring with anger and recriminations. Just looking at him with curiosity, as if he was only really seeing Evan for the first time.

"I thought your arrangement with the new Lady Darnick was purely for your mutual benefit. It seems I assumed wrong."

"Yes and no." Evan hesitated. An avalanche of words were on the tip of his tongue. He was desperate to confess that his feelings for Luz Alana had changed everything for him. That something which at first had seemed like a convenient solution had turned into... No. He could not name it, not even to himself. It would only make losing her that much harder. Because he would…lose her. "I promised her not to keep her in the dark about things that would affect her."

"But you've fulfilled your obligation to her," Apollo said, in a tone that set Evan's teeth on edge. "She has what she wanted. This will be a scandal, to be sure, but what exactly do you think she'll be losing? As you are likely aware, your heiress is a Black woman and a rum maker. I don't expect she imagined the Scottish aristos would welcome her with open arms, regardless of your family's social capital among the peerage."

Evan's hands fisted, and he bolted from his chair. "Watch how you speak of my wife."

"Oh, I see." Apollo widened his eyes, a knowing smile on his lips.

"What exactly do you see?" Evan almost begged his brother to enlighten him, because he was adrift.

"This woman has you in a true predicament, brother. What a time to develop an attachment." That statement was followed by a guffaw of laughter. Evan, for his part, dropped onto the chair, mind reeling.

"No, that's not—" he started, then clamped his jaw shut. "No, it's because deception is cruel. Allowing her to arrive at the ball ignorant of what is to happen does not sit well with me." Which was true…mostly.

"I thought you agreed it was better if our father could not place the blame on others? That it was best if Adalyn, Beatrice and most especially your lady were not aware."

"I…" The words were stuck in his throat. "I was wrong. It was not right to decide for Luz Alana she was better off not knowing, especially when none of this was her problem. And besides, he will think it anyways. If she's there with me, there will be no convincing him she's not somehow involved. I am aware I agreed not to tell anyone about what we were doing, and that I am breaking my word. If there is any consequence here, I will face it. But might I remind you they are your sisters too."

Apollo emitted a wounded sound.

They had rarely spoken about their sisters; anytime they did, Apollo turned almost sheepish.

"Whatever price there is to pay I will be the one to pay it, not Luz Alana." Even as he said it, the bile rose in his throat. Not for whatever retribution Apollo would exact but because he knew it was already too late. Luz Alana had asked so little of him. Trusted him while he continued to keep this from her.

She would not forgive him, and he had earned her scorn.

"You can tell her." Apollo was smiling widely, but his eyes were very serious. "If I had known this was what was troubling you, I'd have understood. Why didn't you say anything?"

"I did tell you!" Evan protested, ready to throttle his brother.

"No, you sent me a note telling me that you wanted to change our plan. Did it ever occur to you that if you'd told me how you felt about her and what your true concern was, instead of trying to send me decrees by telegram, I would've been more amenable?"

Evan was almost grateful for this because at least it gave him an excuse to purge some of this frustration on someone who could take it.

"Oh, yes. I was supposed to infer that from one of the many times you threatened me with my imminent demise if I crossed you."

Apollo was completely unnerved by Evan's outburst.

"I thought by now you knew we are on the same side. I could not accept what you offered." The earnestness in his brother's voice significantly mollified Evan's irritation. Then he opened his mouth again and ruined it. "But if you had told me you'd gone and fallen in love with the woman—"

"Apollo, I am very close to knocking your teeth out," Evan warned, to which the bastard responded by bellowing with laughter.

"Did no one warn you?" Apollo laughed again. "Caribbean

women will turn your life upside down in mere hours, brother. Once you've been bitten, there is no cure."

Evan scarcely understood what was happening to him from one minute to the other.

"If you trust her, then tell her. If my plan is thwarted for any reason, it won't be Miss Heith-Benzan—"

Evan glared.

"Pardon me," Apollo said, with feigned remorse. "It won't be *Lady Darnick* who I will unleash my wrath on."

Evan did not feel any relief at the allowance. Telling Luz Alana would prepare her for what was to come but destroy any chance there was of keeping her. He'd always thought that the most wretched moments of his life were already behind him.

That's why he'd thrown himself into Apollo's scheme without a second's hesitation, but the thought of Luz Alana's disdain, of seeing disappointment in her eyes, that felt like a death. He remembered the sadness in her voice when she'd told him about her father keeping his plans for the distillery from her until it was too late. He couldn't do it to her. He'd rather have her hate him for telling her the truth than for playing her for the fool.

He would not be another man in her life who dismissed her, who kept her on the outside.

"You're really tortured about this." Apollo's words dragged him from his thoughts.

"Apollo…" The menace in his tone only made his brother's eyes light up with interest. With their size and tempers, they'd probably end up destroying the room if they got into a brawl, but Evan almost wished Apollo would push him. "And I've not fallen for her. I don't like to lie, that is all."

"You've had no problem lying since I met you. Don't pretend with me. I've had that fever and scarcely survived the very perilous process of it breaking. Whether you are willing to face it yet or not, that heiress owns you, brother. It would do you good to accept that fact and begin behaving accordingly. Then you'll be able to enjoy the inoculation period."

"She's not a disease," Evan growled.

"I wouldn't say *disease*… *Lifelong affliction without any possible cure?* Definitely. That is why I do not spar with charming women. Too dangerous."

Evan looked at his brother through narrowed eyes, equally irritated and relieved to be able to speak to someone about the depths of emotional turmoil Luz Alana had plunged him into. "One day a woman is going to blow your life to smithereens, and I will be there to laugh in your face."

Apollo's countenance transformed then into an expression Evan had not seen before—yearning, hope?

"That will never happen, but I look forward to witnessing your further descent in the hands of the Dominican firebrand you married."

They'd come together to bring down their father, but in Apollo, Evan had found more than an ally: he'd found a friend. The man was true to his word and a formidable coconspirator. From their first meeting, instead of resentment and loathing, Apollo had given him the benefit of the doubt. He'd been open about his intentions and never placed their father's wrongdoings at his feet. He'd left Evan to prove himself and his integrity.

Apollo was relentless and meticulous in everything he did, but more importantly he was fair and fiercely loyal. Evan respected him for that, and he'd begun to care for this brother who he'd never known yet in fundamental ways seemed like a kindred spirit. So different than Iain, who had never been able to stand up to their father, and whose vices and weaknesses had eventually put him in an early grave.

Evan had always blamed his father for Iain's death. For encouraging his firstborn's proclivities for drinking and gambling. But now he considered the way that Iain had turned a blind eye to their father interring their mother in an asylum. The times he'd thrown up his hands when Beatrice and Adalyn had needed help. Evan could not help but wonder what it would've been like to have Apollo at his side fighting those battles.

"She will never forgive me," Evan admitted, relieved to say it out loud.

His brother considered Evan for a moment, his face serious but not forbidding, and he felt a silent but powerful understanding burgeoning between them.

"Why does it matter, Evan? You no longer owe her anything," Apollo pushed, and Evan resented it as much as he ached to have this truth extracted from him. "If she hates you, all the better for swiftly regaining your freedom and disappearing to the life of whisky-making and the solitude you've claimed to desire."

"I don't want to hurt her unnecessarily. She's already been through too much. She deserves to know."

"Why?"

"Damn you, Apollo." The words were like a dagger blade in his mouth.

Because I care too much about her to hurt her in that way. Because in the last month, her happiness has become more important to me than this fucking revenge.

He clamped his teeth against that truth and let his words hang in the air between them.

"All right, I'll let you keep it all inside, brother. But we both know you're ruined. In honesty, I will call on our sisters this afternoon," Apollo said, to Evan's surprise.

"I thought you wanted to wait," Evan said, not bothering to hide his surprise.

"They should know. It's been weighing on me for some time now." His older brother shook his head, his expression as serious as he'd ever seen it. "You are right to want to protect your woman. I will do the same for our sisters."

"You have my sympathies," Evan said, bowled over by the genuine, deep regard he had for his brother. And legitimately concerned for his safety when faced with Adalyn and Beatrice. "Are you sure you don't want me there?"

"I am. Tell your wife, Evan. Once you have, do whatever is necessary to make it right. That is what men of honor do." Apollo's words hadn't a trace of irony or doubt.

"I'm fairly certain she will shoot me for keeping this from her," Evan confessed, to which Apollo responded by doubling over in a fit of laughter, significantly cooling any emerging warm feelings Evan had toward his brother.

"I cannot wait to get to know Lady Darnick better. She sounds like my kind of woman."

A growl escaped Evan's lips. "I will thank you not to use possessive language when speaking of my wife."

Apollo laughed harder. "You are frankly too easy to rankle. It's getting quite boring."

"You're a bloody bastard." He grumbled.

Apollo looked up and winked. "*That* might be the one thing I am not, brother."

Evan bit his tongue and stood up, feeling like a man about to go to the gallows.

"Are you going to her now?" Apollo asked.

Evan shook his head. "Her trustee has been making a nuisance of himself with her solicitor, demanding compensation for his so-called management of the estate. I thought I'd pay him a visit."

"I thought he no longer had any control over her money?"

"He's a bloody loose cannon," Evan groused. "Luz Alana refuses to let me threaten him with bodily harm, so I will merely *advise* him today and then have my lawyers give him one last warning instead of the horsewhipping he deserves."

Apollo made a sound of distaste, which illustrated Evan's feelings exactly. "If you are attempting to be more honest and establish more equity between yourself and your wife, perhaps heeding her requests pertaining to her business would be a positive step in that direction?"

Damn the man, but his brother was right.

"You are infuriating."

"I am wise beyond measure. You can still have your *lawyers* threaten the rodent. Compromise is the secret to all happy unions."

"And you are an expert in marriage?" Evan retorted instead of admitting that Apollo's advice was sound. "I will talk to my solicitor. Let's hope the man gives up once and for all." Evan was truly out of patience when it came to Percy Childers, but he had more important things to deal with, like keeping his wife, for example. "I will go to her now." Dread gripped him again, alongside something that felt very much like his heart breaking.

"Don't get yourself killed before tomorrow evening," Apollo said with another one of those irritating grins. With that, the man pulled Evan in for an embrace, thumping him twice on the back. "Justice will be done tomorrow. I will not forget what you've risked to help me set things right."

A wave of emotion clogged Evan's throat. He'd honestly never thought there might be a future where his family and their legacy weren't something to repudiate, but he and Apollo might be able to make things different. To use the lands and the holdings that for so long had only served the Sinclairs, to honor both of their mother's lives and to improve the livelihoods of others. He only wished in the end it had not cost him Luz Alana.

"Any decent man would've done the same."

Apollo's derisive laugh vibrated through the room. "We both know that *most* decent men would have done nothing of the sort."

"Then perhaps we should set higher standards for what we consider decent," Evan said darkly as he headed for the door.

Twenty-One

"Are you certain it's another woman?" Manuela asked Luz, who was standing by the bay window in her office, looking out onto Princes Street.

"How could it possibly be another entanglement if the man's in your bed practically every night?" Aurora asked, not one to prevaricate.

"Perhaps it's not another woman," Luz sighed miserably. "But it is *something* because he's different. He has barely looked me in the eye in the last few days. While at Braeburn Hall he felt..." *Mine.* Like they were at the beginning of something rare and precious, whereas now every interaction felt like an ending.

She'd collected her two best friends from Waverley Station in the Old Town an hour earlier, and they'd insisted she give them a tour of her new office. It was the building Adalyn had mentioned near Jenners. In the end she'd leased all three floors. The ground would be a storefront for Caña Brava and Aida's Cordials. The second floor housed her office as well as Adalyn's and that of the secretary they shared. The third floor was, at the moment, occupied by her newest employee, Mr. Grant. A gentleman she'd hired away from Evan—with his blessing—

to assist her with the shipping side of things. But there would be more staff soon.

Her meeting with Seynabou Cisse-Kelly in Paris had yielded not only Le Bureau as a client, but the proprietor of the pleasure palace had referred other merchants in Luz's direction. By the time she'd arrived in Edinburgh she had dozens of orders for Caña Brava from all over England and Europe. So many orders in fact that she was considering commissioning her own ship to make the transport of her products between Hispaniola and Europe easier.

In truth it was far more than mere progress: the gains she'd made exceeded what she'd thought possible in such a short time. And that was in no small part thanks to Evan. Evan who could barely look at her that morning. Evan who even when he made love to her seemed lost to her.

"Luz, you know I love you." Aurora's voice brought Luz's attention back to the conversation.

"You love me, but?" Luz asked, expecting a reprimand of some kind.

"I love you *and* I have very little patience for all this blustering. Talk to the man."

"Aurora, be kind!" Manuela cried, being the more tolerant of her two friends when it came to matters of the heart.

"What did I say?" Aurora asked innocently. "Besides, I thought she said she had no interest in keeping him."

"Clearly that was a bald-faced lie," Manuela retorted as she put her arm around Luz. "For what it's worth, I think you're wrong about him, Leona." Luz shook her head at her friend's certainty and again wished she could be as brave as Manu, who walked around with her heart wide open for the possibility of love, no matter how badly it was trampled. "Every time that man glances in your direction, he looks as if he's just been struck by lightning."

"He does not appear stunned to me," Luz protested.

Manuela laughed at Luz like she was an adorable but utterly hopeless dolt. "Querida, lightning does not simply *stun*, it grips the whole of your body in a web of electric shocks so powerful they can incinerate you from within. Lightning does not merely stop a man in his tracks, Luz Alana, it changes his footprint."

Luz's pulse raced even as she struggled with the temptation of reaching for the spark of hope her friend's words offered. "I don't see it," she said stubbornly. It was not as if Luz didn't have the manner in which Evan stared at her sometimes branded in her mind. She felt short of breath from merely recalling the way that leonine regard roamed over her skin. Rapacious. Like he was cataloging how he would consume every inch of her.

Perhaps she had imagined it all.

"Then you're missing what anyone can see, Leona." This from her other best friend, who seemed to have turned a corner on opining in matters related to male-induced agitation.

"Then what is he keeping from me?" she asked no one in particular.

"Why don't you *ask* him?" Aurora insisted, this time a touch more gently.

The trouble was she didn't know how.

She'd almost done it today when they'd stared miserably at each other outside Bruce's office for what felt like hours. But asking would be breaking the rules they'd both set for this endeavor, and he had given her no indication that he wished to continue after their agreement was done.

She was convinced he was only allowing her the night at the ball before he told her he wanted a divorce.

"I just don't—"

A knock on the door interrupted what she was about to say.

"Come in, Eliza," Luz called, smiling despite her weariness as she saw Mr. Clark's granddaughter at her door. When Luz had requested Evan's help in finding an assistant for her office, he'd suggested his master blender's granddaughter, who had recently finished a typist course and was looking for work. It was just like Evan to be aware of such a thing, but that was the kind of man he was…and it would do her a world of good to stop reciting his virtues at every opportunity.

"What is it, Eliza?" asked Luz when she noticed that Eliza's usual pleasant smile was particularly radiant.

"My lady, Lord Darnick is here for you." It was a sad state of affairs when one's heart threatened to punch right through one's sternum at the mere mention of their husband. Luz was working on drawing a breath when the man himself appeared on the threshold.

"I need a word, in private."

No prelude, no niceties. Not after he'd lied to her that morning. In an instant the misery from moments before turned into indignation.

How dare he demand things from her when he'd treated her like she was invisible for days?

"I don't think so," she told him. "Whatever you want to say, you can do so in front of my friends."

"This is a very delicate matter, Luz Alana," he told her, then glanced at Aurora and Manuela, who had risen from their chairs seemingly ready to escape from the incoming confrontation.

"Whatever you tell me, they will hear about the moment you walk out of here," Luz countered. "As a matter of fact, I'd appreciate if you were prompt with whatever you are here to discuss, as I have urgent matters to attend to." He didn't react to her dismissive tone, not with words, but she saw his jaw clench as he stared at her.

"And what urgent matter is that?" he finally said, voice taut.

"Luz, we could wait outside," Manuela hedged from the corner. "There are those sketches in Adalyn's office—"

"No, you can stay. Lord Darnick won't be here for long." She returned her gaze to Evan. "We've much to do in getting the Heriot Row house ready for our arrival." Both Aurora and

Manuela gasped in surprise, likely because this was the first time Luz had voiced out loud that she was intending to leave Evan's home. It had been the plan, after all, and it was best for her to start facing up to the reality. She had no time for these games.

Was she acting unreasonably? Probably. Would she stop? Unlikely.

"You are planning to move to the house on Heriot Row." Not a question, not exactly, but he clearly wanted answers.

"Correct," she confirmed, now fully invested in this idea.

"Were you intending to let me know?" he asked, stepping into the office and dwarfing it with his presence. His eyes were on her as if he was trying to pierce her mind, but Luz was like a moth circling a flame now. Spoiling, itching for an argument, desperate to tear through this veil of politeness and pained silences that had smothered her for the last week.

"Why would I need to? This was the plan, and as far as I know, nothing has changed," she said as she made her way to where he stood.

Even through the scruff of his beard she could see his jaw working, the muscles of his face clenching and unclenching. Mouth in a flat, unhappy line, but eyes flashing with something very different to that air of irritation he was exuding. He seemed...fearful.

"I would prefer if we did this alone, Luz Alana." The strain in his voice almost gave her pause. But she was done conceding, compromising.

"And I've already advised you that my friends will stay right where they are." She turned to pin the two women with a challenging look. They seemed desperate to flee out the door, but Luz knew they would endure whatever was about to happen. "So what is this important matter you wish to discuss?" She infused each word with a defiance she did not feel. She knew what was coming, could see in his eyes that whatever he was about to tell her would hurt her. But she would not hide from it, and she would not make it easier for him either. He would have to tell her here, in front of her friends, that he was done with her. Evan moved toward her, but she held up a hand.

"No, I need some distance."

He stopped in his tracks the moment she said the words. "All right." If she let him get close enough to touch her, even a brush of the hand, she'd capitulate. And this conversation needed to happen without her feelings for Evan interfering. His face was serious, but he didn't cower or look away. He was ready to face whatever the consequences of his actions were.

"I've kept something from you," he finally confessed, and the way he said it, wearily but almost prideful, planted a seed of doubt in her mind about what he was here to say. Did she have this all wrong? "My intention at my father's ball is not just to demand he give me the distillery back." She nodded, her mouth clamped shut, as she watched sweat bead on his brow. "I…" Evan shut his eyes for a second, and she saw the vein in his forehead pulse from tension. He clenched and unclenched his fist as he struggled with what he'd come to tell her. But when he glanced down at her, there was a determination there that she recognized. Whatever this was, it had to do with something bigger than the two of them.

"I have a brother, an older brother," he explained.

"Your brother Iain?" she asked, confused.

"No." He shook his head, roughly, his gaze still trained on her. As though keeping his sights on her kept him from going adrift. "Remember how I told you about my father's time in the Caribbean?"

"I do," she said warily. Evan told her about the duke's travels when he was a young man. Back then he'd been the ambitious second son of the Duke of Annan. From what Luz had surmised, the man had departed on his journey with the intent of hunting for his own fortune and had returned a wealthy man three years later to claim the duchy after his father and brother had died.

"He married while he was there and fathered a son with a woman in Cartagena."

Aurora's and Manuela's exclamations startled them both. Evan gave Luz a wry look, as if saying *This is why I wanted to speak with you in private*. But her mind was reeling much too fast to address anything other than Evan's revelation.

"My father married a Colombian heiress, likely for her fortune." She could see his throat working, as if the words kept getting stuck. "She died in childbirth, and he left the boy there before returning to Scotland."

"I don't understand," she mumbled, stunned. "He just abandoned the child and absconded with his dead wife's money?"

"Yes, that's precisely what my father did."

Luz could see how much it was costing him to confess this. The shame and self-loathing seemed to roll off him in waves. "What does this have to do with the distillery? With the ball tomorrow?"

"My brother Apollo—"

"Apollo?" Aurora whispered from the corner. Luz cringed, wishing she had listened to Evan and granted him privacy.

"He helped me find my mother's will," he continued, hands clasped tightly in front of him. "She left a copy of it with her nursemaid at the asylum he put her in, and for the last year we've been looking for it. We finally found it just about a month ago." A month ago, or around the time when he'd proposed the arrangement to her. "I promised I'd support him when he exposed my father's secret and claimed his place as heir apparent, in exchange for him helping me find the evidence to take the distillery back from my father."

"Beatrice and Adalyn don't know?"

He shook his head miserably. "No."

She could see the weight of that secret in the slump of his shoulders. "You'll lose your place," she said in a low voice, now truly regretting her insistence that they have an audience for this.

"Yes." A flash of bitterness came over his face. "I know being married to an earl had more appeal, but it seems you were not planning to stay cleaved to my side much longer. I'm just helping you along in your decision."

Now she was truly angry.

"No," she snapped. "Don't make this about me or my designs on your title. You know very well I don't give a farthing about any of that. It's admirable that you've stood by your brother. I respect the sacrifice you are willing to make to make things right, but you've roped me in as collateral damage to your revenge scheme, and I'm supposed to not ask any questions." She was shaking with fury. He'd let her think he was done with her instead of telling her the truth. "I have my sister and my business to think about. This could put all my plans in jeopardy."

"I will not let this touch you," he told her with the confidence of those who didn't know what it was to be the other.

"You have no control over who chooses to take your father's side on this." She was very close to screaming, and astonishingly her outrage only seemed to temper his mood more. "You allowed me to begin a partnership with your sister, when all the while you were working to blow apart your life—and mine in the process." It wasn't that he didn't tell her, not really. Because in a way she understood that. What she resented was that he had let her believe this was about them.

"I have associates, I have allies that will not turn their backs on me. If your concern is that you'll be left adrift because I will no longer be the heir apparent—"

"Your title has never featured in your lists of attributes, as far as I'm concerned," she said through gritted teeth. "It would be wise for you to remember that I am not your lost love, Charlotte. I am the woman you married for business, and you have not acted in good faith. You gave me your *word* that I would not lose in this." If he only knew just how much she'd lost already.

Her heart, her body, her damned senses.

"You're angry," he said with enraging calm.

"I am not angry." She felt the muscles in her face clench and shift as she fought to keep her temper under control. "I am *furious*. You lied to me, again and again."

"I made a promise to my brother, Luz Alana. It was the only way to get the Braeburn. When I agreed to all this, you weren't—" He bit off the words, and she almost shook his shoulders to demand he say them. "If I could do this again, I would never do anything that would hurt you."

Tell me why. Say the words, damn it! Don't leave me out here in the wind.

"You could've let me know that there were things you could not tell me. My business is everything I have, and if it fails…" Her voice went out then. A flickering candle put out by a gust of wind. Whatever he saw in her face made him move, and suddenly he was inches from her. He placed his hands on either side of her face, and they were so cold. Like the blood had gone completely from his body. This close, she felt the tremors racking through his body. He looked at her with wild, fearful eyes.

This man was terrified.

"You have me. You have everything I have. You have *me*." He ground out the words, as if he wanted to etch them into her. And she would not walk toward that mirage, that sad fever dream of a future of love that she'd made up in her desert of solitude and responsibilities.

"You have me. James Evanston Sinclair, your husband." Calloused and devastatingly gentle fingers wiped her tears. "I want you to stay, Luz Alana, in my house with me. We just need to get through tomorrow—"

"It's not that simple." She shook her head stubbornly, fighting the seductive song of his words, of his promises.

"It appears I've arrived just in time!" a male voice bellowed from outside the office, and Evan's entire body went rigid. They both turned in the direction it came from, and there in the doorway Evan had occupied only minutes before stood a man that could've been her husband's twin.

"What in the world?" Manuela cried, leaning dramatically on the wall as she took in the sight before her. The resemblance was uncanny: the same height and wide shoulders, the whisky-colored eyes and wide, generous mouth. But remarkably the thing that made it impossible to deny them as siblings was the eyebrows. The two men were nearly identical but for Apollo's brown skin.

"What are you doing here, Apollo?" Evan asked, in a tone that indicated he was once again close to losing his battle with control.

Apollo raised one of those piratical Sinclair eyebrows and sauntered into the room.

"I knew you'd cock it up and decided to come and offer my assistance before you lost a limb."

"Do you mind watching your bloody language in front of my wife and her friends?" Apollo barely reacted to Evan's bellowing and turned his attention to Luz.

"Cuñada, es todo un placer," the man said before bending to take her hand as if to kiss it, then he seemed to think better of it and brought her in for a buss on the cheek as was typical between family members in the Caribbean. "He'd been very concerned about his confession resulting in being shot," Apollo murmured loudly to Luz with the clear intention of further enraging his brother.

Luz directed an unfriendly look toward her husband. "He should be concerned."

Apollo thought this uproariously funny and threw his head back with a laugh. "I like you, cuñada." His English was very refined, the only perceptible accent was the way he slightly blurred his consonants; but his Spanish, *that* was from the Caribbean.

"Could you please let go of my wife's hand before I divest *you* of a limb or two?" Evan demanded, as he proceeded to shoulder his brother out of the way and place a very possessive hand at Luz's waist. They certainly behaved as siblings, and despite the veritable cyclone of emotions passing through her, Luz felt proud of Evan.

"La bella doctora," Apollo said, turning his attention to Aurora. "Well, this is a serendipitous coincidence. I did not expect to find you here." The man's smile was absolutely predatory and achieved its effect beautifully, because Aurora's face flushed red instantly. She knew the man?

"Fresco," Luz's friend huffed, arms tight against her chest. "You may call me Doctora Montalban." The man's smile deepened. "You disappeared on me at the Mexican soirée, Doctora. I thought you enjoyed our dance." Amazingly, Aurora's faced reddened further, even as she held her chin up.

"You thought wrong." Aurora bared her teeth pugnaciously at the man, who seemed confoundingly delighted by the gesture.

"I never formally introduced myself, enchanted as I was by your charms." Manuela spluttered at the man's choice of words. "Apollo César Sinclair Robles," he said, extending a hand, which Aurora proceeded to glare at for a full five seconds. Luz decided to interfere before blood was drawn, but Evan reacted first.

"We can take care of introductions at another time," Evan said, clapping a hand on his brother's shoulder a bit too forcefully. "My wife and I have important things to discuss."

"Your wife," Apollo echoed. "Did she forgive you, then?" He turned to Luz. "I would not presume to tell you how to carry out your own affairs, but don't let him off the hook *too* easily."

Luz offered him a forced smile and directed her attention to Evan. "Was it his carriage you got in this morning after we left Mr. Bruce's office?" Luz realized there were more important things to discuss, but this was a detail she wanted to be clear on.

"Yes," Evan answered, brows furrowed in confusion.

"Just trying to keep a tally on the number of lies I need to address."

At least he had the decency to appear remorseful.

"I went to tell him that I would alert you to our plan, that I could not let you attend the ball without knowing what you were walking into."

"And what exactly will I be *walking into*?" She looked between the Sinclair brothers and saw that whatever they intended to do, it was no laughing matter. Evan sent a questioning look toward his brother, who responded with a nod. That's when it dawned on Luz that by telling her in front of Aurora and Manuela, Evan had egregiously violated his promise to Apollo, and he'd done it anyway.

That had to mean *something*.

"We plan to expose my father," Evan said vaguely.

"I'm making my grand entrance as the prodigal son with the great and the good of Scotland for an audience." Evan cringed at his brother's words.

"We plan to confront him about what he did to Apollo's mother," Evan continued.

"And to yours," added Apollo with surprising gentleness, then turned to her. "Luz Alana, I need you to understand that my intention is to destroy my father and his reputation. I will expose his secrets and possibly ruin the family's name forever. Evan is not only aware of this but has been instrumental in helping me every step of the way." There was real affection in Apollo's words, and again Luz Alana felt as though she was juggling more emotions than her constitution was built to manage.

"And you will do this tomorrow, at the ball." Matching nods from the brothers.

"If you don't want to come, I understand." So this had been what his reluctance about her attendance was about. The blasted man could've at least told her it was to do with something outside of his control. Evan did love to play the martyr. She would have to divest him of that habit.

"Absolutely not," she said to her husband. "I want to be there when your father sees the consequences of his actions catching up to him. I want him to see that I knew exactly what you planned to do, what you were willing to lose to set things right, and that I stayed by your side." She poked him in the chest for good measure. "That you still have what he never will—the love and respect of the people around you." She gripped the wrist of the hand he'd placed on her face and looked up at him. "I will not be pleased if the Duke of Annan walks away from this thinking he's bested you."

"He will be angry, Luz Alana," Evan insisted.

"I would like to be there with you to see it." She felt more than heard his rumble of approval at her assertion. "I can't think of a better time to take my first steps among Edinburgh society than on the night they learn one of the oldest dukedoms in the land will pass to the son of a Black Colombian woman. I would not miss it for the world."

She thought she heard a mutter from Apollo that sounded very much like *lucky bastard* and bit back a grin. She would enjoy seeing the duke brought down. Luz only wished Evan had trusted her enough to at least tell her that his aloofness was not to do with her. But she was still not done with obtaining answers, and Evan Sinclair was very far from being forgiven.

"What is your plan after the ball?" she asked, looking between the two men.

"We've been acquiring all of my father's debts. He's been borrowing recklessly for years," Evan explained. "If he refuses to recognize Apollo as the heir or allow us to manage the dukedom, we plan to call in all the debts and ruin him. And after, there is much work to do. We need to make the land profitable for the tenants. I'd like to release them from feudal tithes and work together with them to seek more profitable ways to use the land. Apollo wants to use one of the properties to build a hospital for young mothers."

"Para tu madre," Luz said to Apollo, who only grimaced in answer.

"I'd like to build a sanatorium for young women," Evan said after a long moment. "One where they are treated kindly, where they can rest, and family can visit. For *my* mother. My father confined her in one for the wrong reasons, but she was very fragile. I wonder if in her youth such a place could've helped her."

"I," she said and had to breathe through unfathomable emotions, "I will not abide by anything but seeing your father be absolutely skewered by the two of you."

"I do not want you in the crosshairs of my father's ire, Luz Alana. I cannot back away from this, but I will not put you at risk either." He closed his eyes, mouth in a flat line. "Nothing is more important than this." His eyes looked like embers. "I don't want you to go to Heriot Row. I want you and Clarita to stay with me in Queen Street."

Luz Alana truly regretted not throwing everyone out of her office. "We can discuss this later. We should focus getting through the next day," she told Evan as she pressed in closer to him, desperate to believe in the yearning she heard in his words.

"It seems my work is done here," Apollo said, standing from the armchair he'd commandeered. "I must convey myself to visit each of my sisters and inform them they finally have a brother they can boast about."

"Yes, please leave," Evan said with a roll of his eyes but kept his arms locked tightly around Luz's waist.

"Evan!" Luz rebuked her husband.

"Ingratitude is an ugly trait in a spouse, Luz," Apollo said with feigned regret, making her laugh and Evan growl. "And don't think for a second I came here to assist you in any way.

I was only ensuring you could return your focus to what matters to me."

Luz suspected that wasn't entirely true, but she also didn't think Apollo was quite ready to admit he cared for his brother.

"Please be assured that your brother is poised to receive a *thorough* accounting of all my opinions on his behavior in the past week," she said as she glowered at Evan. For a second he looked almost bashful.

It would be a struggle keeping the flames of her anger at the man.

Apollo departed, though only after impressing upon Aurora a few salacious offers for walks and carriage rides, all of which her friend declined with extreme force. She and Manuela did agree to allow Apollo to escort them back to the house on Queen Street. Luz, and Evan at her side, stood watching them go out into the busy walkway of Princes Street and spryly climb into Apollo's very well-appointed carriage.

"What do we do now?" Evan asked.

Luz turned on him in a flash and pinned him to the window, finger pressed to his chest.

"Now, Lord Darnick, you will begin a slow and very detailed explanation of why you couldn't at least reassure me that whatever was happening was not about us."

He grabbed the finger poking his chest and brought her flush against him.

"Is there an *us*?"

"There better be, now that you've got me embroiled in the biggest scandal of the decade," she groused but still let him take her mouth. When he finally pulled back after a series of hungry, breath-stealing kisses, his brow was furrowed again.

"I am worried about how my father will react, Luz Alana. He is reckless, and he will punish me with what will hurt me most."

"I'm not afraid of the Duke of Annan. Justice is important. Seeing your father pay for what he's done matters. Once that's over, we will take what's ours, and we will build, but you need to finish what you've started with your brother."

"I don't deserve you," he said, voice full of awe, and for the first time in many days, Luz felt hope again.

"You don't, but you will, Evan Sinclair." She pushed onto the tips of her toes and wrapped her arms around his neck. "You will."

Twenty-Two

"How does one accessorize for the social annihilation of a duke?" Manuela asked distractedly as she glanced at herself in the mirror one more time.

"Two dozen Colombian emeralds dangling from your neck ought to do it," offered Aurora with a roll of her eyes.

"Do *I* look all right?" Luz asked the other women and Clarita, shamelessly fishing for words of reassurance. In answer, Amaranta leaned over to straighten the hem of her dress and then stepped back with a satisfied smile. "Perfect."

In a few minutes they'd have to depart to Annan House. Luz had been agitated all day, nervous for herself and for Evan. Evan, who had been quiet and resolute since they'd woken up this morning. He had been out of the house at dawn finalizing the last details with his lawyers, who were poised to descend on the duke with what amounted to an avalanche of injunctions and all manner of legal torpedoes. As far as they were concerned, things were at a standstill. The only thing Evan had asked of her was to give him until things with his father were settled before she made a decision about changing her residence to Heriot Row.

There had been no promises or assurances beyond that.

"You look beautiful, friend." Aurora's rare display of emotion brought Luz back to the moment. It was probably best not to dwell but rather to focus on getting through this evening. She took another look at herself in the long mirror in her bedchamber and smoothed out the bodice of her dress.

She was wearing her favorite gown. It was another of her cousin's creations, made in cobalt blue. She'd considered wearing her dress from the House of Worth, but in the end, she'd decided she wanted to walk into that room armed in something made in the Caribbean. She might not have anything to prove, but that did not mean she didn't like to make a statement when she could.

The raw-silk gown was threaded with gold. The embellishment in a luminescent thread at the hem was done to look like cresting waves. It reminded Luz of the ocean at dusk. The bodice started blue and then became almost solid gold as it reached the edges, and the sleeve caps were adorned with smaller, curling waves.

She smiled at the thought of what Evan would say of her dress...because she was a lovesick fool.

"I have Mama's tiara," Clarita announced in a reverent whisper. Luz extended her arm to bring her little sister to her. She was dressed in blue too, no gray or black. In the last couple of weeks, she'd been slowly choosing things of color to wear, and her interests were...well, they were still very much in the realm of the macabre, but it seemed now she was turning her attention to insects, which was...progress?

"You look beautiful, mi cielo," she told her sister before bending down to press a kiss on the top of her head. Even though Clarita would not attend the ball, Beatrice had invited her to spend the night at her home with the twins. They had an evening of games and treats planned, which Clarita and Katherine had decided would work best if they dressed as though they were to attend the ball themselves.

"We all look beautiful," Clarita declared. And they *were* a sight, Luz thought. Amaranta, who usually preferred to stay behind, was for once coming out for an evening with other adults. Her cousin was wearing a royal purple and silver gown that brought out her dark skin. Aurora and Manuela were equally majestic in burgundy and chartreuse.

"No one can say women from the tropics dress to blend in," Aurora quipped as Manuela helped Luz with the tiara. Her mother's tiara had been the last anniversary gift Luz's father had given her before she passed away. It was a circlet of gold orange blossoms with round Dominican blue amber stones set at the center of the flower. There were a few tear-shaped pieces of amber interspersed between the petals that gave the effect of unopened buds. Her mother never got to wear it, and Luz had only done so a few times. Tonight she would on Evan's arm, possibly for the last time as his wife.

A hand instinctually went to her sternum at the thought.

A knock came at the door that joined her and Evan's chambers, and her heart kicked around in that frantic way it did whenever the man entered the room.

"May I come in?" How was it possible that just the man's voice made every bone in her body turn to water?

"We'll wait for you in the drawing room," Amaranta said as she guided Clarita and the Leonas to the door.

Evan stepped inside quietly. He moved so gracefully for such a big man.

"You are…" He never finished his thought, stopping in his tracks to stare at her.

"Oh," she whispered breathlessly as he came into full view. She had not been prepared for James Evanston Sinclair in full Highland regalia.

The Earl of Darnick was a sight in his red, green, blue and yellow tartan. Despite tonight's ball being in his father's honor, Evan had decided to don the pattern of his mother's clan and not that of the Sinclairs. Luz's father, being a Lowlander, had never worn kilts or sporrans, and given the rupture between him and his family, she doubted he would've worn the colors of the Heith clan.

In truth, she'd never had much of a connection to Scottish lore, but she could see how women had swooned for the likes of Malcolm Graeme and Lochinvar. Evan was magnificent in his silk slippers. His socks covered his strong, muscled calves and the traditional sgian dubh was tucked into the one on his right leg. His jacket, which ended at his waist, was molded to his lean torso. He'd trimmed his beard, and his amber eyes shone as he examined her, his gaze carefully making its way over every inch of her. A mixture of that bewildered tenderness and unbridled lust he seemed to evoke in her warred with her more rational self.

She noticed he had a folded piece of Buchanan tartan in his hands.

"I brought this for you," he said, his voice roughened.

"Oh." She knew the significance wearing the family tartan had for Highlanders, and this one in particular was a sacred thing for his mother's clan.

"It will be cold tonight." He came to stand behind her and draped the fabric on her shoulder. It was lined with velvet and felt decadent against her skin. He kept his arms around her, clutching the ends of the tartan in front of her chest, then buried his face in her neck. He inhaled her skin, one deep, long breath as if he wanted to acquire her very essence. He pressed a kiss to her oversensitive skin, and she immediately melted against him. She wanted to turn around and kiss him in earnest, but he spoke before she could.

"Once Apollo arrives, I want you to leave the ball and come back here." She stiffened at the request, but he spoke again before she could voice her protest. "Murdoch will make sure you get out of there safely."

He sounded like a man preparing for war, and she would not make it harder for him.

"All right." She nodded as a hole opened in her stomach. Nerves, and more for him than for her. "Will Beatrice and Adalyn leave then too?" He gave a sharp nod, his nose buried in her hair.

"They will arrive with Gerard."

"Do Gerard and Murdoch know?" she asked, and Evan sighed.

"After telling you and my sisters, I think Apollo is finally starting to believe he has allies in this beyond me."

She smiled at that, glad for Apollo and for Evan both. "Are you sure you want to do this?" he asked…again.

"Evan," she warned, and he smiled despite the worry shadowing his eyes.

"My lioness," he said, pride and something she would not dare name shining in his eyes. He offered his arm to her, and she slid her hand through it, then rose to press a kiss to his lips.

"Take me to the ball, husband."

"Promise me you will not dally once Apollo and I confront my father."

"I promise." He wished he'd insisted on leaving her at home. This was a bad idea, but it was as if he had lost the ability to use the word *no* when it came to this woman.

"*You* will look for Murdoch and board the carriage he will have ready for you, the Leonas and my sisters."

"I like it when you call us Leonas," she said with a satisfied little smile that made a riot of bats—it could not be butterflies— swerve in his chest. "But if anything goes awry as we make our escape, I am prepared." She hiked up the copious layers of fabric in her skirt to reveal a luscious expanse of golden-brown skin covered in a shimmery silk stocking, where she'd strapped that beloved little pistol of hers. His mouth went dry, and his tongue stuck to the roof of his mouth at the sight. His Amazon, ready for battle, ready for anything life threw at her.

He brought her onto his lap, and she immediately wrapped her arm around his neck. His pulse thrummed at the easiness between them.

"You are bloody magnificent, did you know that?" he asked, sliding a hand over that warm skin.

"I am aware, yes." She preened and leaned back on the seat, letting him admire her, like the bloody queen she was.

"If I make very quick work of it, I could have a taste before we arrive," he only half teased as he pressed a hand suggestively to her core. There was enough space for him to kneel…

She shook her head with a groan, even as she pressed into him.

"We'll never get my dress back in order in time," she said regretfully.

"You're right. We'd best leave it for after. I'll want to take pains with you." She moaned and writhed over him in response to his heated promise. He'd finish all this once and for all, and then he'd go home and worship his woman like she deserved.

He'd give anything to be able to keep this. He prayed that he could.

"Don't worry about me. I'll abide to the plan," she assured him, right before brushing their lips together. "When is Apollo arriving?" she pressed, and he felt a smile forming against her lips.

His wife did not like surprises. "I've arranged for a particular song to be played after we arrive. Apollo will be outside in his carriage. Once the piece ends, that will be his signal to come inside."

The carriage pulled to a stop then. Evan's head swam, blood pounding between his temples as they disentangled themselves and stepped down. He tried to breathe through it to no avail, and then a small warm hand slid into his, and he held on to it like it was an anchor in a tempestuous sea.

"Do you need a dram?" she asked, her steady voice an unexpected reassurance.

"No, I am all right."

The line of guests awaiting to enter the ball was a long one. The Duke of Annan's annual birthday ball was a highlight of the year, and everyone came out for the occasion. It was the one event when Scottish high society gathered in Edinburgh. Otherwise, most of the social engagements of the season were hosted in London. And the duke and duchess had lavishly spent Evan's money for the occasion. The entrance to the ballroom was a tunnel made of what seemed to be thousands of white roses.

"Is that her?" Luz Alana asked in a chilly voice as they crossed the threshold into the foyer of the house. From where they stood, there was a clear view to the bottom of the marbled staircase where his father and Charlotte greeted their guests as they arrived.

"Yes, that's the duchess." He tightened his hold on his wife and leaned down to whisper in her ear. "This is the perfect moment to let you know you are the most beautiful woman here."

"You only say that because you'd like to finish what you started earlier." Her smile was that bright, guileless one that made him feel he was in the presence of something too pure for human eyes. But there was a glimmer of doubt in there too. She didn't know where she stood with him.

Impulsively he pulled her out of the line of guests, needing a moment to say the words that were brimming inside him.

"I said it because even after the secrets I kept from you, the pain I caused you with my silence, you are here ready to walk into this nest of vipers with me." Her eyes widened at whatever she saw in his face, but he was done hiding from her. From himself and what he felt for Luz Alana. "Because at every step of the way you've shown me that I had no idea, not an inkling, of what it is to be loyal and faithful and strong. Because *you* have, with your smile—" he traced her lips with his thumb as he breathed through a firestorm of emotions "—and your unrelenting, unshakable spirit have taught me how to hope again." His chest heaved with big, heavy breaths as he poured his heart out to her, before going in to do his duty to his brother. "Once this is done and I've wiped myself clean of the mire of this miserable mess, I will earn the chance to take my place by your side."

"Evan," she gasped, eyes glistening with unshed tears. The words were on the tip of his tongue, needing to come out.

"The Earl of Darnick and Lady Darnick," one of his father's footmen announced, forcing them to cut the moment short. Unhurriedly—his father could wait—he leaned down and placed a chaste kiss on her lips. Then he took her hand and the stairs, and for the first time since all of this started he allowed himself to consider what it would be like to be rid of his title, of the implications of it. The one thing that he felt coursing through his veins was an urgency to be on the other side of this, so he would finally be free to tell Luz Alana exactly what he wanted for their future.

"Ah, the new Lady Darnick." His father's caustic voice pulled Evan out of his thoughts, and he had to fight the urge to place himself like a human shield between the man and Luz Alana.

"Your Grace." Luz Alana curtsied expertly. "It's a pleasure to finally meet you."

"I was beginning to wonder if the news of my son's marriage was just parlor-room fodder." The man pursed his mouth into something he likely thought was a smile but looked more like an ugly sneer. "After years of applying pressure to my son in every way I could—" like threatening to disown him, sell the distillery and squander Adalyn's dowry, all of which he'd done anyway, Evan thought bitterly "—he goes to Paris on business..." he paused on the word *business*, which he'd uttered with the same tone one would expect to hear *vermin* "...and returns with a wife."

"Father," Evan warned, but the older man continued to direct his fictitious graces in Luz Alana's direction. If she was nervous or out of sorts, she hid it perfectly. Her back was ramrod straight. Ready for the arrows she expected to be aimed at her.

"It's all right, darling," she told Evan. "My apologies for not giving you prior warning of my existence before it became an unescapable reality, Your Grace."

"Do you know what the word for *wife* is in the Spanish colonies?" his father asked, surprising him.

"*Former* colonies," Luz Alana corrected with the sweetness of an adder, which his father noted with another one of those sneers.

"*Handcuffs,*" the man said with a bloodcurdling laugh.

"What are you talking about?" Evan spat out, unable to hide his annoyance.

"Handcuffs. It's the same word as *wife, esposas,*" the duke explained, completely ignoring Evan. "The best part is that the word for mistress is *querida,* which means *beloved,*" he added with relish as Evan gritted his teeth.

"It must be jarring." Luz Alana's voice surprised Evan's father, and the older man turned to her with an expression of unguarded curiosity. "The British do love all things to be in their place." Defiance blazed in her dark eyes, and she turned to Evan. "I suppose your father is not accustomed to seeing women with my countenance in the wife box, darling."

She made sure her tone was as bright as the lights flickering on the chandeliers, but Evan did not miss the way his father paled at her words. "Thankfully my husband was able to surmise without any trouble that the woman he desired and the one he married could be one and the same."

Evan's chest puffed up her possessiveness while his father spluttered.

"How delightfully abrupt." Charlotte's caustic observation seemed to ricochet off the walls. At one time Evan had thought her one of the most lovely women in Edinburgh, and she was still that.

But it was such a hazardous beauty.

"She's lovely, Evan," she said, as if Luz Alana wasn't standing right there. He opened his mouth to say something, but Charlotte was not done yet. "You could always find beauty in places others might not."

He rushed to interrupt whatever else Charlotte was intending to say, but once again Luz Alana held her own.

"Forgive me, Your Grace, but I quite disagree with that assessment." His wife's smile could cut glass. "European men have always been quite adept in seeing the beauty in women who look like me. It's our *humanity* they've failed to recognize." That Luz delivered with eviscerating cordiality. "Women like you see it too. How else does one explain the cruelty of so many mistresses to the women who worked for them?"

Charlotte's sly little smile faltered, and the duke's face flushed to an alarming puce. Evan felt some of the tightness inside him loosen. Others might underestimate Luz Alana, but *he* should know doing so was a mistake.

"You've got a sharp-tongued one, Evan," his father said, openly disapproving.

"I'm very fortunate," he said, eliciting a chortle from Luz Alana, but before his father could react the raucous noise coming from the entrance announced the arrival of the cavalry he'd been promised. Beatrice, Gerard, Adalyn, Murdoch and the Leonas breezed in, pushing Evan and Luz Alana out of the receiving line and away from his father and Charlotte. Once the proper greetings were proffered, they all made their way into the ballroom.

"What did you say to Charlotte?" Adalyn asked Luz the moment they reached her, her face alight with curiosity.

"Oh, I just enlightened her on some pieces of history she seems to have missed."

Evan had to swallow a laugh as their group made their way farther into the room, when his sister leaned in, visibly excited. "There's the rear admiral!" she said in a hushed tone that somehow still managed to sound like a scream.

Then in an equally loud whisper Murdoch added, "With the *countess*."

"This is a remarkably unfortunate turn of events," Gerard muttered, just as Luz Alana asked why that was a problem.

"The very, very short version," Addy said through impressively unmoving lips—when it came to sharing ballroom gossip the girl was practically a ventriloquist—"Evan had a...*special friendship* with the Countess of Killian. He ended it. She made her unhappiness about this rupture known quite vocally. She's coming to say hello, and the man with her is Charlotte's uncle, the rear admiral." Adalyn's cringe likely mirrored his own face.

This was not a good development.

"Mierda," whispered his lovely wife, which her friends echoed with equal gusto. "Exactly how many women you've bedded will I have to encounter this evening, darling?" Luz asked sweetly, her eye trained on the countess and the rear admiral who were now only a few feet away. Murdoch chuckled behind them, while Evan's face flamed.

"Lord Darnick." The countess was a beautiful woman, but she was also an accomplished fencer and an outspoken advocate for women's suffrage. She'd even been an adventurous lover, but she'd been fickle and temperamental in a way that Evan had found...trying. Her husband, the Earl of Killian, was almost two decades her senior and did not share her views on almost anything. Taking lovers was one of the ways she rattled the cage she was in. He thought that under different circumstances she and Luz Alana could've been friends, but the pinched expression in his former paramour's mouth told him that was highly unlikely.

"Countess, Rear Admiral," Evan said, aiming for obstinately pleasant. "May I introduce you to my wife, Lady Darnick." He wondered when the urge to pound his chest whenever he called Luz his wife would subside.

"*A wife*. Where have you been hiding her?"

Luz Alana frowned at the countess but extended a hand nonetheless.

"Oh, I wasn't in hiding, I was in the *Dominican Republic*." If Luz Alana's smile could cut, this ball would be a carnage. "Then I was selling rum in Paris."

He was awed by wife's skill in achieving a friendly tone that was also undeniably dangerous.

"Your gown is very pretty," the woman commented, eyes sliding over Luz, assessing. "Not Worth. I know his lines," the woman said haughtily, but Luz remained entirely unaffected. "And it has no bustle, so it must be from an earlier season."

The rear admiral sent his companion a disapproving look at that. It was not the thing at all to comment on a woman's dress in that disparaging way. Evan was about to interject, but his wife gripped his hand in hers in warning. She'd asked him once before to not interfere in situations like these, and he finally understood why.

Soothing his pride mattered less than her ability to stand up for herself. His place was not as her savior but as her sentinel. Luz Alana Sinclair-Heith could fight her own battles.

"As you so cleverly observed, this gown in particular is not from Worth. But when I went for a fitting with Mr. Worth in the rue de la Paix, he personally advised me to forego the bustle," she informed the woman, sliding a gloved hand along the side of her gown. "You see, given my lines," she said as her hand went up her side again, "the bustle would be redundant." She tipped her chin infinitesimally in the direction of the countess's bustle. "The enhancement isn't necessary for me."

Murdoch choked in reaction to the expertly delivered insult, and Bea's and Addy's coloring instantly went to that of ripe tomatoes, while the Leonas looked like a pair of assassins who were only there to confirm their target had been dealt with. His wife simply fluttered her eyelashes, the very picture of a cherub, then turned her attention the rear admiral, who seemed duly impressed with the verbal evisceration she'd just delivered.

"Rear Admiral," she said with that same charming smile, although this one seemed less sanguinary.

"Lady Darnick, it is a pleasure." The man looked genuinely happy to meet her. "Welcome to our city. You are from Hispaniola."

"I am." Her tone changed slightly then, and he saw the shift in her countenance he'd seen when they'd been with Dairoku.

His wife was getting ready to sell her rum.

"Rear Admiral, I hope I am not being too forward," she demurred in that sweet-as-honey way she had of speaking when she was ready to move in for the kill.

This woman was perfectly capable of reaching for her dreams, of making them happen: all she needed was to be allowed in the door. He'd happily spend his life bursting them wide open for her, just to see what heights she could reach. "Lady Adalyn and I are in the process of developing a line of medicinal tinctures, syrups and cordials."

"Is that so?" the man asked, intrigued.

"Yes, and we thought they might be of interest to you."

"With so many sailors, you may be looking for high-quality medicinal drafts to carry onboard," Addy contributed. Evan loved seeing a fire in his sister's eyes again. For so long he thought she'd never regain that old spark of hers, but he could see it now. Once again, he thanked whatever deity was responsible for putting Luz Alana in his path.

"I know you must be familiar with the Dama Juana in Hispaniola, and the syrups are particularly useful for mixing with remedies or tonics."

"That's the concoction with the rum and the roots?"

"It is, sir," Luz confirmed as the man mused over their offer.

"Send me some samples," he told the two women. "I will be placing an order of whisky from your husband soon and can add your products to that order."

"Along with a good quantity of my wife's rum," Evan added, to which the admiral laughed amiably.

"I need to make an escape before this ambush depletes my entire budget," The admiral complained, but his open countenance said he was enjoying himself.

As they exchanged goodbyes, Evan noticed that the countess's combative expression had morphed into something akin to respect.

"Lady Darnick, I host a salon for women in business here in Edinburgh," she told Luz, then turned to Adalyn. "Perhaps you and Lady Adalyn could join sometime."

Luz seemed stunned for a moment but recovered in time to dip her head in assent. "I would like that," she said, sounding genuinely pleased.

After the admiral and the countess excused themselves, the others dispersed to find refreshments and look around the ballroom as they awaited Apollo's arrival. As the orchestra played a waltz, Evan marveled again at how little appetite he had for what would transpire tonight. For months, *for years*, he'd dreamed of finally seeing his father destroyed, and now that he was poised to do so, he only wished he had more time to dance with his wife.

"Always refreshing to befriend my husband's former lovers," Luz Alana said without much heat as they walked to the edge of the ballroom.

"You don't have to attend the salon."

She looked up at him with canny eyes. "I will give her the benefit of the doubt. I am certain I won't be receiving many invitations, so I might as well take up the ones I do get." Her gaze heated then, pinning him to where he stood. "And this might come as a surprise to you, but I don't make a habit of seeing women as my competition. Though it's true I am not what one would call experienced in *affaires du coeur*—" his lips tipped up at her droll tone "—I am not spending my energy fighting for your attentions when I know exactly what I must do to get them."

"Is that so?" he asked, licking his dry lips as he watched her inviting bosom.

"Yes, it is." She sounded a little breathless, and it was requiring every ounce of his self-control not to ravage her on the spot.

"You're playing with fire, wife," he warned, and she taunted him by biting the thumb he was grazing over her bottom lip. He had to suck in a breath and stepped closer. "First you set my blood on fire by alluding to one of my favorite parts of your anatomy in front of the rear admiral." That salacious smile that he knew promised every wickedness—it made him weak. "And now you provoke me in front of all these people?"

"And what will you do about it, husband?" Luz teased. Evan looked down at her, resplendent in blue and gold.

Too beautiful, too pure for him, but he would devote himself to earning the right to call her his own.

"A dance might help put out this fire." He pulled her to him just as the music was changing. After the first notes swept through the room, his wife made a noise of delighted surprise.

"Is that 'Felices Dias' by Morel Campos?" She tipped her head up to him, brows knitted together.

"It is," he said as they moved together, feeling proud of himself for putting that delighted smile on her face. "Apollo knew the piece too, which was serendipitous."

"*You* are a romantic, James Evanston." She pressed herself to him and let him guide her around the room.

"You make me one, Luz Alana."

He truly had never been one before. Always ruthlessly practical, but the moment this woman had come into his life, the things which had seemed all-important simply ceased to matter.

"Mm." She made a happy sound as she burrowed into his

arms, then squealed when he pressed her closer. "Is that your sporran or is the kilt malfunctioning?"

He threw his head back and laughed so hard a few of the dancers around them stopped to stare. "Luz Alana," he said simply. There was nothing more he needed to say. Those two words had grown to mean more than anything else in his life.

"It's almost time," she whispered close to his ear.

It was, merely minutes. A year planning this night, almost a decade waiting for this moment, but this victory tasted very different than he'd imagined. When only a month ago he couldn't see beyond what would happen in the next hour, now all he wanted was what came after. The irony of building a road to a destination he now didn't want to travel.

He'd blaze new trails, for her.

"Stay with me," he whispered, gathering her into his arms, until her feet almost left the ground.

They stayed like that until the piece ended, the last joyful notes echoing in the room before fading away entirely. His heart began beating faster in anticipation as he pulled his wife by the hand to walk off the dance floor with his eyes trained on his father.

He was still standing by the entrance of the ballroom, talking to a couple Evan recognized as the Viscount and Viscountess of Graith. His father was holding court when one of his footmen rushed to him and pulled him aside. Evan saw the confusion turn to anger in his father's face, but before the man could respond, Apollo's booming voice echoed through the ballroom.

"Hello, brother," Apollo called across the crowded room to Evan as the music stopped.

"My brother," Evan called back as every person in the ballroom seemed to freeze at once. "I'm so glad you could join us on this, our dear father's birthday." The duke had turned to where the voice had come from and turned gray when he got a good look as his firstborn's face.

If Evan had had any doubts about Apollo's legitimacy, the dismayed realization in his father's face would've dispelled them. Soon two more footmen appeared with their sights on Apollo, but he kept barreling toward Evan through that tunnel of flowers, emerging from it like he truly was a son of Olympus.

"Go, I'll be all right," Luz told him, tipping her chin in the direction of Murdoch, who was striding toward them and flanked by Manuela and Aurora on either side. Right behind them Evan could see his sisters, Amaranta and Gerard.

"I'll see you at home," she said firmly, before standing on her tiptoes to kiss him on the mouth, while the entire retinue of guests gaped at Apollo in morbid astonishment.

He almost told her then, in an urge to not leave anything unsaid before he walked away from her, but that was not something he wanted tarnished by this moment.

He'd do his duty first.

"Please don't wait. Go now," he whispered in her ear as Apollo reached them with his father and what seemed like every male member of the duke's household staff on his heels.

"Cuñada," his brother said, smiling in Luz Alana's direction.

"Cuñado," she said with a dip of her head and a smile on her lips that did not reach her eyes, as the duke's voice boomed throughout the room. "Please get yourselves back in one piece," she whispered, then turned to the Duke of Annan with a haughty expression. "Your Grace."

Evan ignored his father for another second as he watched his wife walk over to join their family before heading to the exit. His sisters didn't spare their father a second look. They did, however, make a point of going up to Apollo and kissing him on the cheek before making their way up the stairs and out of their childhood home possibly for the last time.

"What is the meaning of this?" his father shouted, for once seemingly unfazed by who might witness his embarrassment. Evan noticed that Charlotte had disappeared right as he opened his mouth to inform his father exactly what the meaning of *this* was, but Apollo spoke first.

"Do you remember Violeta Robles Castillo? The woman whose fortune you stole, you thieving, lying bastard?" Apollo's voice shook only when he said his mother's name, as gasps and maligned protests echoed through the room at whoever dared insult the Duke of Annan.

"Who are you?" the duke demanded, and Evan almost closed his eyes to not have to see the bleakness on Apollo's face as their father looked at him with naked loathing. Another victim caught in his father's endless trail of self-indulgence and destruction.

"He's your son." Evan projected his voice so that everyone in that room would know the duke's shame. He was beyond caring what any of these people thought.

The glass in his father's hand crashed to the marble floor, the sound ricocheting off the walls like a gunshot. For a breathless instant the three of them stared at the mess of jagged shards and the pool of amber liquid spreading on the floor.

Then the duke turned cold, hard eyes on Evan, his face suddenly pale and old. He knew what was coming, but for a second, Evan hoped that for once in his life his father would do the right thing. If only to spare Apollo.

"Send everyone home, and find my wife," he ordered his footmen, turning on his heel and walking out of the ballroom.

Twenty-Three

It was anticlimactic to walk quietly out of the crowded room and down the hallway leading to his father's study. Evan felt as if he was in a dream. The family portraits that had been there since he was a child seemed eerily distorted now. As though every one of them was scowling at him for exposing their treachery to the world.

By the time they crossed the threshold into the study, Apollo appeared unwell, his usual easiness gone, his expression grave. It dawned on him that as much as his brother had prepared for this, he could not have anticipated just how vile their father could be.

Apollo's need to see his mother's death avenged had brought him here, but Evan didn't think there was anything that could arm a man against seeing such hate in his own father's eyes. It could make anyone stumble. But after a lifetime of dealing with his father's cravenness, Evan was utterly unmoved by the Duke of Annan's fits of pique. If necessary he would fight this battle for them both.

"Evanston, you will pay for embarrassing me," his father spat out the moment they entered the room, spittle flying out his mouth.

"We embarrassed *you*?" Evan laughed, and it sounded almost hysterical. He turned to Apollo, who was visibly shaken. "When my brother first came to me and revealed what you'd done, I wanted to believe that perhaps you didn't know. I told myself that there was a possibility you'd really thought your child was dead. That not even you would do something so depraved." The duke's mouth moved without speaking, and for an instant Evan considered the room they were in. The elegant drapery made in the finest damask, the exquisite moldings on the ceiling, the lustrous dark wood tables and supple leather on the Chesterfield chairs. The fireplace made with red Languedoc marble. Every luxury and comfort imaginable for someone who did not deserve it.

How many lives had been laid to waste so that the Dukes of Annan could sit in this room?

"You're a fucking monster," Evan muttered, disgusted.

His father threw his head back, roaring with laughter.

"I'm the monster? I did what I had to for this family, to keep this line *alive*." The older man's words were fueled with the fervency that had always terrified Evan. "My own father forgot his obligations and squandered our fortune for his so-called cause." That last word was delivered with absolute disgust. "And I made sacrifices to fix it, even if I had to put my conscience aside to fulfill my duty."

"The duty of lying, stealing and exploiting others so you can live in opulence," Evan said woodenly.

His father's lips turned up in a bitter smile that chilled Evan to his very core.

"The duty of the *dukedom*. And now like a fool you've gone and thrown away your own legacy. I knew that deluded need of yours to be absolved would end in destruction. You are a disgrace." He'd wondered if he could still feel anything when it came to his father, but the only thing Evan felt was exhaustion.

"If you had any chance of getting the deed to that distillery, it is completely gone."

Evan almost laughed at his father's imperiousness.

"I would be very careful about making threats," Apollo warned, then his lips turned up into a vicious smile. "Why don't you tell our father, brother?"

"I am not your father," the Duke of Annan blustered, and that vicious smile on Apollo's lips turned sinister.

"Oh, we both know that you are," Apollo said with astonishing calm. "And I have plenty of proof attesting to that fact, because if there is one thing that your lot is not, when you go on your feeding frenzies to the tropics, it's prudent. But I'll reserve my own tale for later. Now it's Evan's turn, and I advise you to listen…quietly."

Their father pressed his lips together at Apollo's words, the older man's face turning ashen as he looked between Evan and Apollo, as though he finally realized there would be no denying a truth anyone with eyes could see.

"I have a copy of my mother's will." Evan recited the words he'd spoken in his head so many times and watched with little satisfaction as his father's world began to unravel around him. "I also have a letter in her hand saying that you put her in that asylum after she confronted you for siphoning money from Beatrice's and Adalyn's dowries. You bloody parasite."

His father stumbled, but only for a second. "It will take years to prove those are authentic," the duke countered.

"It's already been validated by the solicitor's son as legitimate. And in the box with the will, Mother left each of us an heirloom from the Buchanan family. Did you not see grandmother's aquamarine ring on my wife's finger?"

His father's eyes bulged, and he cried with outrage. It was so melodramatic and obscene, and yet Evan thought it was the first genuine emotion he'd seen from the man in years.

"Anyone can claim anything," his father said, his typical unbothered demeanor crumbling under the weight of what Evan claimed. "No one will take your word against mine. Neither will they believe this interloper is my son."

"They don't have to believe me." Apollo continued pushing the dagger in without mercy. "But they will have to consider the marriage record I obtained from the priest who married you and my mother. They can't ignore the photographs from the wedding breakfast the Italian photographer took. Or my aunt's testimony."

"Your aunt?" His father recoiled. "She died."

Apollo looked at his father with a mixture of horror and satisfaction.

"My mother had two sisters. The woman you handed me to with orders to get rid of me used your blood money to find the one who still lived." Their father's face was completely devoid of color now, his pallor a sickly gray. His hand, which had been on the back of one of the armchairs, began shaking so profusely the thing began to rattle. "Fidelina took me to my aunt and told her what you'd done, and she raised me as her own. My aunt's husband owned most of the coffee in Colombia and Venezuela, and they had no heirs. I have more money than I know what to do with, and I am willing to use it all to see you destroyed. You buried my mother in an unmarked grave." Apollo's eyes were bleak, the words spilling out of him now. "She had a family, she had a name, and you put her in the ground like she was nothing."

The familiar pain in his brother's voice, the hollowness in his eyes, all but broke Evan.

"Everyone fathered bairns in the colonies," the duke cried, as if the injustice was Apollo's recriminations and not his own actions. "Why do I have to see my legacy ruined over it?"

"Because he is your son!" Evan roared, utterly done. "If all the children the Scots and the English have fathered and abandoned in the places they've gone to ransack arrived here to hold them accountable for their mischief, our population would probably double overnight." Evan spat the rest, uncaring if anyone still left at the ball heard him—hoping they would and that this farce could end, finally. "You are sickening, always so self-important when you're nothing but a common thief."

"How dare you?" his father blustered, but now there was real fear in his voice.

"How dare I what? Tell the truth? That we went to war with the English to fight for our land and our humanity, then we took to the seas and forgot it all. That we became monsters ourselves. All for the sake of this," he said and gestured to the gilded moldings on the ceiling, the treasures that had been bought with money not a single one of the masters of this house had ever worked for. "To continue to sit in opulent rooms with marble fireplaces and denounce mentions of money because they're much too vulgar for polite conversation. After we sold our souls for it!" His chest heaved from his words, and he felt light-headed with rage and repulsion, as his father looked at him through narrowed eyes.

"You have so much to say about our dastardly ways. And yet here you are in your finery, having come from your townhome on Queen Street. You are no better than any of us, Evanston, and don't pretend that you are. That monstrosity, as you call it, is your legacy too."

"It is, and I cannot change it, but I *can* choose a different path. I will stand up with my brother against you, Father. I will see you held accountable for this." Blood pounded in his temples, but Evan felt like he could take a full breath of air for the first time in his life.

"We will be outcasts. No one with an ounce of standing will ever look our way again," his father accused, eyes filled with abhorrence. "You have ruined us, destroyed our family's good name."

"You and I have very different notions of what constitutes a good name."

"You bloody fool." There was almost a note of incomprehension in his father's voice.

"Enough," Apollo bellowed from the dark corner he'd retreated to as Evan and his father rowed. His brother's expression was cold, deadly. There was not a trace of his usual sarcastic humor, or even the placidness from before. This was a man bent on revenge, on destruction. Menace rolled off him, and it was entirely directed toward their father.

For once, the man seemed to heed the threat coming his way.

His brother stopped so that he was standing shoulder to shoulder with Evan and leaned in, finger pointed at the duke, who in the last ten minutes seemed to have aged a century.

"I have spent the last twenty years planning every detail of how I would take everything from you. To humiliate you, sully your name. *I* will replace you."

His father roared with fury, but Apollo's booming voice shut him up. "You took my life, and now I *own* yours."

"What do you mean?" the duke asked in a small, terrified voice. Apollo's grin was chilling.

"We own every debt you accrued, happily, recklessly buying baubles for yourself."

"You can't do this. I am a duke." Their father gaped at them like a landed fish.

"And I am your heir, Father," Apollo declared. "Tomorrow evening, you will come to meet us, and you will sign a statement to be read in the House of Lords, explaining that you had been unaware your firstborn had survived. That you fully recognize me as the heir apparent, and that from now on my brother and I will manage the holdings of the dukedom."

"I will do no such thing."

"This is not a request," Evan shouted. "You have bankrupted this duchy, and it will take money to fix it. The lands and the tenants are in a desperate state. We are not asking you, we are *ordering* you. That is how things will transpire from now on. We give the orders, you obey them, or you will be destitute. You are a puppet now, which should suit you fine," he said with a dismissive flick of his hand. "It's how you've always lived, after all, as if the world is your theater." Evan's gut twisted as his father looked on with the expression of a child who could not understand what he was being told.

This kingdom, *this country*, had waged war and destruction far and wide to keep grown men in this infantilized delusion.

"If it's the last thing I do," his father warned, "I will destroy *everything* you love." Something about the older man's tone, the unhinged wretchedness in his voice, gave Evan pause. There was nothing more dangerous than an entitled man with nothing to lose.

"And what do you love, Your Grace?" Apollo asked, and Evan braced for the final blow they'd wield at their father tonight. "Your duchess? The one you descend further and further in debt to keep in jewels and House of Worth gowns?"

Impossibly the duke's face paled further. "What have you done to my wife?" the duke asked weakly.

Apollo's grin was a blade, ready to draw blood. "Nothing but offer her some options," Apollo said simply, "which she eagerly took." His brother made a show of pulling out his pocket watch.

"Where is she?" the duke asked shakily, standing up from the chair he'd collapsed in and walking to the door, flinging it open. "My wife," he bellowed, as if expecting Charlotte to materialize by command. Apollo clicked his tongue regretfully, his gaze on the duke's pathetic display.

"I'm afraid they may not be able to fetch her for you. If I'm not mistaken, the duchess should be on her way to the Continent with her lover by now."

It took a moment for Apollo's words to take effect, but Evan saw the precise instant his father understood. This time, he saw genuine pain in the older man's face.

Charlotte's betrayal had struck him to the heart.

"Is that what this is all about?" the duke asked Evan. "I took her from you, and now you are taking her from me?"

Evan had not involved himself in this part of the plan but agreed with Apollo that any wife of the duke should have the chance of escaping whatever fate awaited her. Charlotte had not hesitated to take the offer. Evan thought of Luz Alana's words about women's choices, and despite everything, in that moment he wished Charlotte some happiness if she was able to find it.

"There is nothing of yours I want, Father."

"You will pay for this," his father threatened, toothlessly.

"We have all paid dearly already." Evan turned to leave. "Now it's your turn."

Despite the turmoil and worry coursing through him, Evan instantly felt at peace when the carriage came to a stop in front of his town house. He knew without a doubt that Luz Alana would be waiting for him inside.

He wanted that for the rest of his life.

Coming home to this woman could be the North Star of his existence, and he'd die knowing his life had been filled with purpose. Before he made a move to descend from the carriage, he turned to Apollo.

"Will you come in for a dram?"

Evan warmed when Apollo's serious expression changed into obvious pleasure at the invitation. Then he ruined it by opening his mouth.

"I'm not sure it's the right hour to enliven your home with my presence."

This time Evan laughed at his brother's transparent attempt to provoke him.

"Don't you want to make a plan for tomorrow?" he asked, head swimming with the possibilities of what his father could be plotting.

"We have a plan," Apollo reminded him. They did. They'd considered every possible scenario. Even one where his father retaliated with violence. The staff of Apollo's estate near Aberdeen was ready for their arrival if they needed to leave Edinburgh. Beyond that, Evan had a cottage in the north of France also available.

"But we need to—"

Apollo shook his head.

"You have a beautiful woman waiting for your safe return. Our father has stolen too much of our time, Evan. Don't let him rob you of this too." The impact of his brother's words almost made him double over.

"You're right," he said, sounding winded.

"It's about time you started listening to your older, wiser... and better-looking older brother." Knowing Apollo, he was only half joking.

"Do women find this arrogance charming?"

"It's not arrogance if it's true!"

Evan scoffed, turning to descend from the carriage, but a tight hand on his shoulder stopped him. "See you in the morning." He nodded through a constriction in his throat as Apollo tapped the roof of the carriage.

He was so engrossed in his thoughts he didn't hear the noise coming from his parlor and nearly missed his wife rushing out to meet him. She was still in the gown she'd worn to the ball—she hadn't even gone upstairs.

"How was it?" she asked as he took her into his arms.

"Come sit with me," he requested huskily.

"Evan, tell me!" she protested. But she let him pull her by the hand and sank down onto his lap in one of the armchairs.

He almost groaned at the delicious friction.

"Are you regretting your request, husband?"

He answered with a pained laugh, locking his arms around her waist and pulling her in tighter.

"I'm just happy to be home." Her eyes lit and then softened at his words, and then it dawned on him.

Our home. This could be our home. He was still feeling the effects of that when Luz spoke.

"What happens now?"

"Tomorrow we meet with him, and if he is not amenable to our demands, we'll ensure that his mind is changed," Evan said grimly, and Luz sucked in a breath at whatever she heard in his voice.

"If you'd prefer to be out of the city while the dust with my father settles, Apollo and I have made arrangements for you to go to his estate in the Highlands. You can go there with Clarita and the ladies at first light tomorrow."

"I am not leaving you," she said fiercely, as if daring him to attempt to take her from his side. "And I have business to attend to. We have the prototypes for the cordials to see from the glassblower your aunt Odessa put us in contact with."

"Will you at least consider the idea of going to the Highlands?" he asked again, and Luz sighed.

"Evan, what could he possibly do? Your lawyers have already begun the process of repossessing the distillery, and the proof of Apollo's birth is undeniable."

"I don't want any harm to come to you over this, Luz Alana." Warmth covered him, and her arms strongly tightened around his waist. She felt so solid, everything he needed. The one thing he could not lose. "Nothing is worth putting you in danger."

"Your distillery is worth fighting for. The future you and Apollo want to create is worth fighting for," she told him, with that relentless faith she seemed to have when it came to him.

The prospect of living up to that terrified and galvanized him.

He looked out the bay window at the gardens behind the house, then at the inky-blue night of the city he loved so much but that had become unbearable to him in the last few years. It all seemed to have new life now.

In the dark of this room, supported by the love of a woman he almost certainly didn't deserve, he could speak the truth. "I don't know what any of this was about anymore, if it really was about the distillery or just about reclaiming the only part of my family's legacy still worth saving."

Luz made a pained noise. He felt the vibrations of her shudder all over his body. She unclasped her hands at his waist, and he almost gripped her wrists to keep her there. But he knew better now. There was no hiding from Luz Alana. Not anymore.

"Where is your sister?" he asked as they pulled apart, already mentally cataloging what he'd need to have in place in the event there was a need to leave rapidly. Luz frowned at that.

"She's at Beatrice's."

Evan nodded considering. "She will be fine there. My father wouldn't dare incur Gerard's wrath."

Finally ready to take Apollo's advice, he rose from the chair and pulled on his wife's hand. She looked at him in question.

"I'm taking you to bed."

Luz was absolutely done with conversation.

What they both needed was connection, to say with their hands, with their bodies, what they could not otherwise articulate. What she felt for this man at times seemed beyond words. His touch, the way he made her feel had grown from a seed of need and a desire to a flower in full bloom, hungry for sun, for air, for room to grow.

They were so close to that. To the place where they could fully plunge into the future they both seemed to want. Where they could voice without fear what they both knew to be true. She would not rush him—she knew he needed to see things settled with his father—but in his eyes tonight at the ball she'd seen it.

Flames that burned as intensely as hers did.

"This is quite convenient," she said, going to her knees and lifting the flap of his kilt.

She ran her hands up his legs and those broad, strong thighs that could hold so much, that could hold *her*, until the side of her thumb was grazing his hardness. His skin fluttered under her palms.

She loved that he let her see him react to her touch. That he didn't hide his reactions to her. She leaned to press a kiss to that living, breathing marble and smiled at the way his muscles tightened at the contact.

Sculpted and perfect and hers.

"Luz," he said, sucking in a breath when she palmed the tight sac of his scrotum. Without a word, she took his erection in her hand and pressed a kiss to the tip, then lapped it with her tongue. With a groan, he brought his hand to the back of her head and nudged her to take him deeper.

In the past few weeks, she'd come to love pleasuring him in this way. It was a heady act, this, to feel such power and so in control while on her knees. She gripped his shaft and made a line from the base to the head with her tongue. Sucked the pearl of liquid there and still would not take him into her mouth.

"Come on, love. Don't torture me." He palmed the side of her face, a thumb caressing her cheek, as she turned her eyes up to him.

"Take me inside you," he begged, making wetness pool at her core.

"It's so massive," she balked, playing the part of innocent maiden. He groaned loudly and thrust into her hand.

"You like it this massive," he coaxed through gritted teeth, as she continued to tease him.

"I just don't know if I can manage accommodating such..." she flickered her eyes up at him, running her tongue over her bottom lip, as he watched her with an intensity that made her breathless "...heft."

"I'm going to make you take it, Luz Alana," he warned, his brogue thick now, his voice coarse as if he'd just guzzled mouthfuls of burning whisky. The hand that had been behind her head slid down to the pulse point at the base of her neck and began making drugging, hypnotic circles on her skin.

"Is that supposed to be a threat, husband?" He laughed, even as he placed a hand over hers in an attempt to further things along.

Luz would not be rushed.

She loved how openly and eagerly this strong, virile, unflappable man fell apart in her hands. She parted her lips and took him inside as far as he could go, and they both groaned at the joining.

It was always a shock, that invasion, closing her airways, flooding her mouth with the tang of his seed, with the smell of him. It was overwhelming, grounding. When they were like this, her head in his hands, and his hardness filling her, there was nothing else but the two of them.

"So sweet." His breath hitched as he watched her from under hooded eyes. "Heaven, your mouth is heaven." He started to thrust slowly in that give-and-take she loved. She let her throat relax, just as he'd taught her, and Evan groaned his pleasure.

"How you please me, my love," he whispered, caressing her cheek with his thumb, while he took her mouth. "I feel like an animal. I can barely control myself when you give me this. Your sweet lips stretched from taking me." Her nipples tightened at the sounds they made together. She loved this. *Loved him.* Luz pressed in more, taking him farther still.

"Ah, gods," he cried, his voice strangled when she hummed in appreciation at the liquid flooding her mouth. Evan thrust in a couple more times, precise, shallow movements, then pulled out roughly. In the next instant he was lifting her off the floor and had her face-first against the wall.

"I need to be inside you," he grunted hotly into her ear. They worked together to lift the many layers of her dress out of the way. Luz was frantically gathering the fabric and tulle to her waist, when she felt the cool air of the room on her bare skin and Evan's hands gripping her rump.

"I've been wanting to do this since you advertised to the entire ball what you were hiding under those skirts." His voice was low and rough, but she could hear the humor there. A laugh died in her throat as he slid two fingers inside her, one palm pressed to her core holding her in place. "Is this what you need?" he asked hotly as he searched for that place inside that made her knees week. His thumb circled her clitoris and she bucked into him, gasping.

"Nothing is sweeter than this." He kept touching her in the relentless, mind-shattering caress, as he positioned himself at her entrance. She felt the blunt tip of him demanding entry, and she canted her hips eagerly. In one breathless thrust, he sheathed himself to the hilt.

"Luz Alana," he said, and then so quietly she almost missed it, "mi mujer." The way he said the words, reverently. As though he could hardly believe she could truly be his.

And she was, completely, utterly, forever.

They worked together in the practiced rhythm they'd perfected in the past few weeks. He moved inside her first in long drawn-out lazy thrusts that entered her inch by slow inch, and then in a sequence of fevered jabs which ended with her braced against the wall, legs splayed, as he took her hard. Luz cried Evan's name as her walls clenched against him, wanting to keep him inside.

"The way you hold me, mo cridhe, made for me." She felt sweat gathering at her spine and wondered how the windows and doors weren't blowing off the hinges with the force of what the two of them were doing together.

Chaotic, incendiary lovemaking, and she wanted it just like this forever.

Evan gasped, his thrusts intensifying, and soon they were both swept into a blinding, obliterating climax. She slumped forward once she could think again, certain she'd likely crumple to the floor if she attempted to walk, but Evan pulled her to him, holding her upright.

He kissed the side of her face. Her shoulders, the curve of her ear. Every inch of skin he could reach, as he whispered softly to her. With gentle hands he undressed her down to her chemise and carried her to the bed, before divesting himself of his own clothes. Once they were both under the warm embrace of soft blankets and pressed to each other, Luz began to fade. The exhaustion of the day crashing around her, only then did she remember.

She sat up and glanced at his handsome face. His sable hair, which was always groomed to perfection, was tousled, tufts standing up every which way. His eyes, which even in their most intimate moments seemed wary and watchful, were open tonight, almost boyish.

He looked so enticing, her heart felt full to the brim with love.

"How long have you been holding on to *mi mujer*?"

His mouth twitched, but he didn't smile.

"Since the night at Le Bureau, when you asked me if I was at the live copulation show for lessons." He did grin then, and she laughed. "I hope I have since then divested you of the idea I required them."

"You may have made some progress in that area." He brought her up until she was lying atop him. When she looked down at him there was something in his eyes she hadn't quite seen before.

"I never thought of making plans beyond tonight, not really." He spoke into the silence of their bedroom. "You've given me a future to look to."

"Evan," she said, suddenly breathless.

"Once this thing with my father is done, I intend to make a life with you," he told her, and she knew then that bloom they'd made together would become a field of flowers.

"I plan to hold you to that."

He kissed her, slowly and sweetly, until she was gasping for air.

"Let's sleep, cariño." She burrowed into his chest, already half-asleep. "The morning will be here soon, and I'm sure there will be much to do."

But the morning Luz hoped for never came.

Hours later, hard knocks on the door ripped them from an exhausted sleep with the news that Evan and Apollo's plot had resulted in their entire world being set ablaze.

Twenty-Four

"*He is not in London. My men have combed the city. There's* no sign of him," Evan said as he barreled into the room, looking much too presentable for a man who'd barely slept two hours.

"We must get you, Clarita and the Leonas out of Edinburgh."

"I told you I wasn't going anywhere without you," she reminded him, to which he responded with a mulish shake of the head.

"No, leannain." Her resistance buckled somewhat at the endearment. "I need to make sure your rum and my whisky are safe. We're moving them again, farther out of the city. We can't take any chances; the man burned down two of my warehouses." Evan's voice was thin with fury at the mention of the fire that had ravaged most of the three buildings he owned in Leith. It was a miracle half of the port hadn't gone up in flames. The only reason all her rum wasn't gone was that Evan had had the foresight to move their reserves elsewhere, in the event his father tried to retaliate after they confronted him.

"Have you confirmed it was him?"

"No, but who else could it possibly be?" His face, which last night had been so content and peaceful, was pinched with worry.

"I know you don't want to do this, but it would ease my mind to know you're out of Edinburgh for now." He looked so undone, so desperate that she found herself relenting.

"I will go fetch Clarita from Beatrice's house, and then we'll go to the train." He heaved a sigh of relief, the lines of his face softening.

"Good. Why don't I send one of my men for her and you—" That she could not accept.

"Absolutely not, Evan. My sister has gone through too much. If a footman came to get her when I promised I would, she would be scared. I will go and come straight back here."

"All right," he said, pinching the bridge of his nose. "I need to go down to Leith. We are emptying everything we have left in Edinburgh and moving it south to a location Murdoch knows near Glasgow. One of my footmen will accompany you to my sister's. I will return to take you to the train in an hour."

"Carajo," Luz cried half an hour later as their carriage arrived back at the house on Queen Street.

"What is it?" asked Clarita, who had been unusually somber on the drive from Beatrice's.

"I forgot Bisabuela's book. I left it in my office." Luz could not believe she'd forgotten it. Things had been so chaotic this morning, it hadn't occurred to her until now. With her sister safely with her, and Evan taking care of the rum, there was only the book left to secure.

And Evan. She was worried about Evan, fearful of what else his father might try to do. It had been those three things for so long: Clarita, Caña Brava and the book. But now it was four. The four things she had to know were always safe.

Despite the turmoil of the day, she was warmed by that.

"Are you going to send someone for it?" Amaranta asked her as they descended from the carriage, but Luz shook her head.

"No." She pointed in the direction of her office, which was only a few minutes' walk away.

"I will quickly fetch it and then come back here to wait for Evan." Protests erupted around her.

"Apologies, my lady, but I canna let you do that." That came from Clint, Evan's footman, who had taken very seriously his master's orders not to let Luz out of his sight.

"I don't take orders from my husband, Clint. You can accompany me if you'd like, but I *will* go to my office. I cannot leave Edinburgh without my book."

"Luz, I don't want you to go," her sister cried. Luz glared at Clint: he was scaring poor Clarita.

"Nothing will happen to me in broad daylight!" Luz kissed Clarita's forehead and ushered her inside. "I will be back before you are done readying your board games for the train." She held up her hand when Clint seemed intent on arguing. "Evan has a man outside my building, and Clint is coming with me. What could possibly happen?"

"Esto no me gusta, Luz," Amaranta protested.

"I will be perfectly fine. Besides," she said and patted her leg, "llevo mi pistola."

"You are too confident in that Remington," Aurora said disapprovingly.

"Regreso en diez minutos," she called as she hurried up the street to her office with Clint on her heels, looking extremely discomfited by Luz's disregard for the laird's orders. "It won't take but a minute," she told her escort as they hurried toward her office.

It truly only took a few minutes, and soon they were approaching her building. Despite her cavalier attitude, she wasn't reckless and approached the entrance cautiously but didn't notice anything amiss.

She knew Evan had placed a guard in front of her building the night before, but the man must've gone home or to help with the fire. Everything looked as she'd left it the afternoon before. The ground-floor storefront was still not open to the public, and they had to enter the building through a side door. She'd given her secretary, Eliza, the day off, thinking there might be too much happening at home for anyone to get work done, but Mr. Grant had business to attend to this morning and would already be in.

"See? Everything is fine. My employee is likely here already," she told Clint, who didn't look very convinced. The footman had been with Evan for a long time, had started his employment as a groom in one of the stables and was now head footman. He took his work seriously, and despite how irritating Luz found being coddled, she didn't want to make the poor man's life harder.

"Why don't you guard the entrance, and I will run up and procure my book? I won't be long," she promised, pulling a key out of her handbag. But when she turned the doorknob, it swung open. She looked over her shoulder at Clint, adding a smile to reassure him. "See? Mr. Grant is probably up there." Her nerves were frayed enough, and she did not want Clint underfoot in her office.

"Yes, my lady," Clint said unhappily as he planted himself beside the door.

She quickly made her way up the stairs to the second floor, deciding she'd get the book first and then go see Mr. Grant on her way out. Everything in her office was in its place: the two green armchairs in front of the fireplace facing each other; her father's mahogany desk, which she'd brought from Santo Domingo, was just as she'd left it the day before; the decanters of Caña Brava and Braeburn on the cart by the window.

Everything was in order, yet something felt off.

It was likely just nerves, she told herself. With a day—and a night—like she'd had, it was natural to be somewhat antsy. She rushed to the locked cabinet across form her desk, opening it with the key she always kept on her chatelaine. She sighed with relief, tucking the book under her arm, as she locked things back up.

Evan would never know she'd been gone.

As she turned toward the door, she heard the unmistakable click of a pistol being cocked behind her.

"Miss Heith-Benzan, or shall I say *Lady Darnick*." A man with an unwashed appearance stepped out from behind her curtain with the weapon pointed at her. She didn't recognize him, but something about him was eerily familiar. "Don't even think of yelling for help, or you'll be sorry."

"My husband will be here any minute, and there are guards downstairs," she said as calmly as she could manage, her eyes darting to the door of her office.

The man walked toward her, his shaky hands aiming the gun at her chest. "I'd imagine Lord Darnick is too preoccupied putting out fires to venture this way anytime soon."

Oh God, this could not be happening.

"My employee is on the next floor." Luz held her breath and counted backward in an attempt to clear her head. Her mind was racing so rapidly she almost missed the next thing the man said.

"Your Mr. Grant is probably still recovering from getting knocked on the head this morning." That stopped Luz Alana cold, real fear seeping into her bones.

"What? Who are you?" she said, trying to hide how scared she was. Her own pistol was pressed to her thigh, but she feared that if she made any sudden movements, her captor would pull the trigger, and he was now merely feet away from her. Up close, the man looked unhinged. Red-rimmed eyes sunken into his skull, face scruffy as if he hadn't shaved in days. His clothes were wrinkled, and he smelled foul. But the worst part was the loathing in his eyes.

"We never did get a chance to meet, since *His Lordship*—" the man spat out the words with obvious distaste "—sent his dogs after me and threatened to throw me in gaol if I made any attempt to contact you." His face twisted into an ugly sneer, and again she thought she'd seen him before. "That's the thanks I get for minding your trust. Not even a thank-you. Didn't even deign to respond to my letters." He lifted a shoulder, pistol waving in the air erratically. "I had to take matters into my own hands."

Percy Childers. And despite the fear gripping her, the man's gall infuriated her. Minding her trust—more like stealing from her! She should've told Evan about the letters. She'd kept it from him out of spite, and now this man was going to kill her. Nausea roiled in her stomach at the thought of him finding her here, of Clarita. She pushed down a sob, and tried to steel herself. She could not fall apart. She had to walk away from this. She had too much to live for.

A strange but absolute calm washed over her, and she decided that Childers was not going to cheat her out of her future, not after she'd gone and found one for herself. She attempted to slide her hand down to reach for her pistol, but the movement seemed to startle him.

"Lift your hands," he barked, and she resisted the urge to pinch her nostrils shut. The man's breath was vile. "Keep them where I can see them. You and I are going to have a talk, get to know each other. I think we'll go to one of the upper floors where no one will come looking for you." He suddenly stopped short, making the nozzle of the gun press against her back. Sweat ran down her spine, and she had to tighten her muscles to keep from shaking. "I'll advise you on how to properly show gratitude for all the help my family has given you, and this time your protector won't be here to interfere."

A frisson of pure horror slithered up Luz's spine.

"My husband's guards will come for me if he doesn't find me at home." Childers scoffed, dismissing her.

"If it's money you want, I have some upstairs. I'll give you whatever I have." She did have some notes in her safe. If he let her get close enough to it, she'd reach for her pistol. If not, there were a couple of solid gold candlesticks in there she could use to brain the man.

"Go," he said, shoving her hard enough to make her stumble.

He shouldn't have left her.

That was the only thought circling around Evan's mind as he reached the warehouse where he'd stashed the reserves a few days ago. That precaution had saved their most valuable inventory, and though he was glad Luz Alana's rum was intact he realized he could care less about the whisky. The only thing that mattered was keeping his wife safe from his father.

Evan jumped at the pounding of the carriage window and was surprised to see Apollo there.

"He's gone," Apollo said grimly, as he pressed a sheaf of papers into Evan's hands. He scanned the words on the paper in disbelief. He was looking at his father's signature on a legal agreement, releasing the control of the duchy fully to Apollo and Evan.

"He signed them?" Evan asked, shocked. He leafed through the pages and saw that his father had indeed signed everything they'd left him last night. Every document. He'd also enclosed a note addressed to them both.

It was a resentful diatribe disparaging his sons for their vindictiveness but in the end admitting defeat. There was also confirmation that the Duke of Annan had sent a letter to the House of Lords and Scottish Parliament, recognizing Apollo as his heir apparent.

The story to be deployed among Edinburgh drawing rooms in the coming days was that due to his declining health, the duke would forthwith be spending most of his time in the South of France and therefore would relinquish the management of the duchy to his sons.

"He's gone to the house in Nice, and from what he says in the letter it seems he intends to stay there indefinitely. The authorization to transfer the deed to the distillery to you is in there too."

"I don't understand," he said woodenly, and Apollo heaved a sigh.

"The duchess is truly gone. I have confirmation she boarded a train to London with the Italian attaché this morning." One day Evan would have to extract from his brother how it was that he was made privy to all this information, but now there were more urgent things at hand.

He knew he ought to be feeling *something*. He finally had everything he'd ever wanted. He'd won. He should be elated, but the niggling feeling that something was amiss would not go away.

"The fire," Evan said as things started becoming clearer. If his father was giving up, if he accepted defeat, then...

"I don't think it was him, Evan." The tendrils of fear that had been sliding up his spine since he saw the papers gripped him all at once. He had missed something. Something vital, and he somehow knew it meant Luz Alana was not safe.

"I've got to go look in on Luz," he said, thumping the roof of the carriage to alert the coachman.

"Is there anyone who would want to hurt you or Luz Alana?" asked Apollo with urgency, just as one of the men Evan had left at the site of the fire arrived on a horse, riding at a breakneck speed. He practically leaped off the animal as soon as the horse came to a stop.

"Sir," he yelled, his fist extended in front of him as he ran toward the carriage. "We found this in one of the warehouses."

In the palm of the younger man's hand was a silver cufflink, the initials *PC* etched delicately on its face. Suddenly, everything became clear. He knew who'd done this.

He should have killed him when he'd had the chance.

"I have to go," he told Apollo.

"Wait! What do you need?" His brother grabbed his arm, not letting him go, and Evan's throat closed in gratitude.

"Notify the constabulary and tell them to send men to my

house and to Luz's office on Princes Street. Send someone to check with the guards at her bottling plant in Leith."

Apollo clapped him on the back and brought him in for an embrace. "Go. I'm right behind you."

Afterward, Evan barely remembered the carriage ride. In his life he'd experienced many moments of fear, but in the twenty minutes it took to get to Heriot Row, Evan thought his mind would break. He stared at the papers that gave him uncontested ownership of the distillery—the very thing only weeks before he thought he'd give almost anything to possess—and tossed them aside.

Evan was no stranger to loss, but until those moments alone in the carriage, praying to a god he scarcely knew how to talk to, he didn't understand what it was to face the possibility of absolute and total despair. Losing his mother and his brother had been terrible, but Evan had kept his will to fight on, to see justice done. The mere prospect of a world, a life, without Luz Alana engulfed him in such darkness that he was not sure he could bear it. He'd gladly burn Braeburn Hall to ashes and scatter them to the four winds without a moment's thought if it meant finding Luz Alana safe and sound at home.

If that bastard Childers dared touch a single hair on her head Evan would tear him limb from limb with his own hands.

Needing something to distract himself with, he revisited the plan they'd made before he left the house. She was supposed to get Clarita, then pack and wait for him at home. That secured her sister, while he took care of the rum. She'd told him many times that there were three things that she must know were safe: her sister, her business and—

Her grandmother's recipe book.

Evan didn't bother rapping his fists on the carriage roof but stuck his head out and yelled, "Let's take Princes Street on the way to the house. I want to stop by Lady Luz's office." The driver shouted down his understanding and within seconds set them on the new course.

"Where is she?" Evan flew out of the carriage and found Clint standing by the door.

"My lord, Lady Luz asked me to bring her to fetch one of her books."

"Is the guard I had here up there with her?"

Clint blanched. "No, my lord, Lady Luz said he must've been helping with the fire."

"I told you not to let her out of the house," Evan said, fists clenched as he fought for control.

"She would not listen, my lord, said she'd come on her own if I didn't bring her." He was wasting time, and he also knew how stubborn his wife could be. Clint was no match for his lioness.

"We will talk about this later," Evan said, turning to open the door. He pointed in the direction of Queen Street. "Go back to the house and fetch me my pistol. Just run there. It'll be quicker than the carriage."

In the chaos of the morning, he'd left unarmed.

Clint ran off at a lope as Evan took the steps up to Luz's office three steps at a time. The door was open, but he could see she wasn't in there. His heart pounded in his chest, sick dread turning his stomach.

She's all right, he told himself as he tried to think.

Evan opened his mouth to call for her, but something held him back. He quietly walked over to the secretary's empty desk and stepped on something. He removed his foot and bent to pick it up, and that's when fear truly took hold of him. It was a larimar hatpin which had once belonged to Luz's mother. Something about seeing an object she so clearly cherished discarded on the floor made ice run through Evan's veins.

His mind reeled. So much so, it took him a moment to hear the voices coming from the upper floor. One strange, aggressive and deep. The other was a hushed and raspy sound he'd recognize anywhere. Relief flooded him, even as his pulse raced. She was alive, she was here, but something was very wrong.

He hurried up the steps as quietly as he could—and walked into his worst nightmare. Percy Childers, in a blind rage, was shouting threats at his wife while brandishing a gun.

"This is not enough. I know how much money you have. I want what I'm due. I will be compensated," Childers shouted at Luz, who was not moving a muscle.

She saw him the moment he walked in, but the man had his back to Evan and was too caught up in his rant to notice Evan's arrival. He placed a finger over his lips, to which she responded with an almost imperceptible nod. The sight of his wife still whole and, from what he could see, mostly unscathed made Evan want to weep. But that would need to happen later. Soon Clint would come barreling up the stairs, and the last thing he wanted was Childers shooting Luz in a panic.

He noticed she was lowering her gaze as if to indicate something on her dress, while Childers raved about being unjustly removed from his duties. His wife kept her eyes on her skirts and very discreetly slid her right leg forward, tilting her head to the side. She *couldn't* be suggesting…

"No, absolutely not," he mouthed, shaking his head frantically. She had the nerve to glare at him.

If she thought he was going to let her try to go for that damn pistol while that maniac had his gun trained on her…

"Duck," he mouthed silently, pointing to the ground before gesturing toward Childers's gun. Luz Alana pursed her lips, as if he was thwarting her master plan.

Why did he have to fall in love with the most stubborn, infuriating woman in all of the world? And he was in love. Desperately, irrevocably in love.

Evan steeled himself as he took a step forward, one eye on Luz Alana and the other on Childers, and without hesitation he launched himself forward shouting the man's name. Just as the scoundrel whirled around, Evan tackled him to the ground, struggling to rip the gun from his grip.

"Drop the pistol, before I tear off your bloody fingers." Evan viciously twisted Childers's wrist to make him drop his weapon, making the weasel cry out in pain. He quickly flung the gun aside, sending it skittering across the floor while Luz scrambled for her own pistol.

"I've got him, Evan!" she shouted, as she pointed that blasted little Remington at Childers's head.

"You were supposed to go straight to the house, Luz Alana," Evan groused even as he felt the ice that had been running through his veins for the last twenty minutes begin to thaw, now that his woman was safe from harm.

"I needed my grandmother's book," she said in explanation, eyes still trained on her quarry.

"Will you ever listen to a word I tell you? Luz Alana, for God's sake," he rebuked distractedly, pressing a knee onto Childers's back to keep the man still. He was crying now and wriggling like the devil, which forced Evan to turn his attention away from his wife. "If you don't stop thrashing your fucking legs I will break them both, you bloody shitbag." Childers whimpered pathetically, and Evan squashed his head against the floor.

"Did he touch you?" Evan asked, glancing up at Luz. His eyes roamed over her trying to find any sign that she'd been hurt. Cold violence thrummed through him. He took his gaze off her for a second and turned to Childers. "If she has so much as a scratch, I will put you in the ground." The man whimpered in fear at the threat, but Luz shook her head.

"He didn't hurt me. I knew you'd come find me." She glanced at him for a moment, those brown eyes blazing with fearsome love, and Evan thought it would be a bloody ordeal, living with his heart trampling around Scotland and God knew where else outside of his body.

He could not imagine a more glorious future than that.

"You are going to be the end of me," he said, like the hopeless, ruined, desperate sod he was. A secret and very satisfied smile turned up his wife's lips just as what sounded like a pack of wildebeests trampled up the steps.

Apollo must have alerted the entire police force, and they made quick work of Childers, who was promptly handcuffed and carried out of the room still wielding threats and protestations. But Evan didn't have anything to say to anyone, not until he had his wife in his arms. He pushed her into a small alcove in an empty room, just so he could take a closer look at her.

"You cannot do this to me again, Luz Alana," he pled as he ran rough palms over every place he could reach.

"I am all right," she protested, but he saw when the realization of what had almost happened was finally dawning on her and tears filled her eyes.

"I was so scared, Evan," she blustered against his shirt as he held her tightly.

"I would never let anything happen to ye, mo cridhe," he whispered in her ear. "You and I have too much living yet to do." He nuzzled her hair, inhaling her scent deeply. His hands trembled as he ran them over her back. She sighed into his chest, tremors still coursing through her.

"Sir! Lord Darnick," one of the constables called for him, but he shook his head.

"Lord Darnick is my brother and I need a minute in private with my wife," he bellowed, and the men retreated quietly from the room.

"I do enjoy when you employ your earl-in-training-school voice," Luz muttered, looking up at him.

"My what?" he asked, marveling at the fact that he could be smiling at a moment like this.

"That way that you project your voice to send everyone scrambling."

He laughed ruefully and kissed the top of her head. "I'm

not an earl anymore, wife," he reminded her. She only lifted a shoulder.

"The only title of yours I care about is *devoted*, or *besotted*," she informed him before bringing his head down and pressing her mouth to his. "Doting, adoring husband of Luz Alana Sinclair-Heith."

"I've got my work cut out for me, then," he murmured against her warm skin, weightless in his joy. It had happened so stealthily, so swiftly he'd almost been unaware of it until it was a resounding, undeniable fact. Swept away by all that sweetness right into the deepest waters.

This woman owned him. Every inch of him was hers.

"If anything ever happened to you, Luz Alana..." he said breathlessly from the tightness in his throat.

"I'm not going anywhere," she assured him and squeezed her arms around him like a vise.

"I need you safe and by my side, always." He took the palm of her hand and pressed it right over where his heart was only now slowing down. "This is you."

"Are you saying I'm your heart, Evan Sinclair?"

"You are more than that, mi mujer." She smiled a little wetly at that. "You are my heartbeat."

"You are never getting rid of me now." She beamed at him. "Now, kiss me before our entire family stampedes into this place."

He shook his head, heart pounding, dizzy from love, and applied himself to doing just that.

Twenty-Five

"I'm sure some women enjoy being inspected like a champion thoroughbred while they sleep, but I don't," Luz muttered, much later when they were ensconced in each other's arms laying in front of the fire in their bedroom—with everyone they loved accounted for and safe in their beds.

"I wasn't inspecting, I was admiring."

She grumbled, making him laugh, and he kissed her again. The day had been…long. Childers eventually confessed to setting the warehouses on fire and intending to extort money from Luz Alana. He'd be spending the night—the next many, in fact—locked safely away in a cell.

"I'm sorry I didn't tell you he'd sent me letters," she said, remorseful, and he hated seeing that shadow behind her eyes.

"There is nothing to be sorry for. If I hadn't been behaving like an utter ass, you would've felt like you could tell me." She nodded, her bottom lip caught under her teeth. "I hope, next time, you know that there is nothing that I won't do for you. That I would lay down my life, everything I have, to keep you safe."

She looked up at him and pressed a kiss to the scruff on his jaw.

"I don't think I've been more certain of anything in my life."

He clasped his arms around her, making her squeal, and rolled them until she was on top of him. Those beloved eyes blinked open slowly, and despite the smile on her lips he could see the remnants of what she'd experienced today. The urge to be inside her, to affirm this union of theirs, was a yawning need under his skin. He could see she needed it too.

"I love you," she whispered as she bent down to kiss him.

Those words made his heart feel close to exploding.

"En español," he begged, making her laugh.

"Te amo, Evan. Mi cielo, mi hombre." His heart clenched from the strength of that assertion.

"I love *you*," he said, quietly, as if in prayer, and she smiled at him, radiant in the cocoon of their bed.

"I know you do." She bent and bit his lip, hungry as she was, demanding. Setting his blood to a boil instantly. He slid his hands up her thighs, and she pressed her branding heat to his skin. She'd slipped on one of those sinful bits of lace and satin she insisted on wearing to bed.

He'd torn at least a half dozen of them since they'd arrived in Edinburgh.

This one had delicate tea-rose pink lace covering her bosom. The fabric dipped in a V, revealing the valley between her breasts. The satin of the gown split from her thighs, giving him access to that place he could never get enough of. He slid his hands under the buttery material, up and up until he was there. He ran his thumb over the furrow of her. Hot and slick.

"Always wet," he groaned as he parted her with his fingers. She gasped into his mouth. He licked into her, moving his tongue in the same rhythm his fingers pleasured her.

"Evan," she grunted as she bucked into his touch.

"Do you require something of me, wife?" he asked, lazily circling his fingers over her engorged clitoris. Not what she needed to climax, but enough to keep her on the brink of it.

"Don't tease me, husband. This is cruel." She spoke through gritted teeth as she rocked into his hand, searching for more pressure. He laughed and continued that languid, slow caress as she huffed harsh breaths into his ear.

"Is this not enough for you?" He feigned curiosity, knowing full well he could dangle her over the edge like this for hours. He loved this, keeping her on the verge of orgasm as he tasted and licked her into a frenzy.

"You are well aware it's not. I hate this game..." She let the words hang as he moved his fingers faster.

"You were saying?" he teased, then leaned in to suck at her skin, leaving a mark.

"Yes..." she moaned, planting her palms on his torso, gyrating her hips faster. The friction on his cock was enough to blur his vision. He kept his eyes on her, watching her move. Pink lips puffy from his kisses, half lidded eyes still searing him with that hunger of hers. Evan could not recall ever wanting anything this much. Feeling like with every touch, every kiss, his need for this woman, his desire for her, only soared. He reached up to suckle a nipple through the scratchy lace and felt a rush of liquid drench the fingers he had inside her.

"I need a taste," he groaned, gripping her hips roughly.

"I need *you*," she exhaled as he swiftly lifted her up his body until her thighs were on each side on his head.

"Grip the headboard, love," he ordered and promptly heard the crick of the wood as she did what he asked. With one hand he held her open to him and licked into her. One long stroke of his tongue until he'd tasted her completely.

"Evan." Her moans swirled around him, spurning him on as he feasted on her.

"So sweet...can never get enough." He palmed her backside until her heat was flush against his mouth, and he was on her like a ravenous beast. With the flat of his tongue he swiped at her core, drinking her arousal as Luz begged him for more.

"Mas," she demanded, and he knew now what that meant. He wrapped his lips around her clitoris and sucked just as his palm delivered one swift whack to her round bottom. She cried his name and flooded his mouth as her climax swept over her. He worked her with his mouth and fingers for a few more moments, until her moans of pleasure became soft little gasps, and he could not wait any longer. He flipped them both until she was on her hands and knees, looking at him enticingly over her shoulder.

"Ven, cariño."

Come to me.

Without a word, Evan pushed up the negligee until it was bunched up around her waist, his nostrils flaring at the pink swell of her rear. He knelt and pressed his lips to the heated spot, then gently pressed his teeth to it, making her laugh, and his heart did that funny skip again. His hands caressed the curves of her before he covered her back with his chest and sheathed himself until he was so deep he felt like she'd hold him inside her forever.

"Say my name," he pleaded as he cupped her breasts, thrusting inside.

"Evan, mi vida." She sighed, pushing into him wantonly, and his head spun from pure, delirious pleasure.

He'd always wondered about men who forgot their responsibilities when a woman turned their heads. But he knew now that he'd happily dedicate his life to this. To begging this woman to take him inside her. Sinking into the hot, velvet grip of her body was the only heaven he cared to know. He imagined them at the Braeburn years from now. Her hand in his, walking through their land, thinking about their work, dreaming up new passions together.

His Luz Alana, the woman who had made his heart beat again.

"Luz." Her name was a sacred thing, three letters that fed his soul. He moved inside her, and as she clutched him in an exquisite vise, he slid his hand to the apex of her thighs and searched for that place that belonged to him.

"This is mine," he said, recklessly possessive as his fingers moved on her, and she convulsed around him with a broken cry, coming for him again, and soon he was following into a sea of blinding bliss.

Once their breaths were coming more evenly, he scooped her to him and shifted so they were lying on their sides.

"Your beard is very ticklish," she said in that languid tone her voice acquired after they'd done this in a particularly satisfying manner.

It made him think of well-fed felines.

"There were no protestations earlier," he said, sweeping away her riot of curls so he could kiss the back of her neck. "And my beard was in much more sensitive places. Perhaps you were distracted with my ton—"

"Evan!" she yelled as she pulled a pillow and flung it in his direction. Within moments they were wrestling in the bed, tangled in crumpled sheets.

He finally lay on his back with her head on his chest, and for a long while they were silent, contemplative in the sanctuary of their bed.

"Your father is gone, then," Luz asked some time later.

Evan nodded, his eyes looking into the distance.

"He's signed everything over to us and recognized Apollo as the heir apparent."

"Do you believe he'll stay away?"

He shrugged with that faraway look still on his face. "There is nothing left for him here. Everyone knows what he did. They might pretend, for the sake of maintaining appearances, but with Charlotte gone…"

His voice trailed off, and she saw that there was something he wasn't saying.

"What is it?"

Evan shook his head and held her tighter.

"It seems that the one thing he cared about was Charlotte." He sounded utterly flummoxed.

"Do you think he'll try to get her back?"

He furrowed his brows, considering her question, and when he answered she was surprised by his certainty. "No, I don't think he could live with the knowledge that everyone is laughing at him. My father is much too fragile."

"I hope she finds happiness," Luz said after a long silence, and Evan made an affirmative noise in response, then tightened his arms around her.

She felt so safe in his arms. Believed fiercely in what they'd started together.

"I don't deserve you, but I will never, ever let you go."

"You most certainly do deserve me," she protested. "I take offense to the suggestion that the man I love is nothing other than absolutely perfect."

"And most handsome," he added, making her grin.

"Very dashing," Luz added, burrowing into him.

"Aggressively virile," he muttered as he nuzzled her neck, making her giggle. "And with biggest co—"

"That's quite enough," she cried through a bout of laughter.

"Apollo has asked me to help him with the holdings," he told her after they'd quieted down. "Managing them. He intends to divide his time between here and London."

"What about the Braeburn?"

"I plan to ask Raghav if he wants to buy half of the shares. I've been wanting to do so for years, but I didn't like the idea of him being liable if my father got up to any of his tricks with it," he explained. Impossibly, she felt even a bit more in love with him.

"How do you feel about Apollo's offer?"

"I want to do it," he said at length. "We could do a lot of

good, but mostly I want to make a life with you." Her heart melted, ice under the searing sun of his love.

"That you already have," she said with all the strength she could put into that truth.

"It's all I want. You and me and Clarita, in this house. Spending Christmas at the Braeburn. Sailing to go see that island of yours."

"You want to go to Santo Domingo?" she asked, surprised.

He lifted a shoulder and bent down to kiss her nose.

"I must pilgrimage there in gratitude for the gift it's given me."

"That's extremely sacrilegious."

"It's the truth. Everything I believe is in my arms right now. My miracle. I love you."

There could be a day perhaps when hearing those declarations of love from this man would not make her throb with happiness. There might even be a time when the mere glimpse of that fire he always seemed to look at her with wouldn't incinerate her senses, but tonight, in this moment, she was utterly aflame with love for Evanston Sinclair, the former Earl of Darnick, the love of her life.

Her home.

"Te amo, Evan Sinclair. Con todo. Everything I am loves you." Evan's chest rumbled with something lusty and warm, then he hungrily covered her mouth with his, and for a long time there were no more words.

★ ★ ★ ★ ★

A Note from the Author

The idea for this series came from where all great ideas come these days…the internet. In the fall of 2019 I was researching for an upcoming trip to Paris. Randomly, I found an article from a Dominican newspaper where they mentioned the first time the Dominican Republic attended a French international exposition was in 1889. Not only that, but the article said that King Leopold of Belgium snubbed our pavilion because our president, Ulises Heureaux, owed him money…le escandalo! The whole Dominican Republic got the cut direct at the 1889 Paris world's fair, where among other things the Eiffel Tower was debuted. I had to know more. I quickly found an article written by the poet José Martí talking about his impressions of the fair and the presence of Latinx countries. Fast-forward to a month of research, and I had a trove of fascinating information and an idea for a series to boot.

It turns out that at the 1889 Paris exposition, which was done to celebrate the centennial of the revolution, not only was the Dominican Republic present, but another thirteen Latin countries also exhibited. All of them built pavilions showcasing their architecture, and more than 5,500 Latin presenters traveled to France in the spring of 1889. The thought of all those Latin men and women boarding steamers full of products made in their countries to present on a global stage…rum, minerals, timbers, jewels. How could I not throw some boss babe heiresses looking for adventure into the mix?

I would not have been able to write this book without the help from Jhensen Ortiz, the librarian at the Dominican Studies Institute at City College in New York City. I put the call out and Jhensen sent me a treasure trove of articles documenting life in the Dominican Republic in the second half of the nineteenth century and invaluable information about women in trade and business during that time. The writings of Frank Moya Pons, Silvio-Torres Saillant, Quisqueya Lora Hugi, Michel-Rolph Truillot, Lorgia García Peña and Teresita Martínez Vergne, among others, were vital to me as I crafted the character of Luz Alana.

I am grateful for my mother's insistence that I learn French. Being able to read and write Spanish and French were lifesavers in this process. The National Archives of the French National Library was a lifesaver, which allowed me to learn details of what happened in the six months of the exposition, from the notable persons present to the food being served at the various restaurants in the fairgrounds, including one on the second level of the tower.

I can't deny the research part was very fun, but bringing to life BIPOC characters in a historical romance that had space to breathe and live their best lives was a dream come true. It took me a few tries to figure out how to ground my voice and my gaze into a space of romance where characters like the ones I write hadn't really been in before. I hope I did the Leonas and their girls' trip of a lifetime justice!

Acknowledgments

Seeing a Latina on the cover of a historical romance novel has been something I've yearned for a very, *very* long time. To actually write that story and see it on bookshelves—that's not a dream I even thought I could dream. The road to bringing *A Caribbean Heiress in Paris* to life was one I travelled with the help of many. I would like to thank:

My amazing, brilliant, infinitely patient, and unbelievably generous writing community who listened, encouraged, brainstormed, and shepherded me as I attempted to write Luz Alana and Evan's story. Alexis Daria, Sarah Maclean, Tracy Livesay, Nisha Sharma…there are literally not enough Thank Yous. To my accountability partner, JN Welsh, for all the pep talks. To Jen P, my consiglieri and book doctor for *Heiress*, who plucked these two protagonists (and my sanity) out of a ditch more than once.

To my agent, Taylor Haggerty, whose excitement for this story and support as I worked on getting it out in the world were and are invaluable to me.

To my editor, Kerri Buckley, my Day One. Nine books and counting. This one was a marathon, but like always, we made it through and have something we're both proud of to show for it. I will never not be grateful for the way you let me say what I need to say, with my voice and vision intact. I appreciate you immensely.

To Jhensen Ortiz, the librarian at the Dominican Library in the Dominican Studies Institute at the City College of New York. The assistance that you gave me in finding what I needed to write this book was priceless.

To the two friends who inspired these Leonas, Nicole and Indhira. With Nicole I travelled the most tempestuous journey of all: adolescence. Nicole, my sister from another mister. The one who knows all the secrets… And Indhira, my dominoes partner since college. The one who left the Dominican Republic with me twenty years ago. We were twenty-three and striking out on our own so far from home, but we had *us*. We got each other through that first winter in the Northeast, and seventeen years later, she was in the front row at my first author event. Leona is the only word to describe your friendships, love and loyalty.

To my mother, my sister, my abuelas, my tias, my primas. I am and have always been surrounded by the fiercest of women. The kind that don't just tell stories, but who *are* stories.

To my partner and my girl. There is no better hype team in the world. I love you endlessly.

To my readers. The ones who find themselves in these pages. The ones who can see their own family's story in the ones I write. These books are for you, always.